The Prometheus Crisis

Before joining forces to write the phenomenally successful
The Glass Inferno, Thomas N. Scortia was a physiochemist in the
aerospace industry with several novels of science fiction/suspense
to his credit, and Frank M. Robinson was an editor at *Playboy* and
the author of *The Power*, a novel which was made into a film.

D1395969

Thomas N. Scortia and Frank M. Robinson

The Prometheus Crisis

Pan Books London and Sydney

All of the characters in this book are fictitious, and any resemblance to actual persons, living or dead, is purely coincidental.

The excerpt from 'Nightmare, with Angels' is reprinted from *Selected Works of Stephen Vincent Benét*, published by Holt, Rinehart and Winston. Copyright 1935 by Stephen Vincent Benét, copyright renewed © 1963 by Thomas C. Benét, Stephanie B. Mahin, and Rachel Benét Lewis. Reprinted by permission of Brandt & Brandt.

First Published in Great Britain 1976 by Hodder and Stoughton Ltd
This edition published 1977 by Pan Books Ltd,
Cavaye Place, London SW10 9PG
© E.S.T. International Ltd 1975
ISBN 0 330 25330 1
Printed and bound in Great Britain by
Richard Clay (The Chaucer Press) Ltd, Bungay, Suffolk

for Bob Heinlein,
who thirty-five years ago said:
'Blowups Happen'

Foreword

The Prometheus Crisis was conceived in June 1973 while we were still working on *The Glass Inferno*. We interrupted that work to prepare an outline, which was subsequently purchased by a major film studio. During early 1974, when we worked on the screenplay (an unusual reversal of the usual creative flow line), we became increasingly concerned with the shaky assumptions upon which the national nuclear energy policy is based. Even if no reactor failure such as described in *The Prometheus Crisis* ever occurs, or no reactor the size of the Prometheus reactors is ever built, we are faced with the immediate danger of theft of fissionables from power plants and the long-range danger of nuclear wastes entering the world ecology. Since these wastes must be stored literally for hundreds of thousands of years before they 'decay' to the point where they're harmless, the odds for a major leak at some point are extremely high. It is this danger alone that has prompted us to say that the present nuclear programme is potential 'racial suicide.'

To the technically uninformed, the failure of a nuclear power plant means an atomic explosion. The breeder reactors now under construction, because of their high operating inventory of plutonium, could well explode if they fail. But such is not the case with the boiling water reactors we have been building in the United States for the last two decades. Such reactors cannot explode because their fissionable materials are too dilute to form the critical masses of the right geometries needed for a runaway chain reaction. Moreover, the chain reaction of uranium-235 or plutonium that powers such reactors requires 'slow' neutrons. These are obtained by the collision of 'fast' neutrons, produced by the primary reaction itself, with the water within the reactor vessel. This water acts as both coolant and moderator. In case of a failure and the water is lost, the primary fission reaction automatically stops.

The great danger of the conventional boiling water reactor lies in the accumulation of radioactive wastes as the reactor operates. The longer the reactor operates, the greater the amount of waste products. These 'ashes' are a mixture of many radioactive materials (including plutonium), each decaying at a different rate. When a radioactive material 'decays' it does so by fission and/or the emission of a neutron or other atomic particle. This reaction is always accompanied by heat. As a result, the mass of waste materials in a reactor that has been operating for some time generates large amounts of heat. This heat is normally carried away by the cooling water in the reactor.

It has been calculated that should a 'loss of coolant accident' – or LOCA – occur, the temperature of the reactor would rise rapidly. The wastes generate more heat than can be radiated so that the fuel rods in the reactor core would soon melt and after that, the reactor vessel itself. Depending on how long the reactor has been in service without refuelling, and the accumulation of waste products, this process could continue until not only the reactor but all the structures immediately surrounding it would become a molten mass that would begin to melt into the earth. This 'melt' might sink into the ground for as much as a hundred and fifty feet, heading, as the physicists' sardonic joke puts it, for China. This situation has come to be known as 'the China Syndrome'.

Dixy Lee Ray, former head of the AEC, has estimated the odds against a LOCA at one in 300 million while the recent Rasmussen Report has estimated the probability of nuclear-related fatalities as one in 10 million years *per reactor*. The statistical calculations leading to these results, of course, assume that all personnel are operating at optimum and that all routes of failure have been identified. William M. Bryan of the University of California (Davis) has criticized the Rasmussen statistical techniques as being too sensitive to small changes in input data, pointing out that these techniques were discarded by the Apollo Programme for use in calculating the chances of component failure because results were often in error by as much as two orders of magnitude (*i.e.* by a factor of more than 100). A number of statisticians agree that the above figures are probably meaningless without complete identification of failure routes and coupling modes among failure routes. No provision has been made in the calculations for any 'domino effect'.

In the two years since we began work on *The Prometheus Crisis*, the possibilities of terrorists stealing radioactives and the dangers of a loss-of-coolant accident in conventional reactors

8

have become front-page news. Not too long ago, the now-defunct AEC halted the operation of most of the country's reactors because of reported flaws in coolant pipes – flaws that could conceivably have resulted in LOCA's. Intensive inspection of many of these plants revealed flaws similar to those mentioned in our story.

Similarly, a recent television programme was devoted to the problems of guarding the nation's stocks of plutonium. As a part of this programme, the producers commissioned a teen-age undergraduate student to design an atomic bomb, using only information readily available in open literature. Experts pronounced his resulting design workable. The day of the basement bomb may well be upon us.

Neither of us is delighted that fact is so fast catching up with fiction.

In the acknowledgement to *The Glass Inferno*, we said that 'no product of [this] size and scope ... can be the sole product of the authors.' This is doubly true for the present book. We would like to emphasize that we have not at any time had access to classified or proprietary information. We have postulated certain technologies within the story that seemed reasonable to us. For instance, we have mentioned the use of ion exchange resins to recover the fissionables from spent fuel rods, an approach that seemed logical to us even though we were unaware of the existence of such a technique.

We are unaware of a reconnaissance satellite as sophisticated as MIROS. However, satellites do exist using photographic techniques combined with ejection and retrieval of the film that can produce photographs with the same remarkable resolution that we have described. It seemed reasonable, if the television band width were broad enough, or if laser communication techniques could be used, that MIROS might exist.

We have, in some instances, taken auctorial licence. We have used a *deus ex machina* in postulating a shore-to-sea wind during a storm sequence. Such a situation can occur in certain areas of the California coast, but it is hardly common. Most importantly, we have *downplayed* the hazards of radiation to the participants in our story. Had we not done so, few characters would have survived their adventures and our story would have been a very short story indeed.

We have taken some licence in the design of our hypothetical plant both for dramatic effect and for simplification. We would expect, for instance, that a four-reactor complex would norm-

9

ally be contained by four domes, but the single dome is more useful dramatically. We have not extensively described the system whereby in-core neutron sensors operate a variety of 'fail-safe' systems but have merely implied this in the capability of the computer system to SCRAM the reactor automatically. The scenario for the final LOCA disaster is taken directly from a number of government documents.

While plutonium is the most toxic substance known, the metal's solubility in body fluids is so low that workers have survived with large fragments of the metal lodged inoperably in an extremity. We have encountered a persistent story that the Manhattan Project regulations called for immediate amputation if extremity tissues were contaminated, but we suspect that this story is apocryphal. However, soluble salts of plutonium, on entering the body, would be quickly distributed by the venous system to all parts of the body with eventual fatal results. The degree of this hazard and the methods of coping with it are a source of some debate among radiation medical specialists. In the absence of a qualified MD and at an accident site some distance from a hospital, we believe that the use of a tourniquet would not be sufficient first aid in such an accident as we have described in Chapter 22. While a surgeon would probably disapprove of such a primitive and inelegant solution as we have described, a layman might, we feel, choose the more drastic solution.

While the decay heat from the fission product inventory in the Prometheus reactors is sufficient to account for the meltdown described in the novel, we might expect further heat as fuel metals from the reclamation plant enter the caverns and become critical because of the surrounding hydrated limestone. Such a reaction appears to have happened spontaneously in nature. French researchers have recently reported in *Bulletin d'Informationes Scientifiques et Techniques* on the discovery of fossil reactors in the African Republic of Gabon ... beds of U-235-rich uranium surrounded by hydrated minerals and ground water ... which in the geological past have reached criticality and operated for extended periods to produce thermal power equivalent to the operation of a ten-kilowatt reactor for a million years.

Since one of us has some years of experience with technological thinking in government and both of us are still too aware of the recent cover-up scandals in high office, we make no apologies for the attitudes we have attributed to Brandt, Cushing, or the members of our fictitious joint congressional invesigating committee. The dollar investment, both private and Federal, in fission power is now so high that we feel unusual steps will be taken to protect it. A retrenchment from fission power could well bankrupt the major power companies of the country.

We do not believe that geothermal power or solar power – valuable as each of them may become – or any of the other proposed new sources of power can ever be more than supplements to the power demands of a modern industrial nation. The obvious and costly answer to this dilemma is the development of fusion power (although here we encounter ecological problems of thermal pollution). Unfortunately, present funding for fusion research is painfully inadequate and philosophically misdirected because it assumes that the problem is an engineering one. Fusion power has been demonstrated in the laboratory, but as of now the energy needed to initiate fusion is greater than the energy obtained. However, the break-even point is slowly being approached and new techniques such as laser initiation show much promise.

A hybrid-breeder concept (as contrasted with the straight breeder reactors now being built) has recently been proposed. This postulates a near break-even fusion reactor as a source of both power and neutrons which would breed uranium-235 as a fuel for conventional reactors through neutron capture in thorium billets surrounding the reactors. Many of the problems of conventional reactors still remain, however. Proponents argue that such a scheme would allow the eventual phasing out of fission power while providing the money and experience needed to develop a practical fusion reactor. While the concept is technically interesting, we feel that the capital outlay for such plants might better be invested in fusion development *per se*.

We would like to thank Dr James Benford for technical help during the research for this novel and for reading and commenting on the final manuscript. We would also like to thank Dr Reynold F. Brown, Clinical Professor of Radiology and Administrator of Environmental Health and Safety for the University of California, San Francisco, for reading the manuscript and offering criticism on the descriptions of the medical effects of radiation. Thanks are also due Tom Passavant and

Ron J. Julin for assistance in the demanding library research, as well as to Gene Klinger, research assistant, first reader and harried gopher for the two of us while displaying a patience and good humour beyond the call of duty. Finally, we would like to thank Friends of the Earth for technical assistance, as as well as several gentlemen who, for obvious reasons, would prefer to remain anonymous. Despite the inestimable help of the above, errors of fact may well have crept in. For these, we accept complete responsibility.

It should be mentioned that the Atomic Regulatory Committee (ARC) and its subcommittee for Nuclear Reactor Safety are fictitious agencies – as are various others. The knowledgeable reader will, of course, recognize their counterparts in real life.

Finally, a note on creative intent. We view ourselves primarily as story tellers and our purpose was to write a thriller based on the menaces of the world as it now is. *The Prometheus Crisis*, while a 'didactic' novel, is not a polemic, and we would be disappointed if it were viewed in that light. Nevertheless, we hope that the reader, having finished the book, will stop and consider where we are going. It is our sincere hope that *The Prometheus Crisis* is not a scenario for such a catastrophic accident in the near future. We are more than a little afraid that it may be.

March 10, 1975

Thomas N. Scortia,
Sausalito, California
Frank M. Robinson,
San Francisco, California

Prologue

Excerpt from the hearings of the special *Congressional Subcommittee on Nuclear Energy – The Cardenas Bay Incident* (Document No. Y4.NE7/2:Cb/2/979–80). Second Day, Second Session. Senator Clement A. Hoyt (D, Idaho), Chairman. Present: Senators Harold J. Stone (D, Pennsylvania), Robert J. Clarkson (R, Vermont), Clinton E. Marks (R, Connecticut), and Representatives Horace T. Holmburg (R, Indiana) and James X. Paine (D, Massachusets).

Senator Hoyt I would like to thank Dr Caulfield for his presentation of the events following the failure of the initial SCRAM sequence of Prometheus One. Do you have any other pertinent films, photographs or other exhibits to show the Committee?

Dr Caulfield No, Senator. I'll present the detailed casualty and property damage data, as well as the statistical projection of future casualties, as an addendum to my report.

Senator Hoyt Unless my colleagues object, then, you may step down, Dr Caulfield. I think it would be appropriate at this time to recall Mr Parks. For the benefit of Senator Stone and Representative Holmburg, who were absent this morning, would you please state your full name and your position with Western Gas and Electric at the time of the incident.

Mr Parks My name is Gregory T. Parks. I was General Manager of the Cardenas Bay Nuclear Facility during the period in question.

Senator Stone You say you were. May I ask your present position?

Mr Parks I'm no longer with Western, Senator. I'm an engineering consultant now – I guess the term for it is 'self-employed'.

Senator Hoyt As General Manager, I take it you were responsible for the actual construction of the Prometheus complex?

Mr Parks No, sir. Fulton Engineering was the prime contractor for the complex, with Renkin operating as a subcontractor to Fulton.

Senator Hoyt But you were responsible for the overall performance of the complex, the final shakedown of the plant and bringing it on stream?

Mr Parks That's correct, Senator. I was on the scene during the final days of construction and assumed the position of General Manager once the facility was completed. Both I and the contractors were, of course, answerable to the various Federal inspectors such as those from the Nuclear Reactor Safety subcommittee.

Senator Hoyt Then you must have formed some opinion of the performance of these contractors?

Mr Parks I did, sir.

Senator Hoyt What was it?

Mr Parks I guess you could call it one of quiet horror.

Senator Stone That's a pretty harsh indictment, Mr Parks. Do you mean the engineering and construction of the Prometheus facility was that much inferior to other nuclear plants in the country?

Mr Parks No, sir. The history of most other nuclear plants would show a similar lack of engineering quality control. That the carelessness should carry over to the construction of the most recent and biggest reactor complex, I found particularly frustrating – and frightening.

Representative Holmburg I'm not sure I follow you, Mr Parks. Are you implying the job was featherbedded or what?

Mr Parks It's difficult to explain to a layman, sir. In most construction jobs, including that of standard fossil-fuel power plants, you can usually live with an occasional bit of poor design or faulty workmanship. The tolerances aren't that tight. With a nuclear plant, poor design or sloppy workmanship can have disastrous consequences.

Senator Clarkson That was your problem, poor design?

Mr Parks That was only part of it, Senator. At Prometheus we were dealing with a group of vendors and engineers who had no appreciation of what might happen if parts didn't meet specifications or if design problems weren't completely thought out. They didn't give a damn, sir, and that attitude pervaded most of the plant.

Senator Stone Attitudes are hard things to verify, Mr Parks.

Mr Parks That may be, sir, but it was that attitude that led to the Cardenas Bay disaster – too many people simply didn't give a damn.

First Day

1

The pilot's voice was a quiet murmur over the intercom. 'We'll be landing at Cardenas Bay in ten minutes, gentlemen.'

Eliot Cushing loosened his seat belt and stretched. The trip in the Learjet had been a short but uncomfortable commuter hop and he'd be glad when they landed. Unfortunately, every plant he visited was built in the sticks, miles away from decent airports, decent hotels and, especially, decent restaurants.

'Gregory Parks will be meeting us, Eliot,' Brandt said. 'You remember our plant manager, don't you?' His voice was too friendly, too eager to please.

'Really can't recall,' Cushing murmured. He leaned back in his chair and glanced out the window. Brandt and Walton were still visible as half reflections in the glass. He was going to have to deal with both of them, though he didn't anticipate that either one would prove difficult. Gerrold Walton was only a hired flack and didn't matter. Hilary Brandt, ageing and faintly pudgy, might be more of a problem. He was Vice-President for Nuclear Development for Western Gas and Electric but still thought of himself as more of an engineer than a company politician. Engineers tended to be overcautious; as a group they could usually think of a dozen reasons why something should not be done. On the other hand, most politicians had a streak of the venal – a definite asset when a push came to a shove.

Brandt had that worried look on his face which meant that he was sizing up Cushing in return and was about to start asking questions or offering reassurances, either of which Cushing could do without at the moment. Cushing closed his eyes and kneaded the bridge of his nose, forestalling conversation.

Parks was the one he would have to worry about. From every inquiry he had made, Parks was all engineer and no politician. Hard-working, honest, dedicated ... Cushing half smiled to himself. A hell of a combination.

He opened his eyes. 'Tell me about your Mr Parks,' he said softly. 'I've read his reports and for three months now they've been one solid stream of bitches.'

Brandt started to reply when the pilot's voice cut in. 'You can see the plant now, off to the right. We'll be passing directly over it in another minute.'

Cushing held up his hand, stopping Brandt in mid-sentence, and leaned closer to the window. In the approaching dusk the deep shadows below modelled the plant in bold relief against the ground: a sprawling collection of factory buildings, the kind you found on the outskirts of Detroit or Cleveland or a hundred other industrial cities. There was nothing to distinguish them from a hundred thousand counterparts – except for, perhaps, the curious lack of windows.

That, and the dome – a huge hemisphere painted white so that at this time of day it was a blinding half globe, red with the reflected fire of the setting sun. Underneath the almost mirror-like sheen were layers of concrete and steel – almost four feet of concrete laced with massive steel reinforcing bars, designed to contain any commonplace failure of the reactors themselves.

The largest nuclear plant in the world, Cushing thought sombrely. Four reactors of three thousand megawatts each, a total of twelve thousand. The biggest. And the best.

'Your man Parks?' he reminded Brandt politely.

Brandt looked uncomfortable. 'What do you want to know about him?'

Cushing spread his hands. 'Anything you think is relevant.'

Brandt cleared his throat. 'He's probably the best engineer in the company. Took his bachelor's at Illinois, his master's in nuclear engineering at Carnegie Tech. He's been in nukes for almost ten years now. Assistant plant manager at Chippewa Falls, then plant manager here. He's been on the site for a year and a half.'

'I've read his résumé,' Cushing said, faintly bored. He opened his briefcase and took out some papers. 'We keep getting his reports – your office forwards them to us, of course. He's unhappy with the vendors; he's unhappy with the staff; he's unhappy with the plant itself and he's been giving our compliance teams fits.'

'I wouldn't expect him to be completely happy,' Brandt said nervously. His forehead had developed an oily sheen. 'I wouldn't expect a good engineer to be smug.'

'I wouldn't expect him to keep crying that the sky is falling, either,' Cushing said. 'Dammit, you know how much we've increased our compliance standards in the last ten years.' He singled out one of the papers and slipped on a pair of reading glasses. 'He complains that the modifications of the emergency core cooling system haven't been—'

'We don't use that term any more,' Walton interrupted. Cushing took off his reading glasses and stared at him. His only objection to nonentities was when they tried to stop being nonentities, though Walton was a man remarkably easy to dislike for other reasons. A big man, slowly going to fat, dressed in the latest mod fashions – the sort that looked good on smaller men but on Walton only gave the appearance that his pants were too short and his arms were too long. An oddly juvenile appearance for one in his late thirties, though it matched the personality.

Cushing shot an irritated glance at Brandt, then said quietly, 'You don't use what term any more?'

Walton giggled, flustered. ' "Emergency core cooling system." We use "excursion moderator" instead. The word "emergency" has semantic overtones that worry the public.'

'I see,' Cushing said gravely. If the local boniface tried to double him up with this idiot, there'd be hell to pay. 'About Parks,' he said again, 'is he married?'

'In name only,' Brandt said. He had found a handkerchief and was mopping his face. 'His wife didn't come out here with him; apparently she doesn't like small towns.'

'For a year and a half. Interesting.' Cushing made a small notation on a tablet. 'Any hobbies?'

It was Walton's turn to be helpful again. 'He's an antique-car buff. Last time I was here, I got a hernia riding over some of the back roads in his Reo.'

He might be worth his keep after all, Cushing thought, making another note. Parks undoubtedly had a love of machinery, not an uncommon trait in engineers. 'What about your number two man?'

'Tom Glidden.'

Cushing raised an eyebrow. 'Why number two?' Over the years he had met Glidden a number of times. He was a fixture with Western, a man who had made a profession out of avoiding decisions; he had no enemies but neither did he have any real friends.

'He's been with the company a long time,' Brandt said.

Cushing nodded. 'You two started out together. Understandable. What about your third in line?'

'Mark Abrams – younger than Parks, more shrewd than smart.'

17

'Capable?'

Brandt's eyes narrowed slightly, trying to guess what was on Cushing's mind. 'I would say so. Again, not as capable as Parks, but then, he doesn't have the experience.'

He had his own dossier on Abrams, but Brandt's remarks were something to remember. He put the papers back in his briefcase and closed it with a snap. 'Parks is dissatisfied with the operation of the plant; he doesn't think it's ready to go on stream at full power. Is that right?'

'I don't think he's that dissatisfied,' Brandt said cautiously. 'He'd like to see it delayed a few weeks.'

Cushing folded his glasses and thrust them back in his shirt pocket. 'What do you think, Hilary? Is the plant ready?'

'That's why I came along,' Brandt said. 'I want a first—'

'Do you know what's involved, Hilary?' Cushing leaned forward in his seat, not waiting for a reply, and looked at him intently. 'A total of twelve thousand megawatts, enough to supply the electrical needs of half of California. It's equal to importing 144 million barrels of high-grade crude a year. What's low-sulphur oil going for now? Almost twenty a barrel? That's close to three billion dollars a year, quite a chunk in our balance of payments. The plant itself cost five, most of it from the Government. Prometheus, Hilary, is the keystone in our own self-sufficiency, the prototype of a dozen more plants.'

He sat back. 'It's taken us eight years to get here,' he mused. He was silent for a moment, then said, 'Your man Parks is General Manager. If he doesn't think the plant is ready, he's legally authorized to delay it.'

Brandt was sweating heavily. 'He thinks it's risky.'

'Do you?' Cushing was on the edge of his seat again. 'We set a target date three months ago, Hilary, and you agreed to it. A dedication, formal ceremonies, a speech by the President – the works. But the convention is next week and it would be nice if the party could say the country was now self-sufficient in energy and Prometheus was hooked into the national grid.'

A little colour seeped back into Brandt's face; he began to look stubborn. Cushing relaxed, backing off mentally.

'Nobody from the Commission is authorized to overrule us, Eliot,' Brandt said heavily.

Cushing shrugged. 'I never said I wanted to, Hilary. The Government has always held the position that it's the reactor owner and operator who bear the ultimate responsibility for the public safety.' He was conciliatory now. 'The public utilities

18

and the Government have always worked hand in hand; we'll be working together even closer in the future.'

The intercom came back to life again. 'Looks like something's happening down on the beach.'

Cushing leaned toward the window. They were banking over the ocean and flying inland now. It was almost dark but he could make out the phosphorescence of the surf. Just inside it were a number of lights that looked like the headlights of automobiles. Brandt had been looking, too, and muttered, 'Probably some kids on a beach party.'

Then they were past the beach, rapidly loosing altitude. Cushing glanced past Brandt's bulky shoulders through the pilot's windscreen. In the distance, lights suddenly bloomed, forming a long rectangle. At its sides, other lights fanned out over the landing strip.

'Hilary,' Cushing said thoughtfully. 'What's Parks going to do when he finds out he doesn't have two weeks to go on stream – that he only has three days?'

2

You could feel the tension in the room, Parks thought, like the air just before a thunderstorm. Four men who had to cooperate to survive and each one of them had reasons to hate the guts of the other three.

It was Barney Lerner who said angrily, 'I don't get it. Why this soon?'

Parks took the crumpled wad of yellow paper out of his waste-basket and flattened it out on his desk, glancing over it quickly. He handed it to Lerner. 'Take a look for yourself – nothing beyond the fact that Cushing and Brandt will arrive around seven tonight. I'm supposed to meet them; command performance.'

'You said something about a man named Walton when you read it the first time,' Abrams said. 'Who's he?' He sounded relaxed and at ease; Parks guessed there were no sweat stains on his shirt or grease on his hands. Not quite dapper, but close.

'Jerry Walton,' Parks said, not bothering to hide his distaste. 'Public relations expert, so-called. You started with Western late, so you've never had the dubious pleasure of meeting him.'

Abrams nodded, obviously reserving judgement. He reserved judgement on almost everything, Parks thought. He wasn't about to make a mistake in disliking the wrong people – or liking them, for that matter. Mark Abrams – thin, boyish, brittle and reserved. He had never quite forgotten that he had spent two years at West Point before changing his mind and switching over to a civilian school. He wore his background like a uniform; Parks knew without ever checking that his shoes had a spit shine. Brilliant, Parks thought, with no experience or humanity to temper it. Abrams would do fine until he hit a situation where common sense was more in demand than sheer brilliance. Parks was momentarily fascinated by what would happen then. He wondered why Abrams had left the Point, then shrugged. It wasn't any of his business. But he had the uncomfortable feeling that if it were the other way around, Abrams would have made it *his* business ...

'Nobody's answering my question,' Lerner repeated sarcastically. 'Why so soon? The dedication ceremony is two weeks from now. You can't tell me a vice-president of the company and a Federal committee vice-chairman are going to hang around for two weeks until it's time to cut the ribbon. If they do, I'm sure as hell not going to baby-sit for them for fourteen days.'

'Nobody asked you to, Barney,' Parks said quietly. Lerner's face reddened with anger. Red hair, red face, a mass of red strands curling over the neck of his tee shirt – the Red Man, Parks mused. And a pale pink in politics. Parks knew from Lerner's security dossier that he'd been active in a number of student movements during his college days. Every investigation had cleared him, however; his radical views had never gone beyond the level of rhetoric. Unfortunately, at thirty he still hadn't mellowed; he could be as abrasive as a file rasping over bare knuckles. If he weren't so good in his job as Chief of Safety and Quality Assurance, Parks thought, he might have fired Lerner long ago. As it was, his abrasiveness had caused turmoil more than once among his sizeable staff. And his involvement with Karen hadn't made their own relationship any easier.

'It's probably a routine trip,' Glidden said casually. 'It's been months since we've had a visit from the brass, they're overdue.'

Lerner turned on him, bitter. 'What's the grapevine say, Tom? You've got a pipeline. You should know what's up.'

Glidden flushed and Parks felt a twinge of sympathy for him. If Lerner was the red man, Glidden was grey – grey in appearance and grey in mood and attitude. He had been with the company since Day One and his progress up the ladder had been automatic. He had reached his level of incompetence several promotions ago – raises since then had been more in the nature of corporate charity that pats on the back for work well done. A man who was out of his depth, condemned to flounder around until retirement. Even the office boys sensed it. Yet he'd rather talk to Glidden than to either Abrams or Lerner; at least the man was human. Abrams was a threat, idling in the bullpen, waiting for Parks to make that final fatal mistake. And if he did make it, Lerner would be there to tell him about it at the time and remind him of it afterwards.

'I don't know anything more than anybody else,' Glidden said reluctantly. 'Why should I?' He sat there now, oddly vulnerable; a colourless, bluff fat man hiding behind his bulk. Maybe that was his problem, Parks thought. Glidden had always been too big for his own good and usually wound up in a big man's double bind : if he hit back, he was a bully, and if he didn't, he was a coward.

'Because you and Brandt have always been buddy-buddy ever since you both joined Western,' Lerner shot back.

'Shut up, Barney,' Parks said sharply. With his knack for tact, Lerner's political career must have been brief, he thought. And ten to one it was also responsible for his missing front tooth – lost, according to Lerner, when he had served with the Israeli Army at the age of twenty-five. Not a hand grenade, Parks thought, just somebody's hand.

The intercom broke his chain of thought. 'Paul Marical is here, Mr Parks. He says it can't wait.'

Marical, Parks thought wryly, the plant's prime malingerer. Flu, a cold, food poisoning, sinus headaches – if it was going around, Marical would get it. 'All right, send him in.'

Marical was Lerner's size and build, only dark where Lerner was red. A small, unobtrusive man, he would be a definite asset if you could depend on him to show up for work.

'Sorry to interrupt, Mr Parks,' Marical said, glancing apprehensively around the room. 'It's those damned shearer blades Fulton sent us. They're the wrong size. If we don't get replacements soon, we'll have to shut down the whole fuel reclamation line. They say they can fly us replacements tomorrow but there'll be an extra charge.'

'Of course – they screw up and then we have to pay them extra to correct their own mistake.'

Marical held out the requisition. Parks thought momentarily of wadding it into a ball, then grabbed it and signed it. Marical turned to leave and Parks suddenly frowned and said, 'You feeling all right, Paul? You look terrible.'

'I'm OK,' Marical said apologetically. 'A little indigestion – it goes away.' And then, oddly: 'Thanks for asking.'

As soon as Marical had left, Lerner said, 'You know what Fulton's motto is? "You get something extra with Fulton." Brother, do you ever!'

Parks ignored him. 'Brandt, Cushing and Walton,' he repeated ticking them off on his fingers. 'If it were just Brandt, it would be company business. If it were Brandt and Cushing alone, it would be strictly an inspection trip. With Walton along, it's neither of those – and I think I know what it is.'

They were all looking at him now, even Glidden, who for once didn't act as if he had known about it all along. 'I think they want us to chop a couple of days out of the schedule.'

There was dead silence for a moment. 'You've got to be kidding,' Lerner objected. 'We won't be ready for a month yet.'

'That's not true,' Abrams objected mildly. 'We could be on stream in forty-eight hours. Number four reactor is down to quarter power by now. We're raising the jacket and pile temperatures slowly to avoid heavy thermal stresses. The new programming should bring the reactors on stream pretty fast now that the integrity of the structures has been checked.'

'That's right,' Lerner said sarcastically. 'We can perform miracles – but it's risky. In a fast start, it's too damned easy to strain a marginal component.'

'I've got my own objections to it,' Parks said. 'But if they asked you to bring it on stream early, Barney, would any of your safety staff complain? What would *you* say?'

Lerner shook his head violently, his face redder than usual. 'I'd tell 'em to piss up a rope. For the last month we've been relatively clean but if I gave you a report on everything that's gone wrong before then, I'd run out of paper. We had one stainless-steel fitting supposed to be copper-nickel. It was even stamped copper-nickel. But don't believe what you read – it was pure stainless steel. It would have lasted two weeks and then all of Prometheus One would have gone down the drain. Throw in a dozen or two lousy welds that somehow passed a rigorous no-fault inspection and let's not forget the diffuser blade those half-ass klutzes from Renkin bolted in backwards.

You know what would have happened if we hadn't caught it?'

'But we did catch it,' Abrams objected. 'It wasn't that big a deal.'

Lerner's eyes narrowed. 'The difference between you and me, Abrams, is that I keep score and you don't. That's the fourth time in a month that the Renkin whiz kids have flunked simple addition. And Renkin builds half the reactors in the country!'

Lerner had a temperament like rough sandpaper, Parks thought again. 'What's your opinion, Mark?'

Abrams looked faintly uneasy; he hadn't expected to be put on the spot. 'I think it's a hypothetical question,' he said finally. 'They haven't asked us to cut our schedule and I think we're just spinning our wheels talking about it.'

'But if they did,' Parks persisted.

Abrams now had a somewhat furtive look in his eyes and Parks wondered again why he had really left West Point. 'I guess it would depend on the circumstances.'

'I just bet it would,' Lerner said contemptuously.

'Tom?'

Glidden acted as he always did when forced to make a decision. He looked from one to another to see where the power lay and what was expected of him. It was force of habit by now. 'I think we could cut some time, maybe a day or two, if everything went well.' His voice had a let's-all-be-sensible-about-this ring and he settled back with a faintly pleased expression on his face. The Great Compromiser, Parks thought with disgust, in a field where there was no room for compromise.

Which left it up to him. With the exception of Lerner, nobody would back him – Glidden would compromise and Abrams would try to avoid committing himself up until the very last minute. Lerner backed him all right, but despised him for not going far enough fast enough.

He stood up. 'My decision, as usual,' he said wryly. 'Well, we're not going to cut any time. I'm going to ask for an additional two weeks' delay. We're not ready now; we won't be ready in a week or even two weeks. Go on stream when they want us to and we won't stay on stream five minutes.'

There was a gleam in Abram's eye and Parks smiled to himself. 'Mark.' He turned to Glidden. 'And you too, Tom. I want complete summary reports from both of you, covering all of the difficulties to date as well as an estimate on when we may safely go on stream. Barney, have your statistical section give me a complete failure analysis based on the number of probable defective components. I want an analysis of the defects Fabel's compliance teams have turned up. Go through every one of the NRC reports. Make it thorough, gentlemen. These will be part of my report to the top brass.'

Abrams' gleam faded and Glidden looked uneasy. Parks shuffled some papers into his briefcase. 'Barney, you want to help me check out the balcony control system?'

Abrams looked slightly miffed. 'The new computer will handle it. I checked it out myself.'

'Did you check out the operator as well?' Parks asked dryly. 'The computer's no better than the man who's programming it, Mark. You remember – GIGO? Garbage In, Garbage Out?' Abrams' face promptly fell.

He was really tired, Parks thought when he left his office. He had been pushing it for a week and working long hours even before that. So had everybody in the plant and that bothered him even more. Tired men made mistakes, and with Prometheus, mistakes could be disastrous.

For just a moment then, it almost overwhelmed him. A bigger-than-life plant with bigger-than-life problems and he was just one tiny, human being ...

He shook the feeling and smiled to himself. Fatigue also did strange things to your emotional state; for one, it tended to make you petty.

But it had still felt good to put down a potential replacement.

3

Digging for clams after dinner had been a great idea, Rob Levant thought. Willy hadn't wanted to go at first. There was a Creature Feature he'd planned to watch on TV – but then his father and mother had gotten into an argument and Willy had been glad to duck out.

The tide was out by the time they reached the beach. They started digging in the wet sand at one end of the Western Gas and Electric property and worked their way along the beach. It quickly became a contest to see who could find the most and Rob, as usual, was the winner.

'It runs in the family,' he bragged. 'If your old man was a fisherman, you'd know how to find them.' He suddenly changed the subject, looking at Willy curiously. 'What were your folks arguing about?'

Willy shrugged. 'Dad had to work again tonight, he's been putting in overtime for three weeks now and Mom says he's killing himself.'

Fishermen didn't have overtime, Rob thought. You got up before the sun was up and you worked from dawn to late afternoon – every day, unless the weather was so bad you couldn't take a boat out. He suddenly felt Willy's hand dip into his pail; he jerked it away. 'Dig for your own damn clams!' he protested. 'It's not my fault you don't know how!'

For a moment Willy looked guilty. 'Why don't you show me? Afraid I'd find more than you if I knew?'

Rob nodded. 'OK, next time we go out, I'll show you the best spots.'

Willy looked at him suspiciously. 'That's what you said last time.' He suddenly shivered, tugging his windbreaker tighter around him.

'What's wrong?' Rob asked. 'Getting chilled?'

Willy lowered his voice. 'Somebody's walking on my grave,' he whispered in sepulchral tones.

'Oh, crap,' Rob said, feeling very grown-up.

'No,' Willy hissed. 'It feels like somebody's watching me. Ever get the feeling that somebody you can't see is watching you?'

Rob glanced at the cliffs behind them; the fence lights were just going on around the plant. 'Maybe it's somebody up there.'

'No.' Willy shivered convincingly. 'It's something else.'

Rob felt the goose pimples forming in spite of himself; he glanced uncertainly around at the darkening beach. The lengthening shadows were making him uneasy. He wondered if anybody could be hiding in the darkness at the bottom of the cliffs.

Willy suddenly grabbed for his bucket of clams and turned to run down the beach. 'It's your own fault!' he hollered. 'You knew where all the best spots were and you wouldn't tell!'

Rob said, 'God damn you!' He caught up with Willy and aimed a wild punch at his friend. It didn't connect; for a moment he was off balance, then up and running after Willy. His feet like lead in the sand as Willy rapidly outdistanced him. Then he veered over to the hard, damp sand at the very edge of the beach and began to make better time. Occasionally he splashed through the lacy edge of the surf, his sneakers sinking in the softer sand and spattering his pants with water. At one point, he almost tripped over the untied laces in one of his shoes. There was no time to retie them; otherwise Willy would get away and would never stop lording it over him.

He headed away from the surf now, trying to strike a compromise between the water-soaked sand and the drier but even harder-going beach. He dodged a stump sticking out of the sand, leaped a mass of smelly seaweed, then dug in his toes for a final spurt. Willy was slowing down, his breath coming fast and heavy. Another stump lay just ahead of him, half in and half out of the water; he took a deep breath and leaped over it. In midair he felt something grab at him and he sprawled forward on his face.

His loose shoelaces had caught in something. For a moment he lay there, the wind knocked out of him; then he turned and sat up to free himself. A flopping limb of the half-buried stump had snagged him. He swore quietly to himself; Willy would be a block away by now.

Then he yelled frantically, 'Let me go! Let me go!' A man's hand, thrusting from the sand, had grabbed his laces. Someone had been waiting for him and had clutched at him as he had passed.

A hundred feet ahead, Willy came to a sudden halt. 'Rob?' He was a little cautious, Rob had faked him out before. He started to walk slowly back. 'Rob? What's wrong?'

Rob struggled frantically, his heart thumping like mad, and yelled again. The hand flopped back and forth, as if its owner had no control over it. Then Rob had worked himself free. He ran a few feet and turned to see if the man were pursuing him. The figure hadn't moved. It was then that Rob realized the man was buried in the sand up to his shoulders, that only one arm was free. He stopped running and edged back to see if he could make out who it was. He screamed then and stumbled backward. Behind him he heard Willy's own cry of horror.

The moon had risen now, casting just enough light to outline the terrible ruin of what had once been the face of a living man.

4

Parks walked to the end of the corridor and leaned against the wall, his hand poised over the balcony elevator button without pressing it. Lerner studied him, trying to read his face.

'You're really going to ask for a two-week delay?'

'It should be a month.' Parks hesitated. 'You realize they're not going to give it to us,' he said.

'Then they're a bunch of dim-witted bastards,' Lerner said angrily.

It was always so easy for Lerner, Parks thought, resentment building within him. In his own eyes, Lerner was always courageous and everybody else was chicken. 'You know who will pass on your report, don't you, Barney? Brandt and Cushing. But if it doesn't work, we can always man the mimeograph machines – insist that the plant be turned over to the people. People's Energy Plant Number One. "Power to the People." We could even dust off that old slogan; for once it would have some relevance.'

Lerner looked at him, startled and angry but not quite sure what to say. 'That's a low blow,' he said finally. 'You knew my background. If it bothered you, you didn't have to hire me.'

Parks pressed the elevator button. 'I'm sorry, Barney. Chalk it up to the fact that I'm tired and it's starting to show. I knew all about your background and it didn't bother me then and it doesn't bother me now. All the student radicals I ever knew are either selling insurance, planting bombs or making leather belts. You deserve a gold star for at least being different.'

In the elevator, Lerner shifted uncomfortably. Something was on his mind. Parks waited for him to break the silence. 'Karen and I are engaged,' Lerner said abruptly.

'Congratulations,' Parks said after a moment. 'Does she think so, too?'

Lerner coloured. 'You can ask her.'

Parks shook his head. 'If she wants me to know, Barney, she'll tell me. And if she wants to tie a can to me, that's her privilege. I like her as a person and it'll be a pleasure to know her under any circumstances.'

'Even if she no longer goes to bed with you?'

Parks consciously controlled his temper. 'I learned long ago never to date a woman unless I could be happy with just the pleasure of her company. If anything else developed, fine.

Whether it developed with Karen and me is our business.' The elevator doors started to open. 'If you want to discuss it further, Barney, take it up with Karen.'

The observation balcony with its huge glass wall was vacant except for a lone technician sitting at a control console overlooking the reactor room.

'How's it going, Jeffries?'

'Fine, sir, just running some of the subprograms against the readout boards in Control Central.'

Parks stared through the glass at the floor below. The window itself was three inches thick, and with its high lead content more than enough to stop everything but high-energy gamma radiation. Not that he worried about such radiation in the balcony area. The pools of cooling water and the shielding of the reactors themselves handled such problems.

Still, the floor was a potential death trap without the safeguards for handling the hot used fuel rods. They had been operating the four reactors at quarter to half power for over six months as they worked out the bugs and made the necessary modifications to the auxiliary equipment. The present waste product inventory on the floor, either in the reactors or in the holding wells, was close to ten billion Curies, a fantastic mass of radioactive material. Without the cooling water of the holding wells, the fuel bundles would have melted from their own decay heat.

The floor was deserted now, although in another hour it would be teeming with activity. Prometheus reactor number one was now assembled and near critical while the vessel heads of reactors two, three and four had been lifted off by the huge bridge crane that spanned the entire room. The crane now stood motionless above an auxiliary fuel storage cell. Parks could see deep into the pools of water that were level with the flange of the reactors. Wisps of vapour played over the top of the water and occasionally a swell crossed the surface as the cooling pumps surged momentarily.

'Let me handle it a minute, Jeffries.'

He slid into the still-warm seat and pressed the button marked 'Video, Reactor Four', then glanced up at the bank of overhead cathode-ray viewing tubes. On the first of them, the image cleared rapidly and he was looking up from below through the heart of the operating reactor. Bundles of fuel elements filled the centre of the screen while surrounding them were half-withdrawn control rods. The whole interior of the reactor was suffused with an eerie radiance – white on the screen but greenish in reality, the Cherenkov radiation of active fission.

Parks watched for a moment, fascinated by the pulsing glow, then touched the button for Control Central. The scene shifted to the interior of a long, narrow control room; he could see the slowly spinning tape on the computer at the far end. The technicians in the room didn't notice the red light on the camera; they were too intent on their tasks.

Parks said, 'How's the program, Delano?'

A harried man in the foreground looked startled for a moment, then realized the room was on camera. 'Not too good, Greg. We've been bringing Prometheus One up to standby temperature but we're still getting spurious responses on channels twelve through fifteen. I've been on manual twice this afternoon.'

In the background, four technicians hunched over their boards, calling out fuel-rod temperatures in a singsong voice.

'I have eight hundred Kelvin in bundle twenty ...'

'Delta tee at twenty is minus fifty and falling ...'

'Hold it,' one of the technicians suddenly said. 'I have a positive delta tee in bundle one-five-oh.' He checked the board in front of him, then repeated, 'I have a positive and climbing.'

'We've got a hot spot,' Delano said, frustration in his voice. He now ignored both Parks and the camera. 'Automatic override?'

'Hasn't kicked in yet,' another technician said. There was a trace of excitement in his voice.

Parks and Lerner glanced at each other. 'Manual override,' Parks muttered under his breath.

'Manual override, three-quarters rods,' Delano repeated below.

'Delta tee still positive.' Parks imagined he could hear the distant hiss of hydraulic motors operating the control rods.

'I've got a rod hang up!'

'Stand by for a SCRAM,' Delano said quietly. He sounded defeated.

Christ, Parks thought, a SCRAM might damage the fuel assemblies if any were buckling. In a SCRAM all control rods were thrust full in at high speed. He threw the reactor view onto an adjacent screen and hurriedly glanced at it. The reason for the hang-up was obvious.

'Delano,' he shouted into the console mike, 'you've got a cladding failure in two hundred!' In the eerie light within the pile, fuel bundle two hundred was bowing at one side. The Zircaloy cladding of one of the fuel rods had peeled away and the bowed bundle had blocked a control rod.

'Full control rods in quadrant three,' Delano ordered.

As Parks watched, the control rods rose from their seating in the bottom of the reactor and thrust into the quadrant that held the critical fuel bundle. One of the rods struck the bundle and stopped. Its hydraulic motor whined and laboured for an instant and then the rod was through the twisted group of fuel elements.

'I have a negative,' a technician called out.

Parks could sense an almost physical wave of relief sweep the group below. He suddenly realized he had been holding his own breath. He wiped at his forehead; it was greasy with sweat. 'All right, Delano, take it below critical.'

Delano hesitated. 'The program is still—'

'To hell with the program, take it down manually.'

'You heard the man,' Delano said to the room at large. 'Take it down.'

'Nine hundred Kelvin, eight fifty, seven ...'

Another technician: 'We're subcritical.'

'Infrared signature?' Delano asked.

'Strength three.'

'Signal MIROS Control.' Delano looked into the camera. 'That was closer than I like, Greg.'

'Damn close,' Parks agreed, and turned off the camera. He sat there for a moment, then said almost to himself, 'I thought we had a complete outgassing check on all fuel bundles the day before yesterday.'

'Not all bundles,' Lerner corrected him. 'Just a test sampling.'

'Do you have replacements?'

'None with any better pedigree. We don't have the facilities to run complete failure checks on every assembly that comes in here.'

Parks nodded. 'All right, tear her down as soon as she's cool enough. Thank God for the auxiliary cooling system. Five years ago, we'd have to wait for days.'

Lerner said slowly, 'You going to tell Brandt? That was close.'

'I'll tell Brandt,' Parks said, his mind still on the accident. Over the console speaker, he could hear a technician saying softly, *'MIROS Control, MIROS Control, this is Cardenas Bay. We are now at emission strength here.'*

Too close, Parks thought. Too damned close.

5

Five hundred miles to the east of Cardenas Bay and far beyond the stratosphere, MIROS III – Military Intelligence and Reconnaissance Orbital Satellite – was crossing the terminator. At fifteen thousand miles an hour, it was outracing the line below that divided the darkness of the eastern part of the United States from the dusk that had settled on the West Coast. It was ugly, as satellites go, and had the same sort of utilitarian, no-nonsense look about it that a well-designed tank has.

Its purposes were vastly different – but still in the same league.

Almost three hundred miles below and to the west, in Denver, Colorado, in a concrete complex beneath the sprawling plant of Templar Aircraft Corp., a group of men monitored the signals from the satellite. They all wore yellow coveralls across the back of which was stencilled a stylized satellite ringed by the words 'Templar Missiles and Spacecraft Division' in electric blue. They spoke in low voices, taking notes in a cryptic shorthand, and gazed intently as MIROS' televised pictures flowed across a battery of viewing screens.

Frank Tebbets sat slouched in one of the observer seats on the third tier that swept along the back of the pie-shaped room. He sipped at a paper container of coffee, glanced at his wristwatch, then went back to watching the yellow-overalled technicians below him. The new Air Force monitor was late, but then new Air Force monitors were always late. This one, a rather chubby captain named Kloster, was breaking records – the briefing had been due at three that afternoon and it was already five.

Tebbets watched the image on one of the screen projections, then touched a button on his console, picking up the chest set that lay on top. 'You're losing sync, Number Three.'

He placed the button to his ear and heard the technician acknowledge. 'Give me a frame synchronization on camera two,' the man in the earphone said. There was a quiet acknowledgement and the screened image cleared, then began to dim.

'Number three solar panel is losing power,' the voice said in Tebbets' ear.

'It's probably in shadow; rotate the satellite five degrees.'

A wedge of light suddenly cut through the semi-darkness of the room. 'Thanks, I can make it from here,' somebody said. There were scuffling sounds on the rubber-matted concrete and Tebbets debated briefly weather he should give Kloster the standard MIROS Control initiation by leaving a half-filled coffee cup on the seat of his chair. Better not. They were all so damned formal nowadays ...

Kloster eased himself into the chair. By the smell of his breath, Tebbets decided the welcoming party had been a huge success. Kloster sighed contentedly. 'That executive dining room of yours is quite the place.'

Tebbets nodded, smiling in the gloom. 'I brown-bag it myself – ever since the scare three months ago.'

Kloster sobered slightly. 'What scare?'

'Nothing serious – something to do with the potato salad.'

Kloster took off his blue cap with the tarnished silver piping and placed it on the chair next to him. He was silent for a moment, obviously trying to decide if he was being put on. 'Did I miss anything?' His voice was chilly.

'MIROS III just crossed the terminator. About four o'clock there were some good shots of tank manoeuvres on the Siberian-PRC border.'

He could sense Kloster's disappointment. Then, doubtfully: 'From MIROS III?'

'No, MIROS IV.' Well, that was something at least. Kloster knew they couldn't see whenever they wanted to.

'MIROS III is approaching the West Coast now,' Tebbets continued. 'There's not much cloud cover, so our visuals are pretty good.'

'How's your infrared resolution?'

Kloster was no dummy, Tebbets thought; he had done his homework. He spoke into his chest mike. 'Charlie, give us the infrared.'

The image on the main monitoring screen dissolved and reassembled as a ghost image with strange shadings and inverted tone values.

'That heavy mottling to the north is a high-pressure area moving down past Oregon,' Tebbets said. 'The bright mass below Los Angeles is a forest fire. It's been burning for three days.'

'How about those bright spots along the coast?'

'Industrial heat sources – power plants, both fossil fuel and nuclear, plus a number of smelting and cracking plants. They all give out different heat patterns.'

'There's one out in the middle of the ocean,' Kloster said, curious.

'Let's see.' Tebbets pulled out a log book and consulted it a moment. 'That's the *Garfish*, a Poseidon-class submarine out of San Diego. Notice the fuzzy heat pattern? That means she's running half submerged.' Kloster turned on the chair lamp and began to jot down notes.

Another voice spoke in Tebbets' ear now. 'Cardenas Bay just signalled; they're down to strength three.'

Kloster looked up, startled; he had heard the same message. 'You get infrared reports from power stations?'

'Only the nuclear ones. Prometheus is the new twelve-thousand-megawatt facility at Cardenas Bay. They've been running shakedown for six months now. They keep us posted on their infrared signatures so we won't confuse them with an incoming warhead.'

Kloster now looked bored. He doodled a globe of the earth on his pad and said offhand, 'I thought you could get better resolution from MIROS than that.'

One good needle deserved another, Tebbets thought. 'Switch to visual, zoom three, Charlie.'

The image on the monitoring screen reversed and lost its ghost-like quality. The coastline expanded rapidly; the image now showed vast stretches of scrub forests and distant foothills. Tebbets guessed the apparent altitude at one thousand feet. MIROS itself was now over the ocean and Tebbets ordered the satellite rotated for a longer image. Now the screen held a high-angle shot of the Cardenas Bay reactor. It stood out sharply, outlined by its own lengthening shadows. Small points of light were already glowing in the parking lot to the north of the main reactor building.

Kloster seemed impressed. 'That's pretty big for a nuclear installation.' The stylized globe had now become the head of a man hanging upside down from a gibbet. The hanged man in the Tarot deck? Tebbets wondered.

'The buildings in the lower part of the screen are the reactor facility; the reprocessing plant is upper and adjacent to it. Underground passages connect the two for security reasons.'

Kloster glanced up. 'That's interesting.' He carefully added a lopsided grin to his hanging man.

33

Tebbets felt faintly annoyed. Kloster was going out of his way not to be impressed. 'Zoom seven, Charlie.'

'We're losing the image,' the voice in his ear said. 'We're past lateral correction limits.'

On the screen, the first sign of water appeared. 'Full resolution, Charlie.' The beach area with two tiny dots on it leaped up at them; the dots resolved themselves into two young boys. For just an instant, one seemed to be staring directly at them.

Kloster forgot his doodle. 'My God!' he breathed. 'From two hundred miles up and in poor light at that. That's incredible!'

That was more like it, Tebbets thought. 'That's what you're paying us for, Captain; we can see not only the cat but the smile as well.' The image of the boys drifted off the screen and the water's edge crept on. A black mass protruded from the sandy beach. Water washed over it and the mass shifted position as Tebbets watched. There was an uneasy familiarity to it. 'Give me better focus, Charlie. Try the vernier.'

The black mass now had form and definition. Even in the shadows of evening, there was no mistaking what it was.

'For God's sake, that's a body!' Kloster said. He leaned forward in his chair, fascinated.

'Half buried in the sand,' Tebbets added. 'The tide must have uncovered it.' On screen, the right shoulder and one arm were now free. The arm flopped aimlessly back and forth in the surf. Tebbets reached for a nearby phone.

Kloster caught his arm. 'What the hell do you think you're doing?'

'We ought to notify somebody,' Tebbets said, surprised.

Suddenly there was wire in Kloster's voice. For the first time that evening, Tebbets remembered that he was a civilian and Kloster was brass. 'Forget it, that's a breach of security – MIROS is top secret.'

'But we just can't—'

'Sure we can, Tebbets,' Kloster said softly. 'It's only a body; it'll keep.'

6

The night air was cool, a trace too much so, and Hilary Brandt felt chilled. He was really feeling his age, he thought, when the night air could get to him. He stood beneath one of the mercury-vapour lamps that lined the runway, watching the pilot unload their luggage. The man's complexion was pale, almost bluish, in the light from the mercury lamps and Brandt guessed that he himself looked much the same way. The difference between him and the pilot was that he felt the way he looked. Too much pressure, he thought. Sooner or later the doctors would confirm what he already knew, that he was digesting himself from the inside out.

'I thought your man Parks was supposed to meet us,' Cushing said. He sounded faintly irritated, but then Cushing always sounded faintly irritated. Brandt felt a brief surge of resentment at Parks. Tonight, of all nights. He glanced at his watch. 'We're ten minutes early, he's usually right on the button.'

'Like a good engineer should be,' Cushing mimicked, not willing to be mollified.

Then the sound of the evening crickets was drowned out by that of several automobiles turning in the airport gates. A moment later, a station wagon rolled up to the landing strip. Brandt couldn't tell the make of the second car; it had stopped just beyond the circle of light, but it was large and obviously antique. Why the hell hadn't Parks brought the company Caddy? Walton was right about one thing; the Reo rode like a tank.

In the darkness a husky voice said, 'Get their baggage, will you, George?'

A WG and E guard appeared out of the darkness with a dolly and started loading their bags into the station wagon. A moment later, Parks strode into the circle of light. He was just over forty, tall and with an athlete's huskiness softened by the slight shoulder slump of a scholar. His nose was too large for his somewhat narrow face and his light-brown hair was, as always, uncombed.

Then Brandt realized with sudden shock that the pressures were telling on Parks, too. There were lines in his face and streaks of grey in his sideburns. The plant was a grindstone that was wearing them all down, Brandt thought.

Parks' grip, however, was as firm as ever. 'How are you, Hilary?' He gave a perfunctory nod to Walton. There was a moment's hesitation while he waited for Brandt to introduce him to Cushing.

'Eliot, this is our General Manager, Gregory Parks.'

They shook hands and murmured the usual pleasantries, each of them taking the measure of the other. Brandt couldn't tell whether Cushing liked what he saw or not; Cushing's expression was opaque, as usual. There was a slight edginess about Parks, however; he had obviously already made up his mind about the visitor. He couldn't dissemble worth a damn, Brandt thought. In his mind Parks had already labelled Cushing as a paper shuffler and it was only a matter of time until he made it obvious.

'I've got you booked at the Bay Lodge,' Parks said easily. He turned to the cars. 'You can either ride in the station wagon with Mike or with me in the Reo.'

'I've heard you were an antique-car buff,' Cushing said pleasantly. 'I'll opt for the Reo; I don't believe I've ever seen one.'

Brandt's eyes were more accustomed to the gloom beyond the landing-strip lights now and he could make out the high-profiled car parked behind the station wagon, its spare tyres set into the sloping front fenders. Parks ran his hand fondly over the hood. 'It's a 1931 Reo Custom Royale sports sedan – 358-cubic-inch straight eight. Styling by Alexis de Saknoffsky, a real classic.' He loked at Cushing expectantly.

Cushing hesitated, searching for the right thing to say. His interest had been purely political, Brandt thought. Parks wouldn't forgive him for that; he wasn't about to be bought by a casual show of interest in his hobby. 'I imagine it's very expensive,' Cushing said lamely, and got in.

'In money, I suppose so. In terms of love and attention, very few people can afford one,' Parks murmured coldly.

In the car, Cushing suddenly asked in a strained voice, 'Do you have a rag?'

Surprised, Parks handed one back to him. 'What's wrong?'

'Grease,' Cushing said dryly, wiping his hands. 'On the door handle.'

Parks laughed and Brandt could sense Cushing stiffen. 'I was working on it this morning. Just got in a set of original handles and thought I'd put them on.'

In the uncomfortable silence that followed, Brandt wondered if Parks had missed breakfast in his excitement to put on the handles. He also wondered how he was going to manage Parks when he had to give him the new schedule for Prometheus.

They were entering town now and Walton stared out the window, nodding his head approvingly. 'The plant has sure made a difference in the town; they didn't have many street lamps when I was here last. Seems like there are more shops in the business district, too.'

'Three bars and another restaurant,' Parks said. 'The plant's fully staffed now and the town thoughtfully provided some new places to cash paychecks.'

Cushing came alive in the back seat. 'What was the main business in town before they built the plant?'

'It was a small fishing village then – population about two thousand, closer to three and a half now not counting transients from the plant. Except for the bars, it's a pretty dead town at night. The fishermen go out early in the morning and we've been working the plant around the clock. It's strictly early to bed and early to rise.'

The lights of the business district retreated in the distance and Cushing asked casually, 'How are relations between the fishermen and the plant workers?'

'You've heard, huh?' Parks shrugged in the darkness of the car. 'Actually about what you'd expect – bad. The fishermen claim the plant is ruining their fishing and for all I know, they might be right. We're calling in a state fisheries expert next week.'

'We've already checked it out,' Walton interrupted. 'Not a shred of truth to it.'

'It doesn't matter whether *we* think the complaint is justified or not; the fishermen think it is,' Parks said, annoyed. 'They've been picketing the plant off and on and it's been the big story in the weekly paper ever since we went on shakedown.'

'That's bad; that's really bad,' Walton stuttered. 'I think I ought to send somebody in to help you with community relations; what we've really got here is a public information problem.'

'Walton,' Parks said curtly, 'do me a favour for once and don't send anybody at all. Last time you sent one of your flacks, it was all I could do to get him out of town ahead of the lynch mob. If you insist, for God's sake send one with a taste for older women; this is a small town, not your big city.'

'There were two sides to that story,' Walton objected stiffly.

'But the present situation demands action before your corporate image is—'

'Jerry,' Brandt sighed, 'we'll discuss it in the morning.'

They were almost out of town when Cushing broke the silence. 'You love machinery, don't you, Parks?' There was a peculiar undertone to the question that Brandt picked up on but couldn't figure out.

Parks glanced into the rear-view mirror. 'I think every engineer should,' he said quietly. 'Otherwise he shouldn't be an engineer. That's probably what's wrong with the plant; not enough people give a damn about machinery or understand what makes it tick. I'm not about to claim a machine has a soul but I'm not so sure it doesn't have feelings – in a manner of speaking.'

'I used to be an electronics officer in the Navy during World War II,' Cushing mused. 'We had an old radar – a Sugar George model, if I remember correctly – and whenever something went wrong with it, we used to kick it. It worked fine then.'

It was the wrong approach, Brandt thought, pained, and for Parks, it certainly had the wrong ending.

'It would have worked even better with graphite on the interlocks,' Parks said curtly.

Cushing sat silent for a moment and Brandt wondered when he would quit sparring. 'Sometimes, Parks, an engineer can get so wound up in the mechanics of a particular problem, he fails to see the larger picture.'

A faint smile fled across Parks' face. 'I prefer the one that goes, "For want of a nail, a shoe was lost." '

'Let me know when we get to the motel,' Cushing said, and leaned back against the cushions, closing his eyes.

Well, that was that, Brandt thought bleakly, wincing at a telltale twinge in his stomach. They hated each other's guts and sometime within the next few days he was going to have to choose between them.

7

Senator Hoyt This morning, the former General Manager of the Cardenas Bay complex, Mr Parks, testified that there was an undue amount of urgency in getting the Cardenas Bay facility on stream – that it was in part this pressure that led to the disaster that occurred.

Mr Brandt I believe he overstated the case, Senator. At least in the immediate sense. But with all due respect to this Committee, and in defence of Western Gas and Electric, there has always been a historical pressure on the utilities industry for more nuclear power. It was technology the Government wanted to develop, whatever the cost.

Representative Holmburg That's too quick a switch for me, Mr Brandt. We're discussing Western's culpability in this matter, not the Government's. It's not the Government that stood to make a profit, and it's not the Government that's been dragging its feet in building the plants needed to solve our energy crisis.

Mr Brandt Perhaps I've been in the business too long, sir, or perhaps I'm too proud of it, but I have to disagree. The public utility industry has always been well aware of the country's need for power and has always striven to fulfil it. Maybe we would have preferred to do it a different way, but once the die was cast, we did our damnedest.

Senator Stone As far as the role of the Government may have played, Mr Brandt, I'm not sure what you're referring to.

Mr Brandt It was before your time, Senator – no offence intended.

Senator Stone I admit my status as a freshman Senator, Mr Brandt, but your statement arouses my curiosity.

Mr Brandt I don't believe it's relevant, Senator.

Senator Stone I'm afraid you can't take it back, Mr Brandt. You've had a lifetime of experience in the public utility business and I think you ought to explain your statement. Certainly nobody could give us more insight into the politics of power.

Mr Brandt As the Senator may not be aware, various Congressional committees have always injected a degree of urgency into public utility plans for developing nuclear power. But to be inelegant about it, the bulk of the industry never wanted to build nuclear power plants in the first place; they were pressured into it. Certainly the economics of it were not attractive to our stockholders.

Senator Hoyt Mr Brandt, that statement verges on the ridiculous. You're in a profit-making industry; I have to assume that nuclear power contributes its share of that profit.

Mr Brandt In one sense it does, sir. But in another, the

economics of fission power are so involved, direct and indirect Government subsidies so complex, that I'm not at all sure nuclear power would be profitable in the open marketplace.

Representative Holmburg Mr Brandt, you said the power companies were pressured into going into nuclear power in the first place. Why didn't the utility business want to get into it of its own accord?

Mr Brandt One reason was the risk, sir. No civilian insurance company was willing to cover the liability in case of accident.

Representative Holmburg Nevertheless you went into it.

Mr Brandt The Price-Anderson Act limited our liability and also provided Government insurance. The Government also threatened direct competition.

Senator Stone The Government doesn't ordinarily compete with private industry, Mr Brandt.

Mr Brandt There are those who would argue with you, Senator. But in the beginning, the Government threatened to build research and development facilities that would be empowered to sell 'incident electricity' in competition with power supplied by public utilities. And if you recall, in the early 1950s, the AEC claimed that electricity from nuclear plants would be too cheap to meter. The utilities had little choice but to enter the nuclear field.

Senator Clarkson Power too cheap to meter seems wildly optimistic.

Mr Brandt It was but we couldn't be sure of that at the time, sir.

Senator Stone You're claiming the Government used a carrot-and-stick technique. I can see the stick but aside from solving your insurance problems, did the Government provide any more carrots?

Mr Brandt A number of them, Senator. At least initially, the Government contracted to purchase the plutonium made in reactors during their operation – these purchases offset fuel costs considerably; in effect, a subsidy. And there was the provisional construction permit. This allowed a utility to start the construction of a nuclear plant even though all the technical details hadn't been worked out yet. The assumption was that they would be by the time the plant was finished.

Senator Stone Was the Prometheus complex built under such a permit?

Mr Brandt Yes, sir, it was. But I would like to stress that while every nuclear power plant has its own unique aspects, nuclear technology has come a long way. We hardly anticipated any unsolvable, or even difficult, problems.

Senator Stone You've avoided one area in your discussion of costs, Mr Brandt. These tanks in which you store wastes. What happens if you have to replace the tank?

Mr Brandt As a matter of fact, Senator, we'd have to replace each tank about every fifty years. The hot wastes corrode the metal, and since the tank has been made radioactive by its contact with the wastes, we cut it up and bury it.

Senator Hoyt We've been told atomic energy is very cheap; yet now you tell us that every fifty years or so you'd have to cut up and bury an obviously very expensive tank. Has this cost been figured in your price per kilowatt hour of nuclear energy?

Mr Brandt No, sir. At the time these projections were made, storage was handled by the Government.

Senator Hoyt Mr Brandt, if we have to change tanks every fifty years, just how many tanks are we talking about?

Mr Brandt The wastes contain plutonium 239, sir, and plutonium has a half-life of 240,000 years. We'd have to retain the wastes for at least twice that long – some experts estimate ten times that long.

Senator Stone And the cost, Mr Brandt?

Mr Brandt I can't project that, Senator. Obviously the cost of retaining the wastes in tanks would be astronomical. What it might amount to if the Government succeeds in storing wastes in salt formations out west, I don't know.

Senator Stone Mr Brandt, one of the longest lived institutions of the human race was the Roman Empire and it lasted something like two thousand years. Do you honestly believe we can maintain safe storage for half a million or more?

Mr Brandt I admit it seems unrealistic, Senator.

8

The headlights of Kamrath's jeep threw everything into sharp relief – the rippled sand, the black water just beyond and a dozen milling, outraged townspeople. A deputy was holding back the sightseers but the word would spread and Kamrath didn't have enough manpower to handle a really big crowd.

He glanced at the sky. Clouds were blowing across the face of the moon and from the feel of the air, it would start raining soon. That would keep most of the curiosity seekers away. Still it might be a good idea to call the Highway Patrol and ask for help before the crowd got out of hand.

Kamrath made the call on the jeep's transceiver, then got out and stretched his legs. A new assistant, Bronson, hurried up. He was too eager, Kamrath thought cynically; he'd seen too many television shows. Bronson would make a better deputy when he finally realized the good guys got shot and died just as often as the bad guys.

'The body's right up the beach, Sheriff.'

'You sure it's Doc Seyboldt?'

Bronson hesitated. 'Hard to say; most of the face is gone. But I'm pretty sure it's Doc.'

'You wouldn't bet money on it, though; that it?' Kamrath walked down the beach, his boots digging into the soft sand. 'How'd the boys discover it?'

'Fooling around on the beach – digging for clams and playing grab-ass. As soon as they called the office, Pearson and I came down here. We've managed to keep the immediate area pretty clear.'

'Pretty clear,' Kamrath repeated. 'Meaning the souvenir hunters have probably picked the beach clean.'

He walked towards the water's edge. Bronson trailed after him, not quite knowing what to make of his mood. 'I've got some tracks I'd like to show you later,' he said tentatively.

Kamrath nodded. Just ahead was a black mass that looked like a small stump with seaweed draped over it. Bronson turned his flashlight on it and the stump suddenly became the head and shoulders of an elderly man, his damp grey hair plastered against his head. One hand had washed free of the shallow grave and lay palm upward, its fingers clutching desperately at the night air.

Kamrath stared for a long moment, wishing he could cry or at least feel sick. No more nights sitting on Doc's back porch, drinking beer and playing chess. No more evenings browsing through Doc's library and borrowing an occasional book. And no more ... just talking. About the people they knew, about politics, about the weather.

And then the feeling of regret and loss finally came. Nobody dies all by himself, he thought. A little bit of each of his friends dies with him.

'Whoever buried him didn't count on the tide,' Bronson was saying. 'Either that or he was in a hurry. The water undercut the sand on the sea side.' Which eliminated any of the fishermen as suspects, Kamrath thought automatically. It had to be someone who knew nothing about the ocean and the tides. Unless the killer had purposely done a sloppy job to mislead him or make sure the body was found. And either event was rather unlikely.

He slowly paced around the body. The corpse's head lay to one side and Kamrath could see that a good portion of the frontal part of the skull had been blown away, tearing the cartilage of the nose and shredding the flesh of the left cheek. The entire face looked like it had collapsed in on itself. Without being asked, Bronson shifted the flashlight slightly so the rear of the head was in the beam. The entry wound, though small, was quite well defined.

Kamrath hunkered down on the sand for a closer look. 'Hair looks singed around the point of entry – he must have been shot point-blank.' He rocked on his heels for a moment, then said, 'So much of the face is gone, it could be somebody other than Doc.'

Bronson looked at him, startled, but didn't say anything. Kamrath straightened up. 'All right, it was wishful thinking. We still have to get someone to make a positive identification. What about his nurse?'

'Abby? She's an old lady, Hank. You don't want to bring her in on something like this.'

'I was thinking of the one he worked with at the plant – Karen Gruen.'

'I'll have somebody call her.'

'Tell her to meet us at Cole Levant's boathouse. Did you bring the winch jeep?'

'I'll get it.'

Bronson left on the double and Kamrath stood looking down at the corpse. There was a muttering and jostling in the crowd behind him and he could hear other people driving up on the beach. The word was spreading fast; Doc had been well liked in town. Probably equally well liked up at the plant, where he spent two days a week. A vanishing breed, Kamrath thought. Dedicated. One of the few doctors who still made house calls and would accept a dozen chickens in payment for an appendectomy. The last man you would expect to see on a lonely stretch of beach, buried in the sand with half his head blown off.

Bronson came running back. 'Gilmore's calling her; then he'll be right down with the jeep.'

'What about those tracks you were going to show me?'

Bronson walked a dozen feet along the water's edge. 'Right over here. Had a helluva time keeping people from tramping over them – didn't realize there were so many ghouls in town.'

Kamrath shrugged. 'Everybody likes to take a look so they can go home thanking God it wasn't them.'

The tide was still running out and the sand was packed hard enough to walk on without difficulty. Bronson kept his flashlight trained on the sand at the very edge of the beach. Suddenly Kamrath spotted a series of indentations, half filled in by the water, and then a double line of footprints. From their size and distance apart, he guessed they had been made by the boys, running away from the body. He knelt down for a closer look. Both the boys had been wearing sneakers, one pair new enough so the trademark on the sole was imprinted in the damp sand.

Nearer to the water's edge was another set of footprints, fairly close together.

'All right, Bronson, tell me who made them.'

Bronson cleared his throat nervously. 'Two men, walking slowly and in single file.'

Kamrath nodded. 'Do they lead to the body?'

'They come close. The water washed some of the prints away.'

'Any tracks leaving the area?'

'One pair walking away for maybe a dozen feet. We lost the rest to the first people on the scene.' He looked at Kamrath thoughtfully. 'Think Doc knew his killer? They came down to the beach together.'

'Possibly – but they didn't come down here for an evening stroll. Two men, walking single file on a broad beach. The murderer was holding a gun on Doc; he marched Doc down here to kill him. Nobody to see; few people to hear.' He glanced up at his deputy. 'What else?' There was an edge to his voice and he realized he was taking out his own anger and frustration on Bronson.

Bronson looked away. 'You're doing fine so far, Hank.'

'Two men walked down here,' Kamrath repeated. 'One was forced to walk ahead of the other. Then the victim was shot in the head, just behind the left ear – an execution-style killing. The murderer made a quick attempt at burial, probably think-

44

ing the sand would cover the body, and then he walked away.'
He stared down the length of beach. 'Just walked away,' he
murmured.

There was a familiar chugging and Bronson said, 'Here
comes Gilmore with the jeep.'

'You screened the area completely? Any shell casing, anything like that?'

'It's clean; the ocean got any shell casings.'

'OK, start digging him out.'

Kamrath watched in silence as Bronson and Gilmore carefully spaded the sand away from the body. They uncovered half
the torso, then Gilmore knotted the nylon winch rope under
the shoulders, went back to the jeep and started the motor. The
line slowly tightened and bit into the body. A moment later, the
corpse had been tugged out of its pit with a sucking sound.

Kamrath waved his hand and the jeep stopped. Gilmore ran
back to untie the rope. 'Wrap it up and take it to the boathouse,'
Kamrath said. 'Then see if you can get hold of Greg Parks.'

'The two kids are up at the boathouse, too,' Bronson said.
'Cole doesn't like it very much.'

'If they were my kids, I wouldn't like it, either,' Kamrath
grunted. He watched while they wrapped the body in a tarpaulin and carried it over to a waiting station wagon. The first
murder in Cardenas Bay in four years, he thought. He'd seen
a lot of them when he was with the Los Angeles police but
there was no such thing as getting used to them.

It was colder now and he shivered inside his jacket. The
crowd behind him had grown steadily larger but when they
took the body away, it would disperse. He just hoped Bronson
hadn't opened his big mouth and told everybody they were
going to Levant's boathouse.

He turned to the young deputy, busy wiping the sand off his
coat. 'Did you contact the county medical officer?'

'Yeah, he'll meet us there.'

Kamrath nodded, staring at the hole where the body had
been. It was already filling with water, the sandy sides crumbling into the bottom. By morning there would be only a slight
dip in the beach and by afternoon Doc's last resting place
would be lost among the miles of beach. The good didn't
necessarily die young, he thought; they just died badly.

'We ought to get started,' Bronson said in a hesitant voice.

Kamrath took one last look, then walked back towards the

jeep. 'It won't be too hard to find out who did it,' he said, almost to himself.

Bronson looked startled. 'You've got some leads?'

'Several,' Kamrath mused. 'One, whoever did it, did it for a reason. And two – he's a fanatic.'

9

'We're here,' Parks said with a cheerfulness he didn't feel. 'Everybody out.' He cut the motor and jumped out onto the gravelled parking lot. What he needed more than anything else was fresh air – and after that, a drink, a big one. The last ten minutes of the drive had been made in absolute silence. Walton had sulked, Brandt had been strangely silent and Cushing just slouched against the rear of the seat with his eyes closed, pretending to catch forty winks. How many days were they going to stay? he wondered. And how many days of it could he stand?

The bell captain came running towards them and Parks said, 'They're expecting you. The food isn't bad; the fish is fresh and the drinks are first-rate.'

The others had gotten out of the car and were casually inspecting the motel. The Lodge was the first totally new structure in Cardenas Bay for years, not counting the public buildings subsidized by Prometheus tax money. It was self-consciously contemporary with heavy redwood beaming supporting a flat composition roof; railed walkways, weather-protected by translucent plastic, ran the length of each building.

The Lodge was the home away from home for transient engineers and technical staff from Western's subcontractors, who stayed there under a special rate. One definite plus was that the help had learned to cater to Western's VIPs.

Cushing seemed mildly pleased by the Lodge; Parks guessed he had been used to staying in off-the-highway motels when he had inspected nuclear plants in remote parts of the country. He was all cordiality and charm now. 'First thing I want is a shower. See you in the dining room in half an hour?'

'Make it the bar,' Parks said, grabbing Brandt by the arm.

'Mind if I join you?' Walton asked eagerly.

'Sorry, Jerry, this is private business,' Parks said, aware he was being deliberately rude. He steered Brandt towards the tiny bar set in one corner of the dining room. Parks picked the rear booth, an unhappy combination of polyurethane stone and pine intended to resemble a deep-sea grotto.

After they sat down, Brandt said, 'You really dislike Walton, don't you?'

'I didn't realize he was important enough to be nice to,' Parks said sarcastically. 'You want me to be polite just for the hell of it?' He glanced quickly over the menu, then slapped it down on the table. 'I'm sorry, Hilary. I've had six hours of sleep in the past three days and I've been averaging about four a night for the past month. I'm just not ready for Walton.'

The waitress came up to take their order and Parks noticed that she had caught Brandt's eye. She had been pretty once and the echo of it still lingered. Brandt apparently liked them just after they started to go to seed. Odd, he thought, how everybody could always tell the part-time hookers.

Parks smiled at her. 'How's it going, Wanda? This is my friend and boss, Hilary Brandt. Hilary, meet Wanda, the best cocktail waitress in all of Cardenas Bay.'

She smiled back with surprising warmth and Parks dropped his sudden urge to pat her on the butt. There was still something of the lady about her at that. 'The bar's open for business but the kitchen's closed, gentlemen.' She winked. 'I could probably bootleg some sandwiches if you didn't tell the boss.'

'Mum's the word but we'll wait until our friends come down.' She took their drink orders and Parks turned to Brandt. 'All right, Hilary,' he said coldly, 'what's up? I should be out at the plant now and I should have been there all evening. Why is all of this so important?'

Brandt avoided his eyes. 'Inspection trip,' he said casually.

Parks shook his head. 'Not with Walton along. If you've got bad news, I want to hear it now, before they come back.'

The drinks came and Brandt took his, swirling the glass and staring deep into the amber liquor. 'Greg, how ready is Prometheus to go on stream at full power?'

Parks tightened up on the inside. 'It isn't – and I'll put that in writing. In fact, I have put it in writing a dozen times during the past two months. Or haven't you been reading my reports?'

It was Brandt's turn to show anger. 'I've read them – cold, dispassionate reports on the status of the plant with some not so dispassionate comments by one Gregory Parks, facility manager. So you've had problems. You had problems at Chippewa Falls, too, and I don't remember you screaming about that one.

It went on stream right on schedule and it's been producing at peak capacity ever since.'

Parks sipped his drink and smacked his lips. 'Trace too much lemon.' He looked back at Brandt. 'Chippewa Falls wasn't the biggest reactor complex in the world, either. And you know damned well you can't compare one nuclear plant to another, Hilary.' He finished the rest of his drink in one gulp. 'To Fulton and Renkin and the other subcontractors, Prometheus is just another job. They've made so many reactors now, they think they're turning them out on an assembly line. Prometheus is bigger than their last job, probably smaller than their next. It's become routine. And that's what's wrong. When a job's routine, nobody really gives a damn.'

'You've had six months to check it out,' Brandt said sourly. 'Do you realize how much money that's cost the company? Do you realize how hard the Government is pushing for every kilowatt to plug into the national energy grid?'

'Maybe that's part of the problem,' Parks said thoughtfully. 'Prometheus is becoming a political football.' He signalled for another drink. 'It's not my fault we keep running across bad welds, Hilary. It's not my fault we're getting more than our share of bum fuel rods. You didn't hire me to close my eyes and rubber-stamp everything.'

Brandt leaned back, his face frozen. 'At Chippewa Falls, you were assistant plant manager. The buck didn't stop with you. Here it does. Afraid of the responsibility, Greg?'

For a moment, Parks found himself seriously considering the idea; then he dismissed it. 'Lerner agrees with me.'

Brandt made a noise. 'That Commie.'

'Come on, Hilary; you know he got clearance.'

'What about Abrams and Glidden? Do they feel the same way you do?'

'My guess is that they don't. But ask me again in two days. I've requested complete summary reports from them.'

The hostility faded from Brandt's face and he looked suddenly older and very tired. 'You don't have two weeks to go on stream, Greg. There's a national convention coming up and the President wants to announce then that Prometheus is plugged into the national energy grid, that the power shortage is over.'

'The convention,' Parks said, his voice flat. 'That's three days. There's not a chance in hell we'll be ready by then. Not a chance. This afternoon we had another fuel-cladding failure in Prometheus One.'

'Come on, Greg. Cladding failures aren't that uncommon. When it happens, you replace the assembly, that's all.'

Parks drummed his fingers on the table. 'Under the right circumstances, this failure could have been disastrous.'

Brandt shook his head. 'Not likely. You handled it with local damping, didn't you? You didn't even have to SCRAM.'

'Lerner's studies show we're running sixty-seven percent above industry experience,' Parks persisted.

Brandt sighed. 'Statistics can be deceiving. To quote: "Often the sole significance of a statistical improbability is simply that the improbable has happened." '

'Bullshit,' Parks said softly.

'I'm not going to argue,' Brandt snapped. 'How long do you need to get Prometheus One back on standby temperature?'

Parks shrugged. 'With the auxiliary cooling system, you can have the whole reactor below one hundred degrees F in two hours. I'd say four hours to remove the closure and the condenser and scrubber assemblies. We could have the assemblies replaced by noon tomorrow.'

'Which means you could be back at standby temperatures by tomorrow night.' Brandt looked impressed. 'Not like the old days.'

'Those are textbook answers,' Parks said coldly. 'The other problems won't go away quite that simply.' He put his drink down and looked Brandt directly in the face. 'We need more shakedown time, Hilary. The reactors aren't ready to go on full stream.'

Brandt inspected the menu again. 'I can't give you any more time. We have to go on stream – at full power – in time for the convention. Among other reasons, it wouldn't be ... politically wise ... to miss that deadline. We have no choice.'

'Sure we've got a choice,' Parks said calmly. 'At least I do. I quit – and I'll give a full statement to the newspapers as to why.'

'Greg.' Brandt hesitated, searching for the right way to phrase it. 'Would it make you any happier if I told you that I'm not terribly pleased about the whole thing myself? I don't like being under this kind of pressure, either. But next year's an election year and Prometheus is the final link in making the country self-sufficient when it comes to energy.'

'Not quite true,' Parks said quietly. 'But close.' He toyed with his drink. 'That's why you brought Walton along, isn't it?'

'It gave the game away, didn't it?'

'I can see it now,' Parks said, bitter. 'First, Western will run a half-hour promo on nuclear energy – get the networks to bill it as some sort of a news special. The footage has already been shot, hasn't it? Walton will oversee the television cameramen shooting live from this end and at the finish of it all, the President throws the switch.'

Brandt stared into his drink without answering.

Parks sagged back in the booth, too tired to be polite. 'You want me to go to the front desk and see if any camera crews are checked in for three days from now?' He signalled to Wanda again. 'The TV crews should have lots of fun interviewing the local townspeople on how nuclear energy has changed their lives. I can just see what will happen the first time they ask one of the fishermen.'

'They'll be selective,' Brandt said.

'Walton would be better off with a ten-minute bit by some television medicine man telling the audience how radiation is actually good for them.'

'That's enough, Greg,' Brandt said quietly.

He had pushed the old man too far, Parks thought. 'You've got my registration,' he said.

Brandt ignored him. 'You're a damned good engineer, Greg. You're also a damned good plant manager. And you're ambitious. But you have to realize that the further you want to go, the more you have to compromise. And compromising isn't necessarily bad *per se.*'

'In most things probably not,' Parks agreed moodily. 'But what I've got is a nuclear energy plant, the biggest in the world, and I'm having to cut and patch every day to meet a deadline. Right now I think the cutting and patching has reached the danger point.'

'Would you leak that to the papers?'

'If I have to. And if all I've got is three days, then I'll have to.'

Brandt fished in his pocket for a cigar. 'Would you be willing to even try to get it on stream in three days? If you could convince me at the end of three days that we shouldn't go on stream at full power, then I'll back you all the way – even if it means my job, too.'

It was big of him, Parks thought. If he really meant it. But the chances were that Brandt was just trying to defuse an uncomfortable situation.

And then he realized with a sudden pang that Brandt had

him. He really didn't want to blow the whistle on Prometheus. It was the biggest thing he had ever been involved in, perhaps the biggest thing he ever would be involved in. Building something like Prometheus was the ultimate dream of every engineer. Maybe that was the real problem after all. He wanted it to be the perfect machine, a fine Swiss watch instead of the workaday power station it was designed to be.

'All right, Hilary,' he said slowly. 'I'll make a bargain with you. I'll go through the motions of trying to put it on stream. In the meantime, I want you to look at everything I show you and consider very carefully the reasons why I think the on-stream date should be delayed.'

Brandt looked at him shrewdly. 'What happens if you get as far as countdown, Greg?'

Parks felt like he had just stepped in quicksand. 'If it gets that far and one little thing goes wrong, I'll abort the count-down. Otherwise, I'll put her on stream.'

Brandt nodded. 'All right, Greg. Just remember that's a bargain that binds both ways.'

And then another thought struck Parks. 'Cushing. Our Vice-Chairman for Reactor Safety for the Committee on Reactor Design. I've never met him before.'

Brandt looked guarded. 'What do you want to know?'

'Is that all he is? I have the feeling that he has a lot more clout than just that.'

Brandt shrugged unconvincingly. 'He knows a lot of people in Washington, but then he should; he's been there a long time.'

And then Parks had figured it out. 'He's not really coming out here just to inspect the plant, is he? What he's really here for is to make sure we go on stream.'

Brandt sat there in heavy silence.

'Isn't that it, Hilary?'

'What the hell are you worried about?' Brandt asked harshly, stubbing out his cigar in the ashtray. 'You hold all the cards. In the last analysis, if the facility manager feels the plant is unsafe, he has the authority to stop it from going on stream. Those are the rules.'

He didn't believe him, Parks thought slowly. Those were the rules all right but there had to be a catch. Brandt was giving in too easily. He sat there for a moment, staring at Brandt, who gazed steadily back. He couldn't make up his mind. He should hand in his resignation and walk out, he thought. There was no way anybody could get the plant on stream in three days. Except . . . Except he wanted Prometheus more than he had ever wanted anything.

Suddenly Wanda was standing at his side. 'Mr Parks? There's a call for you.'

He turned almost savagely. 'Who the hell is it?'

She shook her head, frowning. 'I didn't catch his name – a man from the sheriff's department. He said it was important.'

10

Tebbets could tell the symptoms. It was a lot like falling in love. First, you ignored her, then became mildly interested, then fascinated, and finally you couldn't leave her alone. Kloster had run the entire gamut in three hours. He had been due to leave an hour ago but had remained, fascinated by MIROS and its capabilities.

'What are you doing now?' Kloster asked.

Tebbets put down his coffee cup. 'We're following a routine scan pattern that alternates between visual and infrared. We tape that and the computer inputs.' He nodded towards the bank of video and high-response digital tapes to the left of the monitoring stations. 'The computers take the digitalized images, introduce high contrast where necessary – the sort of thing NASA used to build up images from the Mars probe – and print out a profile of what's happening below.'

'Profile?' Kloster asked.

'You know – missile firings, temperature inversions, even micro-meteorological patterns. We chart probable fallout patterns for Civil Defense as well as our own military missions. That way, we know immediately how radioactives will be distributed in case of an attack or a nuclear plant failure.'

Kloster looked surprised. 'You mean one of those plants could blow up?'

Tebbets sighed and picked up his coffee cup again. After all these years, you'd think even a layman would know that was impossible. 'They don't blow up, Captain. There just aren't enough concentrated fissionables in a plant for a blowup. The fuel rods contain only 3 percent U-235; the rest is U-238.'

'All right, if they don't blow up, what the hell do they do?'

'In the first place, a failure is pretty unlikely,' Tebbets said, grimacing at the bitter coffee. 'If one did and there was a high inventory of decay products – the "ashes" of a nuclear fire – the plant would melt down because of the decay heat in the reactor. Ask Scott Nichols; he's the expert on it. The nuclear boys call it the China Syndrome. Presumably, the reactor and its fuel would keep melting into the ground, heading for China.'

Kloster had out his clipboard now, doodling a mushroom-shaped cloud on the first blank piece of paper. 'So what's so bad about that? Sounds like a self-liquidating disaster.'

Tebbets drained the coffee and crumpled the paper cup. 'The fallout – your melting plant would be spewing radioactive "ashes" into the air by the ton. If a big city were within a hundred miles downwind, it could get hit pretty bad. A couple of hundred deaths the first week, a few thousand the first week to a month, maybe as high as a million within the first year. And God knows how many cancer deaths from low-level radiation for fifty years after that.' He leaned into his mike to order more coffee. 'It depends on a lot of factors.'

Kloster was fascinated. 'Such as what?'

Tebbets shrugged. 'The obvious things. How big the plant is, how long it's been operating – there are other factors, you'd have to ask Nichols. I know they did a computer study.' He paused a moment, speculating about it. 'If you had an inversion layer, where the air was prevented from rising, I imagine you'd wind up with a nice heavy radioactive smog. That'd be rough. There's the question of what part of the cloud settles on your particular neighbourhood – the edges of the cloud would be lighter in contamination. And it would make a difference whether you're indoors or out.'

Kloster shrugged. 'If you got contaminated, you could always take a shower. Everybody has a shower.'

'It'd work,' Tebbets admitted. 'You couldn't go outside again, of course.'

'Isn't there anything the medics can do?'

Tebbets was a little slower in answering. 'They'd probably use antibiotics to keep down infections that might develop—'

'What infections?'

'You get a dose and the cell wall in the colon starts sloughing off – you're a sitting duck for a lot of diseases then. Blood transfusions aren't too much good, though if the bone marrow has been damaged, there's the possibility of marrow transplants. You can actually do a lot with a couple of surgeons, several nurses and an intensive care unit.'

Kloster was looking at him, disbelieving. 'Come off it, Tebbets – we're talking about millions of people. Where are you going to get the medical help?'

Tebbets nodded. 'Catch 22. It would be just like Hiroshima and Nagasaki where all the hospital facilities were overloaded. Most of the people you couldn't help at all.'

'My God, it could be as bad as an atomic attack!'

'Probably worse,' Tebbets said, watching Kloster out of the corner of his eye. He was beginning to delight in getting a rise out of the pudgy Air Force captain.

'What are the chances of it happening?'

Tebbets yawned; it was getting late. 'Don't make book on it. All the computer studies I've seen on a Maximum Credible Accident put the odds at something like one in three hundred million. Those plants are as safe as you can make them.'

There was a view of central Russia on the main screen and Kloster's attention began to wander. 'There's one thing that bothers me,' he mused, doodling on his scratch pad. 'How do you calculate the odds on something that's never happened?'

11

Parks left the station wagon in the lot and ran for the boathouse. It was damp and getting colder, something that wouldn't have bothered him back East. But he had lived in California just long enough to become acclimatized to the warm winters. When the weather crossed him up, it really cut through him.

The boathouse was a large, barn-like building with a slip down the centre filled with the dark waters of the bay. Normally, fishermen rented it to bring in their boats for major repairs. At the moment, it was empty. The damp wooden walls were flecked with green mould and there was the pervasive odour of rotting fish and diesel oil. Near the far wall were coils of rope, tar buckets and an ancient wood lathe. Closer to the door was a large table and, on it, what looked like a roll of canvas. Overhead was a green-shaded lamp, swinging slightly in the occasional wisp of wind that leaked through the cracks in the walls.

On a card table nearby was a small box; one of the sheriff's deputies was calling out the contents. Cole Levant stood next to him, logging in the items on a clipboard. 'Yellow-knit shirt, J. C. Penney label. Wash-and-wear Haggar slacks, rip in right front pocket.' He hesitated. 'Old-fashioned long johns, I guess you'd call them, no label. Top heavily bloodstained.'

Kamrath was on the other side of the slip, talking to a man whom Parks didn't know. A doctor of some kind, he decided; there was a professional air about him and he carried the standard doctor's bag. Kamrath was pushing sixty but looked younger – a short, squat man who once spent some time with the Los Angeles Police Department. He was dressed like a local sheriff but still looked the big-city cop. Then Parks noted with surprise that Karen Gruen was standing in the shadows behind them.

Kamrath finished talking and crossed over to where the deputy was checking the clothing. Karen and the doctor followed.

'Any hardware, Bronson?' Kamrath asked. 'Money?'

'No wallet, no coins, Sheriff. A key ring with six keys. Looks like it might have been simple robbery.'

'An execution as part of a simple robbery?' Kamrath looked disgusted.

'He never carried much money,' Karen volunteered. 'I usually lent him some when he ate in the plant cafeteria.' She looked like she had been crying.

'Anything else?' Kamrath asked. He noticed Parks and nodded.

'Something that was in his pants pocket,' Bronson said. He held out an envelope, which Kamrath took and opened, shaking out a postal receipt.

'Anybody know what this is for?'

Karen took it and inspected it carefully in the light. 'That's probably the lab in San Francisco where he sent all his blood tests. It's not for anybody at the plant, though; I'd have that in my own files. You'll have to check with Abby Dalton, she takes care of his town office.'

Kamrath started going through the clothing and Parks said, 'You wanted to see me?'

Karen noticed him then, and managed a weak smile. 'Identification first,' Kamrath said casually. He walked over to the canvas-covered bundle on the table and turned back the flap with an oddly gentle movement. Parks abruptly caught his breath. The doctor took out a small pocket flashlight and leaned over the table, inspecting the body beneath the canvas with scientific detachment. 'White male, middle fifties. I'd say about one fifty, five eleven, non-muscular build.' He leaned closer, frowning. 'Point-blank wound in the occipital region behind the left ear, made by a small-calibre bullet which exited about an inch below the right eye. The slug fragmented on entering – there's very little of the face left. Death was instantaneous due to large loss of blood, tearing of the dura mater and severe damage to the brain stem itself and surrounding organs.'

He inspected the body a moment longer, then stepped back. Kamrath said, 'Mr Parks, Dr Pickering, county medical officer.' He pointed to the corpse. 'Do you recognize it, Mr Parks?'

Parks felt a queasy feeling in his stomach. 'It looks like Dr Seyboldt. I don't think I could swear to it – there's not that much to go by.'

Kamrath nodded. 'Miss Gruen gave us a positive identification – a scar on the left forearm.' He re-covered the body.

'Is that it?' Parks asked. Being around Karen wasn't helping his piece of mind and he wanted to escape to the plant.

'Could I talk to you a minute?' Kamrath led Parks over to one side of the boathouse, out of earshot of the others. The usually placid Kamrath looked somewhat distracted and pre-occupied. 'I guess I'm on a fishing expedition, Parks. They found Doc on the beach three hours ago. Apparently executed. So far as I can see, there was no reason for killing him. If there was a better-liked man in town, I don't know who it could have been. But he was also your plant physician and I don't know his relationships up there. I suppose even the best-loved man in town might have an enemy somewhere.'

Parks shook his head. 'He was well liked at the plant, too. He handled a lot more than just in-plant work; most of the men were his regular patients on the outside as well.'

Kamrath smiled briefly. 'Doc was the only one in town; he had a monopoly. What'd his duties at the plant consist of?'

'Usual industrial work, complicated by in-plant radiation problems. Cuts, bruises, crushed feet, broken bones. That's about the size of it. Plus supervising the processing of the radiation-exposure badges and monitoring the safety procedures.'

'Who worked with him?'

'Karen was his chief nurse. A kid named Mike Kormanski helped out; he used to be a paramedic.'

'Any drug cases?'

Parks shook his head. 'None that I know of and I'm sure he would have mentioned it if there were. The plant's a little too sensitive to allow for it.'

Kamrath turned back to the canvas-covered body and lifted up the covering once more. Parks forced himself to be more objective this time. How big you were in life and how small you looked in death, he thought. He felt somewhat guilty then. He hadn't known Seyboldt too well, although the doctor had been plant physician for two years. A quiet, fatherly type, somewhat grizzled-looking and absentminded.

He caught the look on Kamrath's face and said, 'He was a good friend of yours, wasn't he?'

'We grew up together,' Kamrath said. He let the cover roll back. 'A long time ago,' he said slowly, 'my little girl caught something in her throat – part of a sucker, as I recall. Doc performed an emergency tracheotomy with a kitchen knife. She's a senior at Berkeley now.' He glanced back at the canvas bundle. 'I owe him.' For just a moment Parks saw something in Kamrath's eyes that made him wince.

'We'll be glad to help in any way that we can.'

Kamrath nodded absently. 'You handle radioactives up at the plant,' he said. 'No reason why Doc should have been involved in that, is there?'

'Not directly. You thinking about theft?' Parks shook his head. 'Doc never handled anything personally; he never even went near that section of the plant.'

'I had to ask. Thanks for coming down.' Kamrath started to walk away, then noticed Karen standing in one corner, looking lost. He turned back to Parks. 'Could you give Miss Gruen a ride back to town? We'll be here a while yet and I imagine she'd be glad to get home.'

'Did you have to call her in?' Parks asked. 'It must have been pretty rough on her.'

'We needed positive identification. And it would have been even rougher on Abby Dalton; she's near seventy and has already had one heart attack.'

'Sure, I'll be glad to take her back.' Parks walked over to Karen. She was sitting on a wooden bench, staring sombrely into the brackish waters of the slip. 'Let's go home,' he said gently.

She glanced up. 'If it's a bother, I can call a taxi.'

'It's no bother.'

She stood up, wrapping her coat around herself like a cape. 'I'm supposed to meet Barney at the café. He doesn't know I came down here; he wasn't home when I called.'

'Do you want to call him at the café and cancel out? I'm sure he'd understand.'

She shook her head. 'No,' she said, 'I want to see him.'

He nodded. 'I'll be glad to drop you there.'

Outside, she shivered in the night air and pulled her coat up around her neck. Some townspeople had gathered in front of the boathouse to sit on the railings and gossip. One of them waved to Parks and he waved back; then he helped Karen into the company station wagon.

'No Reo tonight?' she asked.

'George dropped it off at home – I'm working on it.'

He got in and started the car. Karen sat on the seat saying nothing and staring straight ahead into the night. She had a knack for making him feel helpless, Parks thought. He didn't know whether to leave her with her sorrow, to let her battle it out by herself, or take her into his arms and try to comfort her.

The latter was out, he guessed, if what Barney had told him was true. And then he wondered why Karen hadn't told him herself. Too much had happened that night, probably. He thought for a minute of bringing it up, then changed his mind. She had enough problems at the moment. Karen had always struck him as a strong person, a woman who wore her maturity like a second skin, but even the strongest have their limits.

He drove silently, glancing at her from time to time. She was in her late twenties and had successfully bridged the gap from the long-legged California coed type featured in the skin magazines to a graceful young lady. As she grew older, he thought, she would look more and more the librarian type. The glasses would become more severe and the hair might be pulled back to a bun but there would always be a certain sensuality about her.

She sat hunched against the door of the car. The cords of her neck were tense and occasionally a thin muscle jumped in her cheek. It had been one hell of a night for her. Without thinking, he reached over and touched her shoulder with gentle reassurance.

It was as if he had touched a button. Tears suddenly sprang from her eyes and she fought for a moment to control the sobs.

But she made no move towards him. Barney had been right, he thought.

After a long moment, she said, 'I'm sorry.'

He had to watch the road and couldn't turn towards her. 'What about? If I had worked with Doc as closely as you did, I might cry, too.'

'I hate myself when I'm weak,' she said forlornly. 'He was a gentle man. I can't imagine why anybody would do such a thing.'

They were coming into town and he said, 'I can switch on the light if you want to repair your face.'

She shrugged. 'Barney's seen me like this before. It'll be no great shock to him.'

'Barney told me that you two were engaged.'

She sat there for a moment without answering, then said, 'I was going to tell you and then tonight ...' She was silent again. 'If you want a reason, I guess I would have to fall back on the one that most women use. I'm not getting any younger. And Barney's available and you're not.'

'I wasn't going to argue,' he said quietly.

'No, I knew you wouldn't.' For a moment he thought she sounded disappointed, then shrugged it off as male ego.

They were in front of the restaurant now; he pulled in at the kerb and stopped. She stepped out, standing in the open door a moment. 'Thanks for the lift, Greg. And ... I'm sorry about the other.'

He managed a smile. 'Congratulations,' he said softly.

She was gone then. He watched her walk across the side-walk – tall, slender, almost regal – and disappear through the door. California girls, he thought. There weren't any others in the world quite like them.

He glanced at his watch. Two hours before the midnight shift started. He didn't have to show but he wanted to be there. Almost as much as he wanted to slump against the steering wheel and go to sleep. Too long a day, and it was going to be much too long a night.

He made up his mind then. The plant would keep, at least for an hour or two. The new headlamps for the Reo were sitting on his workbench at home. He'd install those, catch a few hours of sleep, then hit the plant about the middle of the shift.

They wouldn't be expecting him then. Which was exactly the way he wanted it.

12

Senator Hoyt Mr Walton, let me see if I understand your position correctly. You're a public relations representative working directly for Fulton Engineering?

Mr Walton Industrial communications specialist, Senator.

Senator Hoyt Isn't that the same thing?

Mr Walton Well, yes and no. The position encompasses a great many other functions. I'm concerned with the ordering of interpersonal, interorganizational relationships as they affect the town-government-industry interfaces in a developmental programme. Particularly where it's technically complex and not readily understood by the layman.

Representative Holmburg In other words, a PR man.

Mr Walton If the Congressman finds the term more convenient.

Representative Holmburg I sure as hell do.

Senator Hoyt I'm still confused here. Just who did you work for on the Prometheus complex?

Mr Walton My primary employer is Bagston, Jarmon, Dunner and Finn. We act as consultants to Fulton Engineering.

Senator Hoyt I thought you just testified that your salary was paid for by Western Gas and Electric.

Mr Walton That was for the convenience of accounting. Very early in the history of nuclear plants, Fulton Engineering developed the concept of supplying a complete package when it became prime contractor and vendor on a reactor project. As vendor, Fulton would supply construction engineering, training personnel and even a community interface package. BJD and F provided this service as a subcontractor to Fulton. In short, when Western chose Fulton as prime contractor and vendor, they received the services of myself and my community interface team as well.

Senator Stone What you're apparently trying to say is that Western bought a public relations programme as part of the Prometheus package.

Mr Walton That's quite common in the industry, Senator.

Senator Stone Just why were your services needed in Cardenas Bay?

Mr Walton There was the usual resistance to locating a nuclear plant there, plus Western had the problem of becoming the major employer in a town whose previous primary industry consisted of fishing. Initially, there was antagonism between those who worked in the plant and the men who worked on the boats.

Senator Stone You were successful in smoothing out relations between the two groups?

Mr Walton I would like to think so, Senator. In fact, I'm quite sure we did.

Senator Stone As I understand it from the transcripts, one of the fishermen's complaints was that the waste discharge from the plant polluted the waters of the bay.

Mr Walton Not a word of truth to it, Senator. We had our own men personally test the bay waters for thermal and radioactive pollution and both were well within prescribed limits.

Senator Stone Who set those limits, Mr Walton?

Mr Walton I'm afraid it's a toss up. The Environmental Protection Agency, the Atomic Regulatory Committee, even the Health, Education and Welfare Department claim jurisdiction. Eventually they all seem to fall back on the old AEC standards. I think it safe to say, however, that at least a part of the disagreement between the two groups in town was because of the wage differential between the plant workers and the fishermen. There wasn't much we could do about that except point out that everybody benefited from the taxes paid by the plant.

Senator Stone What about the reaction of the townspeople to the nuclear plant itself? Weren't they worried about what might happen if something went wrong?

Mr Walton Not after we explained it to them, Senator. It was almost a textbook case in solving a major communications problem in a way well tailored to interfacial thinking.

13

It was almost ten-thirty when Parks finally pulled into the driveway of his house. He walked in, dropping his suit coat on the couch. There was no need to be neat, he thought; there was nobody to offend. The shades were pulled and he wondered when the last time was that he had been home long enough to bother raising them. In the dining room, the rug was still rolled up and most of the dishes were still packed in the boxes sitting on the floor. One had been ripped open so he would have enough plates and cups for an occasional breakfast or late-night snack.

The only room completely furnished was the pine-panelled study. He wandered in and snapped on the light. The book-shelves were the first thing he had put up and after that, his toys, as Marjorie called them. A huge light painting behind the small bar, consisting of a grey translucent screen on which were rear-projected constantly shifting waves of coloured light; the Fluid Circle, an eighteen-inch disc containing chambers filled with coloured liquids that spilled into the lower compartments as the disc rotated; and a sculpture welded together of nuts and bolts in imitation of the lovers in Rodin's 'The Kiss'. The prize of them all was a fountain sculpture of shimmering Lucite rods and small copper cups on the ends of revolving arms. At the top was a revolving fountain – the fountain and the arms with the cups moved in an elaborate pattern resulting in different streams of water falling in different cups as the arms revolved. No drop of water had yet fallen on the floor.

Parks stood in the doorway for a moment, watching the light screen. A den was where you want to get away from the kids or even your wife, he thought. It had been his favourite room in the house but he had yet to spend much time in it.

He walked into the kitchen to make a sandwich, then lost his appetite when he saw the dishes in the sink. It would mean washing them so he could have clean ones to eat off and it wasn't worth it. He got a can of beer from the icebox, pulled the tab and took a long gulp. He turned and leaned against the sink, sipping the beer and listening to the stereo playing in the living room; it had been wired to turn on automatically when the front door opened.

There was no other sound. No kids, nobody saying hello or laughing or kissing him good evening or even complaining that he was working too late. What was wrong, he decided, was not that there was nobody around to go to bed with. What was wrong was that there was nobody around to give a damn.

He said 'Shit!' in a low voice, deliberately poured the rest of the beer over the dishes in the sink, then walked into the garage and flipped on the lights.

The Reo sat poised there, gleaming in the overhead lights.

He had bought it from one of the fishermen, in whose backyard it had sat for years, slowly rusting and rotting away. Restoring it had been expensive but he had devoted himself to it with tender loving care. He had waited three months for the paint chemist in San Francisco to deliver the precise shade of greenish black that he wanted. Local machine shops had duplicated most of the broken and corroded parts. She ran, and she ran well, but she was still far from perfect. He looked at it and felt the same surge of pride he always felt. It was easy to fall in love with a machine, he thought.

He glanced down at his shirt and suit pants, thought, what the hell, and picked up a wrench from the tool board. The head-lamps could wait, there was something else he wanted to do first. The transmission was still giving him trouble. He lay down on the dolly board and pushed himself under the high wheels. If he were careful, he could probably avoid the grease.

He had been working on it for half an hour when he heard the taxi pull into the driveway. A moment later someone entered the house and walked through into the kitchen. There was the sound of the refrigerator door being opened and then the clink of ice cubes and glasses.

He pushed the dolly out from under the car. Karen was standing in the doorway, a pitcher of martinis in her hand. 'Barney saw you drive me up,' she said.

'You told him where you had been?'

She nodded. 'He can't help it, Greg. His jealousy is patho-logical. He always lost out when he was a kid and now he can't stand the thought that somebody might take away the one thing he really wants.'

Parks stood up, brushing at his pants. He had lost the battle with the grease, he noticed. 'If he keeps it up, he'll push it away himself.'

'Maybe.' She handed him a glass. 'After a drink, I'll clean up this mess for you.'

He glanced at the sink and shook his head. 'I think I'd rather have you come into the den and just sit and talk. It's the only room in the entire house that's finished. Did you know that?' He laughed, a little of his bitterness showing through. 'In a whole year and a half.'

In the den he lay back in the lounger while she sat on the edge of the desk, after having first pushed back the Wave – a small, plastic-enclosed tube filled with a blue oil and centred on a fulcrum like a teeter-totter; when the ends moved up and down, the oil imitated ocean waves. For once the stereo playing in the living room didn't seem out of place. This was the way it should be, he thought.

'You have a penny?' he asked suddenly.

She nodded curious. 'Why?'

'Put it in the little slot on the cube there.' She did so, there was a whirring sound and suddenly a lid flipped open and a mechanical hand snatched up the penny and retreated back into the box. She giggled. 'You get a kick out of things like that, don't you?'

He grinned self-consciously. 'I like gadgets. I've got an old-time Wurlitzer in storage – not a jukebox; it's a combination player piano, drums, horn and violin. It works by a bellows arrangement and it sounds absolutely terrible.' He chuckled. 'I love it.'

She gave him a long look. 'Did Marjorie?'

He sobered for a moment, almost resenting the question, then realized that after all he had deliberately asked her into the den so they could talk. 'Hell, no. She hated it. When I worked at Chippewa Falls, we lived in Madison, Wisconsin, and I restored a Marmon back there – sold it when I moved here. She hated that, too. I can imagine what she would have thought about the Reo.'

'You love working with machinery, don't you?'

'Sure. I imagine a writer likes writing and a musician likes making music, too. I don't think it's a talent so much as a compulsion. It's what gives you satisfaction.'

She made a guess then. 'Marjorie wants you to give all of it up, doesn't she? It's not just a dislike for living in the sticks.'

He felt uneasy. 'You're pretty perceptive.'

'And you can't make up your mind.' She wasn't picking an argument with him, he thought, she was honestly curious. 'Why?'

He stared at the light screen, watching the tumbling waves of colour flow across its surface. 'I'm not sure exactly. I married late and I thought I had myself a prize. Maybe I still love her.'

She looked surprised. 'After a year and a half of separation?'

'Doesn't absence make the heart grow fonder? In any event, it hasn't seemed as long as that – I've been too wrapped up in Prometheus. Pretty soon we'll be going on stream and then I guess I'll have to make up my mind, won't I?'

'It would be about time.'

He poured himself another drink from the pitcher. He'd have to watch it, he thought; he'd be going back to the plant in another hour or so. 'What about you? I'm doing all the talking.'

'What about me?'

'In the car, you said you hated yourself when you were weak. Any special reason?'

She hesitated, absently swirling the cubes in her glass. 'My parents died when I was young. I had to start taking care of myself at an early age and I guess I've come to believe that that's a cardinal virtue – to be able to take care of yourself.'

'So you hate to show emotion.'

'I guess.'

'You're pretty enough,' he said slowly. 'You're not a youngster but most men aren't that fond of youngsters. And you certainly have strength of character. I should think you would have married a long time ago.'

Her voice was suddenly brittle. 'I was going to at one time. He was an intern. Jewish. Very Orthodox. It was all set and then his family put their foot down. I was Gentile and it was more than they could take ... even after I converted. They broke him completely; he didn't even have the courage to tell me himself.'

The raw emotion in her voice was more than he had bargained for but he couldn't help asking, 'Does that account for Barney?'

She wasn't offended. 'I don't know, Greg, I honestly don't know. If it does, then there's something ghoulish about it. It means I want to win a game that I lost before.' She thought about it for a moment. 'I don't love Barney. I'm fond of him. I think I could learn to love him. And—' She broke off, trying to put her feelings into words. Finally: 'It's time. A man can have children at almost any time during his life. A woman doesn't have that option. The older you get, the riskier it gets and finally there comes a time when you can't at all. Besides, the pickings get slimmer every year. The good men are taken early.'

'What happened tonight?'

'I told you. He got jealous because you dropped me off. He still thinks I'm seeing you.'

'You want me to tell him you're not?'

'It would just confirm it in his own mind.' She put the drink down. 'Besides,' she said, 'I am.'

He glanced down at his own glass and sighed. 'Spite's a lousy reason to go to bed with anyone. It's almost as bad as sympathy.'

'I'll leave if you want me to,' she said without anger. 'I like you in a lot of other ways, too, Greg. But I guess I'm pretty human. I don't belong to Barney and tonight I had a pretty rocky time. I'm not about to apologize because I didn't want to go to bed and have nightmares about Doc and wake up alone. I don't think I have to defend myself. I wanted somebody to hold me and make love to me and comfort me. It's a human thing to want and I went to Barney first. But he was so wrapped up in his own jealousy that he couldn't see that. I was hoping you could.' She shook her head, her face a mask. 'I know – I'm being aggresive and liberated and all of that. And it's not very good for my pride to have to ask.' She laughed. 'I probably wanted you to seduce me.'

He hesitated. 'You're an engaged woman.'

'And you're a married man.'

Much later, in bed, he woke with a start when the alarm clock rang. He quickly smothered it before it could awaken Karen. It was four in the morning, the middle of the night shift. Time to get back to Prometheus. He felt guilty about having been away from it this long.

He sat on the edge of the bed for a moment, trying to shake the sleep out of his eyes. He glanced over once at Karen, who had moaned slightly in her sleep and then turned on her side. Her breathing was shallow and even. He moved the alarm hand of the clock up to seven; she would still have enough time to dress and make breakfast for herself. He'd leave her the keys to the station wagon and drive the Reo in.

The beautiful, long-legged California girls, he thought once more. And then: Who was it who said lovers never should be friends? Or was it vice versa?

He felt around on the floor for his shorts, found them and slipped them on. He had been having a dream, he recalled, about Marjorie, and during it he had discovered an eternal truth. He smiled in the dark. Like most eternal truths you discovered while dreaming, you could never remember them thirty seconds after waking up.

And then it came back to him while he was pulling on his socks. Marjorie and Prometheus were just alike, he thought, astonished at the insight.

With each of them, it was a case of unrequited love.

66

Second Day

14

It was eight a.m. in Denver and Tebbets had settled comfortably into his morning routine. He spent five minutes holding his plastic cup of steaming coffee, warming his hands and smelling the aroma. He was hooked, he thought, luxuriating in the feeling. He was as addicted as any junkie on skid row. It there was some way to inject it directly into his bloodstream, he probably would. He glanced around, suddenly feeling guilty. It was the one lax moment of his shift. He had split his team of six technicians into groups of three, allowing each five minutes to get their own coffee. What was sauce for the goose . . .

And someday, he thought, that bit of information would find its way into a dossier in Moscow or Peking or Damascus and the big one would start because somebody would know that for ten minutes every morning, America's Eye in the Sky was only half open.

He bent closer to the hot, steamy odour drifting up from the cup, inhaled deeply, blew on the coffee and took a long, noisy sip. Morning was finally ready to begin. Except that Captain Kloster was absent.

'Anybody seen Kloster?'

'His car wasn't in the lot when I came in,' one of the technicians said. 'Maybe he thinks we keep Pentagon hours.'

There was a noise in the corridor and the door on Tebbets' right opened. The rest of his shift came in with their coffee, followed immediately by Captain Kloster.

'Sorry I'm late,' the Captain said breezily, sliding into the seat beside Tebbets. 'The expressway was really hell this morning.'

'You think that was bad,' a yellow-clad technician said, 'take a look at it now.'

The image on number three screen suddenly expanded to show the expressway coming into the city. Traffic was bumper to bumper and Tebbets could imagine the steady honking of horns. For a brief moment, the fuzzy faces of exasperated drivers swept across the screen.

'That's enough, Charlie.' Breaking discipline in front of the new Air Force monitor was risky. 'Go back to infrared scan; you're losing your reference point.' He glanced over at Kloster. 'How was the party?'

Kloster looked surprised. 'You know about that?'

'Standard operating procedure for VIPs when they're courting your good opinion.'

'If it had been any better,' Kloster said smugly, 'I don't think I would have made it this morning.'

Tebbets buried himself in some notes. 'I keep hearing about Lysistrata's massage parlour. Is it really all that good?'

Kloster was suddenly miffed. 'We didn't go there,' he said curtly.

Tebbets raised a shocked eyebrow, then went back to his notes, pretending confusion. 'Probably something for colonels only,' he murmured, adding a bit too hastily, 'It's just a place to dry out before reporting back to duty.'

Kloster studied him a long moment, then laughed good-naturedly. 'OK, Tebbets, quit putting me on. What's happening this morning?'

He'd guessed right, Tebbets thought; they could live with Kloster after all. 'Same thing as yesterday. We're alternating the routine scan pattern between visual and infrared. We concentrate on the most sensitive areas, of course. It's been a long time since we took a close look at the Sahara, for example.'

Tebbets was interrupted by muttering from his headset; he quickly put it on. He listened for a moment, jotting down some notes in his log book, then took the set off, frowning.

'What's up?' Kloster asked, curious.

'Prometheus is going on stream the day after tomorrow.'

'So why the long face?'

'Just surprised,' Tebbets said. 'It's two weeks early. Rumour had it they wouldn't be going on stream for another month.'

Charlie had already anticipated him and Prometheus was on screen now, its dome a blinding white in the early-morning sun. Tebbets stared at it for a long moment.

They were really pushing it, he thought.

15

The chill morning fog blew across the Information Building parking lot in ragged streamers. Hilary Brandt huddled deeper in his coat and trudged up the walk to the concrete viewing pad. Cushing and Walton hadn't wanted to brave the cold air and had stayed behind in the car. The plant itself was over a mile away, on a bluff overlooking the ocean, the intervening distance punctuated by erosion crevasses with falls of shattered rock leading down to the beach. The location of the Information Building, Brandt remembered, had been a compromise between the wishes of Public Relations and the demands of Security and had satisfied neither.

The prevailing wind in the small valley below had swept away the fog and he had no difficulty making out the massive bulk of the reactor building. At this distance, its gleaming dome seemed almost toy-like. Behind it, the miniature reprocessing buildings marched towards the sea cliff in military ranks.

He fumbled for a dime and pushed it in the slot of the coin-operated telescope nearby. Now he could see the chain-link fence and the guard post at the main entrance, as well as the automobiles in the parking lot at the side. It was time for the new shift and technicians were filing through the gate, the armed guard carefully checking each ID. A second guard on the other side was even more carefully checking out the night shift as they straggled out to their cars. At the gate, sensitive monitors scanned each man for stray contamination. Nobody could carry out radioactives through such an inspection, Brandt thought.

Foolproof. But what about a smart man?

Cushing's voice suddenly cut in. 'Are you ready, Hilary? I'm freezing.' Brandt had been completely unaware of his approach.

'It's the biggest power plant in the world, Eliot.'

'And hopefully the best. Though apparently not everybody thinks so.'

From below, Walton called, 'We'd better go in. A school bus just drove up and I don't want the kids to beat us to the model.'

Brandt turned with a sigh and picked his way down the path. When he got back to the car, he said, 'Jerry, you remind me of my mother, God rest her soul. She was a worrier, too.'

The Information Building was a large oval-shaped structure with two wings. The tiled façade of the entrance was gold and blue, the Western Gas and Electric colours. To the right of the broad concrete steps leading to the entrance stood three flag-poles, the centre one flying the United States flag. On the left was the California state flag and on the right that of Western, all three fluttering in the morning breeze.

'It's pretty elaborate for a public relations building,' Cushing said dryly. 'Even for the world's largest nuclear plant.'

'It also houses Security and the bookkeeping department,' Walton said nervously. 'We wanted to make every dollar do double duty.' He led the way up the stairs and into the central rotunda of the building.

Brandt paused a moment to catch his breath, then glanced around. The rotunda housed a variety of animated displays ringing a central pit. Each of the displays demonstrated some aspect of atomic power and could be activated by pressing a button on the information board beneath. A recorded voice ex-plained in simple language what the display represented.

The pit in the middle of the rotunda was perhaps twenty feet in diameter and six feet deep, surrounded by a brass rail. At the far end was a small, elevated control console manned by a uniformed guard. Currently he was looking somewhat bemused at a group of schoolchildren clustered around him.

'Damn!' Walton said. He looked both disappointed and furious and Brandt idly wondered why he always got such a kick out of Walton's frustration.

Then the teacher with the children said, 'Let's start at the beginning, shall we?' The children followed her towards another display and Walton scurried up to the pit, followed by Brandt and Cushing.

He nodded to the guard at the console. 'Let's see the whole projection, Goreman.'

'Sure thing, Mr Walton.' He began to press buttons on the inclined panel before him.

'They wanted to keep this in the plant surveillance room,' Walton said. There was outrage in his voice and Brandt could almost see him baring his teeth. If he did, he'd look more like a groundhog than a rat, he thought. 'I wouldn't hear of it, it was too valuable as a' – he searched for the right word – 'teaching aid.'

'Fascinating,' Cushing murmured, staring into the pit. 'What the hell is it?'

Walton's face was glowing. 'It's a holographic model of the

complete plant area – including all of the reactor and reprocessing buildings. Goreman?' In the pit, a ghostly three-dimensional image of the buildings appeared, then solidified. They were startlingly real.

Cushing had allowed himself to become interested, Brandt noted. 'You mentioned that this was originally designed for use in a security system. How?'

At Walton's signal the guard pressed another button and the walls of the model plant suddenly became transparent. Brandt could now see down through all the floors of the plant to the porous limestone bedrock below. It was impressive, he thought. It was impressive every time he saw it. 'You can look into the model layer by layer,' Walton said. The guard worked some controls and floor by floor the model vanished from the top down. At bedrock, the guard pressed another and the complete model reappeared.

'Security,' Cushing repeated. 'How does security fit into this?'

Walton pointed with a finger. 'Notice the moving lights within the model,' he said proudly. 'We have solid-state radiation detectors located throughout the plant and even in the limestone caverns along the underground waste-water discharge channel. We can spot the movement of radioactives anywhere in the plant.'

Cushing looked thoughtful. 'Do that again, Walton.'

The plant promptly dissolved layer by layer. Brandt watched the four bright spots that marked the Prometheus reactors disappear in sections until finally only the storage caverns were left, glittering spots of stationary light in the limestone bedrock.

'That's the cavern area?' Cushing asked.

'The area's honeycombed with them,' Brandt cut in. 'One of the reasons why we built here. We have direct linkage between the two plants underground, invaluable for security reasons. We've enlarged quite a few of the caverns for storage purposes while sealing others off.'

Cushing looked puzzled. 'Sealing them off?'

'In case of waste-water overflow. We didn't want it pooling anyplace; we wanted it to go directly into the ocean.'

Cushing stared at the model in silence, obviously lost in thought. Brandt could see Walton start to fidget. 'It shows the movement of radioactives through the plant at all times?' Cushing asked.

'Yes, sir,' Walton said, looking faintly uneasy. 'The radiation sensors are self-powered, so they work night and day.'

'I see.' Cushing nodded. 'Since this is primarily a security setup, I assume you have men assigned to watch it in twenty-four-hour shifts, logging in all the movements of fissionables?'

Walton blanched. 'I don't believe ... There hasn't been time, we went over budget as it was.'

Cushing turned back on the model. 'I bet the kids love it.' He stared at the far wall where a large animated display showed the progressive fission of a U-235 atom. A ping-pong ball neutron struck an 'atom', which released two more ping-pong neutrons, which 'split' two more atoms to make a visual chain reaction.

Walton looked at Brandt with a whipped-dog expression. Brandt ignored him. Some dogs, he thought, begged to be whipped.

'Hilary?' Brandt turned to see Glidden closing a door labelled 'Security'. Glidden hurried towards him, smiling and holding out his hand. Brandt gripped it briefly and turned to Cushing. 'Eliot, I'd like you to meet Tom Glidden, our number two man.'

Cushing nodded. 'I believe we've met – several times at various conventions, as I recall.' Cushing had a knack for it, Brandt thought. The empty politeness of a man who was going places towards a man who had no place left to go.

'Good to see you, Mr Cushing.' Glidden suddenly looked nervous and Brandt knew exactly how he felt. Cushing also had the knack of making everybody he met feel like a country bumpkin; you suddenly felt that your collar was dirty or that your pants had lost their crease.

'We've got more displays,' Walton was saying, somewhat pathetically. 'Over here is the history of the power plant industry in photographs ...'

'How much time until we see Parks?' Cushing interrupted.

Brandt glanced at his watch. It was working out just right. 'About twenty minutes or so.'

'Good. You have any vending machines here? I could use a cup of coffee.'

Brandt pointed towards the steps, then clapped Walton on the back, giving him a gentle shove in Cushing's direction. 'Why don't you go along, Jerry? You look like you could use a cup – we'll join you in a few minutes.'

Walton looked deflated, Cushing shot Brandt a wry I'll-get-you-for-this look, and they disappeared below.

Brandt walked back to the model, Glidden trailing after, and leaned on the brass railing, staring into the luminous depths below.

'Liz was asking about you the other day,' Glidden said, 'and I told her—'

Brandt cut him off. 'Tom, how bad are things here? Don't bullshit me; just give me a straight answer.'

Glidden picked up on the change of attitude immediately. Brandt's business was to be all business, no remember-way-back-when. 'I'd say everything's up to snuff, Mr Brandt. It's no better nor worse than in any other plant ...'

' "Mr Brandt," ' Brandt repeated softly, looking away. Glidden had spent a lifetime trying to find out what somebody wanted to hear and then telling them. He would equivocate and hedge until he knew for sure what decision Brandt had already made, or was likely to make; then he'd hasten to confirm it. The only thing he would never tell anybody was what he himself thought; he didn't know how to think for himself any more.

'Tom.' Brandt's voice had a ragged edge to it. 'I understand that Parks asked you to give him a report on the plant's readiness. It's due tomorrow. What are you going to say in it?'

Glidden fidgeted and looked ill at ease. 'If you wanted to go on stream today, I wouldn't advise it. Two days from now, I'm not so sure. There's a lot to be done but if everything went right ...'

Why the hell had he kept him on all these years? Brandt thought. For auld lang syne? He had bet wrong. Again. Parks would probably paint a bad picture of the plant because Parks had everything to lose if something did go wrong. He'd do his damnedest to delay, to gain as much time as possible, to make sure everything was letter-perfect. Glidden had a sinecure; he had nothing to lose – or to gain – either way. At the least, he had hoped for an impartial view from Glidden.

Glidden was still searching his face, hoping to read the right answers on it. It still hadn't occurred to him that there might not be any right answers.

'What does Abrams think?' Brandt asked.

Glidden looked slightly relieved. 'My guess is that he feels pretty confident. Like I said, there are things wrong with the plant but Abrams thinks we could probably go on stream.'

'If he had to,' Brandt said slowly, 'do you think Abrams could bring the plant on stream himself?'

Glidden hesitated, mulling it over in his mind. 'I think he thinks he can,' he said finally. 'Theoretically he's qualified but . . .' He shrugged.

'Nothing's impossible for the man who doesn't have to do it himself,' Brandt said heavily. 'That's not original with me, Tom. It's the basis of the Peter Principle.'

'Are you thinking of replacing Parks?' Glidden asked after a moment.

'You think we should?' Brandt countered. 'What the hell *do* you think of him, Tom?'

Glidden looked thoughtful. 'Personally he's a little scratchy. As an engineer, he's a crackerjack. I worked with him at Chippewa Falls and it was a damn smooth operation.' For Glidden to commit himself that much was an overwhelming endorsement. 'His only fault is that he tends to be a perfectionist,' Glidden continued reluctantly. Brandt wasn't sure whether he was recanting completely or just hedging his bets.

'Parks wants a delay. We can't afford one, either financially or politically.' Brandt stared down into the display for a moment longer, then suddenly faced Glidden, catching the man's eyes before he could shift them. 'Straight answer, Tom. Would you bring it on stream if it were you? No evasions, friend to friend.'

The appeal to friendship had trapped him. Something stirred in the back of Glidden's eyes then, something Brandt had never seen there before. He had finally pinned the big man, he thought. Glidden had been a good engineer once; he had been able to make judgements. Brandt found himself holding his breath and waiting for the answer with fascination.

'You wouldn't have me bring it on stream in any event,' Glidden said thickly. 'What you want from me is a kind of insurance. Parks has already made up his mind. Your problem is that you can't make up yours. You want me to say sure, go ahead. Or no, it would be a disaster.' He shook his head sadly. 'I'm not qualified to give you an answer, Hilary, you know that. Why don't you ask the office boy for his opinion? We're both in the same league.'

Brandt started to say something, then spotted Cushing and Walton returning. He felt vaguely ashamed of himself – both because Glidden was right and because he was one of the damned who should never be forced to tell the complete truth. It was like forcing a homely woman to strip naked.

'I've made better coffee on a one-burner hot plate than those machines can produce,' Cushing complained. 'Let's go to the main plant, Hilary. Parks probably has his own private pot.'

'Did you know there was a murder in town last night?' Walton bubbled. 'A Dr Seyboldt – worked right here at the plant. Everybody was talking about it downstairs.'

Seyboldt, Brandt thought, momentarily shocked. He had met him once but couldn't quite remember the man's face. He was part-time in the plant dispensary, as he recalled. He was about to ask for more details when Walton supplied them. 'Executed, right on the beach. Everybody thinks he might have been involved with some kind of drug ring.'

Not in a town this size, Brandt thought. He toyed with the idea that it might be connected with the plant, then discarded it. If Seyboldt had been a technician in a sensitive area, it might be different. He dismissed the murder from his mind. There was no sense borrowing trouble, he had enough of it as it was.

They were halfway to the exit when there was a sudden commotion behind them. Brandt turned in time to see a guard run for the chain-reaction display on the far wall. In front of the display board were a number of buttons that activated various parts of it. One of the kids had jammed several buttons with chewing gum and the board was now racing through a series of fissions. To Brandt, it looked as if the entire board were a mass of electrical fire.

Almost everybody in the rotunda drifted over to watch, except for two schoolgirls who had stopped to stare curiously at the model in the central pit. While they were watching, one of the moving lights abruptly winked out. They giggled and waited a whole minute for it to come back on. When it didn't, they picked up their books from the plastic top and marched off, faintly disapproving.

16

Paul Marical wasn't feeling very well at all. He pulled the electricar over to one side of the corridor and took a small sip from the thermos of tea that he carried with him. The nausea lasted all day now; it didn't go away by noon as it used to. He shivered; the chills made his teeth chatter slightly. Flu again, he thought, then caught himself. Not this time around. He knew better.

He glanced at his watch. Usually he waited until noon, when everybody had gone to the company cafeteria. But with the overtime, the plant's personnel grabbed lunch whenever they could. The ten-minute coffee breaks were still observed, however, and for Marical, they were even better. He had refused to go to lunch with the other technicians, giving as his excuse his desire to lose five pounds. It was a stupid lie – he had hardly been fat to begin with – and nobody would believe it now, he had been losing weight steadily for the last two weeks.

He laughed to himself. What the hell was he worried about? He was completely trusted; nobody kept track of him. He could come and go damn near as he pleased.

'Hey, Paul, do you want to get in on the pool?'

Dan Guberman, the plant's lunchtime gambler and the one man who had gone out of his way to be friendly with him, had come up behind him.

'What pool?'

'The exact time we go on stream.'

It had better be right on schedule, Marical thought grimly. The one they had announced that morning.

'No, thanks, Dan.'

Guberman punched him lightly on the arm. 'What've you got against us common people, Paul?' He sounded almost plaintive. 'You don't eat lunch with us; you don't take coffee breaks with us.' He smiled slightly. 'You won't even let us take your money. How about giving us a break?'

Marical laughed. 'I heard you're pitching pennies in the john now, Dan. Any truth to that?'

He didn't wait for an answer but moved the electricar back into the corridor, turning down the passageway leading to the reprocessing cells. A few feet into the corridor, the cells themselves opened out on either side, fronted by thick plate-glass windows. Inside, automatic shearing machines chopped up used fuel rods. Marical kept the car's speed low, dodging the operators manipulating the outside grips of their master-slave mechanisms.

Then he was into a deserted, fully automated stretch of cells where the chopped rods were dissolved in acids and different radioactives precipitated out.

The radioactives were actually mother's milk, Marical thought bitterly, and the plant was a huge teat that the whole country sucked on. The plutonium that had accumulated in the used fuel rods was extracted by a complex chemical and adsorption process and sold back to the Government for the weapons programme or used for plutonium cycle reactors. It was worth its weight in gold, he thought cynically. Or maybe cyanide was a better comparison.

He hit the first down ramp and sped on to the next. He was now running the electricar at top speed through the almost deserted corridors. Cheap thrills, he thought, enjoying the feel of the air rushing through his hair. There were damn few left for him.

Then he slowed. He was now in the storage area where used fuel rods were kept in huge tanks of water until their inner decay heat had declined to a point where they could be handled. More importantly, it was also the area where they stored the lead casks of mixed uranium and plutonium that they had extracted from the used fuel before it went to the final processing step in the ion-exchange columns. It was impossible to maintain a rigid control on waste radioactives during the process. On the other hand, in the areas where the two metals were finally separated into their pure salts, security and inventory control were more thorough.

He stopped the electricar in front of Cell Twenty, whose inventory record he had been carefully watching. Storage cells were filled and emptied on regular schedules. There was always a period when a cell was changing over and a tiny deviation from the authorized amount of stored radioactives would never be missed. He waited a moment, listening, but there were no sounds of anybody coming down the corridor. He got out, lifted a lead cask from the rear of the electricar where he had hidden it, and placed it on a hand dolly.

He pushed it to the outer door, touched the knob with his hand, then paused, frowning. For some reason he was wringing wet.

He didn't want to do it, he thought. He didn't want to go in there again. It was desperately dangerous. More than anyone else in the plant, he knew just how dangerous. But he needed one more cask. For safety's sake. He laughed then and reached for the doorknob again. His hand was shaking almost uncontrollably.

He shouldered his way in; the light went on automatically. On the security board upstairs, a red light should now be flashing indicating that somebody was in the cell. But chances were that whoever was assigned to watch it was on his coffee break or would merely flick on the intercom and ask who was there.

Once they knew who he was, the risk of their asking more questions was one in a hundred.

In the outer pressure lock white radiation suits hung on hooks, along with oxygen tanks good for half an hour. The suit was designed to conserve its air supply. In case of atmospheric contamination, the radiation sensors in the hood would automatically switch its air-intake filters over to the tank. At one time, he thought sadly, wearing a suit might have saved his life. When he had first started switching casks of radioactives, he had been afraid somebody would notice his long absence; so he had cut his time too close. Too close to take a minute to put on a suit.

But there was nothing he could do now; it was all spilt milk. He donned a suit and strapped an air tank to his back. He tested the system for a moment, then suddenly remembered and took off his radiation safety badge, placing it on a nearby table. He had to be clean – at least for another two days.

Through the thick glass port of the inner door he could see the wide-spaced racks that held a number of lead casks, each three feet long and six inches in diameter, similar to the one he had brought along. It would be relatively easy for somebody on the outside to refine the sludge in the casks into weapons-grade plutonium, Marical thought – if you didn't worry too much about your own skin. And there was enough plutonium in the storage cells to make hundreds of bombs, albeit inefficient and very dirty ones.

He turned and pulled the dolly closer to the door. The cask on it was filled with a sludge from one of the earlier reprocessing stages. It was like kiting a cheque, he thought. Inventories of casks with insignificant plutonium content were seldom made. Inventories of casks containing high amounts of plutonium were made fairly often. But the switch could only be detected by quantitative monitoring of the radioactive contents. Sooner or later his substitutions would be discovered but by then he would have made delivery and vanished.

He glanced through the port again. What interested him as much as the casks was the painted pathway on the floor. Position in life was all-important, he thought grimly. The casks were kept a minimum distance apart; if they came too close together, a mutual neutron exchange from the U-235 content would cause a chain reaction. Even the water in his body as he walked between the racks could act as a neutron moderator with the same result. The marked 'safe' path wasn't too narrow but neither was it too wide. Once a few weeks ago he had stag-gered while carrying one of the casks ... There hadn't been any explosion but for an instant the cell had been filled with a green radiance. He didn't know how much radiation he had absorbed at the time, but the effects had become all too ob-vious. It might take weeks, but he was sure now that it would kill him.

He checked the door radiation detector, noted that the back-ground level was within safe limits, then gripped the knob to open the inner door. Again, the ague brought a flood of sweat that almost fogged the view plate of his hood.

It doesn't matter, he thought harshly, *it's too late ...*

He picked up the cask and pushed through the door, letting it swing silently shut behind him. The pathway was just wide enough but he still felt like a ballet dancer on opening night. He walked carefully along the path until he reached the loading table and remote hoist. All the casks were at the same level of radioactivity; he chose one at random. He set down the substi-tute cask and ran his fingers lightly over the control board. The hoist moved quietly along its tracks, then let down steel fingers to clutch the lugs of the selected cask. A moment later, he had transferred it to the loading table and lowered the substitute into the rack.

Marical disengaged the hoist, then suddenly gripped the table, a wave of nausea washing over him. Not fear this time, he thought, clenching his teeth. It passed; he lifted the heavy cask and carried it through the airlock, then recycled the inner door. He hung the tank and the suit back on the wall, pinned his safety badge on his pocket and loaded the new cask onto the dolly.

He was just putting the cask in the back of the electricar when a suspicious voice behind him said, 'Hello, Paul, what are you doing here?'

For a fraction of a second he froze, knowing full well that hesitation now could be disastrous. He finished covering the cask, then casually turned and said, 'Hello, Mrs Hardy. They sent me down to pick up a cask for quality inspection.'

Her smile was a shade too wide, showing a mouthful of yellowing dentures. 'Everybody's working overtime these days. Myself, I think haste makes waste.'

He got into the car, hoping she wouldn't notice his sweat-drenched shirt. 'You can say that again.'

'Hastes makes—' she started, then sprayed him with a burst

of laughter and continued up the corridor. Marical watched her go. A short, dumpy statistician in her forties with a reputation as a scatterbrain. By late afternoon, she would have forgotten that she had ever seen him.

He started the car and drove a hundred yards farther up the corridor to an access door in the corridor wall. He parked and waited a moment, listening again. The riskiest part of all, he thought. He could explain possession of the cask – but would be hard-pressed to explain why he was taking it into the caverns.

The corridor was empty. He opened the access door into the roughhewn cavern just beyond, propped it open with a rock, then went back to the electricar for the lead cask. It was heavy enough so that his biceps bulged under the weight. He carried it into the cavern, kicking the door shut behind him.

Inside it was cool and moist and quiet, the darkness relieved by a string of naked light bulbs dangling at intervals from a cord that led off into the darkness. A few yards in he thought he heard a noise and glanced quickly around, filled with fear that somebody might have followed him. Because the caverns held much of the piping for the plant, workers occasionally entered them to do routine maintenance.

There was nobody else there.

A hundred yards farther on, a small grotto led off to his left. Several battered clothing lockers left over from construction days stood guard just before the entrance. Marical set the cask down, wiped the sweat off his forehead and rubbed his arms. In the grotto, behind the lockers, he had hollowed out a large cell. In it were three casks, properly spaced to avoid triggering each other. He carefully positioned the fourth, trembling slightly remembering the pale-green blaze of Cherenkov radiation when he made his first mistake.

He straightened up and glanced at his watch. He had been gone a little more than twenty minutes, long enough for somebody to miss him but hardly long enough for anybody to be alarmed.

He heard voices just before he reopened the access door. His nerves started to give way then. Why the hell was he doing it? he thought, panicked. He got sweaty palms and jumped every time he heard a noise.

He waited, then inched the door open, slipped out and ran back to the car. He slid into the seat and slumped over the steering tiller, shaking.

And then he gradually calmed while a growing rage replaced

his fear. He could be many things, he thought coldly. But he could never be disloyal. Not to his memories.

He had just started up the car when the paging device in his pocket bleeped once. He pulled over to a service phone.

'Marical here.'

The page operator said, 'I'll connect you,' and a moment later an annoyed voice complained, 'Paul, where the hell have you been? I need a back-up man for these titrations.'

Marical felt a light sweat pop out on his forehead again. He had forgotten that Van Baketes had asked him for help in the cell.

'Give me five minutes, Van.'

Speeding towards Cell Charlie Three, where Van Baketes was waiting for him, he debated briefly if he should take a pass and tell Van to get somebody else.

He couldn't remember when he had ever felt quite so sick.

17

Kamrath parked the jeep in front of Seyboldt's beachfront home, cut the ignition and sat staring at the house while he finished his cigarette. It was a typical rustic oceanside cottage except for the small brick addition that Doc had built for his office and examining room. A lot of babies had been delivered there, Kamrath thought. And a lot of accidental gunshot wounds sewn up. Plus a few emergency appendectomies and gall-bladder operations and, once, a simple open-heart operation when there had been no time to get the patient to the city. That patient had lived, too – long enough to be transferred to the city hospital where a nurse finally killed him when she confused prescriptions.

All of that was gone now, he thought, stubbing out his cigarette. From now on it would be 'Don't come down with anything that requires a house call and make damned sure you don't get sick on weekends.'

He climbed out of the jeep and stretched. It had been a lousy night and the morning hadn't been much better. He had called Doc's relations and made arrangements for shipping the body. Doc had never mentioned his family and after spending the morning talking to them, he could understand why.

He started up the flagstone walk. The last murder in Cardenas Bay had been almost four years ago – a simple crime of passion, two fishermen quarrelling over docking space and one had stabbed the other with a bait knife. Before that, they had been the best of friends.

Nobody answered his knock and he pushed tentatively at the door. He hadn't really expected to find anybody there but the door opened easily and he stepped inside. 'Abby?' There was no answer and he walked quietly into the small reception area. The light on her desk was on and there were half a dozen files strewn across the top. A small tic of worry started in the back of his head. 'Abby, you here?'

No answer. He felt for the gun in his holster and edged closer to the examining-room door. The door was translucent glass and he could make out a vague form hunched over near the filing cabinets. He was almost ready to throw his weight against the door and burst in when he heard her reedy voice say, 'All right, Hippocrates, if you don't like that, you'll just have to go hungry.'

He turned the knob and eased inside. Abby had been kneeling down, coaxing a calico cat almost as thin as she was to nibble at a bowl of cat food.

'Abby?' He said it much louder this time, recalling that she was somewhat hard of hearing. Her head jerked back and she glanced up at him angrily.

'You shouldn't startle me like that, Hank.' She bent back down towards the cat. 'Honestly, that man has had this cat for five years and I don't think he ever remembers to feed him two days in a row. If it wasn't for me, Hippocrates would have met his Maker a long time ago.' She reached out a thin, gnarled hand to scratch the cat behind its ears. It turned away from the bowl of food and rubbed its head against her spindly calves. She started talking to it again. 'Well, I guess somebody has to take care of you; Doc is always so busy with everybody else's problems.'

She walked back to her office, Kamrath following after. At her desk, she shuffled aimlessly through the files; she didn't look up at him. 'That man is such a trial, he can't keep these files straight for love nor money. I always have to do it for him.' She gathered them up in her hands. 'I really don't know . . .' Her voice began to falter.

'Abby,' Kamrath said kindly, 'Doc is dead.'

She turned away from him so he couldn't see the tears suddenly start to leak down her face. 'It was nice to pretend,' she said. She took some Kleenex from the desk drawer and honked her nose. 'Is there anything I can help you with, Hank?'

'You're still on duty?' he asked her gently.

'He paid me to the end of the month.' Her voice was a tired quaver and he thought she must be older than she looked; the flesh usually got stringy long before the voice went. 'There are prescription refills that have to be approved, referrals to make. And I've got to ship the records out when patients find other doctors in the city.' Her voice drifted off. 'I don't know who else could do it, he would have wanted me to stay around.'

He hated to put her through it but he didn't know how else to go about it. 'Do you know of anybody who didn't like Doc, Abby? Anybody who might have hated him because he failed to save their son or daughter – anything like that?'

She looked indignant. 'He didn't have an enemy in town, everybody loved him, everybody relied on him.'

Kamrath sighed. 'I know that, Abby. He was my best friend. But nobody's loved a hundred percent.'

'Dr Seyboldt was!' Her mouth clamped shut and he could see the muscles become rigid; then she relented a little and became less certain. 'There might have been somebody, I suppose. He had a mean streak or two; nobody knew it but me. But if anybody in town really disliked him, I don't know of them.'

'Can I see his drug cabinet, Abby?'

She nodded, showed him the small storeroom and turned on the light. Neatly arranged on the shelves were dusty cartons and bottles of various pills and liquids and boxes of hypodermic needles. Kamrath touched nothing, merely glanced at the shelves. He would have Abby do an inventory later but nothing looked as if it had been touched. In a drug robbery, you'd expect to see things rifled through, bottles or boxes clumsily replaced or pushed aside. Except for a faint film of dust, the storeroom was neat as a pin. Abby's fine hand, he thought. But the storeroom would be a treasure trove for a thief. Barbiturates, amyl nitrite, morphine Syrettes, tranquillizers, amphetamines, antidepressants ... uppers and downers, you name it, Doc probably had it in stock. And then another thought struck him.

'Abby, Doc did emergency operations here. Could you show me where he kept his instruments?'

She looked faintly disapproving but she showed him into the examining room. Most of the surgical instruments were in an autoclave. Nothing missing, he decided, though he wasn't sure if he would know or not. But then, a thief would probably have taken everything. Again, there was no indication of a hasty search for scalpels or other small instruments that could be pawned or sold. He glanced through Doc's black bag with the same result, and this time Abby confirmed directly that nothing was missing.

Which left the question of whoever had seen him last. 'Abby, how complete are Doc's records?'

She nervously fingered the ones on the desk. 'As complete as I could make them.' She sounded defensive and Kamrath guessed that she had either forgotten appointments or misplaced an occasional record. Doc had been a patient man but he might not be so forgiving on something like that. It probably accounted for Abby's remark about Doc's 'mean streak or two'.

'A lot of the workers from the plant were his regular patients here, too, weren't they?'

She nodded. 'Certainly. Who else could they go to? But we don't have any of the plant records here. That young nurse up there – Miss Karen' – she fumbled for the last name – 'took care of all that. He kept separate records for the plant.' She suddenly looked put upon. 'You have no idea how much trouble that caused. He'd keep their records at the plant and then he wouldn't have them here when they visited him in the evening. A lot of patients would drop by after I left at night and he'd complain in the morning that he hadn't been able to find their records. I kept telling him he should make duplicates. After all, a lot of the workers couldn't see him during normal hours.'

Kamrath remembered the frequent chess games interrupted by patients dropping in for an examination or free samples of drugs that Doc would give away or calling up in panic when Johnny's cough wouldn't clear up.

But someplace he must have kept notes on the man who had seen him last.

'Do you have his appointment book, Abby?'

She sniffed. 'Certainly, though I'm not so sure it will do you much good. He was pretty careless about keeping records on night callers. Sometimes he'd forget to log them in, particularly if it was for something minor or' – she shot him a disapproving glance – 'if he was playing chess. It gave me a lot of headaches when it came billing time, let me tell you.'

'I'd like to see his appointments for the last night,' Kamrath said, adding, 'We didn't play chess yesterday.'

She started searching the desk top and then quickly thumbed

through the letter divider, looked flustered and went through the drawers. 'Just a moment and I'll check the other office.' She disappeared for five minutes and returned looking even more confused. 'I must have misplaced it,' she said, not quite believing she could have done so.

The murderer had probably taken it, Kamrath thought. That was strange in itself. Appointment books were usually left open; all the murderer had to do was lean over and rip out the last few pages. But the entire book had been taken, which meant that if he could find it, the book itself might tell him a great deal.

'I don't know what I'll do,' Abby said, sounding a little distraught. 'I use it for billing.'

'You don't remember who his appointments were with last night?' Kamrath asked hopefully.

'I left at six,' she said. The tears started to flow. 'There was nobody scheduled after that. But that didn't matter; they used to drop by at all hours if they knew he was home.'

Kamrath fished in the pocket of his coat for the postal receipt he had found on Seyboldt's body. 'Do you know what this is for? Karen Gruen tells me he mailed all his blood tests into the city and I imagine he sent in a lot of his other lab work, too. We found this in one of his pockets.'

She took the slip of paper and fumbled for her glasses. 'That's right,' she nodded. 'To Moore Labs.'

'And this receipt was for blood tests?'

She inspected the small slip closely, tilting her head back to look through the bottoms of her bifocals. 'It's for blood tests all right, I remember him filling out three forms.'

'Do you remember who they were for?' He added gently, 'This is no time to protect confidences, Abby.'

Her mouth tightened slightly. 'He coded his blood tests; he always claimed I talked too much.'

'He mailed in the samples on the same day he took them?'

She nodded. 'The results should be back at the end of the week.'

'Couldn't you call up the lab and have them give you the results over the phone?'

She looked dubious. 'I don't think they would have them by today; maybe by tomorrow.'

'You sure you couldn't find out who the blood tests were for?'

She couldn't hide a small look of triumph. 'He always put the code number on the patient's file folder. It might take a little while but I could find out.'

Kamrath smiled at her. 'Would you do that for me? And call me at the office as soon as you find out?' It might be something and it might not, he thought, but it was worth finding out. He hesitated at the door. 'Doc would be proud of you, Abby.'

Which was the wrong thing to say because she started to cry again.

18

Brandt and Cushing were thirty minutes late and Parks' irritation grew by the minute. He finally tracked them to the Information Building – he should have guessed that Walton would want to show that off – and noted with interest the guard's comment that Glidden had been with them. Brandt wouldn't find out much from Glidden, he thought. The grey man wasn't about to commit himself one way or the other.

But when they finally did show up, it was Cushing he had to fence with. He had his secretary brew coffee and then served brandy from the liquor cabinet in his office. Hennessy Five Star; Cushing should appreciate that. When they had finished, he said, 'Everybody ready? The first tour left an hour ago but I think I can arrange another.'

Cushing leaned back on the office couch and crossed his legs. 'I've already had one tour,' he said pleasantly. 'We can skip this one and get right down to business.'

'Seen one plant, seen them all,' Parks murmured politely. Brandt had his sources of information and no doubt Cushing had his. The tour had been his first line of offence and the only reason Cushing might want to avoid it was if he knew in advance what he was going to be shown. It was one thing to read a complaining letter; quite another to be shown the physical evidence on which the complaint was based.

'I'm afraid if we're going to talk meaningfully, we'll have to see the plant,' Parks continued, still polite. 'Besides, I've already ordered up an electricar.'

In the suit-up room, Walton fingered the white radiation uniform with curiosity and a show of distaste. Perhaps he didn't care for the cut, Parks thought. 'I can understand technicians wearing these, but why us? We're not going to be in hot areas of the plant very long, are we? I've got to make plans for to-morrow.'

'Jerry—' Brandt started to say.

'It's regulations,' Parks cut in. 'And don't forget to take along a hood and tank while you're at it.'

Walton looked uneasy. 'I might have to cut it short,' he said tentatively. 'I want to go up to the balcony and figure out some camera angles. We should be able to get some very effective shots from up there.'

'You do that,' Parks agreed. 'Just don't get in anybody's way.' The one plus, he thought, was that Walton would be out of his.

The next stop on the tour was Generator Room Two. They came out onto the catwalk overlooking the floor and Walton gasped. 'My God,' he said, 'it's right out of *Forbidden Planet*.'

Parks smiled. The room was huge and almost antiseptic in its spotlessness. A faint odour of lubricant filled the air although, once the massive turbines and their coupled generators started operation, the more acrid odour of ozone would predominate. The four tandem-compound quadruple-flow reheat turbines were an impressive sight, he had to admit, with their long gleaming housings enamelled a brilliant white. The plumbing from the secondary heat exchanger was buried under the floor. He thought for a moment of taking the party down one of the access passages to see the massive pipes but decided against it.

'I've got to get a crew in to photograph this,' Walton said excitedly. 'The very heart of the generating capacity of the plant.'

'Not at all,' Brandt corrected. 'This unit handles the heat output from Prometheus Two only. There are three other generating rooms just like this.'

Walton shook his head in wonder. For a perverse reason Parks was pleased that the installation had impressed the PR man.

After they left the balcony and returned to the electricar, Cushing asked, 'Theoretically, Parks, if you had no problems at all, how long would it take you to get on stream from a standing start?'

'No problems?' Parks said cautiously. 'The situation doesn't exist, Mr Cushing.'

'Theoretically,' Cushing persisted.

Parks slowed the electricar to round a corner. No matter how he phrased it, his answer could be interpreted as a commitment. 'Right now, reactors two, three and four are on standby. They could be brought on stream in a "hot start" in a matter of hours.' He glanced over at Cushing. 'Is that your new time-table?'

Cushing's lips thinned. 'Don't be ridiculous.'

'I seldom am,' Parks said.

'Bad night, Greg?' Brandt asked pointedly.

Parks shook his head. 'Bad morning.'

In Control Central, he introduced them to a harrassed Delano and crew, then tried to explain the consoles to a Walton who was obviously growing bored and hungry. 'The operator sits in the middle of each console with the readout board in front of him and a console leg to either side. The right leg monitors the turbines, generators and auxiliaries. The left, the water-circulation system, heat exchanger and condensate salvage. We've simplified the system a great deal.' Walton had a glazed expression on his face. 'You getting all this, Jerry? You're the guy who'll have to explain it to the newsmen. If you don't know what you're talking about, it'll be bad for our image.'

Somebody snickered in the room and Walton jerked alert. He pointed at a series of red glass panels ringing the top of the consoles. 'What are those?'

'Emergency alarms. The panel in the main part of the console is hooked up to a neutron-monitoring device. If it lights, then the operator has to SCRAM the reactor – though the computer should already have done it for him.'

'How much time for manual override?' Cushing asked.

'Two seconds,' Parks said slowly. 'Two long, long seconds.'

Outside the control room, he stopped the others by the electri-car before they could climb back on. 'Interesting, wasn't it?' he said with a trace of sarcasm. 'What's even more interesting is that Fulton's subcontractor has rewritten the program for those consoles fourteen times – count them. And there are still critical sequencings that have to be done manually.' He held up a hand. 'That's only the beginning. The boards should show temperature changes at any critical spot in the reactor as well as local neutron fluxes. Fine in theory, not so good in practice. The sensors have a failure rate of about ten a month. And we can't tear a reactor down just to replace a sensor. That means a fuel rod could collapse in the pile and we wouldn't even know it.'

'Greg, we can go through this later,' Brandt said. There was anger in his voice.

'No, I'd like to hear all of it now,' Cushing said. A faint smile flickered about his face. 'Have you had any failures lately?'

He'd been right, Parks thought, somebody had been feeding Cushing information. 'No – but I consider this month exceptional.'

Cushing nodded. 'You had confused me there. I couldn't remember any complaints recently and I was sure if there had been any failures, you would have reported them.'

So much for paranoia, Parks thought uncomfortably. Cushing had read his mind. But he still thought Cushing had an inside man and his nomination for it was Abrams.

He started the electricar and ran it a hundred yards up the corridor, stopping before a set of double doors. Brandt glanced at him in surprise. 'What's this, a warehouse?'

'My museum,' Parks said shortly. He pushed his way through, hitting the light switch inside. The room was filled with wooden racks holding a variety of plant hardware, most of it sections of pipe and a number of valves. Some parts showed signs of corrosion; others were still in the lubricant and plastic bags in which they had been shipped.

Parks walked to a bench at the rear on which rested five large valve fittings, each of them ten inches in diameter. Pinned to the cork wall behind the bench was a large brown envelope. 'All of these fittings are for the recirculating-water inlet to the reactor vessel,' he said. 'They're all brand-new – we never installed them, thank God.' He opened the envelope and shook out a group of X rays. 'If you look at the negatives, you'll see that each of these assemblies contains at least two fracture lines. Anybody want to make book on how long they would have stood up under vibrations from the pumps?'

'Well, Hilary?' Cushing said affably.

Brandt reddened. 'This is why we have shakedown runs – so inferior equipment and fittings show up in actual use. There's no way in the world you're going to get one hundred percent perfect fittings. Recently, Fulton has started using ultrasonic inspection techniques and they've cut the failure rate sharply.' He was obviously angry now, his voice ragged. 'I read your reports too, Greg. You've had no complaint about these valves for the last month.'

'I said these were samples of Fulton's work,' Parks said calmly. 'We haven't been able to check everything.'

Brandt glared at him. 'Your report didn't carry a recommendation. What do you want to do?'

Parks hesitated, then decided to bite the bullet. 'Pull out the entire cooling system for a point-to-point check.'

Brandt exploded. 'Out of the question!'

Cushing waved his hand at the other racks in the room. 'I take it everything here is in the same category – equipment, parts and fittings that didn't live up to specs?'

'Everything I could find,' Parks said.

'Over how long a period of time?' Cushing nodded. 'I know, it's all in your reports. But I can hardly quote from memory.'

'Since I started here, a year and a half ago.'

'How much is current?'

'It depends on what you mean by current. For the last month we haven't had the time to do that much checking. That's one reason why I'm asking for an extension of the on-stream date.'

'I see,' Cushing said coolly. 'You want an extension of the date so you can find more faulty fittings so you can get a further extension of the date. I thought you were running a power plant, Mr Parks, not an underwriter's laboratory.'

'And I thought you were the Vice-Chairman for Reactor Safety,' Parks said angrily. 'I thought the samples here would interest you. They should – but apparently they don't.'

It was Cushing's turn to hesitate. 'They interest me,' he said finally. 'Very much. But the fact remains that you have had no failures of significance for the last month. You may not have been able to X-ray everything but neither have they failed in actual use. If they had, I assume you would have reported it.'

'That's right,' Parks admitted quietly. 'During the last month, no major plumbing part has failed. The last run on Prometheus One was successful enough. Everything seems to be in reasonable shape right now but I can't speak for tomorrow.'

At lunch in the company dining room, Parks found an excuse to sit with Brandt at their own table. Cushing and Walton shared a table with Abrams and Glidden on the other side of the room. Muzak covered their conversation.

'Are you trying to make me look foolish, Greg?' Brandt asked in a low voice. 'If you are, you're succeeding.'

'I'm trying not to make myself look foolish two days from now,' Parks said. He speared a pat of butter for his hard roll. 'You hired me to do a job and this is part of it.'

'All right – do you realize what it would cost us in terms of time and money to pull the entire cooling system?'

Parks spoke around a mouthful of cold hamburger. 'Do you realize what it would cost Western if we had to shut down this plant in mid-run because of a cooling-line failure?'

Brandt shook his head impatiently. 'Under our contract with Fulton, I doubt very much that we could demand such an inspection without footing the bills ourselves.'

'Don't they have a penalty clause in their contracts?'

'Sure they do – but it's a time-performance clause and they could make a damned good case of our forcing them to extend their performance into the penalty period.'

Parks stabbed viciously at another piece of butter. 'Fulton hasn't performed as it should have right from the start. Whoever advocated running the cooling pipes for all the reactors through the same utility tunnel? One of Fulton's resident geniuses?'

'It was done six months before you got here so you can't be held responsible,' Brandt said, unperturbed. 'On even the most expensive project, Greg, you have to watch the dollars.'

'So if one of them goes, they all go.'

Brandt was now angry. 'Come off it, Greg; the odds against that happening are astronomical.'

'You've seen Lerner's staff reports,' Parks said sharply. 'I can give you the tapes for our test runs over the last six months where we simulated system failures, including reactor-core failures. The response time just isn't there. We need at least two more weeks to refine the system and iron out the bugs. Otherwise, you're running the risk of having to take this plant off stream for a year.' He swirled some Coke around in his mouth to kill the taste of the greasy burger. 'What kind of interest would our bank loans cost us for a year, Hilary? And if something went wrong and we contaminated the plant, how much time and money before we could clean it up and bring it on stream then? Or would we still be in business at all?'

'Keep your voice down!' Brandt said sharply. 'All right, I'll talk to Lerner; I'll look at your tapes. But believe me when I say there's pressure to get this plant into the grid – and I do mean the day after tomorrow. You've had over six months for shakedown, Greg. The compliance teams haven't turned up any major discrepancies and they're pretty damn thorough. You want to spend the rest of your life shaking the plant down? You've got to stop sometime; you've got to determine what sort of risk is acceptable. I know all about the risk-versus-benefits arguments when it comes to nuclear plants. A one-in-a-hundred chance is unacceptable. A one-in-a-thousand chance is unacceptable. But what about one in a million? Or one in three hundred million? Where do you draw the line? Western's got half a dozen thousand-megawatt plants on stream and I had to oversee them all. You still haven't convinced me you have a case.'

Parks sat in silence, sipping at his coffee. 'What will it take to prove it to you?'

Brandt shrugged. 'I don't know – but I'll recognize it when I see it. I'll pull it off stream myself, then; you won't have to.'

Brandt sounded more convincing now than he had before and Parks found himself beginning to sway. 'I've asked you once before; what's Cushing's power, Hilary? It's a lot more than his title indicates.'

'He knows his way around,' Brandt said slowly. 'He's well known in banking circles; he made all the right connections when he was at Harvard. He's a specialist in power-plant financing. Any bank will check you out, of course, but a recommendation from Cushing will cinch it. It isn't generally known, but he's arranged for a line of credit to a lot of power companies. His friends have helped Western in our financing. Last but not least, he's the unofficial adviser to the President on nuclear power. I think the Convention speech was his idea.'

'What's he bucking for?'

'What's anybody buck for in that circle? Personal prestige, the power-behind-the-throne-type thing.'

'He's also got a conflict of interest,' Parks said slowly. 'Haven't any of the newspapers picked up on it?'

'You think I could prove anything I've said?' Brandt stared at his plate. 'Conflict of interest. My God, Greg, the whole country's one big conflict of interest. Look at the President! Look at the Vice-President! And if the *Post* or the *Times* doesn't investigate you, who else does? Most reporters are lost when it comes to investigating City Hall, let alone the Federal bureaucracy. The big investigations hit the top, that's it. But what about the next rung down, the managerial level of the Government? There's damned little public scrutiny of it, but that's where the real wheeling and dealing is done.' He shook his head. 'There's no conflict of interest there; there's no conflict at all, Greg, it's all interest.'

Parks finished his coffee in silence; then glanced up to see Cushing making his way over to their table. Cushing looked at Brandt curiously, obviously wondering what they had talked about. 'You're the tour guide, Parks. What's next?'

Parks wiped his mouth with his napkin and stood up. He'd

be tasting that hamburger all afternoon. 'The reprocessing plant – you'll enjoy it. I don't have any major complaint about that one.'

Out in the corridor, Cushing motioned Parks aside. 'You apparently think I'm some sort of ogre, Parks, that I'm here to see you go on stream at all costs. I expect you to tell me everything that's wrong, or at least what you think is wrong. I'm no novice to plants; I've been through dozens of them and I feel fairly sure you can't show me anything I haven't seen at least once before. You haven't yet, at any rate. But I have to juggle possibilities and, as I'm sure Mr Brandt has mentioned, you can't stay on shakedown forever.' He looked at Parks frankly. 'You've got the last word, you know; you're the plant manager.'

He was all patrician poise and openness and Parks found himself desperately wanting to believe him. If he were ten years younger and had less experience, he might, he thought. He nodded without answering and climbed into the electricar.

The trip through the corridors to the processing plant was a good five minutes, the fluorescent lights overhead flowing past with a monotonous regularity. Then they had passed through the safety doors and the reprocessing cells opened up on both sides. The first few cells were vacant and unused.

'We're installing a new deluge system to wet down the radioactive dust in case of an accident,' Parks explained. 'It's the reason for all the plumbing and electrical equipment along the walls.'

He rounded the corner, resisting the temptation to take it on two wheels, then braked to a sudden halt. On one side of the corridor was a workbench with some conduit and electrical switch boxes on it, along with a portable power hack saw. A length of conduit had rolled along the bench so that it jutted out into the corridor.

Parks glanced quickly around to see if the sudden stop had jolted his passengers, then strode over to the nearest cell. The two men inside were dressed in complete airtight radiation suits, dragging lifelines behind them. Parks touched the intercom button beneath the window.

'Where the hell did the electricians go?'

One of the figures slowly turned and flipped the 'talk' switch on the inside. Marical's face peered out from behind the faceplate. 'I guess they broke for lunch.'

Ask a dumb question, you get a dumb answer, Parks thought.

'When they get back, tell them to secure their gear after this.'

Back in the electricar, Cushing said, 'Will this be the subject of a memo, too, Parks?' He laughed easily.

Parks drove slowly along the passageway, watching the operators with a practised eye. On the outside, they went through an odd ballet with the grips of the master-slave manipulators. On the inside of the cell, mechanical claws imitated their movements, picking up a used fuel rod from an inner holding room and lowering it onto a conveyor where the shearer blade chopped it into small pieces. The fragments then dropped into containers that would be sealed later.

Parks kept up a dry monologue, explaining the procedures down to and including the wide-mouthed vacuum bags that sucked up the chips and dust to keep the cell atmosphere dust-free.

Walton dutifully scribbled the details down on a note pad, finally commenting, 'You're taking a lot of precautions. Is it that dangerous?'

'More dangerous than you might think,' Parks said. 'We make doubly sure those linkages through the windows are airtight. The cells themselves are even under a slight negative air pressure so any air leaks will be inward, not outward.'

They were past the cells now and Parks turned a corner of the passageway to drive out onto a broad balcony overlooking a series of huge water tanks. A hundred feet away an overhead crane was unloading used fuel rod bundles from an open water tank mounted on an electricar and lowering them into a larger holding tank.

Walton watched for a long moment, then turned to Parks. 'Those aren't all from Prometheus, are they?'

'We handle rods from all over the country,' Parks said. 'And from plants overseas, too. We have a contract from Fulton Engineering to process used fuel rods from their foreign installations as well.' He fell silent, watching the bundles sink below the surface. 'There are two more rooms like this. And we're constructing a fourth.'

Walton leaned over the balcony railing a moment. 'That's quite a lot of used fuel down there, isn't it?'

'Quite a bit,' Parks said dryly. He looked over at Cushing. 'We're running out of space. Fulton keeps building more reactors and that means more and more used fuel rods come in.'

'And you don't like that?' Cushing said. 'Why not?'

'Partly because it's dangerous,' Parks said. 'And partly because I don't like the idea of the United States becoming the world's nuclear garbageman.' He thought about it for a moment. 'There's a phrase for you, Jerry. Maybe you can use it on your television special.'

19

Senator Hoyt Dr Cohen, as an expert on radiation sickness, would you tell us about the long-term effects of contamination from the Cardenas Bay incident?

Dr Cohen I can't give you as much information on that as you would like, Senator. The most serious studies were those made of Hiroshima and much of that work is suspect.

Senator Hoyt What do you mean by 'suspect'?

Dr Cohen At Hiroshima, we compared the incidence of cancer, leukaemia, child mortality and other radiation-related diseases with the incidence in a control population. Initially the control population was a group of Japanese who lived on the outskirts of the city. We didn't realize then that they were subject to a great deal of downwind fallout from the bomb. As a result, their incidence of radiation-related diseases was as high as that of the test population – or higher. We've since found other more valid control populations. The results are still coming in.

Senator Stone Still coming in? Then the total results of the Cardenas Bay disaster aren't all in yet, either?

Dr Cohen That's right, sir. You have to consider, first, that there is no such thing as a safe or 'threshold' dose of radiation. This is strictly a statistical concept. Radiation exposure is cumulative; any damage keeps adding up. In addition to that, you have to consider that many of the fallout products have extremely long half-lives.

Representative Paine Since my colleague, Representative Holmburg, is absent today, I'll have to ask questions I'd ordinarily leave to him. Exactly what is a half-life?

Dr Cohen Briefly, the half-life of a radioactive element is the time necessary for half its radioactivity to disappear. If a substance has a half-life of ten days, for example, then half of its radioactivity will have disappeared in those ten days. Half

the remaining will disappear in the next ten days and so on.
Representative Paine It doesn't seem like much of a problem then.
Dr Cohen I was using that as an example. The half-life of strontium 90 – it's the radioactive element similar to calcium that cows tend to concentrate in their milk – is twenty-eight years. That of plutonium is approximately two hundred and forty thousand years.
Senator Stone Plutonium keeps cropping up in these hearings, Doctor. Is it really dangerous?
Dr Cohen It depends on how you look at it. Plutonium's an alpha emitter and a sheet of paper would stop its radiation.
Senator Stone Then it could hardly be considered dangerous, Doctor.
Dr Cohen I'm sorry, Senator; that's only part of the story. The truth is that it's one of the most dangerous substances known to man. A speck the size of a dust mote will eventually cause lung cancer if inhaled. A small amount of soluble plutonium salt lodged in an open wound would concentrate in the bones, destroying the bone marrow, the source of your white blood cells. There is no antidote. The victim may die in a week, he may linger for months, but blood cell destruction continues. He will die, perhaps years hence, of aplastic anaemia. But he *will* die.
Senator Stone I'm correct in assuming that one of the reasons for the magnitude of the Cardenas Bay disaster was the sheer quantity of radioactives stored there?
Dr Cohen I was appalled at the total amount. The reprocessing plant at Cardenas Bay serviced not only the Prometheus reactors but reactors all over the world. The inventory of used fuel rods on hand, either in water tanks waiting for their decay heat to dissipate or simply waiting for processing, was terrifying. The radioactive waste ran into the billions of curies – one figure I've heard was higher than fifty billion.
Senator Stone Could you put that into perspective, Doctor? A simple comparison will do.
Dr Cohen A good comparison might be with radon, the gas usually found in uranium mines. One trillionth of a curie of radon gas per cubic metre of air is ten times higher than the maximum permissible dosage for miners.
Senator Stone I'm stunned. I have no idea how all of this happened, how it was allowed to happen.
Dr Cohen For years, it's been common practice for

manufacturers who sell reactors overseas to include a reprocessing clause as part of their sales contract.

Representative Paine We not only sell the groceries; we haul away the garbage?

Dr Cohen That's one way of phrasing it.

Senator Clarkson I can understand the finances but I'm bewildered by the ethics. I should think that past Congresses would have cried out about this sort of thing.

Dr Cohen I'm no psychologist, Senator, but I think the answer to all that is obvious. It's damned difficult for a layman – and with all due respect to members of Congress, both past and present, most of you are laymen – to get worked up about radiation. You can't see it; you can't feel it; you can't smell it. Furthermore, in most cases it represents a danger that might not show up for ten or fifteen years. In the case of Cardenas Bay, however, the future was neither cancelled nor postponed.

20

Parks leaned against the glass of the main balcony and listened to Jeffries' monotonous drone in the background as he ran through the various programs. It was more to check out the console than Jeffries. When it came time to go on stream, he would probably handle the console himself, though all the real work would be done in Control Central.

On the reactor-room floor below, the mantle head of Prometheus One had been removed and placed in a corner, along with the inner steam dryer and other assemblies. The bridge crane hovered over the open reactor, its fuel grapple dipping deep into the water below to remove a buckled fuel-rod assembly.

'Where did you leave our guests?' a voice asked in his ear.

He turned around. 'They're taking a brandy break in my office, Barney.' He glanced at his watch. 'I'll be picking them up in another five minutes to show them the storage cells. Walton has an idea it will be like looking at the inside of Fort Knox.'

'Keep an eye on the idiot running the crane,' Lerner murmured, staring at the reactor floor.

'Why?'

'He's the living proof of Murphy's Law.'

'Murphy's Law?'

' "If anything can go wrong, it will." Earlier today he trolleyed too close to the steam-dryer assembly and the fuel grapple put a dent in the side of it.'

'Any damage?'

'We had to replace part of the lifting lug on the assembly. We lost an hour on countdown.'

'Simmons is a better man than that.'

'It wasn't Simmons.' Parks raised an eyebrow. 'He had accumulated his radiation limit for the month and was transferred to another portion of the plant. We brought in a man from Iron Grove. He's not familiar with this kind of crane. Same old story.'

They couldn't use their regulars on a refuelling operation or a disassembly job where the radiation level might be too high, Parks reflected. So back-up workers were trained in Western's fossil fuel plants and brought in during those periods. It was a good idea – except the back-up workers were never as efficient or concerned as the regulars. But the only alternative was to wind up with critical personnel who had accumulated so much radiation they would have to be retired for a year.

'How many other replacements did we bring in?'

'Around twenty – all for critical jobs.'

There was nothing to be done about that, Parks thought. Except be even more vigilant than he already was. 'How's it going.'

'Read my report. I just dropped it off on your desk.'

There was something in his voice that made Parks glance at Lerner again. He looked sullen and withdrawn and Parks had a good idea why.

'Tell me now, you don't have to recite it word for word.'

Lerner became angry then. A little more angry, Parks thought, than the situation called for.

'You're going to let it go on stream, aren't you?'

Parks turned away. 'I haven't made up my mind yet.'

'For God's sake, you've got all the samples of valves and piping that you need! We've got reports on faulty fuel rods up the kazoo. The operations reports are so bad I'm beginning to think this place is jinxed. You're going to have to pull it – and Abrams and Glidden aren't going to help you do it.'

Parks resented it. 'That's not why I asked them to write out reports.'

'Isn't it?' Lerner thought he had him on a hook and wasn't going to let him wriggle off. 'Tomorrow you're going to see the buck passed so many times it's going to wear out right in front of your eyes. Everybody will want the plant to go on stream but nobody will want to take the responsibility for it. It's going to be a game of musical chairs; who's going to be left with their fanny hanging out while everybody else is clutching a safe seat.' He paused, his eyes narrowing. 'You could call Washington, go over Cushing's head. You could speak with the Chairman directly.' Parks didn't answer and Lerner said, 'What's the matter? Afraid of losing your job?' His voice was heavy with contempt. 'Don't worry, you won't. I will. I'll pull the plant myself if I have to. I've got the authority; so do a dozen others. You're not the only one.'

'You really think you could, Barney?' Parks couldn't hide his sarcasm. 'With Cushing right here on the scene? They'd just refer it to him and then he'd buck it over to me.'

Lerner's face grew tight. 'I don't know whether that's the way it'd work or not. But at least I'd be on record.' He walked away, then hesitated at the elevator. Parks knew what was coming next. Lerner had been waiting to say it all day.

'I had an argument with Karen last night.' Lerner bit his lips, then continued, his face white. 'I went over to her house to apologize. She didn't come home last night. This morning she drove your station wagon to work.'

Parks watched the bridge crane a moment longer – Lerner was right, the operator was obviously inexperienced. 'Do you always check up on her?'

Lerner teetered back and forth on his heels, balling his fists. 'Yeah, I guess I do,' he said flatly.

'Does she check up on you?' Parks went back to staring through the window at the reactor floor. 'She's a grown woman, Lerner; she can do what she wants to do. If that isn't good enough for you, we'll step outside or make arrangements for pistols at forty paces. I'll even buy a set of duelling swords. But we'll settle it outside of company hours, OK?'

Lerner reddened, turned abruptly and walked down the stairs. He was acting more like a kid than a grown man, Parks thought with disgust. Then he suddenly felt pity. There were traumas you had to go through in growing up but they didn't always happen at the same age for everybody. For Lerner, they apparently were happening now.

He waited until Lerner's footsteps had faded, then took the

elevator down. It was time to pick up Cushing and Brandt, in the fuel-holding room just outside the main reactor floor, a group of men using hand winches were unloading a crate of new fuel rods. Parks stopped to watch. There was a sudden hollow ring and the supervisor yelled, 'Watch it there, Vic!'

The man who had dropped the rod wore plain coveralls; he was a replacement for one of the regulars. Parks hurried over to the supervisor. 'Check the bundle for mechanical damage, Walt.'

'Sure, Mr Parks. Right away, Mr Parks.' Then he looked apologetic. 'I wouldn't let it get by without checking, Greg.'

Everybody was tired, Parks thought. They had been on overtime for a month, some of the supervisors working a steady double shift. And then he wondered how many times this had happened before and he hadn't been around to catch it. How many times had a supervisor let it go? How many times had a workman failed to report it? The lazy and the ignorant and those who didn't give a damn, secure in the false knowledge that somebody else would catch their mistakes. And those who did give a damn were being pushed far too hard ...

He felt himself begin to clutch at straws then. Nothing really serious had gone wrong for the past month – nothing he hadn't encountered before. And there was redundancy in the plant. If one safeguard failed, there was another after that and then still another. Brandt had a point. Sooner or later you had to fish or cut bait. If he wanted, he could keep testing forever. The chances of something going wrong were one in three hundred million, wasn't that the figure?

And what was going wrong with *him*? he suddenly wondered.

And then he knew the answer. It wasn't water circulating through the plant's cooling system; it was his blood. He had invested too much of himself and now, in essence, he had to blow the whistle on himself. And he didn't want to. Like Brandt, he was getting to the point where he couldn't admit that anything was irrevocably wrong with the plant. But the bitter truth was that the plant had a bad history; it didn't smell right. The last month had been a streak of good luck, nothing more, and next week or the week after the same succession of small failures and major miscalculations would begin all over again.

Lerner was right, he thought. And whatever his faults, at least Lerner wasn't afraid to stand up and be counted.

As for himself, he was becoming another Hilary Brandt.

21

It was quite a contrast, Kamrath thought. Doc's office in town was strictly down-home. This one looked like something out of a big city hospital – all chrome and stainless steel with an examination room fancy enough to perform operations in.

'I'm impressed,' he said aloud.

Karen Gruen laughed. 'It's the best office that money can buy. It was like a bride furnishing a kitchen in a new house. Doc was allotted scads of money and he ended up buying everything in sight.' She sobered, her smile fading. 'He got a kick out of it but he made fun of it, too. He always claimed that the fanciest pots couldn't help a bad cook and the best-equipped examining room in the world wouldn't save a single life all by itself.'

Kamrath had liked her when he had first met her the night before and he liked her even more now. A tall, willowy brunette, she was probably close to thirty. It was obvious she took time making up in the morning. And she was probably the liberated type, at least the type who thought she was. Rumour had it that Parks was seeing her regularly. And so was one of his assistants.

Funny thing about rumours. If they were about politics, they were almost always wrong. If they concerned sex, they were probably right.

He walked around the room and ended up in front of the medicine cabinet, automatically searching for the same drugs he had seen in Doc's beachfront office. It was a different setup here, he thought. The records would be complete, the appointment book would be up to date.

'Miss Gruen, I don't like to ask you questions. I know you liked Doc pretty well and it probably hurts to talk about him. But I'm going to ask the questions anyway.'

He had a sudden mental image of Abby feeding Hippocrates and the cat rubbing up against her thin legs. What this office needed was a cat, he thought, to take some of the curse off the antiseptic feel.

'If there's anything I can tell you,' Karen said, 'I'll be glad to.'

He caught himself looking at her again with more than professional interest and couldn't help smiling. You're never too old, he thought. Or at least, he'd like to think he wasn't. He wished the room had windows that he could look out of. Sometimes it was easier to think standing by a window and staring off into the distance.

'Did Doc have any enemies in the plant?'

She hesitated. 'I wish I could say "of course not" but it wouldn't be completely true. Occasionally some employees feel hostile towards a company doctor because he doesn't do as much as they would like. A lot of men come in with something that isn't work-connected and think the doctor should take care of it anyway. Most companies are pretty strict about that; you have to have authority from your foreman before you can go to the company doctor. It didn't matter much to Doc but sometimes he'd have to draw the line.'

'Most of the people here were his patients on the outside as well, weren't they?'

'He was the only doctor in town.' Small red spots danced suddenly in her cheeks. 'Actually, his work here was just an extension of his practice in town – except the company paid for it. It hurt his private practice. Some of the men did everything but bring their kids to work. He seldom complained.'

The gossips in town should bite their tongues, Kamrath thought. Karen Gruen was a woman of feeling and what she did in the dark was her own damn business. 'What sort of thing did he usually handle here? Plant-connected?'

'The usual type of industrial accident – cuts, sprained ankles, smashed fingers, pulled discs, headaches, something in the eye – that type of thing. And we never drew the line at handing out aspirins or APC's or making referrals in case of something serious – even recommending psychiatric treatment when it came to that.'

'And the company picked up the bills?'

'It's like hiring a lawyer on retainer. Doc put in two days a week here and was always available for emergencies. Of course, Mike and I were here the rest of the time.'

'Mike?'

'Mike Kormanski. He's in charge of the film badges results. We get those from Lerner's photo-processing group.'

'Anything Doc might have handled that was peculiar to this plant, something you might not run across at any other?'

'Radiation poisoning,' she said immediately. She swept her hand around the room. 'That's why all of this is here.'

'Could you fill me in?'

She wasn't smiling now; she was very serious. The professional Miss Gruen, he thought, a side he hadn't seen before. In her late twenties, she could be all business. By her fifties, she'd be formidable. 'There's always the risk of being exposed to radiation in the plant. You understand that exposure is cumulative. It can actually be a slow process.'

'You're beginning to lose me,' Kamrath said. 'What about radiation sickness itself?'

'Say a man is working on the main reactor floor or in a fuel cell and there's an accident. He could be exposed to a very high level of radiation. If it's heavy enough, he could become nauseous and have diarrhoea. After several weeks, his hair may start to fall out. His white blood cell count will go down and then skin lesions may develop. Eventually he could die – depending on the dosage.' She smiled wryly. 'There's a kicker. He may not die of radiation sickness but his resistance could be so low he might die of any of a number of minor illnesses.'

'Ever had a case of radiation poisoning?'

'At Cardenas Bay?' She laughed. 'Heavens, no. In some areas of the plant there may be some background exposure and then a worker will have to be furloughed for a while because he's gone over his allowance for a month. I believe I told you that radiation was cumulative.'

He frowned. 'Then you have to keep track. How do you do that?'

She leaned over the desk and tapped the plastic disc attached to his shirt pocket. 'They issued you this badge when you came in. Later on, we'll develop it to see if you were accidently exposed to any sort or radiation while you were here. Then we'll enter it in a log – or we would if you were a regular employee.'

'Keeping track of the badges must be a big job. There must be over a thousand a week. Do you do that?'

She called into the other room. 'Mike?'

A moment later, a thin, gangly, red-haired kid in his late teens stuck his head into the door. Six three and a hundred and forty-five in his winter overcoat, Kamrath thought. Mike blinked at them from behind a pair of thick-lensed horn-rims. 'Yes, Miss Gruen?' He had on a lab smock and there was the smell of disinfectant about him.

'Sheriff, Mike Kormanski. Would you bring in a tray of film badges, Mike?' She smiled and Kamrath guessed that, for her, Mike Kormanski would walk a tightrope over Niagara Falls carrying a large elephant on his back.

Kormanski vanished and a moment later reappeared with a black plastic tray divided into small compartments, in each of which was a badge.

'Ordinarily we send these to photo processing once a week,' Karen continued. 'We keep a log for every man employed here. During a refuelling period such as we're having now, we process certain badges every day.'

'We furloughed two regulars in the last week,' Kormanski said.

'I thought you told me that you had no serious accidents?'

Karen shook her head. 'The exposure wasn't that serious; they just exceeded their maximum for the month. Sometimes we assign them to other areas of the plant. We keep them away from the reprocessing cells and the main reactor floor. In these cases, we thought it best that they simply stay at home.'

Kamrath said, 'I'm not sure I understand—' and then broke off.

In the corridor outside there was a sudden loud clanging and Karen abruptly went white. A moment later a wall phone rang and she snatched it up. In the meantime, Kormanski had ducked back into the lab with the film tray and returned with two white hoods and a doctor's bag. His face had suddenly acquired a tense look.

Karen hung up. 'Where is it?' Kormanski asked.

She was already out from behind her desk, running for the door. 'Cell Charlie Three in the reprocessing plant. A bad spill.' Kormanski ran after her, banged into a desk, swore loudly and then was out of the door.

'Hey, wait a min—' And then Kamrath shut up. They had already disappeared down the corridor.

They had never had a serious accident, he thought.

At least not until now.

22

Parks had just finished explaining the painted pathway on the floor of a storage cell to a titillated Walton when the sound of the alarm rolled through the passageway. His first reaction was one of astonishment more than anything else. He had never heard it before except in drills and he was totally unprepared for it.

'What's wrong?' Walton bleated. 'What is it?'

Parks ignored him, his ears straining for another sound: the effluent-gas alarm, the loud klaxon that would signal the evacuation of the plant. Finally, he moved over to the intercom on the wall and signalled the switchboard. He listened briefly to the operator and then he ran from the outer chamber to the car. The others were waiting for him.

'What's happened?' Brandt demanded.

'Bad spill in Cell Charlie Three; that's one of the cells where they handle dissolved wastes.' He leaped into the driver's seat.

'How bad?' Brandt was standing in front of the car, unintentionally blocking him.

'I don't know,' Parks snapped. 'Get out of the way, will you?'

Brandt stepped on the running board. 'I'm coming along,' he said, his face tight. Still the working engineer after all, Parks thought. Cushing jumped on and Walton followed, looking from one to another, trying to determine how dangerous it might be.

'None of you are going,' Parks said firmly. 'I have no idea how bad the spill is. I don't know if the cell itself will hold – I don't know what's wrong there but it could be dangerous. If the window linkage has been perforated, the area could be contaminated.'

Walton now looked considerably less sure of the wisdom of his actions and took a tentative step off the board.

'I think it concerns all of us,' Brandt said.

'It won't be entertaining,' Parks said grimly. 'Check your radiation hoods back there, you might need them.' Depending on the nature of the accident and how serious it was, it might actually work to his advantage, he thought. There was no such thing as a hundred percent safe industrial plant and maybe it would shake Brandt's and Cushing's confidence.

Parks pushed in the electric clutch and turned the car around. He retraced his path down the corridor, accelerating in the straightaway. Soon they passed technicians, many of them in white suits, running away from the area. He shouted at one man, 'What happened?' and got a mute, frightened look in response. He slowed to round a corner, then saw Cell Charlie Three just ahead. A small knot of people had gathered around the outside. Thank God, he thought, at least the leak was contained within the two chambers of the cell.

He slowed the car to a halt and jumped out. He pushed his way through the group before the cell. Paul Marical was leaning against the wall, his face white. 'Paul, what the hell happened?'

Marical opened his mouth to speak, looked as if he were going to be sick all over the corridor and clamped his jaws shut.

'Come on, Paul, what happened?' Parks asked again, a little more gently.

'I had just taken off the rad unit,' Marical gasped. 'I came outside to work the master-slave grips. We had a beaker of stuff from the precipitation vats and were running titrations to determine the concentration.' He stopped for a moment and swallowed convulsively. 'We were taking a sample with the remote pipette, the helium-pressurized one, and the remote helium discharge jammed. Van went in to fix it and the damned fool spilled the whole beaker on himself.'

'You don't go into those cells without a safety clearance. What the hell got into Van?'

Parks looked through the window. Van Baketes' white suited figure stood silently, one hand scrubbing at the surface of the suit. Parks hit the intercom button and said, 'Van, are you OK? Did any of the solution penetrate the suit?'

The figure inside shook his head slowly. Van was obviously frightened. Thank God, Parks thought. If the suit was intact the decontamination would be relatively simple. 'There's no secondary leakage,' Parks continued; 'so we'll follow standard procedure. Go into the first airlock and shower down. Shower for five minutes and use the detergent head. When you're through, go into the section lock. Strip down at the door and leave the stuff in the first lock in the waste chute. Shower for another five minutes. Use plenty of detergent. Finish off with a Versene shower and then water. Got that?'

The suited figure waved uncertainly. He looked unsteady on his feet. Pure funk, Parks thought. 'After that we'll monitor you.'

Lerner eased in the door past Marical and Parks turned. 'Barney, get a scrub team down here with Versene. He'll probably miss a lot, especially mucous membranes. We'll need a safety crew, too.'

'I've already ordered them,' Lerner said.

'Damn fool,' Parks said. 'What the hell do you teach these guys in your safety meetings, Barney? Van knows better than to go in there without a standby safety crew. They're supposed to rehearse every move they're going to make before a man ever enters a cell.'

'They're regulars,' Lerner said, pale. 'They know the rules.'

Inside the cell, Van Baketes turned and stared towards the door, dragging his heavy air lines behind him. At least he'd had the sense to use the air lines rather than depend on bottled air, Parks thought; otherwise his suit supply would have been exhausted by now.

'Marical,' Parks ordered, 'move the pipette assembly out of his way.' Marical grabbed the grips of the manipulators and moved them in. The assembly was a heavy metal and Teflon structure ending in a glass pipette whose centre bulge was filled with liquid from the beaker they had been sampling.

Marical was using a remote hand to swing the assembly out of the way. Parks could see that his hand was very unsteady. At this moment one of Van Baketes' airlines fouled against the metal table leg. Unconsciously he pulled at it and for a second he was off balance. He stumbled as the line came free. He automatically stretched out his hand to break his fall.

It was at this moment that the pipette assembly swung free of its constraining mount and jabbed into Van Baketes' arm. The sudden pressure against the glass triggered the helium, and liquid spewed out over Van Baketes' suit. Clumsy fool, Parks thought. He wasn't sure whether he meant Marical or Van Baketes. Then he realized that the suited man was not moving.

Van Baketes was staring down at the glove of his hand in horror. The glass stem had ruptured and the sharp end had penetrated his glove. He stared at the blood slowly welling from the wound.

'Did he get any?' Lerner asked, leaning forward.

'That thing's like a hypodermic,' Parks said appalled. 'He must have got some of the stuff into the tissues.'

'Van,' he said into the intercom, deliberately keeping his voice calm, 'how bad is it?'

Van shook his head. Apparently just a surface wound, Parks thought. Which was just as bad as a mortal one if any of the solution had been injected into the tissues. Parks felt an icy calm then. There was so little time ...

Lerner was still standing in the vestibule. Parks said, 'Barney, is Karen out there?'

'She just came up. Kormanski's with her.'

'Send some of your men for white suits or some plastic coveralls. And fill Karen in on what's happened.'

Through the double windows, Parks could see Barney giving

orders to some men, who got into an electricar and sped away. Then he turned to Karen, who nodded silently, her face professional and cold.

Parks turned back to the intercom. 'Van, don't worry about the cut. Get into the airlock and shower down. Quickly.'

Van resumed his slow progress. Parks, still fighting to keep the tension out of his voice, said calmly, 'On the double, Van. Forget the five rinse-downs, two will have to do.' There was a fleeting glimpse of Van Baketes' face through his airtight hood. He was wide-eyed and obviously frightened now. He moved as fast as he could to the airlock door, disengaged the air hoses and disappeared inside.

Karen was waiting for Parks in the corridor, Kormanski behind her. Her face was grim. 'You know what this means, don't you?' Parks asked. 'We're too far from medical help. We can't risk a tourniquet's doing the job. If the stuff gets into his system, he's dead sooner or later.'

'I don't have the equipment,' she said, her voice shaking. 'I know enough but I don't have enough equipment, not even clamps. Besides, if it got into the venous system . . .'

'Can you do it?'

Her face was bloodless. 'I guess. I'll need your help.'

Parks was aware of Brandt and Cushing standing close behind him. Walton was at the fringe of the crowd, not wanting to get close but, at the same time, afraid he would miss something. 'We don't have time to send him to the city,' Parks said in a low voice. 'It'll have to be done here, now. We'll have to improvise. Has anybody alerted the hospital what to expect?'

She nodded. 'I sent one of the technicians to phone ahead.'

'You've got plenty of gauze?' She nodded again and he turned to Brandt. 'Get me some alligator clips.' Then back to Karen. 'They'll have to do, I guess. It's the only thing I can think of.'

'Greg.' He could see that she was trying to control her trembling. 'You know this is nothing but butchery.'

'We've got no choice,' Parks said carefully. 'If we wait, he'll die. You know that. He may be dead already.'

She agreed with a barely perceptible nod of the head. Parks turned and checked the signal lights through the glass outer wall of the cell. In the vestibule, the second red light suddenly glowed as Van Baketes moved into the second airlock and shower. Lerner appeared at his side and said, 'We've got the coveralls.'

'Can you help, Barney? You know what we're going to do?'
Lerner said quietly, 'I've seen blood before.'

'Mike? We'll need another man – down here with me.' He glanced around at the group. 'And one more man, please. It'll be messy.'

'What about me?' Brandt asked suddenly.

Gutsy old bastard, Parks thought. 'No, I appreciate it, Hilary, but we need a younger man in good physical shape.' Brandt nodded agreement. Parks finally picked one of the electricians, who reluctantly agreed.

'What are we going to use?' Karen asked. 'It will have to be quick and it will have to be something heavy-duty.'

He didn't answer her but said in a louder voice, 'Everybody out of the area but those of us concerned here. When Van comes out, he's going to be hot.' They started to move back, slowly and reluctantly. A few minutes ago, most of those in the corridor had been poised to flee for their lives; now they were afraid to miss the show. At the very edge of the small group, he could see Walton scurry halfway down the corridor, then start to edge slowly back.

He handed out the plastic coveralls. 'Get these suits on. After we're through with Van, we'll have to scrub down ourselves.'

'Will we need respirators?' Karen asked.

'I don't think so.' In a louder voice: 'Who's got a counter?' Somebody ran into a nearby office and returned with one and passed it to up him. Parks turned back to Karen. 'Anything hot will be adhering to his skin. We'll have to monitor the whole area afterwards, however – probably have to run it through a thorough cleaning.'

They silently donned the coveralls. As soon as they were all suited up, Parks pointed to the electrical equipment still standing against the far wall. 'Barney, get that power saw and plug it in over here.' He gestured at a grounded wall outlet near the cell door. Karen gasped softly. He shot her a warning glance. 'You can't faint; you can't have hysterics. If you do, you'll kill a man. Can you do it yourself?'

'I wasn't going to faint,' she said. 'But I can't do it. The skill is rudimentary but it also takes a lot of physical strength.'

'Can you tell me how?'

She took a breath and nodded.

The corridor was silent now; everybody was waiting for the last cycling of the airlock. Parks found himself counting. It was taking forever. Then the door finally opened and Van Baketes stumbled into the vestibule. He was naked and shivering, the goose pimples showing plainly on his skin. He was holding his left hand, blood welling up between his fingers and dripping on the floor.

'Christ,' he mumbled, his voice shaking. 'I guess I cut myself in there.' He spotted Karen, looked foolish a moment and reddened.

Then he noticed the group waiting for him and said, 'No, for God's sake!' He glanced wildly about, looking for a place to run. Parks and Lerner jumped him and wrestled him to the concrete floor. A drop of blood flicked against Parks' glasses and he tossed his head so they flew off and went skittering down the corridor.

'Stop it, Van,' Parks said firmly. 'You struggle and the stuff spreads up your arm that much faster.'

Van Baketes was weeping now, still struggling on the floor. Suddenly he went limp, his eyes wide and glistening. Parks had seen the same look once before in the eyes of a deer he had shot but hadn't killed. It knew that it was going to die and had lain quietly, waiting for the final bullet. Van swallowed once and nodded. Lerner knelt on the wounded man, one knee on each side of the elbow. Kormanski held the other arm while the electrician sat on his legs, carefully averting his face.

Van Baketes had closed his eyes now. He was trembling, his lips moving in a silent prayer.

Cushing suddenly said, 'Aren't you going to give him morphine or anything?'

'There isn't time,' Karen murmured, not looking at him. She knelt by the injured man. 'There's a morphine Syrette in my bag; we'll use it afterwards.

'Get me the tourniquet from the bag.'

There was a second's pause, then Mike's voice, nervous: 'It's not there; it wasn't packed.'

Karen bit her lip, then looked up at the men standing in a semi-circle around her. 'Somebody give me a belt,' she asked calmly. 'Quickly, please ... and that piece of pipe.' She pointed towards a piece of pipe laying on the floor.

Brandt handed his belt down to her. She wrapped it loosely around Van Baketes' upper arm, then shoved the short length of pipe beneath it and twisted, tightening the makeshift tourniquet.

'Greg?'

Parks picked up the power saw and flicked it on; its whine

110

filled the passageway. He looked at Karen for instructions.

'Just below the elbow, Greg. There are too many bleeders in the upper arm.' The muscles in her cheeks suddenly tightened. 'Now. As quickly as you can.'

To Parks, the roar of the saw was deafening. He wanted to close his eyes and hold his hands over his ears. Then the blade caught and it was all over with. He turned the saw off. Van Baketes had mercifully fainted.

In the sudden silence he heard the sounds of somebody vomiting. Walton, Parks guessed.

'Hold the tourniquet, Greg,' Karen ordered. He placed the saw on the floor and held the steel pipe tightly. Karen leaned over, laid back the torn flesh with a scalpel and began to set the clamps improvised from alligator clips, her fingers dancing a skilful ballet. She was all cold professionalism now, oblivious of the blood that spattered her coveralls. Parks prayed that they had been in time, that no soluble plutonium salt had moved too far past the original cut. And then Karen had finished. Kormanski moved in with the morphine Syrette and plunged its needle into his upper arm.

'We'll have to get him to a hospital. As fast as we can.'

She stood up, suddenly looking weak and faint. Parks moved over to grab her but it was Barney who got there first.

23

'Here, this will help,' Parks said. He handed Karen a water tumbler half full of brandy and she took a big swallow. Her hair was still damp from the multiple showers they had taken after discarding the bloodstained coveralls. She was shivering.

'I'm sorry,' she said. 'Every second breath, I think I'm going to become hysterical.'

'You were just great,' he said. 'Drink some more.'

She did and had a sudden fit of coughing. 'It burns,' she gasped.

Parks smiled and turned away from the liquor cabinet. 'OK, just sit down and sip it for a while.'

'Van should be at the hospital by now,' Lerner said from across the room. He had been watching them closely and Parks guessed that he was jealous about his giving Karen the glass of brandy.

'What chance do you think he has?' Brandt asked.

Parks sat down at his desk and leaned back in his swivel chair. The day sure as hell hadn't gotten any easier. 'Hard to say. If any of the plutonium got into his venous system, he'll die' – he shrugged – 'soon.'

Walton had been brooding in the corner of the room. 'That was the most brutal goddamned thing I've ever seen!' he suddenly burst out. 'Did you have to do it? My God, you might have murdered the man!'

There was a sudden, embarrassed silence. Parks said quietly, 'Had it been pure metal, we could have used a tourniquet and cleaned out the debris. The pure metal isn't that soluble in body fluids. With water-soluble salts I just don't know. Maybe a tourniquet alone could have stopped the stuff from spreading into his system until we could get him to a hospital, but we couldn't take the chance.'

'What if he had cut his torso?' Walton demanded, still outraged.

Parks sighed. 'Maybe Solomon would have an answer in a case like that; I don't.'

'I'll check in with his family on the way home,' Lerner said, getting up to go.

Walton said, 'Just a minute.'

Lerner looked surprised and said, 'Just a minute what?'

There was going to be trouble, Parks thought with a mental groan. Walton had the cornered-rat look on his face. 'I think we ought to discuss this before you visit the family.' He looked quickly at Brandt and Cushing for backing. Cushing's gaze was noncommittal but steady; Brandt looked away. Lerner walked back to the couch and sat down.

'Discuss what, Walton?' Lerner asked coldly.

'I think we all know how damaging bad publicity can be before we go on stream,' Walton began nervously.

Lerner's voice was dangerously tight. 'Damaging in what goddamned way?'

Parks had a hunch he knew what Walton was going to say and if it was what he thought it was, it would be a dead heat between him and Lerner to see who hit the little bastard first.

'We've got a difficult community relations problem here,' Walton said hesitantly. 'The man in the street is frightened by nuclear power plants. He can't distinguish between a typical industrial accident that just happens to involve radioactives and accidents that are inherent in the nature of the plant.'

112

Lerner glared. Parks said, 'You're drawing a rather thin line, aren't you, Walton? It's true Van contaminated an open wound. Such an accident could probably have happened in a number of different plants, but it wouldn't necessarily have resulted in amputating his forearm. It was the presence of radioactives that made that imperative.'

'I don't see what the hell difference it makes,' Lerner said. 'What are you trying to do, hush it up?'

'It's the day before we go into the grid,' Walton stuttered. 'If we let this get out, it'll give us a black eye from which we'll never recover.'

'So I shouldn't tell his family,' Lerner said, now dangerously calm. 'He just had an "industrial" accident, right? For Christ's sake, Walton, what the hell do you think the hospital is going to tell them?'

Walton was sweating. 'Why should they have to know, either? If you caught the man in time, then for all practical purposes, he's just a simple injury case, isn't he? There's nothing to be gained by emphasizing the radiation aspects of it all. Isn't that right?'

'What if we didn't catch it all?' Parks asked.

Walton looked from one to the other, not understanding why they couldn't see his viewpoint. 'Then he'll die in a few weeks anyway. There's nothing to be done; you said so yourselves.'

'Why do you want to cover it up?' Parks asked. 'Just because of bad publicity?'

Walton looked shocked. 'Just bad publicity? Do you want to see pickets outside your plant tomorrow? We can't afford any community action against this plant, not just before the President is going to . . .' His voice trailed away.

'I don't know about anybody else,' Karen said suddenly, her voice slightly fuzzed both by anger and by the brandy. 'But someplace along the line I took a pledge. I'm not even sure we should have committed such butchery; maybe a tourniquet would have been enough. But one thing I do know. You bastards can do anything you want to, but a complete report on the incident will go into the hospital from me. If there's anything I can do for Van, I intend to do it.'

'It would be simple to handle,' Walton said desperately. 'I can prepare a routine press release. We could at least keep it to a relatively minor incident, downplay the story. I have several friends at the wire services; they'll help.'

Parks swirled the brandy in his glass and said, 'Walton, if Van Baketes winds up a terminal case, what happens when it becomes obvious what he's dying from? There's no way you're going to hide that, you know.'

'We'll be on stream by then,' Walton said. He looked fairly pleased with himself. 'It'll still be bad publicity but it won't be fatal.'

The room was silent. Parks could hear the drip of the faucet in his wall bar. Walton's slight smile faded and he looked over at Brandt, who had suddenly become absorbed in studying his fingernails. He then shot a desperate glance for help at Cushing. Parks noticed it and said, 'Mr Cushing, surely you have some thoughts on this?'

Cushing looked quickly around the room and Parks guessed he was getting the emotions of everybody there. 'Frankly, I can't see the sense in publicizing the cause of Van Baketes' accident. It certainly won't restore his arm. As far as any malpractice traceable to the plant, granted it will look bad in the public eye, but we all know this was an isolated incident in which two men violated company regulations.'

'You want to cover it up?' Lerner asked hotly.

Cushing shook his head. 'I'm not entirely familiar with medical ethics or hospital practice. I think we ought to leave it to the young lady. She knows more of the medical aspects than we do. And as she said, she took a pledge.' He bowed slightly in Karen's direction.

There was a pause in the conversation and Cushing took advantage of it to light a cigarette. Walton sat there with his mouth slightly open; he seemed stunned. Cushing didn't bother looking in his direction.

Walton must have been given his orders earlier, Parks thought. Cushing would have preferred that the whole incident be shut up but he could hardly push for it outright, so he had set up Walton to try and convince them. But it hadn't been a very good attempt and in the long run it didn't really matter that much anyway. So Cushing had shrugged and let it drop.

Poor Walton, Parks thought with a smile. He had just walked the plank for Cushing and hadn't even realized it.

24

Senator Stone You were with Western Gas and Electric for how many years, Mr Glidden?

Mr Glidden Thirty-five years and four months, sir.

Senator Stone But you're not presently employed by them?

Mr Glidden They offered me a chance for early retirement and I took it.

Senator Clarkson One month after the Cardenas Bay disaster, I believe.

Mr Glidden That was coincidental, Senator. I had been trying for it for a long time.

Senator Stone How long did you spend with their nuclear division?

Mr Glidden I was with it since the division started – some twenty-five years, I'd say.

Senator Stone Then you would certainly have an opinion on Gregory Parks' effectiveness as plant manager?

Mr Glidden I don't believe you could have found a better plant manager in the industry. He knew his job; he got along with the men but he was still a stickler for detail and safety.

Senator Clarkson Considering what happened at Cardenas Bay, that statement sounds somewhat contradictory. Could you tell us about safety in nuclear power plants in general? I'm not thinking of Cardenas Bay specifically.

Mr Glidden You can break safety problems down into two kinds – those caused by the personnel and those caused by the equipment. Some things you learn to expect. Accidents usually come in clusters. And sometimes there's a domino effect. One worker will make a mistake and just let it go, thinking that Joe will catch it. Then Joe will let it go, thinking the same thing, and so on. And you're bound to get more accidents on the night shift or on weekends. Mondays are usually a bad time and so are start-ups after vacation periods. The first day back on the job, a man has to learn caution all over again.

Senator Clarkson What about the technical side?

Mr Glidden The human factor is involved there, too. You have automatic safeguards but sometimes human failures occur independently and in rapid succession and they multiply so fast the automatic equipment can't catch them.

Senator Stone Did any of this apply to Cardenas Bay?

Mr Glidden I would say so, yes, sir. We'd been on overtime for more than a month and the men were tired and edgy. And, of course, we'd had trouble with vendors – parts and equipment not meeting specs; I think there's been testimony on that score. The thing you really have to remember is that this was a nuclear plant and something that might have been trivial in a different sort of plant could be critical at Cardenas. A nuclear plant is more of a precision plant, you might say.

Senator Hoyt What about accidents at Cardenas Bay? According to Mr Parks, you seemed to have a larger number of them, even for a nuclear plant.

Mr Glidden More than our share, sir.

Senator Stone Let me pose a hypothetical question, Mr Glidden. If it had been your responsibility, would you have taken Cardenas Bay on stream?

Mr Glidden That's a question that has to be pretty carefully weighed, Senator. It was difficult to tell about Cardenas. There were a lot of problems but until the very end, I wouldn't say that any of them were that unique.

Senator Stone I understand that, Mr Glidden. But if you had been in Mr Parks' shoes, would you have taken the plant on stream?

Mr Glidden As I said, Senator, things look different to the man in charge. If you're an underling, you might look at something in a completely different light than if you're the boss. And sometimes there are small bits of information that only the man in charge may have.

Senator Stone You were Mr Parks' second in command, weren't you? Was there any substantial piece of information that he might have had that you weren't aware of?

Mr Glidden No, I can't say there was. What I'm trying to explain is that you might look at something one way if you don't have the responsibility for it and quite another if you're the top man.

Senator Stone All I'm asking is that you put yourself in Mr Parks' shoes. It's a simple question, Mr Glidden. If you had been Mr Parks, knowing what he did, would you have brought the Cardenas Bay facility on stream?

Mr Glidden I keep trying to explain, Senator, that's a tough one to answer. I don't know how to put it ...

Representative Holmburg For God's sake, Mr Glidden, do you always find it this difficult to make up your mind?

25

Barney Lerner drove slowly down Main Street, wondering if he should go straight home and clean up for dinner or just drop in at the Skupper, have a hamburger and a beer and play the bowling machines. He'd had other plans but Karen had begged off. The accident had been more than she could handle ...

All at once he wanted to beat the steering wheel with his fists. The sweat popped out on his forehead and his hands tightened on the wheel until the muscles stood out like cords. The accident had been too much for her, coming on top of Doc's death. She needed sympathy and understanding, and chances were better than even that Parks was supplying both right then. He debated driving out to Parks' house and confronting them, then dropped it. He'd lose Karen for good if she were there; there'd be no making up later.

What was it his mother had always said? Never make a wedding gown out of soiled linen ... But his mother had been from the old country and a lot had happened to morality in the intervening thirty-five years. So Karen slept around; everybody slept around. A girl wasn't a whore because she had slept with a few men.

But he felt like crying at the thought. He knew down deep that was how he had been raised and that was what he really thought. And the real trouble between him and Karen was that she knew it was the way he thought. He couldn't drop her; he loved her so damned much it was torture to work in the same plant with her.

What the hell was he going to do? What the hell *could* he do?

He slowed the car. Just ahead was the flashing sign of the Skupper with its flickering manhattan glass complete with red neon cherry. He pulled into the parking lot, already two-thirds filled. There'd be a lot of noise and a lot of excitement in the Skupper and he could lose himself in the crowd. It was a hangout for the fishermen; not many plant workers went there, and that was just fine. He didn't want to see anybody who would remind him of the plant. The fishermen would ignore him and that was fine, too.

Inside, he filled his lungs with cigarette smoke and the smell of stale beer. Counterpointing this was the faintly rancid odour of the Skupper's special hamburger – a quarter pound of good chuck with everything on it but Tabasco sauce and you could have that if you wanted. Along one side of the room was a bar and opposite it, against the far wall, small wooden booths. The room broadened at one end for dancing, a jukebox, a cigarette machine and a long electronic bowling game, one of the Skupper's main attractions. A group of fishermen were already clustered around the bowling machine, shouting advice to a player who had sprinkled the miniature alley with powdered wax and was now hunched over the end, taking aim with a steel puck. By the looks of the crowd, it'd be a while before he got his chance at the machine.

He sat down in the one empty seat at the bar, next to a huge redwood beam, so there was nobody on his left. Best seat in the house if you wanted to be alone, he thought.

'Buy you a beer, Barney?'

Not tonight, he thought. Jesus, of all nights and of all the people he didn't want to talk to.

'What the hell brings you here, Glidden?'

'The ribs – best in town. Thought I'd spend an hour here before going back to the plant. You want that beer?'

'Somebody leave you a fortune?'

The grey man shrugged. 'It's only sixty-five cents a bottle; it won't break me.' He glanced over at Lerner sympathetically. 'It's been a rough day. You could use a beer. Stay away from the hard stuff; if you haven't eaten yet, it'll knock you on your ass.'

Lerner hesitated and Glidden said, 'Look, for an hour we can forget we know each other. We're just two guys who met in a bar, OK? And don't try the hamburger tonight, they're frying them in yesterday's grease. Like I said, the ribs are good.'

The idea of barbecued ribs hit the spot and Lerner found himself warming towards Glidden. He'd take the big man at his word and try and forget they worked together.

'Anybody hear anything about Van?' So much for his good intentions, he thought.

Glidden paused to rub some barbecue sauce off his chin with an undersized napkin. 'I called up half an hour ago and the doctors say they can save the rest of his arm. Parks cut it off below the elbow, so he'll be able to use a prosthetic.' He noticed the look on Lerner's face. 'Sorry I mentioned Parks.'

'For two guys who were going to pretend they didn't know

each other, we're not doing too well.' Lerner's beer came and he drained half of it in two gulps.

Glidden noticed it. 'You've got a long night ahead of you, Barney. Whatever's bugging you, I'd forget about it and relax.'

'Nothing's bugging me,' Lerner snapped. Glidden gave him a sideways look and didn't say anything. Halfway through his plate of ribs, Lerner said, 'Parks is going to take it on stream, isn't he?'

'I don't know,' Glidden said noncommittally. 'He'll try to meet the deadline but I figure if it looks too risky, he'll decide not to.'

'You really think so?'

'You're asking me to read another man's mind,' Glidden said calmly. 'I imagine a lot will depend on what happens between now and then. He's got all the brass staring over his shoulder, so the pressure on him is pretty strong. I figure in the end, he'll do the right thing.'

'And the right thing will be to take it on stream, that it?' Lerner asked.

'Barney,' Glidden said slowly. 'That isn't my job; they're not paying me to make that decision.'

'You couldn't if you had to.'

Glidden belched quietly and signalled to the bartender for another beer. 'Quit trying to pick a fight, Barney. Tonight I'm unpickable.'

Lerner switched from beer to straight Scotch. After he had downed it and ordered another, Glidden said, 'The plant's not what's bothering you, is it?'

'It bothers me,' Lerner said moodily. He was starting to feel the alcohol now. He should quit, he thought, he still had to go back to the plant.

It bubbled to the surface then. 'It's Karen.' He swung around on the stool so he was facing Glidden. 'She's engaged to me but tonight she's sleeping with Parks.'

'You're sure of that?' Glidden said. Lerner nodded, for a brief moment afraid he was going to start crying. 'Thing's aren't like they were when I was your age,' Glidden continued. 'I think your problem is that your morality is thirty years behind the times. I guess a lot of women nowadays consider an engagement as meaning an intent to marry, not necessarily a pledge to remain loyal until they do so. Have you talked about it with her?'

Lerner shook his head dumbly. He was into his third Scotch now and feeling like hell.

'If it's any satisfaction, Barney, while it's none of my business, I don't approve.'

Lerner motioned to the bartender for another Scotch and sat there nursing it for a long moment. His thinking was fuzzier now and he kept coming back to what Glidden had said. Finally he figured it out. 'Who the hell are you, passing judgement?' he said angrily. He turned away from Glidden and slid off the bar stool. He weaved over to the bowling machine, still clutching his glass. Two of the regulars were playing it, a couple of fishermen named Halsam and Jefferson.

The older man, Halsam, glanced up and said, 'How about it, college boy? Want to try your luck? Buck a game?'

'Sure.' Lerner clutched the edge of the machine for support, placing his drink on a nearby table. 'I can take your ass any day. It's all a matter of ... a matter of math and ballistics.'

'Catch those big words!' Jefferson said in mock admiration.

'I'll even pay for the game,' Lerner said, slurring his words. He dug in his pocket for three quarters

Halsam nudged his companion. 'The last of the big-time spenders,' he said cheerfully.

Lerner fumbled at inserting the quarters into the slot and Halsam had to help him. Then he squatted at the end of the machine, squinting over the varnished surface. There seemed to be a slight list to the midget alley but Lerner guessed it tilted a fraction more to the left than to the right – the floor was probably uneven – and there was a barely perceptible hump in the middle. He stood up, clutching the machine again to steady himself, and dusted the lane with powdered wax. Then he squatted once more, placing his eye level with the lane and resisting a desire to just lay his head on it and go to sleep.

'You're not splitting atoms, sonny; it's just a bowling game,' Halsam said.

'Mind your goddamned business,' Lerner said thickly. Then, almost to himself: 'Stinking fishermen.' He stood up, grabbed at the puck and let fly. The lights lit up at the far end of the board and there was a loud buzzing sound. Strike. He barely waited until the pins were upright, then let fly again. A second strike. He grabbed the puck a third time and suddenly Halsam's heavy hand was on his wrist.

'It's my turn, sonny.'

Halsam's face seemed to be swaying back and forth. 'Take

your goddamned hands off me,' Lerner mumbled. He opened his eyes wider, trying to get Halsam into focus. There was a part of him that realized he was falling-down drunk.

Halsam's eyes narrowed. 'You guys move in; you take over the town; you poison the fish and then you try and take over our bar. Why don't you just buzz off and go smash atoms someplace?'

Halsam's face now looked oddly like that of an older Parks.

Lerner spent a second or two trying to think of something original, then gave up. 'You old bastard, you smell like your stinking fish.' A portion of his brain now registered that Sheriff Kamrath had come in and was moving towards them.

Halsam let go of his wrist and said, 'That's all she wrote, sonny.' Lerner was still trying to lift his hands up when Halsam's fist caught him on the right side of the face and the whole bar suddenly tilted up and over.

26

Marical lay on his bed smoking, watching the thin grey stream curling towards the ceiling. Once he stubbed out the cigarette in the ashtray on the floor, pulled a pillow over his head and tried to sleep. Ten minutes later he gave up, turned the radio down low and went back to smoking and staring at the ceiling. It was still early in the evening and outside he could hear the occasional slam of a car door. Once he heard two boys fighting, and then huskier voices as their fathers intervened, followed by two heavy slaps, sudden wails, and then silence. He felt sick but didn't bother going to the john for Alka-Seltzer. It wouldn't do any good. Not any more.

He stared at the ceiling and imagined shapes in the rough plaster as he used to do as a boy, lying on a hill and watching the clouds drifting by. The shapes he imagined in the ceiling weren't nearly as pleasant as those in the clouds; he closed his eyes again, hoping to drift off to sleep. He didn't put out his cigarette this time. Mattresses must give off some kind of gas once they were set afire, he thought; he couldn't ever remember anybody dashing from a house screaming that their mattress was burning. Usually the firemen found them right in the middle of it ...

It was his fault, he thought again. He should never have let Van go into the cell. Van knew it, too, but they both thought they could save time. He shouldn't have been in there in the first place; he had been too sick and his hands had been shaking. Now there'd be an investigation. They'd probably suspend him and that would mean the end of weeks of labour.

But maybe not, he thought again. They were going on stream tomorrow night; they wouldn't have time for an investigation. That much, at least, they'd postpone ...

He had just begun to doze when there was a light tap on the door. He lay half asleep, unmoving, hoping whoever it was would go away. The tap came again. Then he remembered what day it was and the time they had agreed upon. He shifted slightly on the bed and looked at the clock on the bed table. Right on time.

But he didn't want to see her that night; he didn't feel up to it. Then he thought, what the hell, she had reserved the time for him; she might even have turned down another john.

He yawned, rolled off the bed and walked to the door. 'Come on in, Wanda.' She swirled in, smelling vaguely of strong perfume and the faint odour of the restaurant, and plumped herself down in the chair by the bed. She kicked off her shoes and very methodically began to roll down her stockings. She didn't wear panty hose; she had once told him they were too binding.

He closed the door behind him. 'You want to get right down to it, don't you?'

She stopped in mid-movement and looked up at him startled. 'I thought you always wanted it this way, Paul. Quick, fast, no preliminaries.' She half smiled at him. 'Just the main event.' Then she peered closer at him. 'You all right? Stomach acting up again?'

He was taking it out on her, he thought. He wasn't being fair. 'I'm all right.'

She continued rolling down her stockings, slower this time. 'You look a little pale. The accident at the plant?' Surprisingly, there was concern in her voice. He wondered at that; nobody had shown any great concern for him for a long time.

'How'd you find out about that?'

'It's all over town.'

He walked to the dresser and started to unbutton his shirt, pausing a moment to look at the snapshot stuck in the edge of the mirror. A diminutive brunette stared back at him, flanked on one side by a young boy and on the other by a girl. It had taken her a long, long time to die, he thought sadly. He worked the photograph out of the wooden framing and turned it face down on the bureau.

'What happened to her?' Wanda asked.

'What happened to who?'

'Your wife,' she said simply. 'Lots of men do what you just did – turn their wife's photograph face down.'

'I don't want to talk about it,' he said.

'Moody, Paul?' She stood up, waiting for him to start their private ritual by helping her off with her dress. 'You're moody a lot lately.' Her voice again, was concerned and sympathetic.

He thought again of telling her not to bother tonight. 'Things haven't been going right. And I can't kick this.' He pointed to his stomach.

'It's all the overtime. Maybe you're getting an ulcer.'

'No,' he said, and even he could hear the regret in his voice. 'No ulcer.'

Her dress was a cheap synthetic and the zipper had stuck on some strands at the side. It was a moment before he could free it. Then the dress was a heap on the floor and she stepped out of it and turned to him, smiling tentatively.

There were times when he could flatter her but tonight wasn't one of them. Wanda had a dumpy body, one that went best with two bottles of beer and a lot of imagination. She might have been pretty twenty years ago but she was fading fast now. Her long hair was brittle from overprocessing; too many years of using too much make-up had ruined her skin and the span of belly between her black panties and bra showed the purple-red stretch marks of periodic weight losses.

But he couldn't have slept with her if she had been really beautiful, he thought. She would have been competition for a memory and he couldn't have allowed that.

'You ready Paul?' She took his arm and pulled him gently towards the bed. She tried to arouse him while she undressed him but it was no use. She drew him into bed and tugged the covers over them. For a moment he just lay there, shivering against her warm flesh.

'You're cold,' she said. She rubbed his stomach and held him close, kissing him lightly on the cheek. 'She must have been something very special.'

'She was,' Marical said.

'You worked together, didn't you?' she said.

He tensed. 'How did you know?'

'Just a guess.'

He lay there in bed, remembering, and then felt her fingers touch his face. 'You're crying,' she said. There was no surprise in her voice.

Marical didn't answer and she moved closer to him and kissed him again on the cheek and then on the neck. There was no fake passion as there had usually been in the past. She was warm and understanding, with an empathy that seemed as much a part of her as her arms or her breasts. For the first time in months, he felt himself responding naturally.

When they were through and she had dressed, he held out a twenty-dollar bill to her. She folded it back into his hand and said, 'Please don't, Paul. Not tonight.'

'No,' he said roughly, 'a deal is—'

'Please,' she repeated.

He hadn't wanted to accept anything from her; he had always wanted it to be cash so there could be no possibility of involvement. He hadn't wanted her to give him anything where he might feel compelled to give her something back.

And then he realized it was too late, that she already had.

'Thanks,' he said.

He watched her disappear down the hallway. He had given her something, too, when he had taken the money back.

He wondered how long it had been since she had been to bed and hadn't played the whore.

27

Tebbets eased open the door of the monitoring room and slid in, waiting a moment until his eyes had adjusted to the dim light. Captain Kloster was at the front of the room, leaning over a table, riffling through a series of computer printout sheets.

He walked up behind Kloster and glanced over his shoulder. Upcoming weather data. 'My God, don't you people ever sleep?'

'The Air Force never sleeps,' Kloster grunted. 'Twenty-four-hour alert and all that. I popped in an hour ago just to see what high noon looks like on the other side of the world.' He let the stack of printouts fall back on the table. 'I answered yours; now you answer mine. What are *you* doing here?'

'One of the technicians called me when you showed up,' Tebbets said, 'I have spies everywhere. If you insist on the truth, I was driving past and I usually stop in for a few minutes at night anyway.'

'Actually,' Kloster said with a straight face, 'you run the day shift with such a tight rein, I thought I'd come back to see how lax the night crew is.'

'Next shift, I'll slip something in your coffee,' Tebbets murmured. 'How's it looking?'

'The crew or the screens?'

'Night crew's the best one we've got,' Tebbets said blandly. 'I meant the screens.'

'There's a storm off the coast and, if I read the IR screens right, they've got a brownout in the Midwest and it's spreading.' He sounded serious.

Tebbets suddenly became alert. 'Did you check out why?'

'Pretty high industrial demand – the entire Midwest seems to be running a night shift – and the fossil fuel plant at Iowa Falls just dropped out of the grid. Turbine failure.'

'The Midwest will have to buy Canadian power then,' Tebbets said. 'Happens all the time.'

'What about tomorrow?' Kloster asked. 'Demand will be even higher.'

Tebbets yawned. Tomorrow was always another day and had a comforting habit of taking care of itself. He glanced around the room. The night supervisor wasn't around; probably in the john. But his cup of coffee was still warm. Tebbets confiscated it and sat in the nearest chair, stretching out his long legs and making himself comfortable.

'It gets to you after a while, doesn't it, Captain?'

Kloster sat down one chair over, absorbed in the different images flowing across the viewing screens. 'What gets to you?'

Tebbets waved a hand. 'All of this. Here you sit, God in His tower, looking down on the world through His All-Seeing Eye.' He sobered slightly. 'Actually, it's pretty awesome to be able to look anyplace in the world without having anybody look back. A Peeping Tom would give his you-know-what to be in your seat. "Voyeurs of the world, unite!"'

'The brownout worries me,' Kloster said.

Tebbets waggled a finger at him. 'That's the occupational hazard here, Captain. Once you're able to see everything, you start wanting to do something about what you see. Impossible, forget it. You're just a spectator in the drama of life – one with a ringside seat. And forget the brownout while you're at it – Cardenas Bay goes on stream tomorrow night and that's going to plug one helluva gap in the grid.'

'If everything goes right,' Kloster amended.

'Don't borrow trouble, Captain.' Tebbets tried the coffee and made a face. No sugar. 'If it doesn't go right, our President's going to be on network television with egg all over his face. You knew there was going to be a Presidential address at seven to announce it?'

'Where'd you hear that?'

'Where do you hear anything that's important? The grapevine. Also, this evening's paper.' He changed his mind then and drank the rest of the coffee just to annoy the night super. 'I suppose our beloved Leader will take all the credit for it, even though it started with the previous administration.'

'That's the way the game is played, I guess.'

'You sound like somebody who voted for him.' Tebbets couldn't hide the sour grapes in his voice.

Kloster suddenly grinned. 'Didn't everyone?'

Third Day

28

A voice said, 'Greg. Greg, it's time to get up.'

He had just gone to bed, he thought hazily. Not more than five minutes ago. He slowly came awake and shifted to a sitting position on the mattress. Karen was standing by the side of the bed, fully dressed. 'It's almost four o'clock,' she said. 'You wanted to be at the plant by five.'

He yawned hugely and rubbed his face for a moment, then sniffed. The smell of coffee and fresh toast. And bacon. He looked up at her and she smiled. 'Eggs over easy, crisp bacon and make sure the coffee is black. Did I remember right?'

'Yeah.' He yawned again and rolled out of bed, standing in the middle of the room naked. He scratched an armpit, yawned for the final time and shook the last of the sleep out of his eyes. 'Be right there – soon as I shower.' Just before he ducked into the bathroom, he said, 'Did I thank you for staying over?'

'Several times.' There was a strange tone to her voice and under the hot needle spray he found himself wondering about it. Then he lathered up, revelling in the feeling of having a woman around the house. If Marjorie . . .

But that was a dead-end line of thought. Marjorie wouldn't – period.

He had finished his second piece of toast and was admiring how clean the kitchen was – really, for the first time since he had moved in – when Karen said, 'I won't be coming here again, Greg.'

He put the toast down and looked at her, wondering why it hadn't come as a complete surprise. 'You've decided you're still engaged after all.'

'I guess so. If Barney still wants to consider himself engaged to me. He's not the forgiving type.'

'I had hoped . . .' he started, then let his voice trail off. He had never been good at deep conversation early in the morning.

She looked at him, curious. 'Hoped what? That I would move in on an unofficial basis?' She shook her head. 'Not in this town, my dear. You ought to know that. It wouldn't work as far as the town was concerned and sooner or later, it wouldn't work for me.'

'Last night you seemed to think it might.' He hated himself when he said it; it sounded as if he were whining. It was something Barney might say; abruptly he wondered who was being the juvenile after all. It was he who had been acting like a carefree teenager while Barney had been trying to stake out territorial rights.

'You'll forgive me if I say this morning is not last night,' Karen said quietly.

'You needed me then,' he said ironically. 'But not now.'

She thought for a moment and nodded. 'I needed you as a friend needed a friend. Sex was a part of it; it frequently is between a man and a woman. I like you. I like you very much, and I wanted to be with somebody I liked.'

'You take what you want, don't you?' he said flatly.

'Don't you?' She couldn't keep back the smile. 'Come off it, Greg; you're sounding like Barney. But you're not that hurt.'

She was right. He wasn't and he felt guilty because he wasn't. 'All right, I'm off base. But you don't love him.'

She hesitated. 'I'm not sure,' she said slowly. 'Somebody once said, if you can analyse it, it isn't love. But if I'm not in love with Barney, I know I can grow into it. My mother didn't love my father when she married him. It was something that grew between them.' She nibbled at a piece of toast. 'Can I give you a compliment?'

'I think I could use one.'

'You're nice; you're really very nice. You're an excellent ... companion. You're really very good in bed and you're a very attractive man. You'll probably be attractive in your dotage. You'll totter down the street with a cane and little old ladies will throw themselves at your feet. In the park, they'll give you their bags of breadcrumbs so you can feed the pigeons.'

He sighed and poured himself another cup of coffee. 'I'm not sure I should take all that as a compliment.'

Her voice was smaller then. 'I once thought I loved you.'

'When was that?'

'The first day I saw you in the plant. I'd heard about your wife and I decided you needed somebody.'

'I still do,' he said seriously.

She shook her head. 'What's wrong is that it wouldn't have been ... equal, Greg. I need a husband; you don't need a wife. You need a friend you can take to bed once in a while.' He

128

glanced at her sharply. Her eyes were large and sympathetic. She wasn't putting him down. 'You restore cars; you collect gadgets; you put plants on stream. There's not much of you left over for a full-time wife.' She hesitated a moment, thinking. 'I guess what I'm trying to say is that Barney needs me and you don't. It would never be a partnership with you, even if you were free to marry. It couldn't be.'

He drained his coffee and stood up. 'I'll be late,' he said. At the door he kissed her, holding her for a moment. He said quietly, 'I wish you the best of luck; I really do.'

She looked up at him. 'That easy?'

He shrugged. 'What can I say now? Maybe I'm just a good loser.'

She laughed, but there was a trace of sadness to it. 'No, you're not. It's just that you're not really *that* interested. It's trite to say it but the plant's your mistress. If it wasn't, you'd have done something about Marjorie months ago.'

29

Kamrath got the phone call at nine-thirty, between his second cup of coffee and third doughnut. It took him a moment to recognize the high-pitched, quavering voice at the other end of the line and when he did, he immediately reached for a scratch pad.

'I have the information, Hank,' Abby said.

'You got the report back on the samples?'

'Right after I fed Hippocrates,' she said. 'Let me see, I've got it right here. Didn't take as long as I thought, I remembered two of his callers.'

'You checked the identities then?'

Her voice sharpened. 'I just told you I did. Two samples perfectly normal – for Mr Bernard Lerner and Miss Karen Gruen; she's that nurse up at the plant, you remember?'

Kamrath frowned. 'What did they get tested for?'

'For heaven's sake, Hank, when a young man and woman come in together for a blood test, what do you think it's for?'

He smiled. 'I'm in the wrong business, Abby. What about the third sample?'

She sighed. 'The third one's not so good. A low white cell

count, really low – the number of leucocytes is far below fifty percent of normal. And there's extensive damage to the red blood cells. The lab even asked if something might have gone wrong with the sample.'

'What would all that mean, Abby?'

'Well, I'm not a doctor, Sheriff. I wouldn't rightly want to say. But Doc and I were talking about his work at the plant one time and he said if anything happened, if any of the workers got exposed, that's what their blood sample would be like. If I remember correctly, that's what he said.'

Kamrath's hand tightened on his pencil. 'Who was it for, Abby?'

Her voice faded for a moment. 'Let me see here.' He could imagine her adjusting her bifocals. 'A Paul Marical. I think he works at the plant. He was a regular patient of Doc's.'

Something ticked in the back of his head then. 'What do you mean by a regular patient?'

'Just that – a regular patient,' she snapped. 'He'd come in once, twice a week. Doc couldn't figure out what was wrong. He kept coming down with everything in the book: flu, colds, all sorts of infections. I suppose Doc took a blood sample to see what was going on.'

'What was the date on it, Abby?'

'Let's see . . .' There was a slight pause at the other end of the line. 'The day before Doc . . . The day before they found . . .'

Kamrath said quietly, 'I'm sorry, Abby,' and hung up. The older you got, the easier you cried, he thought. At seven and seventy, you had come full circle.

He sipped his coffee and leaned back in his swivel chair to think about it. Paul Marical. Chronically sick. Every indication of radiation sickness. And he worked at the plant. All of which meant nothing more than that Marical was a very unfortunate man. Or, it could mean a lot more.

He was still mulling it over, when he saw Greg Parks pull up in the company station wagon. Kamrath automatically poured an extra cup of coffee and waited for him.

Parks came in and Kamrath pushed the cup at him. 'I've got an extra doughnut if you want one.'

'I accept.' Parks pulled a chair over to the desk and said, 'I just found out about Lerner.'

'Nothing major, drunk and disorderly in the Skupper last night. Got into a fight with one of the clammers – guy named Halsam, old enough to be Lerner's father.'

Parks looked his surprise. 'Did he hurt him?'

Kamrath scoffed. 'Halsam? He's tough as a keg of salt pork – decked your boy with one blow, though he was so drunk anybody could probably have done it. I take it you want to get him out.'

'We need him at the plant.' Parks sipped at his coffee. 'Anything new about Doc?'

Kamrath hesitated. He could tell him about Marical. If the man was suffering from radiation poisoning, he'd have to tell Parks sooner or later. But there were a few things he wanted to check out first. He didn't want to go off half-cocked.

He turned and shouted into the back, 'Bronson, bring out the prisoner.' He pushed a form towards Parks. 'You want to sign for him, he's all yours. I can't imagine anybody pressing any charges and in a fishing town it's ridiculous to arraign anybody for being drunk.'

A moment later Bronson came in with Lerner. 'I'm releasing you to your boss,' Kamrath said, trying to hide a smile. 'After this, stay out of the Skupper. I hate to say the town's prejudiced but it is. They generally don't like the plant workers in there.'

'It's a free country,' Lerner mumbled.

Kamrath nodded. 'There's some debate on that.' When they got to the door, he said, 'Oh, congratulations, Barney. She's a lovely lady.'

Lerner looked at him, then pushed out without saying anything. After they had left, Kamrath went back to thinking about Marical. There were, he thought, other ways of checking up on him. He dialled the phone again, got the switchboard operator at the plant and asked to be put through to Karen Gruen. A moment later she was on the line, her voice throaty but businesslike.

'You have files on all the workers at the plant?' he asked.

'I'm not sure – what kind are you talking about?'

'The film-badge files you showed me yesterday. The ones that show if a man has been exposed to radiation.'

'We have records going back to the day the plant opened.'

'Could I check the records for one of the men there?'

She sounded mystified. 'Of course. Who did you have in mind?'

'Paul Marical.'

'Just a moment.' He heard her in the background talking to Mike Kormanski. There was a moment's pause and then she

131

was back on the line. 'I have his file right here. What did you want to know?'

'Any record of overexposure anyplace along the line?'

'I'm looking.' A longer pause. Then: 'None at all. He should have registered high for yesterday when we developed the badges after the accident. He had left his off for some reason and drew a reprimand. But for the length of time he's worked at the plant, he's been remarkably clean. Any reason why you ask?'

It was Kamrath's turn to hesitate. 'Just a routine check. I'll probably be asking you about others.' Then another thought occurred to him. 'Did he ever see Doc at the plant because of illness?'

She laughed. 'All the time. He must spend more time in bed than he does at work.'

He hung up then and sat back, his coffee forgotten. The records indicated that Marical had never been overexposed to radiation. The blood test indicated that he was suffering from radiation sickness. But it had never shown up on the badges, meaning that Marical had obviously taken pains to see that it didn't. Which meant that there had probably been times when he hadn't worn his badge. Or . . .

Or what?

He almost called the plant then, to have Parks call him back as soon as he arrived. And then he hesitated. There could be a perfectly logical reason and if he called without having checked it out, it might go hard with Marical.

And there was another factor. He wanted to wrap something up; he wanted to find somebody – and know that he had found him beyond any shadow of a doubt.

He called the plant then and asked for the personnel department. Marical, it turned out, lived in a run-down hotel just off Main Street. There were things to be done first, Kamrath thought, but that afternoon he'd stop by the hotel. Before Marical came home from work.

30

In the car, Parks avoided mentioning Karen; he knew instinctively that Lerner would bring it up. There was little that he himself could say and probably nothing that Barney wouldn't

132

take the wrong way. It was up to Barney, now, to figure out where he stood. Karen had certainly made her position clear.

When they were within sight of the plant, Lerner said sullenly, 'You still plan to go on stream?'

'It depends on how the final checks go.'

'You're copping out. Have you read my report yet?'

'I will when I get back,' Parks said. He wondered for a moment if he really was copping out, then dismissed the thought. That was something he wouldn't know until the very last moment.

But one thing he didn't want was Lerner looking over his shoulder for the rest of the day.

'Barney, just for today, you do your job and I'll do mine.'

They sat in silence the rest of the way to the plant.

After he had parked the car, he went directly to his office and told his secretary he wasn't to be disturbed. The morning was going to be frantic, he thought; the afternoon even worse.

The reports from Lerner, Abrams and Glidden were on his desk and he thumbed quickly through them. Glidden's report was absurd. A collection of 'ifs' and equivocations, all designed to make it look as if Glidden heartily approved if they did go on stream but there were, nonetheless, serious risks involved. The imponderables were such, possibilities unknown at the moment, risk factors involved even though a probabilistic approach, etc., etc.

Abrams' report was far cleverer, frankly listing the drawbacks but at the same time pointing out that, aside from faulty fuel rods and troubles in ironing out the programming, no major equipment failures had occurred in the last month. As for those that had in previous months, there were numerous similarities to other plants that had gone on stream successfully. While many things had gone wrong in the past, none of them were unique. Similar plants with similar problems had gone on stream with no difficulty.

On the surface a logical statement that, too coincidentally, echoed Cushing's own thinking, Parks reflected.

Lerner's report didn't mince words. The plant, as it now stood, was unsafe and he recommended delaying start-up – unequivocally. Parks looked over the lists and charts in Lerner's report carefully, then finally threw the report on his desk and leaned back in his swivel chair, closing his eyes.

Lerner was right, he thought. Lerner was absolutely right. He was still thinking about it when there was a knock on his door and Abrams came in without waiting to be asked.

'Walton wonders if you can come out to the balcony so he can tape some footage on you before the show tonight.'

Parks came upright in his chair. 'Tell Walton he can shove it.' He gestured at the reports on his desk. 'Did you read these?'

Abrams nodded, a cautious look creeping across his face. 'I didn't think you would mind.'

'I don't. What's your opinion?'

'Glidden's wasn't worth much – not to knock a fellow worker. According to Lerner's report' – Abrams shrugged – 'we've got a lemon on our hands.'

'What do you think?'

'I told you what I thought. There's been nothing new in anything that's happened; in one sense it's all old stuff. The odds are with us.'

'Would you bring it on stream if it were up to you?'

Abrams sat down on the couch and laced his fingers behind his head. 'That's not my decision, Greg. It's the one thing you have no right to ask me. That's what they're paying you for.'

And he was right, Parks thought. As Brandt had once said, the buck stopped with him. If you can't stand the heat, and all of that.

Abrams was now curious. 'What are you really worried about, Greg? If something goes wrong, you SCRAM a pile or maybe even pull the plant. The President will look foolish but what the hell; it will hardly be the first time. Any deadline is arbitrary, you know that.'

'If you were in my shoes, you wouldn't be nearly as worried, would you?'

For once, Abrams seemed perfectly open. 'No, I don't think I would.' He was slightly condescending now, the West Point background coming out like sweat. 'You and I look at the plant from two different viewpoints. For me it's a job, a serious, important job. Someday I hope to be as good at it as you are.' That was a little too gratuitous, Parks thought, but let it pass. 'For you, Greg, it's an obsession.'

There was too much truth to it, Parks thought. And it hurt. He caught a glimpse of himself in the mirror at the other end of the room. His face was a little more lined than it had been when he had first reported to Cardenas; there was a shade more grey in his hair. And he knew he had put on a few extra pounds of weight. Twenty years from now, he'd be Hilary Brandt all

134

right. He was well on his way to dedicating his life to something and giving up everything else in exchange.

'Someday you'll have my job,' he said to Abrams.

'I've been training for it,' Abrams said casually. 'Someday they'll boot you up or out and I'll have it. And the same thing will happen to me after that. That's the way it goes; that's the way it's always gone.'

After he had left, Parks wondered how right Abrams might have been. If things didn't go right, you just pulled the plant. What the hell was he worried about?

What he was worried about, he thought, was that it just wouldn't be that simple.

In the corridors outside, the atmosphere was one of subdued tension. The supervisors were on edge, the workmen and technicians jumpy. They sensed the same thing he already knew: the plant wasn't ready. He went down to Control Central to check with Delano on the reprogramming. Delano was staring gloomily at console number three. Every bank of its warning lights was glowing a bright red.

Parks looked at them with alarm. 'What the hell's going on?'

'Undamped feedback from the left-quadrant sensor channels on reactor one,' Delano said curtly.

'Number five grid bias is out too,' Melton added from the far end of the room, his face peeping above the rear panel of one of the computer banks.

Parks sighed. 'Well, can you fix it?'

'What the hell do you think we're trying to do?' Delano snapped. Then he leaned against the console and slowly shook his head. 'I'm sorry, Greg, we've been plagued with sensor overloads all morning.'

'Can you find out what's causing them?'

'I'm doing my best. I could use more time.'

'We don't have more time. Check it out and tell me when it's operational.' Parks stalked out. Behind him Delano began to swear. He did a quick walk-through of the rest of the plant and everywhere it was the same: frayed nerves, tempers rubbed raw. He had the conviction they suspected what he already knew: the plant simply wasn't ready.

By eleven-thirty the assembly of Prometheus One was complete. Parks stood on the balcony and watched the withdrawal of the work crews. Over the last twenty-four hours, the other three reactors had been brought up to standby temperatures and now Control Central reported that Prometheus One was climbing slowly to the standby temperature. Delano was in a slightly better mood; his big problem with the sensor channels had been solved.

Parks glanced at his watch. They were scheduled to go on stream that evening at seven Pacific time, which would be ten in Washington. The Cardenas complex would officially become a part of the national power grid at seven-ten, coinciding with the President's announcement.

Back on the reactor floor, the workmen disassembled the last personnel shield and towed it through the great double doors. Moments later, the overhead crane trolleyed to the far end of the track to its standby position and the double doors closed with a muffled clang.

It was all over now, Parks thought. The inspection certificates for boilers and heat exchangers were all in order; the ubiquitous compliance teams had departed. Whatever the trials had been in the last week, the doors had finally closed on them and there remained only the final standby checks, bringing the reactors up to full temperature. He flipped the intercom to the turbine room. Everything there was in order.

He walked through the plant once more. There was a slight change in attitude now; the die had been cast. There was a certain air of relief among the people he met, as if the job were now done and all that remained was the throwing of the switch.

He even felt a good deal better himself. There was still the period of going on stream and keeping it there. Maybe after that, everything would be routine. He thought for a moment of looking up Brandt and Cushing, lost somewhere in the bowels of the building with Walton and the camera crew, and having lunch with them. Then he decided against it. He was still too much on edge; he'd have a sandwich sent up.

Back in his office, he ate his lunch and followed it with a quick chaser of brandy, then sat back down at his desk. The reports were still spread across the top. He arranged them in a neat pile, then picked out Lerner's and fingered it for a moment. Finally he settled back and read it through for the third time.

Half an hour later he realized his feelings of relief at having buttoned up the plant were strictly illusory.

31

Kamrath's first impression of Marical's room was one of spartan simplicity. There was no spread on the single bed but it was neatly made, with the blanket folded back in three precise folds and a pillow resting on top. The blanket and sheet, where they showed at the head of the bed, were folded into hospital corners. Atop the enamelled dresser, a comb and brush were precisely lined up with the centre of the mirror hanging on the wall behind.

In the opposite corner of the room was an exercise board and a barbell set flanked by two cast-iron dumbbells. Here, too, there was order. The barbell was positioned at the head of the folded exercise board with one dumbbell on each side.

Kamrath started to open the closet door and Elton, the elderly hotel manager, whined, 'I think you ought to get a search warrant, Sheriff.'

Kamrath shook his head. 'Come off it, Elton. I can get a John Doe warrant on the grounds there are stolen goods in this rattrap and go through every room you've got. We'd both probably be surprised at what I'd find.' He threw open the door. 'Why'd they ever call it the Elite Apartments, Elton? I haven't seen anything elite about it yet.'

Inside the closet, several worn but clean coveralls were hanging neatly on hooks. Three well-brushed and pressed suits were on hangers on the clothes pole. There was a thin layer of dust on the suit-coat shoulders, and the pants were deeply creased by the hanger. The suits probably hadn't been worn since Marical had moved in. He flipped open one of the suit coats to look at the label. 'Jacobson Clothiers, Mohawk Bluffs.' Probably the town where Marical had lived or worked before. Or perhaps a town close by.

He wandered back to the dresser. A photograph lay face down on the surface. From the creased corner, he guessed it had been stuck in the edge of the mirror. It showed a slim brunette with glasses, flanked by a young boy and girl. Something about the woman's face struck him and he stared at it for a moment. Pretty but with a firmness to it, a no-nonsense expression. A business woman, he thought, or maybe a lady doctor. At least she had that kind of look.

A sister, maybe? Or perhaps a wife, one that he had divorced – or vice versa. Marical was compulsively neat and few women could live with that for long.

'Does he ever go out much, Elton?'

Elton shook his head, apprehensive about the possibility of his tenant returning at any moment. 'With the overtime, he reports to work at eight and usually doesn't get back here until eight in the evening.'

'What about the weekends?'

Elton thought about it for a moment. 'No, can't say he goes out much then. Maybe for meals or to get some groceries for the hot plate. And he's been sick a lot, so he stays in.'

That figured, Kamrath thought. But something else didn't. 'They pay them pretty well at the plant and I gather he's got a responsible job – how comes he's living here? Any ideas?'

Elton looked offended. 'This isn't such a bad place . . .'

'If the highway were washed out and there wasn't a motel within five miles, you'd be right.' Kamrath pulled open the drawers of the bureau and methodically went through them. The shirts were precisely folded and stored next to the underwear, the tee shirts also neatly folded. One pair of white boxer shorts, Kamrath noted, had been neatly mended with white thread.

Divorced and paying alimony? Kamrath wondered. That might account for the good salary and the frugal living. Alimony, child support, it'd eat it up all right.

He glanced over the room again. The wastebasket was neatly in line with the wall and completely empty. There was a small radio on the bed table, along with an alarm clock.

'Where's the john, Elton, down the hall?'

Elton drew himself up. 'Every one of our rooms has its own private bath, Sheriff.' He went over to what Kamrath had thought was another closet. A toilet, a white tub, cracked, on cast-iron legs, and a medicine cabinet. He gave the room a cursory glance, then opened the medicine cabinet. It was something of a shock – a small drugstore, the shelves crammed with patent medicines. Marical was a hypochondriac, he decided. Or maybe not, he thought slowly, maybe his sickness was genuine.

'Does he ever get any mail, Elton? Magazines, anything?'

Elton thought for a moment. 'An occasional letter, that's about it. Someplace up North. Kid's handwriting on the outside.'

'Any friends here in the hotel?'

Elton shook his head. 'He keeps pretty much to himself; I don't think the other people on the floor even know him.'

138

'What about friends on the outside? Anybody drop in?'

Elton hesitated a fraction of a second too long. 'No, I wouldn't say he has any friends. No friends come to visit him, at least.'

Kamrath sat down in a chair and made himself comfortable. 'He's in his middle thirties, Elton, and at least until recently, he was a healthy man. Maybe he still is and he's just a hypochondriac. He's got no steady lady friend and there's no sign of any involvement around the room. No curlers, hairpins, stockings hanging on the bathroom shower rod. So I think there's a good chance he sends out for room service. Who's he seeing, Elton?'

'I don't know if he's seeing anybody,' Elton said defensively. 'Why should I?'

'Because you sit behind your damn desk downstairs like it was a military checkpoint. A tenant couldn't smuggle a canary in here without you knowing it. Besides, you used to run a couple of girls and I can't imagine you not offering their services to a lonely tenant. Now come on; who is she?'

'I cleaned all that up a long time ago,' Elton said nervously. 'You know that.'

Kamrath shook his head. 'All I know is that I dropped your case because I thought it was smarter to know where the action was than to have to keep looking for it.' He stared at Elton shrewdly and made a guess. 'What about Wanda?'

Elton paled. 'You can't prove a thing, Sheriff. She has several boy friends and maybe some of them live here, but you can't prove a solitary thing.'

'I'm not interested in busting Wanda, Elton, and as far as you're concerned, let's say I'm convinced you introduced them as a favour and no service charge was involved. But I'd like to talk to Wanda and the sooner the better.'

'She works at the Lodge in the evening,' Elton said nervously. 'During the day, she's at the Acme Café down the street.'

'How about asking her to come up to see me? Right now?'

Elton disappeared and Kamrath glanced around the room again. Somebody stayed there but nobody really *lived* there, he thought. And it had all the appearance of something temporary. No books, no newspapers, no magazines. Damn few letters. Almost no connection at all with the outside world. A man who ate, slept, worked and possibly listened to the radio before drifting off to sleep. Not much humanity there, none of the little things you would expect to find.

And most discouraging to him was the complete lack of any radical literature, anything suggesting the terrorist executioner he was looking for. So far the most he had was a little man who had possibly been divorced and was sick a lot.

There were voices out in the hall.

'Elton, why the hell can't you keep your mouth shut for a change . . .?'

Then the door slammed open and Wanda stormed in, her mouth tight and her eyes burning. 'Why don't you leave me alone, Sheriff? I haven't done a damned—'

'I'm not interested in what you've been doing,' Kamrath said quietly.

'That's what I've been telling her,' Elton said dolefully.

'I want to know about your friend,' Kamrath continued.

Wanda suddenly looked apprehensive and Elton said, 'I've got things to do,' and ducked out the door.

Kamrath closed it behind him and motioned Wanda to a seat on the bed. 'You've been seeing Paul Marical?' he asked gently.

'We're friends,' she said evasively.

'Don't beat around the bush with me, Wanda,' Kamrath said. 'I don't care if you're friends; from the looks of it here, he could use one.' He paused a moment, giving her a little longer to settle down. 'You've been seeing him on a regular basis?'

She nodded. 'Every Wednesday night. Nine o'clock.'

'Cash deal?'

She didn't say anything and Kamrath nodded. 'It doesn't matter; it probably is. Ten to one he insists on it.' He hesitated. 'Does he like you?'

'Who likes a whore?' she suddenly asked, cynical. 'You're used, like a toothbrush or a washrag.' Kamrath didn't say anything and she sighed and nodded, staring at the blanket on the bed. 'I'd like to think he does.'

'Does he ever confide in you?'

'Me?' She looked surprised. 'He's never told me much of anything. A lot of men, they just want to talk more than anything else. Whatever Paul has to say, I have to worm out of him.'

Kamrath walked over to the bureau again. 'Who's the photograph of?'

'His wife. The kids are his, too.'

'Divorced?'

She shook her head. 'I'm pretty sure she's dead. They used to work together and I think she died in an accident. He doesn't talk about it.' She fumbled in her waitress uniform for a pack of cigarettes. 'The kids are in the East somewhere, probably staying with relatives. He sends them every dime he can spare.'

You dug deep enough, Kamrath thought, and you always came up with a handful of tragedy. 'How long ago did his wife die?'

'Just before he came out here. She was pretty sick, I guess, and for a pretty long time. I think he's still paying for the bills on that.'

The room began to make a little more sense. 'He's been kind of sick himself lately, hasn't he?'

She gestured towards the bathroom. 'Look in the medicine cabinet. He's got more pills than the local drugstore.'

'Did he ever see Doc Seyboldt?'

'Sure. A couple of times, I think. Maybe more than that.'

A little bit at a time, he thought. 'Wanda, where does he keep his valuables? You know, watches, jewellery, bankbook – he must have a bankbook. There's nothing in the bureau.'

'He has one of those little boxes like you find in a stationary store. Small steel box with a lock on it.' She frowned. 'I think it's under the bed. I started cleaning in here one night and got that far and he chased me out.'

Just like a hick cop, Kamrath thought with chagrin. Look in all the places but the obvious one. He knelt down and felt under the bed, then pulled out a small cashbox. The hasp was secured with a cheap lock. He took out his pistol and hit the lock with the side of the muzzle.

Inside there were about a hundred dollars in bills, an old pocket watch – Kamrath guessed it was an heirloom – miscellaneous papers and two wedding bands. One from his dead wife, Kamrath thought.

And at the bottom, a thick black book labelled 'Appointments.' On the lower right-hand corner of the cover, in gilt, was 'James K. Seyboldt, MD.'

Wanda had been watching his face while he went through the box. 'Paul's in some kind of trouble, isn't he?'

Kamrath quickly leafed through the book to the day of the murder. There were two appointments scheduled in the afternoon – Lerner and Gruen – written in Abby's crabbed handwriting. Then there was one for six-thirty that had obviously been pencilled in by Doc himself. Paul Marical.

Kamrath thought about it for a moment, then thumbed through the back pages. Marical had been Doc's best patient in the past few weeks. He went to the last entry again. Doc must have written it in before he discovered that when Marical had walked in the front door, it wasn't a business visit.

But Marical had always come up clean with the badges, he thought. He went through the contents of the lockbox again. There was another photograph, similar to the one on the bureau, but this time there was a man in it. Marical, Kamrath thought. A short, slender man, maybe in his middle thirties. Thick horn-rim glasses and something of a baby face. The kind who had been called four-eyes since he was a kid and had taken to building up his body with the weights. He memorized the face and put the photograph aside. Beneath it was a plain white envelope he had overlooked when he had spotted the appointments book. The flap was folded in and he shook out the contents. Three film inserts for the safety badges. They would explain Marical's low exposure; he had been substituting film inserts.

Which meant that Marical had been working around radio-actives and hadn't wanted anybody else to know about it.

Amateur all the way, Kamrath thought. But Marical could afford to be. Everybody at the plant obviously trusted him. You don't suspect your neighbour of murder and you never imagine a friend as being a thief.

He glanced at his watch. Marical was still at work, it wasn't five yet. He decided to stop by the office and make a phone call to Mohawk Bluffs. Then he would call Parks and go out to the plant to pick up Marical.

'Paul's in trouble, isn't he?' Wanda repeated in a low voice.

He looked up at her, read her eyes and said, 'I'm not sure.'

She touched him on the arm before he got to the door. 'I'd like to help him,' she said quietly. 'Any way I can.' She reddened slightly and Kamrath realized with a minor shock that she was blushing. 'I like him a lot,' she said simply.

At the desk downstairs, Kamrath paused a moment to shake Elton out of a slight doze. 'Shame on you, Elton – I thought you said he didn't have any friends.'

32

It was late afternoon and Parks was on the balcony listening to readouts from Control Central. Prometheus One had reached precritical thermal equilibrium. In a few hours computers would take over, bringing all four reactors to full operating capacity.

There was a commotion by the elevator and he turned around to see Walton getting off, followed by several men bearing heavy chests of equipment. The balcony had already been rigged with lights and the cameras were in position. 'What now, Walton?'

'Just some additional taping equipment. Could you lend us one of your men to help position the crew? We don't want to get in your way.'

Parks sighed. 'How many in your crew?'

'About ten, counting film and television camera crews.' Parks swore, not so quietly, to himself and Walton said petulantly, 'There'll be a few reporters in addition.'

Parks had a vision of himself, Cushing, Brandt and Walton up there during the critical phases of going on stream, surrounded by TV crews and half a dozen inquiring reporters, with everybody getting in the way at the last moment. 'You can have two television and one film crew on the balcony,' Parks said. 'Your taping facilities will have to be on the floor below. Pick three reporters for up here; the rest will have to watch the monitor downstairs.'

'But—'

'That's it; I need the space.'

'Those reporters will be mad as hell,' Walton said angrily.

'Not so mad as I'll be if they get in my way.' Parks stalked off the balcony and went back to his office. Cushing and Brandt were waiting for him. Cushing looked more dignified and saturnine than ever. The perfect Man Who Gets Things Done.

'I see you're ready for the big show,' Parks said.

'Everything going all right?' Cushing asked dryly.

Parks shrugged.

Cushing looked at him quizzically. 'Come on, Parks – don't be a spoilsport. Are you going to be disappointed if everything *does* go right?'

Parks half smiled then. 'I've been acting like a dog in a manger, haven't I?'

'I didn't say it,' Cushing said. 'You did.'

'OK, gentlemen.' Parks walked over to his wet bar and pulled out three brandy snifters. He half filled each and passed them around, then raised his own glass. 'Here's to Prometheus,' he said slowly. 'May she be the answer to all our problems.'

They drank silently and he glanced at Cushing. 'Better?'

Then his mood darkened. Over Cushing's shoulder he could see his desk and on it, Lerner's report, bound in red.

33

Karen Gruen had hoped to leave at five. It had been a long day and she had had time for little more than a bowl of soup and coffee during the lunch hour. She had seen Barney once during the day, just long enough to determine that he was capable of a grudging forgiveness, and she had wanted to have dinner with him that night. She had expressed some concern for his black eye and bruised face and that had helped. A quiet evening spent over steak and a glass of wine would help even more.

But Barney was trapped in the process of getting the plant on stream and it seemed unlikely he would be free before eight. Supper – and candlelight and roses – would have to wait. They'd had one brief conversation and it hadn't set too well with her. It was obvious that as the months wore on, he would be more and more insistent that she leave her job. He was typical of most of the liberals and activists she had met, she thought. They were all strong personalities, with strong outlooks on how the world should be run. They were very willing to concede a woman to her place in the world – until that woman became their wife. Then the old tribal rules suddenly became the order of the day. A woman's place in the world was actually in the home.

Mike Kormanski came out of the inner lab and glanced at the clock. 'You sticking around until after we go on stream?'

She nodded. 'I thought I might. Barney won't be leaving until afterwards anyway.'

'Going out to dinner then, huh?'

She looked surprised. 'How'd you know?'

'Just a wild guess. Steak and a bottle of wine at the Lodge and he'll drop a week's salary on you.' He winked. 'What kind of a ceremony are you going to have? Breaking the glasses and all that? A friend of mine is Jewish and when he got married, it was a real blowout.'

She nodded. 'He wants a rabbinical ceremony and a marriage contract. I'm not so sure I'll agree to that. If I had been raised as a Jew, I might feel differently.'

Kormanski studied her for a minute, then grinned. 'You'll be surprised what you'll agree to.'

She was just locking her door when the desk intercom buzzed. Just time to relax and now somebody had a splinter in his finger. She flipped a switch. 'Dispensary.'

'Karen,' a voice said. 'This is Jensen in Maintenance. Tremayne just fell from the main cooling line in corridor B, section 2. His leg is broken – you can see the bone.'

'Don't move him. Is there an emergency stretcher in the area?'

'Yeah, I can see one from here.'

'All right, make him comfortable but above all else, don't move him until I get a chance to put splints on that leg.'

She disconnected and looked up at Kormanski, who had been listening, his face intent. 'Corridor B, Tremayne slipped and broke a leg. Get me the bag and make sure there're some morphine Syrettes in it.' She took down two commercial splints with white surgical canvas webbing from a shelf. They'd have to take him to the hospital, too, she thought. She glanced at her watch. One hour until they went on stream. She'd be there for the reactor countdown in spite of herself.

'Do you want me to come along?' Mike asked.

She shook her head. 'No, just hold down the fort here until I get back.'

There wouldn't be any candlelight and wine after all, she thought.

34

It was five-thirty when Kamrath got back to the deserted office. Bronson had already left and it hadn't been a duty day for Gilmore, who worked part-time. Kamrath threw his coat on a chair and dialled the long-distance operator. Somewhere he had seen Mohawk Bluffs mentioned besides on the labels of Marical's suits. Probably in the newspapers; in fact, he was sure of it. Not a big story or an important one but enough of one so the name rang a bell – and in the right context.

He didn't know the state and the operator became politely non-cooperative until Kamrath mentioned it was police business. Five minutes later he was talking to the local operator in the town and in another five minutes he had the information he wanted. They were working overtime there, too, he thought with relief.

When he was through he put the phone back on its cradle and sat for a long moment, thinking. His first thought was that Marical was a very sick man in more ways than one. An angry, sick little man who had already committed one horrifying murder. A man who had nothing to live for and who, in fact, might even be dying. His second thought was that the possibilities after that were numerous and all of them frightening.

He could guess what Marical had probably been doing and then wondered how he could have gotten as far as he had. Simple, he thought. Nobody had ever checked. And now Marical was probably within an ace of succeeding. Or had been.

Then Kamrath sat bolt upright in his chair. The Prometheus complex was due to go on stream in little more than an hour. Ten to one the on-stream time would be important to Marical. Everybody would be busy; everybody would be distracted, their normal suspicions would be dulled.

He picked up the phone again and dialled the plant. Every line was busy. Probably reporters were tying them up. He had the operator break in and caught the night girl on the switchboard. No, she couldn't disturb Mr Parks right then. Mr Parks was on the balcony conducting the last of a series of reactor checks. No, under no circumstances ...

He slammed down the phone and debated if he should call back Bronson and Gilmore, then decided against it. It would take time and he had a hunch he was running against a deadline as it was. If he needed manpower, there were armed guards at the plant. He took a riot gun from its locked rack on the wall, grabbed a box of cartridges and left.

By the time he had topped the rise and could see the plant below, the storm that had been threatening all day broke above him. Heavy gusts of wind pushed the jeep to the left and he had to hold the wheel at a quarter turn to compensate.

At the plant gate, the guard waved him through. He drove up to the administrative wing of the building and made a dash for the door, holding the shotgun under his coat. Once inside, he shook himself like a dog. A guard was manning the information desk and Kamrath ran over to him. The guard looked up, recognizing him. 'Hi, Sheriff, why all the artillery?'

'Can you plug me through to Parks?' Kamrath asked tensely.

The guard shook his head. 'Not a chance, not for any reason. They've started the final countdown.'

Kamrath started to explain, then shut up. He didn't have the time and the guard wouldn't understand anyway.

'What about Tom Glidden?'

The guard looked dubious. 'He's up there, too, but I'll see if I can get him.' A moment later, he said, 'I was wrong; he's not on the balcony and nobody seems to know where he is.'

Kamrath could feel the sweat start to soak his shirt beneath his plastic raincoat. 'What about Barney Lerner?'

'Probably the same story as Parks, but I'll try him.'

The guard was still trying to track down Lerner when Kamrath noticed an open door at one end of the lobby. He walked towards it and looked in at the plant floor. The heavy emergency doors to the reactor room were closed – he had seen them once on a tour – but the rest of the floor was a beehive of activity: technicians making last-minute adjustments at control boards, workmen lugging away the remains of metal shields and what looked like hexagonal steel channels. And darting through the chaos were half a dozen of the small electricars.

Then Kamrath caught his breath. One of the figures driving an electricar looked familiar. He narrowed his eyes and then was sure of it. Marical. Kamrath stood there for a moment in an agony of indecision. He could wait until the guard contacted Lerner and then wait still longer while Lerner figured out if he had the right to authorize a couple of guards to accompany Kamrath when he went to pick up Marical. And chances were that Lerner would have to get that final OK from Parks – and that wouldn't be considered until after they were on stream.

If he waited, he thought, Marical could get away. The image of Doc lying half buried in the sand on the beach was suddenly sharp in his memory and he made up his mind. 'Marical!'

There was no indication that the little man heard. The electricar buzzed on its way, hit a pair of swinging doors in the far wall and disappeared.

Kamrath ran the length of the floor towards the double doors. He pushed through and found himself in a long, wide corridor. He stopped a nearby technician and asked, 'Did you see Paul Marical come through here?' The technician looked at the shotgun, glanced at Kamrath's 'Sheriff' arm patch and shook his head.

Then Kamrath thought he heard the buzz of an electricar around the far corner and ran towards it. Three more inquiries and ten minutes later Kamrath realized he had not only lost Marical; he had lost himself as well.

35

'Do you have enough light? Can you get a view of him by the console? What about a shot through the window, at the reactor-room floor? Any reflections?'

Walton's voice buzzed in the background, directing the cameramen and giving asides to the half-dozen reporters on the balcony. Parks shifted uneasily in the console seat. It was the final minutes of countdown and he was growing more and more tense. He had the power of veto but in a larger sense, he didn't even have that – a computer could overrule him if its multiple sensors and electronic reflexes detected something that he missed. His only real function now was simply to monitor the different crews. And those in Control Central and the generating plant had been through the countdown drill a dozen times.

In the last analysis, Parks thought, the future of the plant was preordained on the high-response tapes two floors below. He ran his fingers lightly over the controls and watched the different control-room scenes flick over the viewing screens above the console. Behind him, he could hear the soft voice of a reporter droning quietly into a microphone. It was the same level of voice they used when they reported golf tournaments on TV and didn't want to distract the player – a heavy half whisper that probably drove him up a wall.

'*Prometheus is completely automated in the final stages of countdown ...*'

Parks switched to Control Central. He could see the sweat on Delano's face.

Delano wiped his forehead with a huge handkerchief. 'Stand by for power-up – remove function bypasses.' Then: 'Give me a console status report.'

The voices of Melton, Carr, Reynolds and Young cut in now.

'Power calibration completed.'

'In-core temperature holding.'

'... *the great steam turbines that will take the raw heat of the reactors and turn it into electrical energy that will surge over the national power grid tonight ...*'

A short delay. 'SCRAM sequence?' Delano snapped.

'SCRAM sequence standby and operative.'

Ten, fifteen minutes now before full operating pressure, Parks thought. In his mind's eye he kept seeing Barney's red-bound report lying on his desk.

'In-core neutron flux monitoring on line at SRM level, all reactors.'

'Dynamic tests complete.'

'Coolant flow nominal.'

'Rod control checks complete.'

'ECCS nominal.'

There was hesitation down below now. 'What's wrong?' Parks asked.

Delano looked up at the camera, his face strained. 'Sensors in One acting up.' He turned away from the camera. 'No, they're OK, they just blinked there. It's got to be minor; the computer would have cut in if it weren't.'

Parks hesitated, then made up his mind. This was it, he thought. He had promised himself: one screw-up, however minor, and he would abort. He leaned towards the intercom mike. 'Delano, give me a hold on countdown.'

Delano glanced up. 'We've used up all but eight minutes of our accordion, Greg.'

'I'll give you a go-ahead or abort in five,' Parks said. He turned to Abrams. 'Take over. I have her on hold at computer interface checkout.'

He left the balcony without a word and walked quickly towards his office, Cushing and Brandt following. Once in the office, Brandt slammed the door and said in a harsh voice, 'What the hell's wrong, Parks?'

For the first time in weeks, Parks felt calm inside. 'You

149

heard Delano. I told you that if one damn thing went wrong, I'd abort the countdown. That's what I'm going to do.'

Brandt was white. 'Over a momentary flicker that could have been caused by anything? Delano didn't suggest aborting it; the computer didn't report any failure.'

Parks leaned his knuckles on his desk. 'Forty-eight hours, Hilary. Forty-eight hours to check out those sensors and find out why they flickered.'

'You can't have them, Parks. In a few minutes the President is going to announce that Prometheus is on stream, that his party has the solution to the energy crisis within its grasp. And you want to pull the plant because some sensors winked.'

'Hilary,' Parks said calmly, 'you've read all my reports. You know the history on valve fittings and fuel rods and pipe welds. If everything had gone exactly right, I would have risked it. But everything didn't go exactly right.'

Brandt poured himself a stiff slug of brandy from the wet bar and took a huge gulp of it. 'Did you listen to the news to-night, Parks? The national power grid is already in trouble. There's a brownout in New York and they're feeling the strain in Philadelphia and St Louis as well as a lot of other big cities. The demand's too great. They're waiting for Prometheus.'

'We can't take the chance,' Parks said tensely. 'Not even the President has the right to take that kind of chance.'

Brandt wavered, turned to Cushing. 'Eliot,' he said uncertainly, 'we've a serious decision to make.'

Cushing shook his head. '*You* have a decision. I'm not a part of any decision-making process.' He looked thoughtful for a moment, obviously sizing up Brandt. 'The President is all set to announce Prometheus coming on stream tonight. With elections coming up this fall, you know how important this is.'

'I'm aware of the political consequences.'

'And the economic ones,' Cushing said dryly. 'They can cut off funds if you embarrass them. You'll have trouble with your insurance and the compliance teams will start inspecting everything including your typewriters.' He hesitated. 'I can put you through to the Commission chairman.'

Brandt nodded tiredly. Cushing took the phone and dialled. A pause, then: 'Well, where the hell is he?' Another pause. 'How about Commissioner Dann?' He waited another moment, then cupped the phone and turned to Brandt. 'They're all at the White House for the dedication.'

'Let's try there,' Brandt said, nervous.

Cushing dialled again and Parks thanked God that the decision hadn't been dumped in his lap. He desperately wished he were most sure of himself. Maybe Cushing was right; maybe he was an alarmist ...

Cushing hung up. 'Nobody knows where they are.'

'That leaves the President himself,' Brandt said suddenly. He was sweating heavily; Parks could smell it halfway across the office. 'He's putting the prestige of his office on the line tonight. And it's his goddamned broadcast that's forcing our hand.'

The look on Cushing's face was one of contempt, Parks thought. He despised weak men and Brandt was visibly cracking before their eyes. 'You'll have to go through Bateman, the President's appointment secretary. After that, you're on your own.'

'Put it on the amplifier,' Brandt said. Cushing switched it on, dialled, and a moment later the ringing of a distant phone filled the room.

'Bateman here,' said a slightly nasal British voice.

'Eliot Cushing, Len. I've got to speak to the President.'

'Sorry, Eliot – he and Meisner are in the Oval office, preparing for tonight's broadcast. He goes on in an hour you know. The chopper's waiting to fly him to Camp David immediately afterwards to meet the Premier.'

Cushing bit his lip. 'Len, this is important.'

Parks could sense the tension in his voice and wondered if Cushing himself were wavering.

The amplifier said, 'Meisner would skin me alive.'

Brandt suddenly spoke up. 'Mr Bateman, this is Brandt of Western Gas and Electric. It's imperative we speak with the President.'

Parks could almost see Bateman shrug at the other end of the line. 'I'll have his secretary call Meisner out.' A pause. 'He won't be happy.' There was a brief cut in the connection and then a harsh, Southern voice said: 'Eliot? This better be good – the Man doesn't like interruptions.'

There was no emotion in Cushing's voice. 'I'll make it short. The people here want the President to cancel his speech.'

Meisner sounded confused. 'You mean they're not going to meet the deadline?'

'They can meet it '

'Then what the hell's the problem?'

Cushing nodded to Brandt, who said in a shaky voice: 'Mr Meisner, we've run up against a situation that suggests it's wiser to postpone going on stream.'

He went into detail. There was a pause when he finished and then a querulous Meisner said, 'Eliot, I'm no scientist; I don't understand all of this. What do you think? You're right on the scene there.'

Cushing hesitated for only a moment and Parks wondered at the human computer behind his eyes. 'If I thought it was unsafe, I would have pulled it, Jack. But that's only my opinion. It's up to management here.'

Cushing had shot them down again, Parks thought, with rising anger. It was up to them ... And, finally, it would be up to him.

There was a tone of relief in Meisner's voice. 'Eliot, they've been telling us for three and a half years how safe it is with built-in redundancies and all the fail-safe factors.' He hesitated. 'You know that advance copies of the President's speech have already gone out to the press?'

Brandt suddenly exploded. 'Mr Meisner, just call it to the President's attention with my recommendations. I don't give a damn about the press.'

There was sudden frost in Meisner's voice. 'I'll call you back.' The amplifier clicked, ending the conversation.

There was a moment of silence in the room. 'I hope you appreciate that I stuck my neck on the block as well?' Cushing said.

'Did you really?' Parks asked sarcastically. 'I hadn't noticed.'

Cushing looked away and lit a cigarette. A few moments later the phone rang again. Meisner was on the line, sounding very angry. 'Eliot, have you ever seen the Man when he's crossed?' He didn't wait for an answer. 'It's absolutely out of the question. We're getting partial brownouts in Washington and they're feeling the outage in Chicago, St Louis, Phila- delphia ...'

Brandt interrupted. 'We may have to pull it on our own,' he said harshly.

There was a second of silence, then: 'It's your funeral, Mr Brandt. I can't tell you how to run your company – free enter- prise and all that crap – but if I were you, I wouldn't want the Man sore at me.'

Cushing cut in. 'Thanks for trying, Jack. I felt I owed it to Mr Brandt.'

'I won't say "any time," Eliot,' Meisner said sourly. 'He's going to be on my back the rest of the night.'

The phone abruptly went dead.

Cushing put down the phone and looked at Brandt. The expression on his face was one of no concern. Pontius Pilate, Parks thought. He had washed his hands of it. 'It's your ball, Hilary. What are you going to do?'

'I don't think Meisner ever talked to the President,' Parks said.

Cushing shrugged. 'Maybe not. I don't know how you can prove it.' He looked at his watch. 'You have less than an hour to decide.'

'I can pull it myself,' Parks said slowly. He looked at Brandt. 'I've got the authority; you know that.'

Brandt stared back without expression, then turned to Cushing. 'Eliot? What do you think?'

'I'm a member of the Atomic Regulatory Committee,' Cushing said slowly, choosing his words. 'I've seen nothing that would cause me to certify Prometheus as being unfit to go on stream – if I had, I would have told Washington. But neither is it my responsibility if you do go on stream. That's up to you, Hilary.' He stood up and nodded to both of them. 'I'll be on the balcony.'

When he had left, Brandt said, almost pleading, 'What do I give as a reason, Greg? A couple of faulty sensors? You're putting your own judgement above that of Delano – and he's lived with the equipment as long as you have. You're putting yourself above the computer, a multi-million-dollar installation whose major purpose is to tell us when we're wrong.'

'It's not your responsibility,' Parks said quietly. 'It's mine. It's my authority I'm using.'

Brandt grew cold then. 'You think you're the one who's going to suffer if we abort? You're naïve, Parks. You don't cross the White House and come out of it with skin on your back. In two years Western would be in receivership. That's the other side of the coin, and I'm not willing to flip it to see if it comes up.'

'You said that if anything went wrong, you'd back me all the way,' Parks said thinly. 'Even if it meant your job.'

'That's what I said.' There was a hoarseness in Brandt's voice now that wasn't just from the brandy. 'I didn't mean that I would put my career on the line for a couple of sensors.' He fought with his feelings for a moment, then said, 'You'll carry through with the countdown, Mr Parks. That's a direct order.'

There was sweat on Brandt's forehead and his hand that held the glass of brandy was trembling. He had probably never gone back on his word in his life, Parks thought. Not until now.

'I can't accept the order,' Parks said quietly. 'I'm going back out there and tell Delano to shut down immediately.'

The brandy in Brandt's shaking glass sloshed up to the edge and a few drops rolled over and fell to the carpet. Brandt stared at him for a long moment, then abruptly walked over to the office phone. He put the glass of brandy on the desk and dialled a number. Three digits, Parks thought. An in-plant call.

'Mr Abrams? . . . Hilary Brandt. Can you continue the count-down? . . . Very well, do so. You're in complete charge . . . That's correct. Mr Parks has just been relieved.'

He hung up the phone and turned to a stunned Parks. 'You only have the authority to pull the plant if you're facility manager, Mr Parks. As of right now, you're not. You no longer work here.'

For a moment Parks thought Brandt was going to say more. That he was sorry it was necessary, that he didn't want to do it. Instead, he picked up the brandy glass, drained it, then walked out of the room, leaving the door open behind him.

Brandt had caved in, Parks thought. Completely. He stood there, wondering if he should clean out his desk, go home, or what. Then he walked out and back up to the balcony. He stood in the balcony doorway listening and watching, his mind an emotional blank. The newsmen were still taking notes, the ubiquitous cameramen catching every shot. Abrams was sitting at the console checking out Delano below. Cushing was at his side while off in the far corner Brandt was arguing with Lerner. Brandt was brief and harsh, whatever he was saying, and suddenly Lerner looked like he had been backhanded. Lerner had had his say and Brandt had finally found a reason to fire the 'Commie.'

Parks strained his ears to make out the conversation over Abrams' intercom.

Faintly, Delano's voice: 'How's the power system?'

'Turbine checkout complete, all four units.'

'Begin power-up.'

The cameras were focused on Abrams now and Parks could imagine the expression on his face. He had just jumped five years in professional time.

'Begin control rod withdrawal sequence, reactor one.'

'By the numbers. Ratcheting control rods – five level.'

It hurt, Parks thought. He should have been able to see it coming and he hadn't. Firing him had always been Brandt's final way out. Why had he thought the man would never do it?

'What's the computer say?'

'Right at programmed level.'

'Steam entering chamber.'

Abrams' voice was smug and full of triumph. 'Baby's behaving all right,' he said in a low voice. Behind him, Cushing nodded approvingly and Brandt had started to lose his drawn appearance.

Where was Glidden? Parks suddenly wondered. He glanced around the balcony. The grey man wasn't there. Come to think of it, he hadn't been there at all. He must have known that nobody would miss him and had carefully avoided a scene where somebody might ask his opinion or thrust unwanted authority upon him.

'OK, let's take her up.'

'Notch in core.'

'Power going up, all four turbines speed one thousand nominal.'

'Power to grid.'

'Twenty percent power level.'

'Take her up.'

'*In one minute we take you to Washington and the Oval Office in the White House ...*'

It was over with as far as he was concerned, Parks thought. He turned and slowly pushed his way through the technicians and workmen who had crowded onto the balcony after him. Nobody seemed to notice him, their eyes were fastened on the console and Abrams.

'Give me a reading on power-density distributions ...'

'... ECCS operational ...'

'... *where the President of the United States in a major address on the energy crisis ...*'

'... power at eighty-five percent ...'

'... coming up fast, let's not overshoot her the first time out ...'

'... we're at ninety-eight percent level. Saturating ...'

And then Abrams' voice, a triumphant shout: 'That's it! She's on line!'

There was spontaneous applause on the balcony. Prometheus One was now on stream, feeding power into the grid. Two, Three, and Four would follow as quickly.

He had been an alarmist, Parks thought with a sickening feeling. He had tried for a Swiss watch after all and it hadn't been necessary. And he would never know whether he had merely erred on the side of caution or whether Cushing had been right, that he had intentionally kept seeking delay after delay because, in the last analysis, he hadn't wanted to take the responsibility for something this big.

He shook his head. He wasn't going to feel sorry for himself. He had done the best he could; he had called the shots as he had seen them. Maybe the one good thing about it was that he could now go back to Marjorie. She had won by default.

And then he realized for the first time that he really didn't want to go back to her, that whatever relationship he'd had with her had died years ago.

He was almost to the steps when suddenly Abrams' voice cut through the babble behind him. It was too loud and there was a thin note of fear running through it.

'We've got a hot spot in Prometheus One!'

Parks turned and ran back to the balcony door, shoving his way through the suddenly silent crowd.

Something had just gone horribly wrong.

36

Self-congratulatory conversation on the balcony had stopped; the men clustered around the console were as motionless as bees in amber. Barney Lerner looked startled, Jerry Walton confused. Brandt's expression was midway between shock and rage, while Cushing's face was icy ... noncommittal.

Abrams half rose from his seat and stared, confused, at the board in front of him. The console murmured and Parks realized the intercom was still open; the speaker buzzed with muffled commands from Delano in Control Central below. Then the voice of the main computer broke in, its tone unemotional and mechanical, reeking of steel and oil.

'... temperature is now eight hundred forty degrees Fahrenheit in sector ten and rising ...'

Temperature inclines suddenly lit up Abrams' board. The sensors were signalling a sudden heat rise in sector ten of the core.

A beat, then: *'... eight hundred eighty ...'*

Parks stood stunned at the balcony entrance. He had lived with the possibility of a major problem long enough. Now that it was actually happening, he couldn't believe it. This wasn't a simulated test; all four reactors were now on stream.

Abrams, his sweaty face shining in the light from the overhead fluorescents, was on the verge of panic. 'We'll have to SCRAM the pile ...'

For God's sake, be quick ... Parks thought.

Brandt was at Abrams' side immediately, his face flushed and angry. 'Use your damping mode. Move, damn it!'

Parks realized suddenly how much of a strain Brandt was under. The man had made a choice years ago and each step along the way he'd had to reconfirm it. Now, in his own mind, there were no acceptable alternatives open to him. The plant was going to remain on stream no matter what – any other course of action was inconceivable.

Cushing cleared his throat and licked his lips hesitantly. 'I don't think ...'

Brandt turned on him. 'You don't think what? Do you want to try the President again?'

Cushing looked offended, shut up and faded to invisibility. The perfect bureaucrat, Parks thought grimly.

'... eight hundred ninety, rising ...'

The computer sounded remote and unconcerned. Tinny, muffled cursing came from the console loudspeaker as Delano battled the controls below.

Abrams' hands flashed over the control panel, ordering readouts from new sectors within the pile. His voice was a whine. 'We don't have a choice, Mr Brandt. The computer will SCRAM it automatically with these neutron fluxes.'

A television monitor on a table behind Brandt suddenly came to life. Lines shot across the screen and resolved into the familiar view of the Oval Office.

'Ladies and gentlemen, the President of the United States ...'

The balding, fatherly figure appeared behind the lectern. He briefly riffled the papers in front of him, then glanced up at the camera, his face calm and reassuring. *'My fellow citizens. On this historic night ...'*

It was Lerner who reached over and snapped off the sound. On the screen, the now mute, puppet-sized figure waved his arms, as if in anger at being silenced.

'... temperature is nine hundred ten, rising ...'

157

'I can't stop it,' Abrams muttered, hysteria stitching through his voice. 'This is just an observation board . . .'

Abrams had been his mistake, Parks thought, agonized. Brandt's choice, perhaps, but he should have tried several men in the position and run psychological profile to weed out those who might crack under the stress of a real emergency.

'Parks.'

Brandt had spotted him by the door. His voice was almost a whisper. It took a second for Parks to respond to it. Brandt was looking at him with a strange expression. It was a plea, he finally decided. But this was probably the first time in his life that Brandt had ever asked anybody for anything and his face mirrored the pain of his decision.

'. . . *nine hundred fifty* . . .'

Abrams looked sick. 'We're going into automatic sequencing.' He stared numbly at the board, his hands at his sides.

Too soon, too soon . . . Parks ran forward and shouldered Abrams out of the way, sliding quickly into the still-warm seat. One close-up glance at the board and he knew that it was too late – the SCRAM panel for Prometheus One was red. In the depths of the reactor, the control blades were already thrusting up between the fuel rods, shutting the pile down completely.

'. . . *one thousand, rising* . . .'

The board was registering what should have happened, not what had, Parks thought, startled. But it gave him a chance to do what Abrams should have done right at the start. He glanced at the CRT map of the fuel core, locating the co-ordinates of the glowing red area that was the hot spot. He thumbed the intercom switch. 'Parks here, Delano. Cut in the manual override and reduce generator power to three-quarters. Isolate Prometheus One.'

He waited a moment for the acknowledgement. Then : 'Give me emergency damping on control rods eight and nine. Automatic sequencing for coastdown didn't work.' There was still a chance he could damp that section of the pile.

He turned to Lerner. 'Get Glidden back up here, we can use him.' The plant superintendent knew machinery; despite their differences, he'd be invaluable right now.

The murmur of background conversation started up again. They had faith in him, he thought wryly – but they were hardly out of the woods yet.

'. . . temporary malfunction, gentlemen. We'll be back up to full power in just a few minutes . . .'

'... don't understand what you mean by malfunction, Mr Walton. Just exactly what's wrong?'

A swirl of questions and answers and the smell of relaxation. And then Delano was back on the intercom and the balcony chilled.

'Hang-up on rods eight and nine. They've impacted on something.' Parks could hear him clearing his throat for the big one. 'Some of the fuel rods have probably collapsed.'

'... *eleven hundred, rising* ...'

Parks' hand hovered over the red-lit panel button for a moment, then reluctantly swept it down. 'Manual SCRAM of Prometheus One, Delano.'

The balcony was suddenly silent. Brandt stared at him, a tic in his cheek working furiously. Cushing looked lidded and calculating. Abrams was shaking with reaction. Walton was obviously angry at being crossed up in his reassurances to the newsmen.

Brandt said, 'You had to?'

It was more of a question than it should have been. 'Three-quarters of a loaf is better than none,' Parks said tensely.

'... *eleven hundred fifty* ...'

Delano was on the intercom immediately: 'SCRAM aborted. None of the control blades will penetrate.' Pause. 'We've got more hot spots now.'

Parks glanced back to the CRT diagram of the pile. It had developed a bad case of measles; the in-core sensors showed temperature rises at a dozen different spots throughout the core. And each one had its own computer voice.

'... *temperature is nine hundred Fahrenheit* ...'

'... *twelve hundred ten, twelve hundred twenty* ...'

'... *eight hundred fifty and rising* ...'

Parks hit a switch and the chattering voices from the computer's speakers blended into one.

'... *average temperature is now twelve hundred and fifty* ...'

For a moment, Parks' mind filled with thermal distribution curves and heat transfer equations and then he gave it up. He felt oddly bitter. They thought they had eliminated the possibility of human error by entrusting all the safeguards to a computer. But somewhere a two-bit relay had welded itself shut. Or a resistor had burned out. Or an IC circuit had been jarred just enough to break its connection. Or some unknown inspector in some electronics plant had had a morning hangover and blinked his eyes once too often, okaying a defective bit of chip circuitry.

He glanced uncertainly over the board, then back to the intercom. 'Sensors indicating any leaks? I can't tell up here.'

'A dozen of them, none serious.'

At the pressures now present in the reactor vessel, it wouldn't be long before the leaks opened.

Brandt clutched him by the shoulder and squeezed so hard it hurt. 'What the hell are we going to do, Parks?'

He had never thought that he would see the anguish now written on Brandt's face. He glanced at the others. Cushing was obviously nervous. Walton looked as if he had been betrayed. Abrams had closed his eyes and was rocking slowly back and forth on the balls of his feet. And the tiny puppet on the television set kept pounding one small hand onto the other to make a point.

All except the puppet were waiting for him to tell them that everything was going to be all right.

'... *temperature is fourteen hundred ...*'

The warning panel along the entire back of his control board flashed red and dimmed out.

Delano was back on the intercom, screaming, his voice seeming to come from miles away. 'We've got a LOCA!'

Parks' stomach knotted. Behind him, he heard a groan like wind scything through a field of wheat. Without looking down at his board, he knew that the other reactors were SCRAMing, that Cardenas Bay had just dropped out of the national power grid.

37

Senator Hoyt Mr Parks, for the benefit of the Committee, would you explain again how a reactor core functions? And please remember that we don't have the benefit of your vast experience and education.

Mr Parks I'll try to keep it as simple as possible, sir. The core is actually composed of stacked bundles of twelve-foot-long, dowel-thin metal rods that contain uranium fuel pellets. The fuel pellets emit neutrons but these are so-called fast neutrons – they don't cause fission. Collision with the water surrounding the reactor slows them down and reflects them back into the fuel core. These slowed-down neutrons cause fission, that is,

160

they cause atoms to split in two, which in turn releases energy that heats the water.

Representative Holmburg I'm not sure I understand what a neutron is.

Senator Hoyt Rather than have the witness explain it now, I would like to call the attention of the honourable Representative from Indiana to the testimony of Professor Caulfield three days ago. To go on, Mr Parks, what role do the control rods play?

Mr Parks They absorb neutrons. The pile is brought to critical by flooding the reactor with water and then slowly withdrawing the control rods. This regulates the amount of fission taking place in the pile and therefore the amount of heat being developed.

Senator Hoyt I think I see. And shoving all the control rods back in the pile stops the reaction, is that right?

Mr Parks That's essentially it, Senator, though it's somewhat simplified.

Senator Hoyt And you couldn't shove the control rods back into Prometheus One, is that it?

Mr Parks That's correct.

Senator Stone Mr Parks, let me ask you if the fuel rods themselves met specifications?

Mr Parks Yes, they did, sir.

Senator Stone I mean by actual test, Mr Parks, not by virtue of inspection documents from manufacturers. We've had cases in the past where these have been falsified.

Mr Parks By actual test, Senator.

Senator Hoyt I think we're getting sidetracked here. Why wouldn't the control rods operate in Prometheus One?

Mr Parks The answer's somewhat complicated, Senator. Under high heat and the bombardment of neutrons, the fuel pellets tend to shrink in size and clot in the tubes, leaving empty gaps that may be inches long. The pressure within a reactor is extremely high and can cause a fuel rod to buckle at the point of a gap. In some cases, the rods warp and swell for reasons we're not quite sure of. If they get out of alignment, or if they swell excessively, the control blades may have difficulty entering the core.

Representative Holmburg Then it's actually the fault of the fuel manufacturers for making pellets that don't meet specs.

Mr Parks I wouldn't say that, sir.

Senator Hoyt Why not? It seems obvious to me that the vendor is at fault.

Mr Parks The vendor met the specifications on the fuel pellets, Senator. It's just that we're not quite sure yet exactly what goes on in the heart of the reactor core.
Senator Hoyt I'm afraid I find that answer inadmissible.

38

Two hundred miles north of San Francisco, at the grid-system centre in Eureka Falls, senior dispatcher Robert Moore studied his power map of the western half of the United States. The mimic board showed the main generating plants and switching stations, as well as the interconnecting transmission lines. One of the thin lines flashed red, indicating a transmission line overload; then the computer automatically juggled the output of half a dozen plants and the line faded back to a normal green.

It was going to be a bitch of a night, Moore thought. Every company in the country seemed to be working a night shift. Throw in fifty million electric blankets and television sets and electric stoves and you had one helluva load. If it hadn't been for Cardenas Bay, they would have had to make plans to reduce voltage or else institute a rotating brownout. As it was, even with Grayfield down for repairs, they would end up with a spinning reserve. If the Midwest needed to borrow, for the first time in his memory they would be in a position to lend.

He stared at the board a moment longer, fumbling in his pocket for a handkerchief. The room was kept a constant sixty-eight degrees but he was a man who perspired easily and small drops of sweat kept running down the bridge of his nose and spattering on his desk.

He wiped his face and glanced quickly around the room. It was too hectic a night for anybody to be goofing off. At the far end of the huge room, in a recessed pit, were the giant relays and bus bars for the incoming and outgoing transmission lines. The relays were automatically actuated by computer but several technicians were on standby for manual. If the operation of the grid was too important to leave to human beings, it was also too important to leave to the vagaries of electronics. The usual compromise, Moore thought: Twice the protection at four times the cost.

Nearer to him were the junior dispatchers who listened to the reports flowing in over their headsets and checked the rank of cathode-ray display tubes in front of them, ready to make corrections that slipped past the computer. None of them were looking his way and Moore surreptitiously snapped open his tube of five-milligram Valiums and swallowed one. A night like tonight, his tachycardia could act up and this close to a full pension was no time to be carted away to the hospital.

Everybody was intent on his own screen and Moore punched his console keyboard for the system-load-and-operating summary. The screen flickered and the graph appeared. Ordinarily it would have indicated a power-consumption drop after five, when the industrial plants shut down, but demand had held steady. The power load given up by industries shutting down for the night had been picked up by home users.

He punched another combination on the keyboard and a different diagram appeared – the transmission-and-generation summary, which showed everything from the amount and cost of the power generated by the different plants in the system to the weather and the water levels in the reservoirs for the hydroelectric plants.

A bitch of a night, he thought again, but at least the operation was cool. He lit a cigarette and started to relax when an excited voice over his headset announced, 'Cardenas Bay just dropped out of the grid!'

The computer had picked it up already and was flashing the alarm across the display screen, the words forming rapidly in electronic hieroglyphics. He growled into the mouthpiece, 'What do you mean they just dropped out? They just came on.' It couldn't happen, he thought. Cardenas Bay was generating one-half of the electricity for the entire state. One-half! His heart suddenly started to triple-time. He held his nose and blew out, hard; his heart slowed and fell back into its regular rhythm. Go ahead, scare me to death, he thought, his eyes watering. 'George, what the hell happened to Cardenas? See if you can raise those hotshots, keep trying.'

Emergency readouts flickered rapidly over the face of the console tube. The computer had switched in the spinning reserve but the six thousand megawatts wouldn't be able to make up for Cardenas – they'd probably have to go to brownouts after all. A system diagram now flashed on the screen, one of the transmission lines a bright red. Above it, the legend read: 'Hlsdle 7 to Lawrvl 8' – the line from Hillsdale to Lawrenceville, one of the largest in the state. While he watched, nearby lines also flashed red.

163

'Anybody answering at Cardenas?' He had no idea what had happened at the huge complex but instinctively he knew they wouldn't be back in the grid that night.

Then it hit him and he felt his heart lurch once more. The largest transmission line of all ran through Cardenas and it was now down. The spinning reserve was overloading the rest of the system – the computer was trying to meet the power demand without the lines available to carry it. It should have backed off seconds ago but who knew what the sudden current surge had burned out?

The sweat was now a steady stream down the bridge of his nose. He called for more information from the computer data banks and watched intently as the numbers magically appeared and then erased themselves from his screen.

The system diagram flashed back on the screen. The Hillsdale line was down – the system was vulnerable. His headset now crackled with disaster.

'Overload on Meyersville, they're going out. Sacramento can't carry the load, they're going black, too.'

'Portland just blinked. Seattle's gone.'

'Switching transformer at Ukiah couldn't take the surge. All lines in and out are dead.'

The mimic board danced with flickering red lights that dimmed and died. They were going down like dominoes, each loss putting an additional strain on the rest of the grid. He'd have to do something quick or it would leap the Rockies. If that happened, the entire continent might black out. The national power grid was, in effect, a single unit. An outage in Omaha and Nebraskans might have to draw on electricity generated at Niagara Falls. The spider's web: tug on one strand and you felt the tremors a continent away. Only in this case, the tremors would build up until they were a wave that could threaten the entire grid.

He would have to amputate, he thought. He might be able to save San Diego and everything east of it, but the entire coast above El Cajon would have to go black.

He tore off his headset and picked up the phone to the control room. 'Joe, cut the grid at junctures three-two-nine and eight-seven-zero.'

There was a moment's hesitation. 'You sure you know what you're doing? The whole coast will shut down.'

'Do it. My responsibility.'

On his display screen, a small marker floated across and

touched the system map at two points. Between them, the remaining diagram faded from view.

Suddenly one of the dispatchers clutched at his headset and shouted, 'We're losing security!' At the far end of the room, at the switching banks in the recessed pit, a sheet of blue flame played about a giant relay, momentarily blinding the technicians and dispatchers. Moore blinked and shielded his eyes with his hand; he could smell the acrid stink of ozone and feel his hair stir uneasily at its roots. Deep within the building, he could hear the whine of a generator as it started its quick climb into inaudibility.

The lights flared and went out.

Moore let out his breath and sagged back in his chair, letting the tension drain out of him. He loosened his tie and placed his headset on top of the keyboard console. The collapsing grid was somebody else's baby now.

In the darkness, a voice said, 'Anybody got a flashlight?' There was nervous laughter and another voice said, 'How about a candle? Maybe somebody's got a candle.'

Moore sighed and rummaged around in his bottom drawer for the pint he kept in reserve. It was going to be a long night, the people in San Francisco and Los Angeles were going to need their candles.

But it wasn't all bad, he reflected, unscrewing the bottle cap. His heart felt just fine.

39

'How's the President doing?' Tebbets asked.

Kloster shrugged. 'I watched it for a while upstairs. They plugged in Cardenas and you'd think it was the greatest thing since Armstrong walked on the moon. Other than that, you hear one Presidential speech, you've heard them all.' He looked at Tebbets curiously. 'Just dropping in again?'

'Working a double shift,' Tebbets said. 'Malcolm came down with the flu and they couldn't dig up a replacement soon enough.'

'You must get sick and tired of this.'

'It's better than watching television.' He said it as a gag and was startled to realize there was an element of truth to it. He had the feeling it was the same for Kloster and that the Captain had settled in for at least half the night.

'How are the brownouts?'

'They're not getting any worse – and with Cardenas in the grid, they can only get better. You want the overview?' He spoke into his chest mike and an outline map of the United States appeared on the screen, covered with a fine network of lines linking large bright-red dots. 'That's a simplified power grid showing the major transmission lines and generating stations. The really large one on the coast is Cardenas.'

He had just gone back to swirling the grounds in the bottom of his cup when Kloster said, 'There's something wrong with the screen.'

Tebbets looked up immediately. 'You're putting me on. What?'

'The red spot that's supposed to be Cardenas. It just went out.'

40

In San Francisco, the penthouse party at the Mark Hopkins was in full swing. The last of the theatre crowd had arrived and the waiters had broken open the second case of champagne. Suzanne Fast stood by herself on the small balcony overlooking the city. You could see everything from up here, she thought – the bay and the bridge and, twinkling on the far shore, the lights of the Berkeley hills. *Wanted: cty w vu.* Like everything else she'd gotten out of life, she'd had to pay for it. A quarter a look. Perhaps if she bought one of those sightseeing telescopes, she could amortize the apartment.

'Lonely?'

No knight on white charger, no big butter-and-egg man to take her away from all of this. Just Peter Maxey, the accompanist for the ballet troupe. Fifteen years her junior and a regular at all of her parties. According to the gossip columnists, he 'adored' her. Well, a cat could look at a king, she supposed. So Peter Maxey could look at a woman. And a fat lot of good it would do either of them.

'I'm always lonely.'

'That's because you want to be.' He leaned his elbows on

the railing and looked down at the city with her – a thin young man who was charming despite some of his associations. He at least had the saving grace of being full of life, something of a rarity in her circles.

'Sue.' He glanced at her in mock reproof. 'This is the first dull party you've ever given.'

She couldn't make up her mind whether to be offended or amused and on pure whim chose the latter. 'You don't invite actors to a party in hopes that they'll be interested in you, Peter. You're supposed to be interested in them.'

She turned back to look out at the city and it was at that moment the lights went out.

The music stopped inside the apartment and there was a sudden hubbub of voices. Odd, she thought. There wasn't a light anyplace, not even on the bridge. And then she remembered her party. 'I've got some candles, Peter. I better go in and find them for the guests.'

He moved closer to her. 'Why not let them look, Sue?'

The faint odour of lime. She approved of that. 'I suppose I could. But the food will get cold.'

'Not crêpes. Not unless the sterno runs out.'

It was getting to be fun. 'This happened in New York once, remember, Peter? They had a baby boom nine months later.'

He smiled at her and she wished it was another man who was standing on the balcony with her. She was tired of playing bosom buddies. 'Without television,' he said, 'there's not much else to do.' He put his arm around her waist and for the first time in years she felt something close to astonishment. 'It's a dull party,' he reminded her. He seemed oddly earnest.

'So you want to short-circuit it.'

'You're lonely,' he said. 'And you shouldn't be. You're a very attractive woman—'

'—for a woman my age.'

'For any age,' he said. He lightly brushed the hair away from her ears.

'I appreciate the effort, Peter,' she said, suddenly very tired. 'And that's the point – I know it's an effort. You're not exactly a ladies' man.'

She regretted it the moment she said it but he wasn't offended. 'Whether or not I go to bed with someone,' he said, matter-of-fact, 'depends on how much I like them.'

Coldly: 'And tonight you want to go to bed with me. You've got to be kidding.'

167

'Right on the first count,' he said cheerfully. 'And wrong on the second.' He kissed her for a long moment and she realized with sudden shock that he wasn't kidding after all.

Well, there was plenty of champagne and crêpes. And the party *was* dull and, perhaps worst of all, nobody would miss her if she left. Besides, she remembered, taking Peter by the hand, she had always promised herself that when the end of the world came, this was the way she was going to go ...

On the Santa Monica freeway, Joseph Yarbro pushed his rig close to the fifty-five-mile-an-hour speed limit, working the gears with the skill of twenty years on the road. He wanted to reach the warehouse before it was completely dark. The doctors had told him he had poor night vision and he didn't want to push his luck. He half smiled to himself. Pile this rig up and there would be the biggest omelette Los Angeles had ever seen, right smack in the middle of the freeway.

He squinted his eyes against the rays of the fading sun. Tricky time to drive, right at dusk. Then the highway lights came on and he sighed with relief. Every little bit helped. He started jockeying over into the far lane and looking ahead for the off ramp. The Caddy on his right wasn't going to let him in; he dropped back and then started to cut over. Thank God the off ramp was well lighted. Sometimes they could sneak up on you ... He glanced at his watch. Five minutes more and he'd be at the warehouse, relaxing.

He ground gears and crept over the top of the hill. On the other side, he plunged abruptly into darkness. The city around him had vanished; the sky ahead was pitch black and blazing with stars. The highway lights were off, as were those in the houses on either side of the road. There were no lights at all, none except for those of the automobiles coming towards him. Power failure someplace, he thought, a massive one. His pupils struggled to open wider. He leaned closer to the windshield, peering frantically out at the side of the road. It should be right about here ...

He spotted it and tugged at the wheel, then panicked when he realized he was going too fast, that the off ramp was too close. He braked and the rig began to fishtail. He tried frantically to straighten it. Suddenly he felt the trailer behind him break free. He wasn't going to make it to the warehouse after all, he thought with mild surprise.

What he was going to do was jackknife across four lanes of oncoming traffic.

In Beverly Hills, Gloria Marks locked the doors of the Acme Theatrical Agency, Inc., and impatiently pressed the button for the elevator that would take her to the basement parking lot. It had been a long day – there had been contracts to go over and then there was the brat whose mother thought she was another Shirley Temple. Commercials, she had kept repeating, the money's in commercials, not modelling kids' clothes for a department-store catalogue.

'Working late, huh?'

She hadn't heard him come up. Big, early thirties, heavy five-o'clock shadow. She had seen him before and he had always given her the eye – a peculiar look that had made her glad other people were around. Tonight, however, they were alone.

She gave him the cold-fish look. 'Yeah.'

'You an actress?'

Not by ten years, twenty pounds and a whole helluva lot of talent, she wasn't. 'Guess again. Just a secretary.'

'My name's Harry.'

Bored. 'That doesn't mean I have to tell you mine.'

The elevator came and she got in. He followed right behind her, standing close. She punched the lobby button instead of the parking lot. No sense asking for trouble. She'd shake the creep, then come back for her car.

The cab started down. It was between the tenth and ninth floors that the lights went out. The cab jolted to a halt.

She just stood there in the darkness, for the moment too puzzled and bewildered to be frightened.

'I think we ought to get to know each other better,' a voice said in her ear.

Burt Fields caught the BART train at the MacArthur station in Berkeley, found himself a seat and immediately turned to the stock-market reports. In ten minutes or less he'd be at the Montgomery Street Station in San Francisco and then he'd grab a cab to North Beach – he was already late for dinner with Diane. He settled back and concentrated intently on what Polaroid and Xerox were doing, shutting out the world and his fellow passengers and especially the knowledge that he was zipping through a three-point-six-mile tube that was buried under millions of tons of water. If he let himself think about that, his claustrophobia would get completely out of hand.

He had just started doing some calculations in the margins of the page when the lights began to flicker and the train unaccountably to slow. His stomach lurched a little. Not a stall beneath the bay. It had happened to him once before and for the five minutes that he had sat there, it was all he could do to keep from screaming.

Other passengers began to murmur. Then the lights went out for good. He was in complete darkness while the train gradually coasted to a halt. This time he knew it wasn't just a temporary stall, that they'd be there for ... hours.

Matches flared throughout the car and died. In the blackness that followed, he couldn't see his hand in front of his face. Here I am, underneath the bay with ... millions ... of ... tons ... of ... water ... pressing ... pressing ... pressing ...

It took three passengers to stuff a handkerchief into his mouth to smother his screaming.

In Santa Barbara, Frank Johnson opened another can of beer and settled back on the couch to watch the President's speech. What had the papers said? Something about the energy crisis being solved?

'My fellow citizens ...'

The common touch, he thought approvingly. Nobody'd had it since Truman. He took a long gulp of beer. The speech was supposed to take fifteen minutes and afterwards there was that Hawaii cop show. It was going to be a great night for watching the tube and drinking cold beer and just plain relaxing.

'... at the very moment that I am talking to you, the Prometheus nuclear complex is feeding twelve thousand megawatts of electricity into the national power grid. By itself, this complex could supply the entire energy needs of Los Angeles and San Francisco combined. And without using a single barrel of oil!'

'You hear that, Martha?'

There was an indistinct reply from the kitchen.

'... just the first of a series of standardized plants to be constructed ...'

And then the sound went out. The picture on the tube wavered for a moment, shrank in towards the centre and vanished.

He took another sip of beer and waited for the picture to

reappear – it was a new set, it had to be station difficulty.

'You going to sit all night in front of that thing? Go check the circuit breaker.'

He could barely make out his wife, standing in the kitchen doorway. He struggled to his feet, feeling a little foolish. The set was completely dead and there wasn't a light on in the house. It also seemed oddly quiet – the hum of the dishwasher and the furnace was missing.

'I'll be damned, Martha.' He waddled over to a nearby window. It looked like all the lights in town were out as well. He turned and glanced accusingly at the television set.

What the hell had happened to all those mega-whatevers?

41

For a brief moment, there was absolute quiet on the balcony except for the sound of Delano's voice crackling over the intercom. Parks sensed the fear in his voice.

Behind him, he could hear the chief of the television crew asking, 'What happened? What's a LOCA?'

Walton, his voice strained: 'It's a loss-of-coolant accident – a pipe bursts and we lose all the water in the reactor vessel—'

'Is that serious?'

Parks leaned towards the intercom. 'Give me a situation report, Delano.'

Delano's voice was tight and controlled. 'Guillotine cut in a recirculating pipe to Prometheus One. Can't check – access to the utility tunnel is impossible, the blowdown is flooding it. Estimate ten percent water will be left in the reactor vessel in fifteen minutes.'

The nuclear reaction would stop without the water, Parks thought. But the decay heat of the plutonium and other reaction products in the fuel rods would raise the temperature of the core twelve degrees a second.

Brandt was breathing in his ear. 'The cause, goddamnit!'

'What did it, Delano?'

'Don't know for sure. Peterson thinks it's a failure of the pipe at the weld to the reactor vessel. Flexing and a hairline crack would probably do it.'

'... *average temperature is now twelve hundred degrees* ...'

The steam and water blowing out through the broken pipe had reduced the heat somewhat but the temperature was rising again. Parks started to sweat. The emergency cooling system should have come on seconds ago, unless the massive blow-down had crippled the water-level sensors. The longer the delay, the worse it would get. Some of the fuel rods were probably perforated and leaking by now because of internal gas-pressure buildup.

'... *thirteen hundred eighty* ...'

'Greg.' Delano was on the intercom again, sounding relieved. 'The board shows the sprayers and pumps have just turned on; we should be able to flood the core.'

'Not very damn likely,' Brandt muttered. 'Not with a three-foot-diameter pipe broken in two and stream pressure behind the water head.'

'The sprays will wet down the fuel rods,' Parks said. 'They'll be forcing nine thousand gallons of water a minute into the reactor vessel.'

There was the rumble of a small explosion from far below. The cold water hitting the hot core must have flashed immediately into steam and blown back the rest of the coolant, Parks thought, fighting down his panic. He wondered if the vapour barrier would prevent any more water from reaching the core.

Delano was chattering over the intercom, his voice hoarse. 'The explosion blew out the sparger rings. We're not getting any spray!'

On his control board, the cathode-ray display screens for Prometheus One had gone blank, as had a whole section of panel light indicators. Almost all of the in-core sensors must have been destroyed, Parks thought.

'... *fourteen hundred twenty* ...'

That was the average. There were sections of the core that were closer to two thousand. And Zircaloy melted at a little over thirty-three hundred degrees, uranium oxide at around five thousand. They had, at most, five minutes before the core started to slump and melt into the bottom of the reactor vessel. My God, and then there were Prometheus reactors two, three and four ...

He lunged for the intercom. 'Delano – did the computer SCRAM the other reactors?'

Hesitation. 'Our indicators down here say it did – at the same time we dropped out of the grid.'

'Don't trust your indicators – try a manual.'

'Can't – steam explosion's knocked out the main and back-up systems, the drive mechanisms for the other control rods won't activate.' Parks could almost see Delano shake his head in frustration. 'We can't try it by hand, either, Greg. The corridor outside is filled with live steam.'

Parks stared at the intercom. Then, inanely: 'Can you and your men get out of there?'

There was sudden static on the intercom and Delano started to fade in and out '... depends ... water ... boil away sometime ...'

Parks sank back into the console seat, the disaster for the first time assuming a human dimension. He was only vaguely aware of the newsmen arguing with Walton in one corner of the balcony.

'... don't know what the hell is going on but you guys are in big trouble, aren't you?'

'... told you – it's a temporary malfunction. We'll be back on stream in the morning.'

'... bullshit – I've covered nuclear plants before, you'll be shut down for six months.'

Brandt cut in. 'Get them to hell out of here, Walton. Now.'

It sounded too much like thieves falling out. Parks turned away to stare through the thick, lead-glass windows of the balcony at the main reactor room below. Something was happening on the floor. Half a dozen men were standing around uncertainly, their heads cocked as if they were listening to something.

Brandt jogged his elbow. 'Any chance of flooding it manually?'

Parks shook his head. 'Not unless you stood on the top and hosed it down by hand. I don't think you'd find any volunteers for that job.'

'How long will the meltdown take?'

Parks did some quick mental calculations. 'In a few minutes the rods will begin to melt, give a few more for the fuel itself to start to go. Ten minutes to an hour for everything to drip or fall on the grid plate, another hour for the debris and the grid plate to melt through or collapse to the bottom of the vessel head. Maybe another sixty minutes to melt through the vessel head, probably less. Then there's five feet of concrete. A few hours, maybe a few days to break that down and breach the containment.'

'... *sixteen hundred and fifty* ...'

'The variables?'

'Too goddamned many,' he said tensely. 'It could go a helluva lot faster than that.'

The intercom sputtered back to life. '... vibrations ... other recirculating pipes ... tunnel's flooded ... steam backlash ... a lot of voids are hitting those pipes.'

That had been what the technicians had been listening to, Parks realized. The superheated steam and the air bubbles in the boiling water, pounding at the other pipes in the common utility tunnel. They weren't built to take that kind of punishment – even discounting fracture lines and the possibility of metal fatigue and subsequent embrittlement.

'If you know of any experts on core meltdowns, Brandt, now's the time to call them.'

'There are no experts,' Brandt said slowly. 'We relied on computer model studies. We should have tried the Admiral's test. Actually melt one down and see what—'

Delano's static-filled voice cut him off. 'LOCAs! Reactors two and four ... steam explosion in the utility tunnel.'

Cushing, Walton and Abrams edged closer to the intercom to listen. Parks glanced up at the frightened public relations man. 'You had your chance to leave with the newsmen, Jerry. Too bad you passed it up.'

Cushing said, 'The piles were SCRAMed, weren't they?'

Parks shrugged. 'It doesn't matter whether the control rods were in or out – you lose your water, the reaction stops. But the decay heat will be as bad as in Prometheus One.'

Delano was back on the intercom. '... no emergency cooling ... reactor water supply knocked out ...'

'Christ – Delano, get out of there!'

There was a burst of static from the speaker and then it died.

'... *eighteen hundred degrees and rising* ...'

They looked at each other for a long moment and then Brandt said, 'Do you think they stand a chance of getting out of there?'

'No,' Parks said desperately. 'No, I don't think they stand a chance in hell.'

42

In Control Central, the steady hum of computer tapes filled the air, counterpointed by an irregular clicking as the CRT display screens switched to different views within the reactor cores. Almost all of the views were blank; most of the in-core television pickups had been destroyed – the two pickups still operating in Prometheus Three showed a close-up view of eight inches of fuel rod bundle. In the background, the voice of the computer recited the core temperatures in a low, mechanical overtone.

'Situation report on reactor two, Carr.'

Carr's voice was high-pitched and nervous. 'Temperature climbing, no slump yet. Estimate half the fuel rods perforated and leaking. Effluent-gas detectors also inoperative, but we must be getting lots of hydrogen and noble gases.'

Reactors three and four were as bad; Delano dutifully reported it over the intercom. It was then that he realized that Parks was strangely silent. He placed a telephone call to the balcony and verified that the phones were also cut. The one place where there should have been redundancy, there wasn't any. All the communication lines had been bundled together and when one of them had gone, all of them had gone. They were now completely cut off. He decided not to tell the others.

He made meaningless scratches on his clipboard, then doodled a figure of a tree and another of a little girl. *Wait until your daddy gets home* ... He could hear Edith telling Jennifer that right now, it was a regular suppertime refrain. But Daddy would be just a little late tonight ...

He glanced at the others in the room. Carr would be the first to crack, he thought. Carr and Melton. The would-be comics always blew up first; they never had much self-discipline.

His job was to keep them from panicking so they could take advantage of a break if any came their way. Slim chance, but where there was life ...

'Prometheus One, Reynolds.'

'All indicators are out, no screen displays available. Estimate clad melting has started; core slump in two to three minutes.'

Reynolds was married and had two kids, one going to UCLA. Literature major. Reynolds had wanted him to go into engineering but the kid wanted to be a writer. Looked like a writer, slump-shouldered, with thick glasses ...

'Give me the views on three, Melton.' At least he could actually watch a core melt. If they did get out, the observation would be invaluable.

The view came on and Delano switched it over to his own control board. The screen showed a section of fuel rod bundle held together by rod-spacer clips. He watched for a second. Nothing. That particular section might not be hot enough, he thought, and then he caught it. A slight shininess and the slow formation of a drop of metal near a spacer clip. A moment later the drops were a steady flow and he could see the rods visibly grow thinner.

'OK, Melton, switch it.' The view had been unnerving. He couldn't tell what the others were thinking about the melting rods but it must have pushed them out of shape. They were getting hard for him to read, which was bad. He wasn't sure what was going on behind their carefully blank faces.

He felt somebody looking at him and glanced up from his clipboard. Reynolds was staring at him, his face white. 'Max, I think the grid plate is going in Prometheus One.'

It couldn't be, Delano thought, startled. The core melt in Prometheus One should be proceeding by steps, at least according to every computer study they had ever made. It should melt partway down the inside of the reactor vessel, solidify, then melt again. It would take time for the core to melt and collapse on the grid plate, then the plate itself would have to melt through and that would take even more time.

The others were watching Reynolds silently. Several seconds passed and Delano subconsciously noted that the computer loudspeaker had announced the meltdown temperature for the fuel rods in the other reactors.

'Any other indicators registering, Reynolds?'

'No, sir, almost all of the sensors are out. One stress sensor near the grid plate was reading high.'

There might be two hundred tons of debris on that plate, Delano thought. Maybe more. And who knew how much metal fatigue the plate had suffered during the last six months of low-level operation? You couldn't pull it out and test it.

'Report on Prometheus Two, Carr.'

Carr spun out of his chair so Delano had a clear view of the red-lit bench board. 'Why don't you look for yourself, Max?'

'I didn't ask you to show me, I asked you to tell me.'

Melton turned around in his seat, leaned back against the

Prometheus Four Console and lit a cigarette. 'Who you kidding, Max? All the cores are melting and there's nothing we can do about it; there's certainly no point in logging it all down. We can't get out of here – we're trapped.'

'No smoking,' Delano said quietly. 'Put it out.'

Reynolds cleared his throat. 'Max, what's going to happen?'

Melton caught on when he hesitated a moment too long before answering. 'The phones aren't operating, are they? And I'll bet the intercom isn't either, is it?'

Delano ignored him. 'What's happening – what will happen – is that sooner or later they'll cut off the water, and after the remaining boil-off, steam won't be a problem. The cores are melting but the grid plates should hold up the debris for an hour or so. Even if the cores should fall into the vessel heads, it will be a few hours before they melt through.'

'There's water in the bottom of the reactor vessels,' Carr said, his voice full of suspicion. 'There'll be steam and we'll be running the risk of hydrogen explosions.'

Delano shrugged. 'It won't matter, Carr, because we'll be out of here by then. When the boil-off is over, we'll leave. It'll be hot but we should be able to make it to the exit stairs.'

There was a clicking from Reynolds' bench board and he turned to look at it. He sucked in his breath and said, almost inaudibly, 'The grid plate's gone.'

God would forgive him, Delano thought, shaken. He had done what he could. A moment later the explosion came, rocking the control room. Cracks snaked down the walls and a hot, wet fog began to seep into the room.

Carr muttered, 'I'm getting out of here.' He bolted for the door, Melton and Reynolds close behind. Delano clutched at Reynolds, got a handful of damp shirt, then let go when Reynolds threw a wild punch at him. A second later all three were racing down the fog-filled, steaming corridor. Delano stopped in the doorway, listening to the muffled sounds of their footsteps, the scorching steam soaking his shirt and trousers. He started to yell at them to come back but the words died in his throat. Come back to what? They might even make it. He waited a moment, the steam burning his face, and then, in the corridor far ahead, hidden by the steam, he heard the three men screaming.

Carr suddenly stumbled out of the fog, his face blistered and glowing. He clawed at Delano. 'Help me,' he mumbled, and collapsed at Delano's feet. Delano heard other faltering footsteps in the fog. He stepped back and slammed the door.

'You're locking them out!' Young yelled.

'Yeah, I'm locking them out.' Delano shivered with reaction. 'The last explosion breached the primary containment, some of the fuel spewed out, along with the steam.' He shook his head, wanting to cry. 'Carr was covered with it, there was no way we could have decontaminated him – we'd only have contaminated ourselves.'

The lights in the room abruptly flickered out. Small, battery-operated lanterns in the corners came on automatically, throwing gigantic shadows towards the centre of the room. The air conditioning had stopped. The room was now deathly quiet and, Delano realized, stifling hot. He lit a match to read the wall thermometer. A hundred and ten degrees and rising as he watched. A line must have ruptured close by; the room was turning into a steambath.

Someone was pounding at the door; the pounding dissolved in muffled and strangled shouts. Delano and Young stared at each other; neither made a move towards the door. Delano had become oddly philosophic and detached. The possibility of death made you heroic, he thought. The probability made you selfish and weak and desperate, even when you only had a little longer to live yourself – the reason why most heroes were young.

Carr and Melton and Reynolds. Dear Jesus . . .

A hundred and fifty degrees and rising rapidly. It was very real now – he was roasting, his eyelids were beginning to puff and he couldn't breathe. He gasped, 'The shower,' and they both ran for the decontamination stall in the corner. They fought briefly, without shame, for space in the small cubicle. Delano won and twisted frantically at the faucet; water gushed out and he filled his lungs with the now breathable air around him. Young squeezed in beside him and the warm water soaked both of them.

Delano threw his head back, letting the water run down his blistered face and chest. *I'll be a little late—*

Then the water turned to live steam.

43

The calls started coming in immediately from the outlying sections of the complex. Parks took them on the console phone, his eyes constantly flicking over the readout screens and meters. After the last call, he put down the phone and said, 'That was O'Malley in Reprocessing. He wanted to know what everybody else wants to know – if we're going to evacuate. I said no.' He glanced at Cushing. 'Did I tell him the right thing?'

Cushing's face was a mask. 'That's your decision.'

'I should have known better than to ask.' He didn't bother with Walton.

Brandt found it difficult to meet his eyes. 'I couldn't blame you if you ordered it, Parks.'

'*You* can order it if you want to,' Parks snapped, then realized that Brandt could never bring himself to do it.

Walton asked nervously, 'Are we in any immediate danger?'

'You mean the plant and everybody in it,' Parks corrected, 'not just "we." The answer is no, not yet. Emergency doors have blocked off the lower levels; that should contain the steam and any contaminants. If radioactives get into the air up here—' He shrugged. 'Then we'll have to get out.'

'So what do we do now?'

'There's nothing we can do,' he said tightly. 'We can't run the plant from up here; both the intercom and phones to Control Central are out.'

'What about the security camera?' Abrams asked.

He had forgotten about that. At least they could see what had happened down there. He switched on the small monitor above the control panel. The screen showed only swirling clouds of white. 'Steam from the blowdown and the ruptured steam lines.' They watched as the camera slowly scanned the room. Rifts appeared in the cloud; the room was baking out. Parks could see the bench boards – the camera was designed for low light levels – but not much else. The room looked deserted and for a brief moment he thought that Delano and his men must have gotten out.

'The corner,' Brandt said suddenly. 'The decontamination shower.'

Parks stopped the scanning and adjusted the zoom. They stared for a moment and Abrams said, 'Oh, my God . . .' Then the camera lens fogged over. Parks turned the monitor off.

He'd have to tell the families. He'd have to go hat in hand and say, About your husband, Mrs Delano . . .

'There'll be a Congressional investigation,' Cushing said.

'You'll get your chance on the stand, if that's what you're worried about, Eliot – and so will I,' Brandt muttered. He hunched forward in his chair and kneaded his knuckles. 'The explosions shouldn't have happened that soon.'

Parks was still thinking about the scene in Control Central. The other men must be dead, too, even if he hadn't seen their bodies. He shook his head, trying to clear his mind of the picture on the monitor. 'It must have been a steam explosion – the grid plate probably collapsed and dumped the molten debris into the water at the bottom.'

'It was too soon,' Brandt said again, almost to himself. He sounded old and lost and querulous. The plant was down the tubes and Western Gas and Electric, the company that Brandt had saved a dozen times in the past, would probably go with it. Parks didn't know whether he felt pity for Brandt because of the loss or because the man had aged so much so quickly.

'There could have been four hundred tons of debris on that plate. The weight plus the heat and any metal fatigue could have done it.'

'What about the other reactors?'

'They could go the same way, probably will. Number three is still intact but it will go. And there'll be more steam explosions.'

'There's also the danger of radioactivity,' Cushing added sharply.

Parks snapped then. 'No shit, Cushing! Goddamnit, what the hell do you think I've been talking about for the last three days? Did you ever bother to read my reports? There'll be one helluva lot of radioactive gases plus tons of vaporized uranium and plutonium; tomorrow this plant will be leaking like a sieve. If any explosion breaches the secondary containment . . .'

'I'm familiar with the possibilities, Parks.'

'No, you're not, Cushing. For one thing, your computer studies are ten years out of date. For another, you're not dealing with just one reactor – you're dealing with four, and any one of them is the largest in the world. Multiply your computer study by four and you might come close.'

'Take it easy, Parks,' Brandt said quietly.

For three days he had put up with the bastard; he was too angry to take it easy. 'You called Washington again, Cushing –

what are they going to do besides send us some experts in the morning?'

'I tried to reach the Secretary,' Cushing said stiffly. 'He was out for the evening – they took the message; he'll get it as soon as they can locate him.'

'You tried to reach the Secretary,' Parks mimicked. 'Is that the special plan in case of disasters? Make a report and have a team sent to investigate?'

Walton said, 'Look, Parks, you're not the only one who's under a strain.'

The ex-college quarterback trying to keep his teammates from fighting, Parks thought. 'All this means to you is bad publicity – right, Jerry?' His voice was acid.

'It'll give the company a helluva black eye,' Walton said.

Parks could feel himself shaking on the inside. The control board was nearly blank now, almost all of the connections to the main control room had been cut. There was nothing he could do, he thought, sick with frustration. And none of them, not even Brandt, realized what could happen. Everything about the complex had been outsize from the beginning, including the potential for disaster. But nobody seemed able to grasp the possibilities in terms of human life. It wasn't just a matter of a five-billion-dollar plant or twelve thousand megawatts. Delano and Young and the others were just the first instalment of what might be a far more tragic disaster.

The voice of the computer had been droning in the background but Parks ignored it. Now, in the silence, he was abruptly aware of it again.

'. . . thirty-five hundred degrees and rising . . .'

'Parks.' Brandt had the pleading look on his face again, only this time it seemed more natural. Everything came easier with practice, Parks thought. 'What do we do?'

'We stay right here. Until we have to leave. We can't walk away but we can't stop it, either. Do you understand that, Hilary? There's nothing we can do. Nothing.'

A rumbling shook the balcony from somewhere below, followed by the heavy, almost subsonic feel of a major explosion. The balcony shivered and there was a splintering sound from the thick balcony windows. The plant floor below buckled suddenly and a sudden gout of steam spewed from the base of reactor three. They were all gone now. Concrete and dust and steam drifted into the main reactor room.

The console broke into a steady beep-beep-beep. The radioactive-gas alarm – effluents were leaking into the building proper.

Parks hit the red EVACUATION button on the control board; loud klaxon horns echoed throughout the plant. He slipped from his seat and yelled, 'Get the hell out, take the chute!'

Cushing and Walton sprinted down the corridor. Brandt was leaning against the balcony windows, staring at the floor below. He looked as if he were in shock.

'Brandt!' There was no answer. Parks dashed over and shook him, then grabbed him by the shoulders and jerked him around, slapping him as hard as he could.

The look of shock faded and Brandt said thickly, 'Which way? I . . . I can't remember.'

'Follow me.' He turned again and ran down the hall, feeling other explosions ripple the floor beneath him. He sensed that Brandt was right on his heels.

Heavy blasts shook the building as he slid down the emergency chute to the ground. More steam and hydrogen explosions, he thought, blowing apart the reactor vessels and their primary containments and rupturing the walls of the building itself.

The very worst had happened. The plant was now spewing a heavy stream of radioactive steam and gases and vaporized fuel into the night sky to be caught by the gusting winds. And down below, in the bowels of the complex, thousands of tons of molten uranium and steel were eating their way through the concrete containments and melting into the ground beneath.

44

Senator Hoyt Mr Parks, at the time of the disaster there were three people on the plant balcony in a decision-making capacity. You, Mr Brandt and Mr Cushing. I think it's important that we know how you would characterize your relationship with the others.

Mr Parks I'm not sure I understand you.

Senator Hoyt Did you like them or dislike them, did you respect their opinions – I guess that's what I'm driving at.

Mr Parks I respected Hilary Brandt. I can't say the same for Eliot Cushing.

Senator Hoyt I take it you disliked Eliot Cushing.

Mr Parks I did and do, Senator, but I don't see why that's especially important.

Representative Holmburg I think it's pretty simple, Mr Parks. You made a number of unilateral decisions without consulting either Mr Brandt or Mr Cushing.

Mr Parks That isn't true, sir. They both ranked me, they could have countermanded my orders at any point. Hilary Brandt had even relieved me and then asked me to return. But it doesn't matter, there was damn little to consult about. There was nothing anybody could do.

Senator Hoyt That's difficult to believe. From the testimony of Mr Caulfield, the plant had numerous backup control systems. You mean to say that all of them were out?

Mr Parks That's right.

Senator Hoyt You mentioned that the failure of the grid plates was the reason for the initial steam explosions and indirectly for the final hydrogen explosions that destroyed the plant. Would you explain?

Mr Parks The grid plate holds up the fuel assembly. During the course of a meltdown, the molten fuel – that portion which didn't actually flow through the grid – unmelted fuel pellets and pieces of zirconium rods and steel channels would collect on it. Our computer studies indicated that it would take approximately an hour for the grid plate to melt through. Apparently, in this case the failure was mechanical – the grid plate collapsed under the weight of the debris, which I would estimate at four hundred tons. The debris fell into the pressure suppression pool at the bottom, resulting in the steam explosions. There were some hydrogen explosions as well.

Representative Holmburg Hydrogen explosions?

Mr Parks A superheated metal immersed in water will cause a water-metal reaction – the water will break down into hydrogen and metal oxide. The hydrogen builds up and you then run the risk not only of overpressurization but of actual explosions.

Representative Holmburg Maybe some of my colleagues can make sense out of that statement but I'm afraid you've lost me.

Mr Parks It's simple high school science, sir.

Representative Holmburg I'm sorry to say that when I was in high school, I spent more time on the football field than in the science lab.

Senator Hoyt I'd like to get back to that grid plate, Mr Parks. I don't want to sound like I've got a one-track mind but this strikes me as another vendor problem. In previous testimony, you said that your fuel pellets weren't acting as specified but for some reason that I still don't understand, the vendor was not to blame. Now you're telling us that the grid plate didn't act as specified. I suppose the vendor's not to blame in this case, either?

Mr Parks That's correct, Senator. Everything may meet specifications and still fail in the reactor. Maybe I should say that since much of what happens in the core of the reactor is unknown to us, it's difficult to draw up specifications in the first place.

Representative Holmburg It sounds like you're saying that the disaster was nobody's fault at all, that it was an act of God.

Mr Parks Maybe it was – but an act of God that had a lot of assistance from sloppy workmanship, incompetent vendors and a deadline that didn't give us adequate time for testing prior to going on stream.

Senator Hoyt You're making a speech, Mr Parks. Was it somebody's fault or wasn't it?

Mr Parks I think you want simple answers, Senator. Unfortunately, it wasn't a simple situation.

45

The first major explosion reverberated through the underground corridors within seconds after Paul Marical had left the reprocessing plant. There had been a minor explosion minutes before. The technicians exchanged worried glances and stopped work, waiting for an announcement over the loudspeaker system. The plant intercom remained mute and they gradually resumed working, but Marical could sense the underlying tension. Something had gone wrong but nobody knew what. Minutes later, the lighting system shifted to emergency power. Marical detected a brief flicker in the lights; if he hadn't known what it was, he wouldn't have caught it.

This time the explosion was a heavy one, the sound of it rolling down the corridor and shaking dust from the ceiling.

Marical pulled his electricar over to one side of the long passageway and listened, frowning. What the hell was up? For a moment it was ominously quiet and then the evacuation alarm sounded, its piercing *whoop-whoop-whoop* echoing throughout the plant.

He heard the sound of running feet in the cross corridors and several electricars roared past him. One of the drivers leaned over to yell, 'Get your ass out of here, Marical – there're radioactives in the air system!'

Of course there were, he thought – that was what the evacuation alarm was all about. What had happened? He puzzled about it for a moment, then edged the car back into the corridor and accelerated down the passageway, passing deserted storage rooms and empty reprocessing cells. Finally, he turned into a dead-end corridor. He parked the electricar at the small access door at the far end, got out and leaned against the wall to listen.

Nothing, not a sound. The plant was completely deserted. No technicians, no typists, no supervisors and no guards. Nobody who would wonder about the deserted electricar, nobody who would think to check up on him. It couldn't be better if he had planned it that way.

But what the hell had gone wrong up above?

He opened the access door and quickly slipped in, then walked hurriedly down to the grotto. He had smuggled in a kid's wagon months before, carrying it in piece by piece and rebuilding it on his lunch hours whenever he could slip away, carefully bracing it so it could carry hundreds of pounds. Most of the weight would be lead, the rest would be twenty-five pounds or so of partially refined plutonium. He hoped to hell the wagon would hold together; it was going to be rough travelling.

He opened the clothing locker and took out a white radiation suit, complete with boots and gloves and the special hood with its filters and miniature life-support system. If there were radioactives in the air-conditioning system, he was all set. He checked the oxygen tank – enough air for almost half an hour if he needed it.

Behind the small cell he had hollowed out for the lead chests, hidden beneath crumbled limestone, was the wagon. What'd they call them when he was a kid? American Flyers? He dragged out the lead chests and arranged them in the wagon, then pulled it towards the grotto entrance. The limestone was a blessing; if the wagon were on soft ground, it would sink up to its hubs.

The cord of lights stretching away into the darkness marked the path. It was the logical way to the sea exit through which the plant pumped its waste water. But he had explored it on one extended lunch break and knew it would be impossible to get the casks out that way. The path was too rough and at one point a deep crevasse ran across it, the boards that had bridged it lying in a jumble at the bottom. He found another way – the only other way, to the best of his knowledge – that would be difficult but at least passable. He would have to manhandle the casks across the small gullies and reload the wagon on the other side, but it shouldn't take two hours. He'd be at the sea exit long before his contacts were due to meet him with a boat. Even if he were late, they'd wait. They weren't about to leave before he got there.

He'd take the money they had promised him for the fissionables and slip ashore, and that would be the last anybody would ever see of Paul Marical. It would be a man with a different face and a different name who would listen to the radio and read the newspapers with pride about what one Paul Marical had done.

Maybe. If he were still alive.

He heard the rumble of another explosion and small chips of limestone rattled down from the cavern roof. He glanced up. What the hell was happening up above? Whatever it was had emptied the plant and had given him a free hand – freer than he had planned on when they had moved up the on-stream date – but it was also making him damned uneasy.

Still another explosion. He waited while the sound of it echoed throughout the huge cavern, and then the thought struck him that perhaps the plant had been sabotaged. He considered it for a long moment – as far as he was concerned, the more things that went wrong the merrier – then dismissed the possibility. Plant security was laughable; the complex could be sabotaged any time but he couldn't think of anybody there who might want to do it. Not even the Israeli, the plant's captive radical. Lerner was always shooting off his mouth about the state of the world, Marical thought, but he had pinned him once in an argument. Underneath, Lerner was like all the other radicals he had ever met – Republicans with guilt complexes. They all wound up selling insurance and raising their kids in lily-white suburbs.

Raising their kids . . .

The echoes dwindled in the distance and he made up his mind; he dropped the handle of the loaded wagon and retraced his steps to the access door. He'd have to check it out and not just because of curiosity. Whatever was going on could conceivably affect his delivery at the sea exit and he'd invested too much blood and too many months preparing for it.

He stopped at the clothing locker and rummaged around in the bottom for the pistol he had hidden. He found it, checked it and shoved it into the pocket of his radiation suit. He could afford to take no more chances; he could spend no more time in explanations or in trying to calm somebody's suspicions. A man who was already dead couldn't play around when it came to death, he thought. Which wasn't very funny at all . . .

He opened the access door and stepped casually back into the corridor, one hand on the gun in his pocket. He listened very carefully this time, cupping his left hand behind his ear and moving his head slowly from side to side.

And then he froze. Somebody else was down there.

46

The explosions had shaken Kamrath and for a moment he debated returning to the main reactor room. There had been that minor thump followed by the flicker of the lights but at the time he hadn't paid much attention. The last explosion almost knocked him off his feet; he knelt with his hands on the corridor floor to steady himself. An alarm bell began to clang deep within the plant; moments later the first of a stream of technicians, many of them clutching personal belongings, ran past him. A wide-eyed chubby man stumbled near him and Kamrath ran over to help him to his feet.

'What's happening?' he demanded.

'Let me go,' the chubby man gasped. 'Got to get out!'

'What's happened?' Kamrath asked again, tightening his grip on the man's arm. The smaller man winced in pain.

'Can't you hear the alarm?' He was so frightened it almost came out as a sob. 'The air – it's hot. There's hot stuff in the air!'

The man tugged free and slipped back into the stream of

fleeing technicians. The last of the running figures disappeared around a bend in the corridor and he was alone. For a moment he debated following them but the thought of Marical brought a new flicker of anger.

Kamrath felt an irritating tickle in his nose and throat and coughed. The air was faintly hazy with a damp-plaster smell to it, the kind you sometimes got when a hot-water pipe burst in the walls of your house.

If he went back to the main floor, he knew he wouldn't be able to return. And Marical was down here, somewhere in the maze of corridors that wove between the reactor complex and the reprocessing plant.

Unless he had evacuated with the others.

Kamrath thought about that for a moment and decided it was unlikely. He was in the main corridor and everybody who'd left had to pass by him. Marical hadn't been among them. There was also the nagging thought that Marical hadn't been due to report for this shift but had come in anyway. Unfinished business? And if so, what?

The alarm was still clanging and for a moment he wavered. The emergency above was serious enough to evacuate the plant, which meant if he stayed below, he could be trapped. He wasn't that familiar with the corridors and there was nobody around to give him directions or tell him where Marical might have gone.

But if he didn't go after him, he agonized, he'd probably never find him. And he wanted Doc's murderer very badly. The world was full of nuts and psychopaths and self-appointed executioners. This was one that wasn't going to get away.

He made his decision then. A good hound dog never left the scent, he thought. Not when the fox was just up ahead.

He cradled his riot gun in his arms and walked somewhat uncertainly down the deserted corridor.

47

'How is he now?' Glidden asked.

Karen Gruen felt Tremayne's pulse. Slow, but that could be due to the morphine. He was only half-conscious, only vaguely aware of where he was. 'He'll make it all right – people seldom die of broken legs.' She didn't like Glidden and wished he hadn't undertaken his 'rescue' mission when he heard she was down here. It wasn't necessary for one thing, and for another, the least he could have done was commandeer an electricar – which he hadn't. Glidden was the bluff, ineffectual type, she decided. He probably referred to his wife as 'the little woman' and liked to play Big Daddy.

'How much further, Miss Gruen? I don't think I can carry him too much further.'

'Not far, Bildor – about a hundred yards.' Which was a lie. From where they had picked up Tremayne, it was closer to half a mile – but she didn't want to discourage him. Of all the technicians she could have asked for help, she had to pick on Bildor. Rossi, who was carrying the front of the stretcher by himself, was all right – an overgrown, likeable kid who worked in the metal analysis division. Bildor, she had found doing an inventory check in one of the reprocessing cells. The thin, stoop-shouldered technician hadn't wanted to leave, even to help with Tremayne. She'd told him anybody could count the damned fuel pellets and almost dragged him out of the cell by force. Both Bildor and Glidden were holding up the back of the stretcher. Tremayne was enormous; he weighed well over two hundred pounds and no one man could have brought up the rear alone, not even the bulky Glidden.

They started up the flight of stairs leading to the main corridor. Glidden swore quietly as he and Bildor struggled to lift the stretcher to shoulder height to keep it level. Karen was only vaguely aware of their problems. Something was bothering her and it took her a minute to pin it down. There had been that minor thump a few moments back; since then she had felt a slight but steady vibration in the passagewey that seemed to get worse the closer they came to the reactor room. She wondered if Glidden had noticed but he didn't seem aware of it.

The first major explosion caught them halfway up the stairs; Bildor almost dropped his corner of the stretcher. He looked frightened, ready to run.

'Don't pay any attention, Bildor; just keep right on going.' What she needed, she thought, was a whip.

They had just entered the main corridor when the rumble of the second explosion shuddered along its length. The evacuation alarm sounded almost immediately afterwards. They set the stretcher down close to the wall as frightened technicians streamed past, few of them even noticing the little group huddled there.

'That's the evacuation alarm,' Bildor stuttered. 'It means there are radioactive gases in the air supply.'

Karen pointed down at Tremayne. 'I know what it means – how far do you think he can run?'

Bildor looked sly. 'We can always come back.'

'Forget it,' Glidden said bluntly. 'Pick up your end and let's get going.'

The corridors were deserted now and Rossi, Glidden and Bildor worked up to a slow jog. The jostling must be hard on Tremayne but there were other things to worry about now, Karen thought. She didn't know the extent to which there might be radioactives in the air. She might never know – until she came down with leukaemia or cancer of the lungs or had a miscarriage sometime in the next decade. Or started losing her white blood cells next week. She glanced at Glidden again. She had a hunch he knew what was happening above and that was why he had started to jog. The question was whether he would level with her or keep it from her, thinking that he would only frighten her.

They were within sight of the reactor-room doors now. Three electricars were parked before them. One was deserted but the other two had drivers, as well as a number of passengers who were clinging to the side rails.

Rossi slowed to a walk. 'Shit!'

Karen saw it then. The huge emergency doors had closed, sealing them off. Ahead, the two electricars suddenly turned and roared towards them, passed and continued on down the corridor.

Bildor stared after them, confused. 'Where the hell are they going?'

'Probably to the reprocessing plant,' Glidden said slowly. 'Maybe they can still get out there.'

'They didn't build emergency exits down here?' Karen asked.

'Never thought we'd need them.'

Karen walked over to the deserted electricar. Tremayne would fit in the back, the others could hang on to the sides. 'Anybody know how to drive one of these?'

'I can,' Rossi said. 'I used to fool around with one on my lunch hour.'

Karen briefly checked Tremayne. He was still under. 'All right, let's see if we can get out the other exit.'

They made Tremayne as comfortable as possible in the rear

of the car; then Rossi climbed into the cab while Karen, Glidden and Bildor clung to the sides. The car jerked to a start. They went roaring back the way they had come, Rossi adding more speed as he mastered the controls. Storage rooms and reprocessing cells flashed past; Rossi was now running the car at top speed through the empty corridors.

Five minutes later they were within sight of the reprocessing plant entrance. A small knot of people and electricars had gathered around the corridor exit. They were still a hundred yards away when the last of the technicians slipped through. A moment later, the emergency doors clanged shut.

Glidden jumped off the car before it had even stopped moving and ran to the intercom station at one side of the exit. He dialled, listened for a long moment, then let the phone fall. 'No answer.'

Karen pointed at his belt. 'What about your walkie-talkie?'

'Thanks,' he said with a trace of annoyance. He spoke into it briefly. Another long moment and then he shrugged and hooked it back on his belt. 'Nobody's monitoring the frequency.'

Bildor said, 'We're trapped down here, aren't we?'

Another explosion rumbled down the corridors, the heaviest of them all, and fracture lines spread up the walls. In the silence that followed, Rossi asked tentatively, 'Is there any way out at all?'

'That'd be asking too much,' Karen said dryly.

Glidden surprised her. 'I think there is. There are a number of maintenance access doors leading to the limestone caverns. The one on this level is a little ways in from the reactor room. We might be able to get out that way.'

'You sure there's an exit there?' Karen asked.

Glidden frowned. Karen guessed that he didn't like negative people as a matter of principle and that in his book she was definitely negative. 'We've got a choice,' he said slowly. 'We can stay here where we know there's no way out or we can try and find a way out through the caverns. There should be one.'

Bildor jerked his thumb at Tremayne, who had started to moan in the back of the electricar. 'What're we going to do with him?'

Karen was slower in answering this time. 'We'll have to do the best we can,' she said at last. Tremayne was beginning to come around. She slipped into the back of the electricar and

191

gave him another injection. He was just too big a man, she thought. Too big for them to carry any distance through the caverns.

She slowly closed her kit. Maybe the only one with a grasp of reality was Bildor after all. She had been running too fast and had been too worried about Tremayne to really think about their present situation. They were trapped – with no way out except the somewhat dubious one through the caverns that Glidden had mentioned. And then there were the radioactive gases . . .

'Miss Gruen?'

She glanced up. Glidden was watching her, waiting. 'Is it all right to start? He's ready to move?'

She nodded. 'Yes, we can move him.'

Rossi was fiddling with the electricar's controls. 'The batteries are almost dead; we sure as hell can't make full speed.'

Glidden looked worried. Give the devil his due, Karen thought. He was thinking about Tremayne, too. 'Did you check the others?'

'Yes, sir – they're no better than this one.'

'Take it at slow speed, then. We'll walk along.'

As they started, Karen touched Glidden's arm and motioned for him to fall behind. Bildor didn't notice, which was what she hoped. She said in a low voice, 'Do you know what's happening up there? And I realize it's not ladylike to say it, Mr Glidden, but for Christ's sake, don't bullshit me!'

He didn't smile. 'I'll try not to. What I think has happened is a loss-of-coolant accident – probably a recirculation pipe burst in one of the reactors, maybe more than one. That would account for the vibrations.' He nodded. 'I felt them, too.'

'That doesn't account for the explosions.'

'The first ones were steam explosions, the heavier ones were probably hydrogen explosions. And there are probably radioactive gases leaking into the plant – I can't think of anything else that would set off the evacuation alarm.'

He fell silent for a moment and Karen said, 'You're not telling me everything.'

'You sure you want to know everything?'

'It's my life – I have a right to know what might happen to it.'

She could sense Glidden struggling with himself. 'The reactor cores are melting down, that has to be what caused the explosions.' He hesitated. 'That's a lot of tonnage of radioactive metal.'

He was driving at something. 'How much?'

His face looked greasy in the cold light from the fluorescents. 'Maybe ten thousand tons. It'll take time but it will melt through the steel and concrete of the containments and then it will start sinking through the ground.'

'And?'

Glidden took a breath. 'If you've noticed, we're walking at a slight grade uphill. The way the complex was laid out, the generating plant was built at the top of a small hill, the reprocessing plant below it.' He paused. 'I don't really know how much time we've got,' he confessed. 'We're below that ten thousand tons of melt.'

She could understand now why Glidden hadn't wanted to tell her. And there was far more to it than just their tragedy below – there was the plant above. Everything that Greg had feared had come true. For a moment she wondered exactly who had ordered the evacuation of the plant and then realized it had to be Parks. Cushing would never have given the orders, and Brandt probably couldn't have. Not from what Greg had told her about them. He would be the fall guy, of course. A good man, she thought – one who deserved more out of life than it had given him.

Then she wondered what Barney was doing and suddenly the two men came into sharp focus in her mind. Greg was a good friend, she hoped he always would be. There was nobody she enjoyed talking to more; he was warm in bed and more than just good company when they went out. But he would never be loyal to her, nor would he think of demanding loyalty from her. Barney was jealous to the point of being juvenile, though at times it was painfully obvious that he believed in the double standard. And he was hypocritical; beneath his radical exterior, he was orthodox to the bone. He had a plan in life that included family, home and a future that would expect a great deal of her. With Greg, she knew she could always count on warmth and consideration. With Barney, there might be less consideration but there was also passion and a peculiar strength.

She didn't understand it and she doubted that she ever would. Perhaps it was simpler than that. Maybe it was just that, for her, the nice guys were always losers; she loved the bastards. It was Barney that she wanted desperately to be with at that moment.

'I'm sorry,' Glidden said, misreading her expression. 'I didn't mean to upset you.' He sounded defensive. 'You asked me for the facts and I gave them to you.'

'I'm glad you did.' She changed the subject. What Glidden had told her was that unless they were very lucky, they would probably die. No need to go over the same ground again. 'We've still got lights. Why didn't they go out?'

'We're operating on emergency diesels. They probably won't last much longer.'

Ahead of them, Bildor turned and said accusingly, 'Hey, what are you two talking about? Anything I should know?'

Karen was suddenly acutely aware of the oppresive quiet and the deserted corridors and the now stuffy air. 'No,' she said. 'Nothing you should know.'

48

Instead of doing the dishes immediately after dinner, Abby decided to stack them up in the sink while she and Ed watched television together. Funny, she thought, you did change as you got older. There had been a time when a dirty dish in the sink would have bothered her all evening. But the shows were good tonight and she would sit in her chair and do her tatting while Ed would read the evening papers and watch the screen over the top of his glasses. And halfway through the evening, he'd fall asleep and the papers would slip out of his lap and onto the floor.

But that was all right; it had been happening for years now and she didn't mind it any more. It felt good just to sit there and not say anything but still be together. And there wasn't all that much they had to say anyway.

It was in the middle of the detective show – she wasn't sure which one, they all seemed alike to her – that the lights went out. The picture on the television screen suddenly vanished, taking the trench-coated, slow-speaking detective along with it.

'Abby? What the hell happened, Abby?' Ed had jerked awake. She could hear him in the darkness, plucking at the papers on the carpet.

'You stay right there, Ed; I'll get some candles.' She couldn't remember where they kept the fuses but she could look for them in the morning.

She had just lighted a candle and was letting the wax drip in the bottom of a saucer to hold it upright when she heard what sounded like a distant explosion. She wasn't quite sure; her hearing wasn't all what it should be, though she had never let Dr Seyboldt know for fear he'd get some young snippet to take her place. Afraid she couldn't answer the phone, that sort of thing. She sighed. It wasn't fair to keep on pretending; there really were calls she had difficulty handling and someday soon she was going to have to tell the doctor.

Then she remembered and the tears started to come. She bit her lip. It didn't do any good to think about it ...

'Did you hear that, Abby? Sounded like explosions.'

Well. That was different if Ed had heard them, too. She went out to the kitchen and opened the back door for a moment, standing in the doorway and filling her lungs with the fresh air. It was raining slightly – the heavy clouds were skimming in front of the moon like sailing ships under full canvas.

Then she glanced around, suddenly curious. All the lights in town were out but across the inlet she could see the Western Gas and Electric plant plain as day, its lights blazing.

She stared at the plant, frowned, then adjusted her glasses and tried squinting. Something wrong, hard to say just what. Looked like people were running on the grounds. She strained her eyes for a moment longer, then shrugged. Shadows played tricks on you at night and if the truth be known, her eyesight wasn't that much better than her hearing.

She stood in the doorway and let the night air wash over her. It was fresh and damp and cool and ... She sniffed and made a face. It was also a little gritty and something had tickled her nose. She'd go back inside and since they had a gas stove, maybe she could heat up a pot of tea for herself and Ed. No telling when the power would come back on.

She had just turned to go back in when she heard a soft *plop* behind her. She couldn't make out exactly what it was, just something small and dark on the patio behind her, something that must have fallen out of the sky. Or maybe from a tree. She nudged it with her toe and it cheeped softly. It was a bird, poor thing.

She picked it up and cradled it against her blouse, smoothing its feathers. They were wet and oddly warm to the touch.

And gritty.

49

Tom Peterson had been running for the emergency chute when the last explosion buckled the floor beneath him. He stumbled and the tile floor came up to meet him at the same time, throwing him out hard against the wall. He felt the bones snap in his arm and ankle. There was remarkably little pain – so long as he didn't move.

It would have been difficult to move in any event. Part of the floor had crumpled back on top of him, shielding him from the now open reactor pit. He lay there for a long moment, stunned, listening to the alarm gradually wind down. He could feel his uniform slowly dampen from the wet steam that filled the containment. Gradually he got his wind back. He tried shouting for help, even though he knew there was no one around to hear him. Then he wriggled slightly, wincing at the pain. He was pinned, he couldn't get out from under. He peered around the corner of the small mound of floor tiles that covered him – enough to see the reactor pit and the balcony where the VIPs gathered to watch the plant operations. The Eagle's Nest, the other technicians called it. Above that towered the containment dome and the hulking outlines of the bridge crane that was used for refuelling.

A dozen feet away the figure of another technician lay motionless on the floor. God only knew what had happened to the man, Peterson thought, but in a few minutes he might envy him.

The pit was spewing steam and what seemed like a faint rain of ash and tiny metal droplets. Spalled concrete and uranium fuel, he thought. Oh, Jesus, the radioactive fuel . . . He struggled violently against the weight of the tiles for a moment, then gave up and relaxed against the floor. You could make your peace in moments, or spend the rest of your life doing it, he thought. He had no choice. In a few minutes, he was going to die.

There was more activity in the reactor pit now; gouts of molten metal exploded from it and hit the walls of the containment. A piece of half-melted metal landed a few feet away from him. He recognized it as part of a steam-dryer assembly.

He heard creaking from above and for just a moment a draught of cool air touched his face; then he felt it begin to blister again. He craned his neck and glanced up. Parts of the containment dome were glowing white hot where molten fuel had splashed against it and one section had melted away; fragments of steel and concrete were now thudding to the floor a dozen feet from him. The gap in the dome was venting the steam and the fine spray of metal droplets to the air outside. He twisted his head further. At the opposite end of the reactor room, the supports for the bridge crane were glowing a dull red and bowing slightly in the middle.

More of the containment dome was falling around him now. The air was searing his lungs. He could feel nothing below the waist and, strangely enough, the blisters on his face and arms didn't bother him. He was aware of a growing lassitude and a lack of concern. It was going to be easier to die than he had thought ...

A flicker of movement caught his eye. He slowly moved his head, trying to locate it. A slight, wavery line on the balcony. Some of the fuel had struck there and the thick balcony windows were melting in their frames; the wavery line marked where the glass itself was slumping.

Below the floor level, he knew the reactor vessels were melting, that hundreds of tons of steel and uranium fuel were pooling in the bottom. The offices on the balcony were burning now from the intense heat of the spattered fuel. The supports would melt and eventually the metal desks and chairs and filing cabinets would puddle and flow towards the great red gaps in the main reactor room floor. And then the floor itself would join the tons of metal below. The entire plant would eventually cave in upon itself, melt and flow to join the cancer eating its way into the ground.

The sharp cry of metal against metal filled the air. He twisted his head further to see what it was.

He was just in time to watch, unconcerned, as the huge bridge crane buckled and slowly toppled towards him.

50

'So we spend all day out on the sound and we don't come back with enough fish to make a good stew.' Clint Jefferson took a can from the tub of ice and tossed it to Cole Levant. 'Have a beer, Cole, at least *that's* filling.' Jefferson tugged at the ring on his own can. 'I can remember coming back from a morning on the sound with my old man and we'd be so loaded down water would be sloshing over the gunnels.' He upended the can and downed half the contents in two gulps. 'And I ain't that old, either.'

Levant settled back in his tattered deck chair. It was almost dark and he could relax. Overhead, a light rain drummed on the tarpaulin that roofed most of the deck. The chill air was damp and penetrating and the nets that had been hung out to dry now sagged in moist folds against the side of the boat. In spite of the weather, this was the time of day that Cole liked best: early in the evening, just after sunset, when the air was thick with the familiar dock smell of fish and the faint odour of diesel oil.

Clouds scudded across the horizon, threatening a much heavier downpour. The wind, unusual even for the winter months, was blowing off the land to the sea. Old Halsam squatted on the deck and nodded. 'Catch sure as hell ain't what it used to be and you know what you can blame.'

'Come off it, Frank, the catch has been declining for five years now. The fish have shifted their spawning grounds. Maybe they'll be back, maybe they won't. Depends on how lucky we are.' Levant had to raise his voice above the sound of the rain.

'Luck's got nothing to do with it, Cole.' Halsam scratched an itch hidden deep in his grey whiskers, then reached in his lunch bucket for a mirror and held it up so it caught the light from the nearby Coleman lantern. He took a pocket comb and a small pair of scissors from the rear pocket of his Levi's and started to trim his ragged beard closer to his face.

'Mirror, mirror, on the wall, who's the fairest of them all?' Jefferson said gleefully. 'Give up, dummy – it's still Snow White!' He fell against the deckhouse, roaring with laughter. 'That mirror ought to sue you for cruel and unusual punishment, Halsam!'

'OK, Frank,' Levant sighed. 'What do you think has happened to the fish?' It had been the same conversation, with variations, every night for the past six months.

'It's that goddamned plant.' Halsam jerked a gnarled thumb in the direction of the lights of the power plant across the inlet. 'All that waste water flushing out into the sound – that water's ten degrees warmer now. And once they're operating at capacity, it's going to get worse.'

Rob Levant stirred in the shadows of the deckhouse where he had been sitting, chucking bits of fish at a gull perched on the fantail. 'The man from the state said it was only two degrees.'

'Depends on where you measure it,' Halsam said shortly. 'They can say all they want to about how the fish can still live in warm water but the point is, the sound's no longer home to the fish. It's like when I first moved out here from Illinois. No winter and no thunderstorms and believe me, the Coast wasn't home for one helluva long time. I figure fish are the same way. I don't think they're ever going to come back, I think they found themselves a home someplace else.'

Jefferson slapped his scale-encrusted pants in admiration. 'Damn, Frank, that's pure poetry – how come the bastards never listened to you when they had the hearings?'

'Never got a chance to testify,' Halsam said, spitting over the side. 'They picked the people they wanted to listen to – heads they won, tails we lost.'

'You know, Frank, the plant's done a lot of good for the town,' Levant said thoughtfully. 'We don't have to pay much taxes, we've got a new school, a new fire engine. We wouldn't have them otherwise.'

Halsam snorted. 'When's the last time we had a fire in town – nineteen thirty-six? The town got a new fire engine at the expense of you getting a new boat, Cole.'

'There's nothing wrong with the *Taraval*,' Levant said.

'And with such a fancy school,' Halsam continued, 'how come my niece's kid still can't read?'

'He can't read 'cause they don't have the same stuff to read nowdays,' Jefferson said. 'When I was a kid they had them eight-pagers and we learned how to read real quick!'

'You didn't read 'em, Jefferson,' Halsam said. 'All you did was look at the pictures.'

'Cut it out in front of the boy,' Levant said quietly.

Jefferson looked abashed and turned to Rob. 'Sorry, Rob, sometimes I got a big mouth.'

'That's all right, Mr Jefferson,' Rob said, very grown-up. Then he giggled. 'Besides, I've seen them all anyway.'

Levant set his can of beer on the deck. 'Who the hell showed them to you?'

'I ain't no snitch, Dad.'

Kids. 'You tell Willy he shows you any more dirty pictures, I'll have a talk with his old man.' There was a moment's uneasy silence and Levant realized he had embarrassed Rob in front of the men. Damned if you did and damned if you didn't, he thought unhappily. He changed the subject.

'What the hell happened to that guy you decked in the bar last night, Halsam?'

'The little guy? Lerner? I heard they sprung him this morning, they needed him at the plant.' He finished trimming his beard and put away the mirror. It was dark now, the only light that from the deck lantern.

'Cole, what do you think is going to happen to the fish after that plant's been operating full blast for a week or more?'

'I don't know – we'll find out.'

Halsam spat over the side again. 'Well, I can tell you – there won't be any fish at all then.'

Levant went back to his beer and didn't bother answering. For better or for worse, the future would take care of itself.

'How far up the coast do you think we'll have to go before we'll run into decent catches again?' Halsam persisted.

Levant shrugged. He was about to answer when there was the distant, muffled sound of explosions. He set his can of beer back on the deck and listened carefully. There was another explosion, then another, the echoes rumbling across the waters of the sound. They all seemed to be coming from the direction of the Prometheus complex.

Halsam was on his feet. 'Holy shit, what was that?'

Levant said, 'Get my binoculars, Rob – they're in the cabin.'

A moment later, he was focusing the glasses on the plant. The complex leaped across the inlet towards him. The lights were still shining; he saw men running across the parking lot, away from the plant. A lot of men. It looked like the entire shift was running away. He swept the plant with the glasses and finally found what he was looking for – the emergency chutes, thick with men sliding down them. They were evacuating the plant.

Halsam and Jefferson were waiting for a chance at the field glasses. 'What the hell's happening, Cole?' Halsam asked. 'The explosions coming from the plant?'

'Yeah,' Levant said, still looking through the glasses. He finally turned them over to Halsam. 'I think I'll run over and see what's happening. Anybody want to come along?'

Halsam and Jefferson gave each other long looks and shook their heads. Halsam said, 'If it's all the same with you, Cole, I think I'll hang around the boat.' He unrolled his sleeves and made a show of buttoning them. 'You see that Lerner fellow, you give him my regards.'

Rob was all ready. 'Let's go, Dad.'

'Forget it, you're not going,' Levant said gruffly. 'You're going to chase on home and go to bed.' And then, for no reason he could think of, he suddenly changed his mind. Since Leona had died, Rob was all he had and he wanted the boy with him. 'OK, come along.'

The wind was blowing stronger now. 'Button up your slicker,' he told Rob, 'and your hood.' It wasn't until he was on the dock that he noticed all the lights in the town were out. He glanced up and realized that the land-to-sea winds were carrying clouds that had passed over the plant. A sudden intuition made him turn back to the boat and shout, 'Everybody into the cabin!'

Rob was already in the pickup. Levant debated ordering him back to the boat, then changed his mind. 'Close the windows, Rob.'

Later, driving up the coast highway to the plant, he found himself flooring the gas pedal in frustration. Whatever had happened at the Cardenas Bay complex was damned serious. He had no business bringing Rob along. He thought of turning around but they were almost to the plant. From the looks of the men milling around, the situation was grim.

And not just for the people who worked there, he thought.

51

Senator Hoyt We'll try to take as little of your time as possible, Mr Levant. I understand you've been quite ill. What I want to know is how the townspeople and the workers at the Prometheus complex got along. Would you say the relationships between the two were friendly?

Mr Levant Well, before the plant located there, Cardenas Bay was pretty much of a fishing community. When the plant came in, a lot of townspeople went to work for it. So what you had, eventually, were two groups – those who worked for the plant and those who didn't. Most of those who didn't were fishermen. But they were all townspeople and in the end we all suffered.

Representative Holmburg Mr Walton has already testified

that there were two groups in town. I think what my colleague from Idaho was driving at was simply whether they got along.

Mr Levant We got along. If you mean, did we like each other, the answer's no – although I would have to qualify that.

Senator Hoyt You imply there was friction between the two groups. Why?

Mr Levant Once the plant started operating, even on a small scale, the fishing got bad. We blamed it on the waste discharge from the plant heating up the waters of the sound.

Senator Clarkson There's no scientific evidence that the thermal pollution of the bay waters chased away the fish, Mr Levant.

Mr Levant Something sure as hell did.

Senator Clarkson Fish have changed their spawning grounds before for no known reason.

Mr Levant In this case, it wasn't hard to put two and two together, Senator. But I was asked why we didn't like the plant workers and that's the answer.

Senator Hoyt You said you had to qualify your dislike of them. Would you explain?

Mr Levant A lot of us would end up drinking with them at the same bar. I guess it's like with anybody; once you get to know them, they're not so bad. And many of the plant people pitched in for our community activities. I think Mr Parks was probably responsible for some of that.

Senator Hoyt But it would be fair to say that some of the fishermen hated the plant and the people who worked there.

Mr Levant It'd be fair to say that, sir.

Senator Hoyt Perhaps hated the plant enough to try and sabotage it?

Mr Levant I don't think anybody would have tried to sabotage the plant. I don't see how they could have.

Representative Holmburg When Mr Walton testified, he implied that he and his public relations people had done a great deal to smooth the relations between the fishermen and the plant workers.

Mr Levant That's not true, sir. None of us would've bought a used car from Walton. We thought he was trying to sell us a bill of goods and as it turned out, he sure was.

Representative Holmburg The magnitude of the disaster was unprecedented – all of us on the Committee realize that – but I want to assure you, Mr Levant, that the Government is doing everything possible to help the victims.

Mr Levant It may be out of line to ask at this hearing, but what about my boat? They promised me a new boat if I took the *Taraval* up to the sea exit.

Senator Clarkson Mr Levant, by law the Government's liability in disasters of this type – and especially this one – is limited. We would like to make an exception in your case, considering your services throughout the incident, but the law doesn't allow for it. The moneys allotted by the recent special act of Congress will be distributed as equitably as possible, though I can't estimate what that might amount to in individual cases.

Mr Levant I can, Senator. It'll be about two cents on the dollar.

Senator Clarkson I'm sorry, Mr Levant, but no matter how tragic the disaster, it would hardly make sense to bankrupt the rest of the United States for the benefit of the survivors.

Mr Levant What you're saying is that we were taken right from the start.

Senator Clarkson I appreciate your feelings but that's not exactly true. The Prometheus complex paid approximately eighty percent of all the property taxes levied in Cardenas Bay for the last four years – from the inception of construction on. These tax receipts provided the town with a municipal sewage system, a new school building, new equipment for the fire department and would have provided for a small hospital in the near future.

Mr Levant I'm sorry if I don't sound grateful, Senator. Maybe it's because the sewage system, the school and the fire truck no longer exist. That tax money was blood money – a lot of people died in that first forty-eight hours. The others, you'd think they were going to be all right and then a week or two later somebody'd get sick and a week after that, they'd be dead. No kid under five survived and the old folks died almost as easy. Abby Dalton passed away in my arms – she was Doc Seyboldt's nurse and the town baby catcher before Doc started to practise there. She brought my son into the world. There wasn't a damn thing I could do, nothing anybody could do. Did you ever see somebody die of radiation poisoning, Senator? It's the ugliest way to go that I know of, you bleed—

Senator Hoyt The witness is excused. I think all of us are familiar with personal tragedy, many of us fought in the Korean and Vietnam wars—

Mr Levant How many, Senator?

Senator Hoyt I said you were excused, Mr Levant.

Mr Levant You never saw your home town bulldozed and

203

dumped into fifty-five-gallon drums to be hauled away and buried—

Senator Hoyt Will the Sergeant at Arms please remove the witness?

52

Parks had jackknifed going down the chute and hit the ground, hard. He lay on the wet grass, stunned. It was dark on the lee side of the building, away from the parking lot, and light gusts of rain sleeted across the lawn. Occasionally the moon would stare from behind the racing clouds. Parks could see the shadowy figures of men running around him. He flattened out against the grass, his hands and knees deep in the mud that had been churned up by the men who had hit the lawn before him.

'Parks?' Brandt was somewhere close by in the darkness; his voice had the strained ring of pain to it.

'Over here.'

'I think I twisted my ankle.'

The cold rain against the back of his neck was like an ice pack; the building and the figures around him had more form now. 'You'll live. Where're Cushing and Walton?'

'Right here.' Cushing was a dozen feet over on his left. For once, he sounded shaken. 'I'm all right.'

There was no answer from Walton. He had probably hit the ground running and kept right on going, Parks thought.

There were muffled explosions from the plant behind him. The floodlights that bathed the corners of the building flickered and went out; the emergency diesels had finally died. For the moment, Parks' mind was merely recording what was happening; he didn't want to think about the plant, about what might come next.

Another sound cut the night air now. Above the explosions and the rustle of fleeing men, he heard the sound of cars being started in the parking lot.

Parks glanced skyward. The clouds were blowing away from them, out towards the ocean – and directly over the parking area.

He bounced to his feet, shouting, '*Stay away from the park-*

*ing lot, you'll be right under the fallout! Get out of the god-
damned lot – forget your cars, they're contaminated!'*

A voice shouted from the darkness, 'Who the hell are you?'

'Greg Parks, goddamnit! *Meet at the Information Building!
Tell the others!'*

He ran desperately for the exit gate, hoping to beat any cars
that were trying to leave. They'd be coated with radioactive
ash and droplets of metal, including plutonium, from the exploding reactors. At the gatehouse, the guard was holding a
flashlight and gaping at the building behind him. A ruddy glow
showed through cracks in the walls.

'Give me your pistol!' Parks snapped.

The guard flashed the light in his face, recognized him and
handed the gun over. Parks fired twice in the air. *'Nobody
leaves this lot! Your cars are contaminated! Get out and meet at
the Information Building!'*

He gave the gun back to the guard. 'If anybody tries to drive
a car out of here, shoot at their tyres. If you have to, shoot at
their gas tanks – stop them!'

He left the frightened guard and sprinted up the road for the
Information Building near the highway. There was no light
at all except for the glow from the headlights of the cars in
the parking lot and from an occasional appearance of the
moon. The chill, misting rain ran down the back of his neck and
seeped into his shoes; he was shivering and winded by the time
he got to the Information Building. A few dozen men had
already gathered outside and more stragglers were showing up
all the time. Parks tried the doors. Locked. He kicked at them.

'Let me try.' The little man was difficult to make out in the
darkness. Then Parks felt an odd surge of relief. Lerner. 'Give
me some room, Greg.' He backed up and Lerner hit the door
with his shoulder. It sprang open and Parks pushed in,
followed by the other men. The rotunda was cold and deserted,
the exhibits motionless in their glass cases. He felt along the
wall for an emergency electric lantern – he could've sworn
there was one there – then gave up and groped on the round
entrance desk for the stack of information pamphlets. He took
a dozen and rolled them tightly together, then lit the bundle
with his pocket lighter.

The corridor had filled with technicians in water-soaked
smocks and workmen in the blue coveralls of Western Gas and
Electric. In the light from his torch, they were a frightened,
pathetic group, their smocks and coveralls coated with mud

and grass stains. They milled around him, waiting for instructions.

He recognized Abrams in the crowd and said, 'Abrams, get the gate guard – tell him to give you his check-in lists.' The first thing he'd have to do was find out who had made it out of the plant – and who had been left behind. He glanced quickly over the crowd. Karen wasn't there.

'Lerner, see if you can scare up some electric lanterns. There should be some in the storeroom downstairs. Break down the door if it's locked; take anybody you need for help. Smith, Gerrold – check the lunchroom and see if there are any sandwiches left. Bring them up if there are. Break open the candy machines and take all the bars you can find. Start making some coffee if we've got any on hand.'

He couldn't remember whether the stoves were gas or electric. Pray for gas, he thought. The water-pumping station was probably out, unless it had emergency power. Even if it didn't, there might be enough left in the pipes for coffee. If not, they could ladle water out of the commode tanks. The men could piss outside. They'd have to anyway if the water was cut off.

Ten minutes later two technicians were serving hot coffee and sandwiches and the building was jammed. Parks had broken down the door to the small executive office and made himself comfortable at the desk. Brandt and Cushing were at the other end of the room, busy on the two phones. He didn't know what about, they were keeping their voices low. Lerner had come back from downstairs with a stack of newspapers. Parks took one, wadded it tightly and placed it on the large desk ashtray. Once lit, its flames cast dancing shadows over the desk and the chairs.

Lerner nodded towards the rotunda, where they could hear Abrams reading off the check-list and the occasional voice answering 'here.' 'There are a lot of men who didn't make it. I saw Peterson on the main floor, half buried under tiles ripped up by the explosions.'

'It was impossible to help him?'

'I suppose I could've. Then we'd both be dead.' He knuckled his forehead for a moment. 'There's the Control Central crew and McGrath, who was doing electrical maintenance work in the utility tunnel. He must've got it right away.'

'Did you get a good look at the men when you came back?'

Lerner shook his head. 'It's not good. A lot have radiation

206

burns. I think some took doses up to six hundred roentgens, maybe more. There are a couple who are vomiting. One man's already reported bloody stools – he'll probably be dead by morning.'

'Barney.' There was tacit acknowledgement in his voice that in this area Lerner knew more than he did. 'What's the progression? What can we expect?'

Lerner looked pale. 'Figure that a person gets a background dose of five roentgens during the first thirty years of his life. A whole-body dose of a thousand "r" or more will kill you within a week, maybe less. Some men out there probably got more than that. Six hundred "r" will kill you within a month. Three hundred "r" will kill about a quarter of those exposed, seriously injure the rest. It goes down from there.' He hesitated. 'You understand : we were all exposed to some degree.'

'What are the symptoms?'

'For a lethal dose, nausea, followed by vomiting and sometimes diarrhoea. All within a couple of hours to maybe as short as half an hour. Exhaustion, fever and delirium might follow. It might not. You might think you've recovered; a doctor will tell you that the number of your white blood cells has diminished. A few weeks later, you'll start losing your hair. Then you'll notice small haemorrhages in the skin and in the mouth; you'll bruise easy, you might bleed from the gums. You'll lose your appetite, start losing weight, come down with a high fever. Your resistance will be almost zero; some minor sickness a healthy person could shake off will kill you. If you make it through all that, you might discover you've got a cancer – twenty years later.'

'Any threshold dosage?'

Lerner shook his head. 'There's no such thing as a safe dose; you know that. For any dose you get, you trade so many days of your life. Maybe the insurance companies have a formula for it.'

He couldn't dwell on it, Parks thought. It would drive him crazy.

'How much do you know about decontamination?'

Lerner's eyes were large and liquid, without expression. He had already seen too much, Parks thought. 'More than the Government thinks I do. Not as much as I would like to. It was my specialty in the Israeli Army – just in case. Along with some other unpleasant duties.' Lerner hesitated for a moment.

'What you're thinking won't be easy. Decon includes checking body dosages with a Geiger counter, burying clothing if it's contaminated, scrubbing down with heavy detergent, shaving any body hair if it's necessary. You tell me how I can do all that, I'll start.'

Parks thought for a moment. 'One of the exhibits in the rotunda has a working counter. Break the glass and take it off the mount. The maintenance locker should have a drum of heavy-duty detergent for cleaning the floors.'

'What about water? We got the water for the coffee from the johns.'

'There's plenty of it falling outside. We're upwind from the plant; so it should be OK.'

'Dry clothes?'

Parks spread his hands. 'There might be some janitor's uniforms around. Save them for the worst cases only. The rest will have to sit around naked.'

'You're not worried about pneumonia or exposure?'

Grimly: 'We can cure that.'

At the door, Lerner said, 'I'll need some help.'

'Take Mike Kormanski – he was Karen's assistant, he must know something about medicine.' He paused, staring down at the desk. 'Look, Barney. I don't want to ask – but if you had seen Karen in the plant, you would have told me, right?'

Barney's face was flat with no trace of antagonism. 'I didn't see her. I looked.'

She must have gotten out, Parks thought. She must have.

Brandt was back from his phone call. Despite his soaked clothing and fringe of plastered-down hair, he looked more like the Brandt that Parks remembered. Commanding, in control. Only the slightly haunted look in his eyes gave him away.

'Lines still working?'

Brandt nodded. 'Phone companies usually have emergency power – doesn't take that much to keep them going.'

'What did Washington say?'

'They're sending a detachment of CBR marines – chemical-biological-radiological teams.'

'From Washington?'

'That team will be out in the morning. The marines will be airlifted from Fort Nicholson.'

'And until they get here?'

Brandt eased himself into the chair that Lerner had vacated. 'Hold our breaths, I guess. Contact local authorities.'

Parks laughed shortly. 'I would if I could. Nobody's seen Kamrath.'

Brandt closed his eyes and kneaded the bridge of his nose. 'Nobody seems to realize ...' His voice trailed off.

Cushing had finished his call and was walking towards them. He pulled a chair closer to the desk and sat down, automatically tugging at his trousers to keep the nonexistent creases from being stretched out of shape. 'You don't have to worry about newspaper reporters showing up.' He sounded faintly pleased with himself.

Parks could feel the anger boil up again. 'That was hardly my main worry. But if any do show, we refer them to Washington, right?'

'I said there wouldn't be any showing up,' Cushing said shortly. 'There'll be no TV cameras covering this, no news leaks. The bit of film that was shot earlier will be confiscated.'

'News blackout?'

'That's right. Complete.'

Parks had the uneasy feeling that he was at a Mad Hatter's tea party discussing absolutely nothing that really mattered. 'They can't make that stick.'

'I think they can.' Cushing rolled up a newspaper, tucking its ends in tightly; then lit it and dropped it on the tile floor. He leaned closer to the burning paper for heat. The shadows playing over his face lent it a thin, saturnine expression.

'I can think of a dozen other things I would have asked Washington,' Parks said, angry again. 'Why is this so god-damned important?'

Cushing stared into the flames. 'Parks,' he said sombrely, 'I don't like you and I'm well aware that it's mutual. You're a very bright and courageous man in your way; I understand what you're up against better than you think I do. But I don't believe you've thought this one aspect through – and it's not a minor one. If word got out of what had happened here, the most natural result would be panic – people fleeing the vicinity of perfectly normal plants, and fleeing tonight. And there would be another, delayed, panic after that. People would sell their homes and move out if they lived close to a plant, there'd be a public clamour to close down all the nuclear power plants in the country. We couldn't afford to do that – a third of the nation's power is generated by nuclear plants.' He held his hands over the dying flames and for a moment his face was lost in shadow. 'We wouldn't have a recession, Parks. We'd have a full-fledged depression and no way out of it – a permanent cut in the standard of living that would last for generations.'

He was interrupted by a scuffle and swearing at the door. The gate guard entered, pushing a man ahead of him. 'He was trying to drive out of the parking lot, Mr Parks. I told him he couldn't leave and he insisted, so I shot out his tyres.'

It was Jerry Walton, red-eyed, wet and angry.

'You've got no right to keep me here, Parks.'

'I have every right to keep you from spreading radioactive contamination to other parts of the country, Walton.'

Walton shook loose of the guard. 'You know what the newspapers are going to say about this, Parks?'

'Sure. Nothing. According to Mr Cushing here, there's a complete news blackout.'

Walton and Cushing exchanged looks and then Walton turned back to Parks. It was fascinating watching a chameleon change colour, Parks thought. From red-faced anger to dubious acceptance to a groping for the new – and correct – party line. 'I'm sorry, Parks, is there anything I can do?'

'See Barney Lerner in the rotunda. You've been out in the parking lot; there's a good chance your clothes are contaminated. You might even have received a fatal dose.' Walton promptly looked sick. 'If Barney tells you to strip, strip – your clothes may have to be buried. After that, go outside and scrub down with detergent. If Barney has an extra janitor's uniform, change into it. If he doesn't, you'll have to go bare ass probably until morning. Then come back and I'll give you the casualty list. We'll have to announce it sooner or later and maybe you can think of the right words to go with it.'

Walton hesitated, then suddenly looked oddly humble and out of character. 'Could I see it now? Some of the technicians were friends of mine.'

He handed it over and Walton glanced down the list of names. 'You've got Karen Gruen listed as missing. Didn't she get back?'

Parks gripped the desk. 'Get back from where?'

'She went down to the reprocessing corridors. A technician named Tremayne had broken his leg down there.'

'Why didn't you tell us at the time?' Parks' voice was shaking with relief.

Walton looked embarrassed. 'The newsmen were around. It wouldn't have looked good to mention a workman had broken his leg on the same night we went on stream. We've been trying to avoid anything like a jinx image.' He frowned. 'Besides, I did tell you.'

'I'm sorry, Walton, you didn't,' Parks said angrily.

Walton was confused. 'I told Mr Glidden and he went down after her to see if he could help. I thought sure he'd call back up and report.'

It was like Glidden to have gone after her, Parks thought. The plant politician chasing his votes.

There were more explosions now and Parks rushed to the door, followed by the others. Lerner was already there, watching. A few hundred yards away, the containment dome was glowing white. As he watched, pieces of it collapsed inward. Steam and other vapours streamed up into the night sky.

Parks told Lerner about Karen. Karen and Glidden and Tremayne plus a few technicians were in the corridors between the reactor and reprocessing plants, probably trapped – but also probably alive. Lerner listened without comment, then said, 'There are five men up here who won't last until morning. Maybe more, unless we get lucky.'

Parks only half heard him. He'd caught Cushing and Brandt's eyes. Then he glanced skyward again at the glowing stream high up that flowed with the night air across the parking lot and then the inlet and then over the town of Cardenas Bay and out to sea.

Then he looked at the plant that was slowly, inexorably, crumbling in upon itself and melting down into the ground.

There was no way he knew of to stop it, but that was going to be his next problem.

53

Senator Hoyt Mr Walton, we've heard testimony of deepseated antagonisms between the fishermen in Cardenas Bay and the workers at the Prometheus complex. Didn't you state earlier that you had tried to smooth over the difficulties between the two groups.

Mr Walton We did our best to show the townspeople that the plant would stimulate their economy. As it turned out, many of the municipal improvements in Cardenas Bay would have been impossible without the taxes paid by the plant. Perhaps some of the fishermen were hurt – though that has yet to be proven – but they were a small minority.

Senator Stone There were hearings held before the plant itself was built, weren't there?

Mr Walton The Commission held extended hearings at which we heard from the Sierra Club, Friends of the Earth, the National Resources Defense Council, Another Mother for Peace—

Senator Stone Did the Commission listen to everybody, Mr Walton? Were any representatives of the fishermen witnesses?

Mr Walton You can't listen to everybody, Senator. The hearings would have dragged on for ever. They were restricted to representatives of organized groups.

Senator Stone Groups the Commission approved of?

Mr Walton I'm sure they tried to include a representative sampling, Senator.

Senator Stone I gather your job was to convince the town that the plant was good for it. I'm curious just what your propaganda consisted of.

Mr Walton I don't think it's fair to call it propaganda, sir – it was a straightforward presentation. We had a speaker's bureau that gave talks to civic groups, schools, that sort of thing. And we had press conferences and public progress reports. We made technical information available to the townspeople on the benefits of the plant and, of course, once the facility was built, we had guided tours of the less sensitive areas of the plant as well as an Information Centre. We wanted to make the townspeople feel that it was their plant, that the plant was a Good Neighbour. We had an ad campaign to that effect that we ran in the local papers.

Senator Stone And, of course, you made sure the townspeople realized the tax advantages that would accrue.

Mr Walton That was hardly a crime, Senator.

Senator Stone I assume you were just as energetic in describing the possible drawbacks of the plant.

Mr Walton I'm not sure what you mean by drawbacks.

Senator Stone I think I would consider the Cardenas Bay disaster as something of a drawback, Mr Walton.

Mr Walton I regret the disaster as much as anybody, Senator – more so because it makes future assignments enormously more difficult. It was difficult enough before.

212

Senator Hoyt What would you classify as difficulties, Mr Walton?

Mr Walton The language, for one thing.

Representative Holmburg What's wrong with the language?

Mr Walton The language surrounding any discussion of nuclear power plants, sir. Some scientific terms tend to scare people. You can't build up the confidence of a community in the safety of your product if you keep using terms such as 'SCRAM', 'Maximum Credible Accident', 'rads', 'exposure limits' and so on. They're just not conducive to confidence.

Senator Stone What words would you use in talking about nuclear power, Mr Walton?

Mr Walton Well, it's clean power, sir – there are certainly no atmospheric pollutants such as there are with coal or even oil. And I think it's reliable and economical, a Good Neighbour – which is what we say in the ads.

Senator Stone And of course you wouldn't use 'rads' or talk about 'radiation exposure limits' – you would refer to 'sunshine units.' Isn't that the phrase you use?

Mr Walton I know I've been criticized for using the term. I didn't invent it but I think a case could be made for it.

Senator Stone I'm afraid I can't agree with you, Mr Walton – on practically anything. The Cardenas Bay accident would certainly indicate that nuclear power is far from reliable and that there are definitely pollutants involved. The death toll was – Well, what word would you use, Mr Walton? And I would hardly call it economical; the last estimate of the total damage caused by the accident is staggering. And I'm only thinking of urban losses, I haven't taken into consideration the farmland that will have to lie fallow for years, perhaps centuries, before it can be safely farmed again.

Senator Hoyt With all due respect to the Senator from Pennsylvania, I think that he's badgering the witness.

Senator Stone I have only one more question. Did you think it was justifiable to keep the details of the disaster from the general public, Mr Walton?

Mr Walton Certainly – at least initially. The disaster might have attracted sightseers from outlying communities, if the news had been broadcast. The resulting panic might have been duplicated around a hundred other plants throughout the country. At least that was our thinking at the time. We had no inkling of what would eventually develop.

Senator Stone In the light of everything that's happened, do you still believe in secrecy concerning any aspects of nuclear power?

Mr Walton Don't you, sir? And if you don't, then why are these hearings closed to the public?

54

Katherine McNear stretched and yawned. It had been a long ride from Denver but in ten minutes they would be landing at Los Angeles International. She was getting older, she thought – two-hour plane rides got to her, even with a few martinis to take the edge off the boredom. At least Martin was meeting them at the airport. She should count her blessings, she wouldn't have to fight the lines waiting for a cab.

And for once, Jennifer had been a doll; she had slept the whole flight. In the car, she'd probably be wide awake and have a case of the babbles. But even that was better than Martin boring her all the way to Bel Air with every insignificant thing that had happened at the studios during the past two weeks. His one lovable quality was that he really didn't expect her to reply to everything he said – so long as she stared at him with complete adoration. And after ten years of marriage, faking that had become second nature.

She glanced out of the window. Los Angeles should be coming up soon. As jaded as she was about some things, the sight of LA at night always took her breath away. The lights spread out over the hills and the Valley made the coast look as if a giant had spilled his bag of jewels over it.

Strange, the entire coast looked overcast: there wasn't a light to be seen. And that was ridiculous, she could see the stars – in fact, she could see them better than she ever had, so there weren't any clouds. Unless they were all beneath them. But the plane was too low now, or was it?

The coast may have been blacked out for some reason, she thought, suddenly fearful. She glanced quickly around the cabin. People were putting magazines back in the seat pockets and snapping shut their briefcases. Apparently nobody else had noticed anything strange. It had to be her imagination.

'Ladies and gentlemen, this is your captain speaking. We are detouring south and inland to avoid choppy air ahead. There

will be a slight delay in our scheduled arrival time.'

That was so much airline b.s., she thought. They were being rerouted to another airport. Then she felt that quiver of suspicion again. They never announced choppy air until they were well into it. She rang for the stewardess.

The stewardess came down the aisle, all competence, long limbs, spotless uniform and the Smile. Did they ever realize how many of the women passengers hated their guts? she wondered. 'Yes, ma'am, is there anything I can do for you?'

She was upset – and angry at herself because it made her bitchy. 'What's wrong? I know there's something wrong; there are no lights below. Why is the captain detouring?'

The Smile remained just as gracious and frozen as before. 'It's only a routine detour, ma'am. We do it all the time in the event of storms.'

The girl must think she had never ridden on an airplane before. But there was no chance to argue, the stewardess was gone.

Next to her, Jennifer began to stir underneath the light blanket tucked around her. She turned and looked out the window, then said in a sleepy voice, 'Look, Momma – the whole sky's on fire.'

She glanced out the window again. Jennifer was right – a glow seemed to stretch for miles in the darkness.

She wondered what it was and if it had anything to do with the fact that there were no lights below. Probably a forest fire. Maybe it had cut the transmission lines somehow.

They'd be landing out in the boondocks all right and how in the hell was Martin going to pick them up then?

55

The foam-filled cups were stacked up on the arm of Tebbets' chair to the point where they teetered precariously on the edge. He reached for the nearest one and discovered he had already drained it half an hour ago. He launched a brief search for one that still contained drinkable coffee, untainted by a snuffed-out cigarette butt. He found one and leaned back in his chair, glancing briefly over at Captain Kloster to note his reaction to the flow of disaster reports. The chubby Air Force captain was white. Hang in there, old buddy, Tebbets thought. Things were going to get a lot worse before they got better.

The screens in front of him flickered briefly as a voice in his ear said, 'Switching over to emergency power. Eureka Falls transmission station is now out of the grid.'

Kloster heard the same news and paled even more. 'Not much left of the grid, is there?'

Tebbets drained his cup, crumpled it and potted it at a nearby wastebasket. A rim shot. 'Just the West Coast is going black – along with part of the Rocky Mountain area. Eureka Falls cut the grid before any surge hit the Midwest.' He inspected the screens. The plants and switching stations had gone down like a house of cards once Cardenas Bay had dropped out of the grid. 'San Diego is still with us. At least the naval base is safe.'

'Thank God for that.'

Kloster had gone back to nervously doodling on his note pad when one of the technicians cut in. Tebbets held his microphone closer to his mouth and said, 'Repeat that, please'.

'There's been a sudden increase in the Cardenas Bay infrared signature.'

Tebbets leaned into his mike, his voice tense. 'They're coming back on stream?'

'Negative. Too many transmission lines are out. I'm not sure what the hell it is.'

Tebbets caught Kloster's eye. 'Let's take a look. Screen three.'

The familiar infrared view of the coast came back on, this time oddly dimmed; the number of red dots had diminished drastically – except for one large splotch in the centre that had to be Cardenas Bay. It was far larger than any infrared signature should be. Tebbets stared at it, puzzled. 'Switch to visual, zoom six.'

The screen streaked and then showed the vague outlines of the plant as seen from several thousand feet up. It was difficult to make out the outlines of the reprocessing plant or even the coastline itself but the containment dome was plainly visible, parts of it showing very bright on the screen. From one side of the dome and to the left of the screen a heavy phosphorescent cloud slowly drifted away from the plant.

Tebbets looked at it curiously for a long moment, then breathed an almost inaudible 'Holy shit!'

Kloster said, 'What the hell's happening, Tebbets?'

Tebbets' mouth felt dry. He moistened it slightly with cold

coffee, then decided that that kind of dry had nothing to do with moisture. 'The containment dome at Cardenas has been breached. The cloud you see is radioactive steam and probably all kinds of radioactive gases – plus a lot of vaporized uranium and steel, zirconium, powdered concrete, you name it. And plutonium. Radioactively speaking, that cloud's hot as hell.'

'Lethal?'

'I'd hate to be under it.' Tebbets put down his coffee cup, knocking one of the small stacks of empties to the floor. He didn't notice. 'Give me the coordinates on that cloud from the Prometheus complex.'

The voice in his headphones rattled off a string of figures. Tebbets made a face. 'Forget it – how about an outline on a visual of the coast?'

A long view of the coastal area appeared on the screen and superimposed over it was the outline of the cloud. It was blowing out to sea, Tebbets noted with relief, but the size of the cloud seemed to be expanding even as he watched. They'd have to analyse the content and how long the radioactive particles would remain aloft; he guessed the fallout would cover an area at least a hundred miles long and fifteen miles wide. How wide a dispersal pattern would depend on the winds. He suspected that his own estimate was on the conservative side.

Kloster had been staring thoughtfully at the screen, too. Now he suddenly jerked and hunched over his own microphone, his voice panicky. 'Captain Kloster here. I want the weather forecast for the Cardenas area for the next twenty-four hours. Everything you've got – the winds aloft at the height of the cloud and their velocity and direction. Also, how heavy the rain is and how long it's going to last.'

Kloster started filling his pad with computations as the information came in. Tebbets watched with interest. Kloster finally finished and said into his mike, 'No, no further data needed.' He turned to Tebbets. 'My speciality's weather. Too old and too fat to do much flying any more.'

Tebbets pointed to the pad. 'What were you figuring?'

Kloster was obviously proud of his figures. 'Wind velocities, dispersal patterns. And wind shifts.' He was silent for a moment while he quickly checked his figures. 'How long before they get Cardenas under control?'

'Under control?' Tebbets looked his surprise. 'Captain, you're not going to blow that out like you do an oil-well fire.' He motioned to one of the technicians to bring him another

cup of coffee. 'There's no putting it out, Captain, it's just going to go on and on and on. At least for a couple of weeks.'

Kloster looked as if he didn't understand. 'You mean that
Cardenas is going to continue spewing out radioactive particles
and steam?'

Tebbets stirred in some sugar and powdered cream. 'I told
you. It's not the kind of fire you can put out.'

'The steam *has* to die out!' Kloster insisted.

Tebbets leaned forward slightly to speak into his mike. 'What
are the geological formations around Cardenas Bay?' He
waited a moment. 'Thought so. Thanks.' He turned to Kloster
and shook his head. 'It'll keep on all right. Those are limestone
cliffs. The water of crystallization in the rocks will provide lots
of steam.'

Kloster gestured helplessly at his note pad. 'You know what
this means, Tebbets?'

Tebbets buried his face in his coffee. 'You tell me, Captain.'

'At the moment, we've got a pretty unusual situation,
weatherwise. The prevailing winds are from the sea to the land,
unless we've got a Santa Ana – and then they're hot and dry
because they blow off the desert. Currently, the tail end of a
northern storm front is pushing southerly winds ahead of it.
The unstable air behind is blowing out to sea and we've got
showers. But it won't last long. Another twenty-four hours, or
less, that wind is going to shift.'

Suddenly Tebbets knew what he was going to say.

'Sometime tomorrow,' Kloster continued, his voice edgy,
'Los Angeles is going to be downwind from that nightmare.'

Tebbets sat for a long moment, staring at the slowly expanding cloud on screen three. Then once again he ducked his head
towards his chest mike. 'Get me General Whitmore. Break in
if you have to. Triple-A priority.'

For the first time that evening, he was personally frightened.

56

Stragglers were still showing up at the Information Centre but
Karen remained among the missing. There was no way out for
her, Parks thought, or for Glidden, either. Then he closed his
mind to it. He had enough to do to keep the living alive.

The men coming in now were, for the most part, badly wounded – burned or scalded by steam. 'There's got to be a medicine kit around,' Lerner said. 'Most of the visitors here are kids; they've got to have something here for skinned knees and the like. It won't be much, but there must be *something*.' They found the small kit in the desk at the entrance to the rotunda and a carton of reserve supplies in the maintenance locker room, behind a box of toilet tissue. One roll of the tissue was immediately confiscated by a technician, who disappeared outside into the rain, to reappear, cursing, five minutes later.

Shortly after they located the first-aid kit, Lerner reported the most serious problem among the wounded. He motioned Parks into a section of the rotunda where he and Kormanski had sequestered the wounded behind one of the exhibits. Lerner kept his voice low.

'Stewart just showed up. He worked with Peterson in maintenance; same story – trapped on the reactor-room floor except he managed to work loose.'

'How bad?'

'He got a heavy dose, a really heavy dose.'

Parks was puzzled. 'So have him strip and wash down. Any smocks he can wrap up in?' Some of the technicians had escaped from the plant with minimum exposures and had contributed their lab smocks to the usable clothing available for those who had to strip completely.

Lerner looked impatient. 'You don't understand: he's badly burned. He can't possibly strip off his own clothes and he won't be able to scrub himself down, either. He'll have all he can do to keep from screaming his bloody head off even if somebody else washes him down.' He took a breath. 'That is – if we can find somebody. If I have to, I'll do it myself, but there are a lot of men still coming in who need attention.'

'How about asking for volunteers?'

Dryly. 'You can't ask for volunteers without explaining the dangers. And once you do that, there aren't any volunteers.'

Parks felt his skin begin to crawl. 'Nobody's going to help him out? Come on, Barney; they're not all bastards.'

Lerner made a visible effort to keep his voice low. 'Stewart has radioactive particles in his clothing, in his hair, probably under his fingernails, undoubtedly coating large portions of his skin. You're asking for somebody to touch him – somebody who may currently be clean but willing to go through decontamination all over again. If you handle Stewart, you re-expose

219

yourself; there's no getting around it.' He leaned against the wall, the intensity draining from his voice. 'We're kidding ourselves, Parks.' He waved his hand around the rotunda. 'All of this is a farce. It's next to impossible to keep a decontamination centre radiologically clean. It's like honey spreading around a kitchen once you open the jar. There've been cases of doctors unintentionally spreading radioactives all over a hospital, even taking them home. And we're hardly set up as well as a hospital.'

'Everybody turned you down?'

A ripple of anger fled across Lerner's face. 'For Christ's sake, Parks, I haven't had time to ask everybody. Those I did said thanks, but no thanks.' He lowered his voice again. 'During the plagues in London the nearby towns used to post armed guards to keep the refugees out. It's the same thing. Stewart's got the plague.'

'You want me to try and force somebody to help?'

'I don't know what I want you to do.' Lerner suddenly turned away. 'Ah shit, what the hell am I worried about? He got a full-body dose, way over six hundred "r". He won't live a week and every day of it will be hell.' He was silent for a moment, then made up his mind. 'Get me the gate guard's pistol.' He caught the look on Parks' face. 'It's nothing I haven't done before; it's not that difficult.' Parks stared at him in silence and he finally shrugged. 'Americans! We want him to live so he can suffer. What do we *have* against the human race, Parks? Even dumb animals are kinder to their own!'

Parks said, 'Would you really do it, Barney?'

Lerner looked at him defiantly. 'Once upon a time I had to.'

Mike Kormanski had been standing nearby listening to the conversation with growing agitation. He suddenly cut in. 'You didn't ask me, Barney. I'll strip him down and scrub him.'

'I didn't ask you,' Lerner apologized quietly, 'because you've done more than your share so far. You've already risked your life to a far greater degree than you probably realize.'

Kormanski shrugged. 'Nobody else is going to help Stewart.'

'You a hero?' Lerner sneered. 'Or just plain dumb?'

'You testing me?' Kormanski asked.

'You're right,' Lerner said, softening. 'I don't like to see somebody do something brave for the wrong reasons. They get halfway through and then they realize what they're doing; they chicken out then and it's worse than it was before.'

On the way back to the office, Lerner said, 'You're going to say, "He's just a kid." Live in Israel awhile and you realize kids are just like adults. They're just as brave and they die just as easily.'

Parks walked past the office where Cushing and Brandt and Walton were deep in conversation, hesitated, then walked on by to the building's entrance. He slipped out and stood on the porch for a moment, smelling the air. The stink of too many people in too close a space, he thought. But outside, the glare from the melting containment dome and the acrid smell of fire were just as bad. He sensed that Lerner had followed him and said, 'How's it stand now?'

'Five that won't make it; ten that are touch and go. Another dozen with burns and scalds ranging from minor to first degree. They should all be in hospital. Almost everybody was exposed to some degree of radiation but there's no way of really assessing how much. If you live longer than your parents, be thankful. If you cut out before they did, blame it on tonight.' He changed the subject. 'When do the marines get here?'

'Maybe another twenty minutes, maybe half an hour.'

'Try and arrange an airlift to get the wounded out; you might ask them to send in doctors, too.' He ducked back inside.

Parks stood in the doorway a moment longer, huddling in his suit coat against the occasional blast of rain that whipped around the corner of the building. The sound of moaning drifted from the gatehouse; he pulled the collar of his coat tighter and went to look. Cassidy, the gate guard, was holding an electric lantern while a nude Kormanski helped a man out of his clothes and began to wash him gently with detergent. Kormanski was a hairless white in the light from the lantern: a thin, red-headed kid, all knees and elbows and hollow chest.

Nobody was going to give him a medal, Parks thought. Maybe real posterity was just living in somebody else's memory. Like Kormanski would live in his.

He turned and walked back into the office, folding into the chair behind the desk. Someone had brought them an electric lantern, he noted. 'Half the containment dome is gone. If anybody's got any ideas, now's the time to spill them.'

'You already spelled it out,' Brandt said dryly. 'We can't walk away from it and there's nothing we can do about it, either.'

221

Parks glanced at Cushing, who shook his head. 'Don't look at me, Parks, I'm not that much of a technical man. The team from Washington will undoubtedly have some answers.'

It was difficult for Parks to think; he kept seeing Lerner and the wounded in the rotunda. The smell of burned flesh stayed with you, he thought; it was worse than that of rotting potatoes.

'You were being sarcastic when you talked about flooding the containments manually,' Brandt said. 'What about it now? Another hour or so, there'll be nothing but a hole in the ground with the collective melt at the bottom. What about flooding it then?'

'Because it might do just the reverse of what we want it to. The water could act as a moderator and keep the reaction going.'

Brandt started to say something, then hesitated, and finally blurted, 'What about criticality?'

'Possible,' Parks admitted. 'It all depends on how the melt pools – the cross-sectional areas.' He closed his eyes for a moment and ran the familiar equations through his head. 'Before it's over, there'll be something like ten thousand tons of melt down there. We don't know how diluted it will be with steel and zirconium and God knows what else, and we don't know what flow patterns it might take. I suppose if we ever get emergency power in here, we could follow it on the model.' He shrugged. 'I just don't know with all the extra radioactives from the processing plant.'

'What happens with criticality?' Walton asked curiously.

Parks opened one eye. 'Hello, Jerry – I'd forgotten you were here. No offence.' He thought for a moment. 'Criticality, Jerry, is when you have just enough fissionables in just the right position that an atomic reaction starts. In the reactor, it's controllable. Outside of it, at least in this case, you'd have a run-away atomic reaction. Not an explosion but a lot of radioactive material would get splashed around the landscape; our fallout cloud would get more lethal, if that's possible.'

'So what the hell do we do?' Brandt exploded. 'Twiddle our thumbs until the cavalry arrives?'

Cushing was unperturbed. 'The team from Washington will be here early in the morning – they're assembling the various experts now. The AmRad CBR team should be here any minute. In the meantime, if you want to go out and pee on the containments, Hilary, go right ahead.'

'Sometime between the arrival of the marines and the team

from Washington, somebody's going to ask us what went wrong,' Walton said casually. 'Specifically, they're going to ask you, Mr Parks.'

Parks was suddenly aware that all three of them were watching him. 'I suppose they will,' he said slowly.

Cushing cleared his throat. 'If they do, what will you say?'

It was Mad Hatter time again, Parks thought. 'I haven't thought about it – and I can't understand why anybody else has. There are dead and dying men out in the rotunda; the reactors are gone and we're leaking radioactives over half the county.' He fell silent for a moment, then said sarcastically, 'I haven't thought about it for a moment, not one goddamned moment.'

It was Cushing's turn. 'I can't help the dying, Parks. The CBR teams will do what they can when they get here. And apparently there's nothing we can do about the reactors. But there's no point in sitting here twiddling our thumbs when there are important things we could settle now. What you might say to a Federal investigation team or in front of a Congressional committee is damned important.'

'I'll tell them the truth,' Parks said simply.

Cushing leaned forward. 'Just what is the truth, Parks?'

There was an odd tension in the room that Parks couldn't figure out. The others were too intent on what he was saying. Brandt was sweating and grim, Cushing had the aggressive air of a prosecutor in court. 'I'd say what I've been saying all the time. The accident was due to sloppy workmanship, too tight a deadline, defective parts – and trying to push technology too fast. And I've got some dandy examples to back them all up.'

Cushing looked politely curious. 'Really? I'm afraid all your examples are either melting down or have been irradiated to the point where nobody in his right mind would inspect one unless it was under lead glass or could be handled by remotes.'

'There are my letters to the Commission.'

Cushing nodded. 'That's right. There's a volume of correspondence from your office to Washington, listing your complaints, Parks. But without any actual proof to back them up, they're paper complaints. I might believe all of them. As a matter of fact, I believe most of them – but almost everybody else is going to ask for physical proof. If you can't provide it ...' He shrugged. 'You forget the lobbyists for the vendors and the power companies, Parks. Without physical proof they'll do a job on you that you wouldn't believe.'

'What are you leading up to?' Parks could sense that Cushing was in his element now and making the most of it – the clever manipulator, the political animal who knew his way around the dens and warrens of a political Washington.

'Parks.' For the first time since his arrival at Cardenas, Cushing sounded conciliatory. 'Let's assume you're correct in your accusations – defective parts, bad workmanship, all the hundred and one things you've complained about.'

'All those accusations are on file,' Parks said angrily.

'Are they?' Cushing was getting to the meat now and his voice was like a carving knife. 'I wouldn't bet money on it, Parks – and believe me when I say I had nothing to do with it if your reports have disappeared. Inspection records are falsified, correspondence is leaked or altered or stolen – It happens all the time. Too much is at stake and there's no way to guarantee the honesty of every clerk in the Commission. Most of them make small salaries and lobbyists have an awful lot of money to spread around.'

People were dead and dying, Parks thought. Cushing himself may have had a couple of years chopped out of his life but his primary concern now was to protect his back. But the game always went to those who thought of the answers for the next crisis when they were in the middle of the current one.

'What's your point, Cushing?'

'You're making the assumption that defective parts and the like were responsible for the loss-of-coolant accident in Prometheus One. It's a valid assumption but it lacks any real proof – I assume any real proof has melted by now – so it's just an assumption.'

'What the hell's your idea?'

Walton said, 'It could have been sabotage.'

There was silence in the room. They were waiting for him to buy it, Parks thought. He nodded. 'That's convenient, isn't it? Then it's nobody's fault. Western Gas and Electric gets fined twenty or forty grand for poor security and that's it. Everything goes on as before.' He paused. 'What do you have to back you up, Cushing? Maybe my proof is gone and the records have conveniently disappeared. What do you have to back you up?'

Cushing started ticking them off on his fingers. 'Somebody murdered your Dr Seyboldt.'

'The murder doesn't have to be connected with the plant.'

'No, but it's an attractive idea. Two, there's the problem of the missing radioactives.'

Parks felt on the defensive. 'What missing radioactives?'

'The plant's cumulative MUF – material unaccounted for. The microscopic amounts that disappear daily so that by the end of the year, in a plant this size, it's enough to make a bomb or two.'

Brandt shook his head, worried. 'That's pretty thin, Eliot. I still don't think anybody will believe it.'

Cushing turned on him, his voice savage. 'They'll believe it because there's no real alternative to believe. They're going to want to hang somebody, Hilary, and if you don't want it to be you, you better provide them with another body.'

He faced Parks. 'You once asked us to have an open mind; now it's you who have a closed one.' He was conciliatory again. 'I can't believe you have a vested interest in blaming the disaster on the faults you discovered in the building and the operation of the plant.'

'You're forgetting future plants, Cushing.'

Cushing leaned closer, breaking off his words. 'Have you ever dealt with Congressional committees, Parks? They're not made up of scientists and engineers, they're made up of lawyers. They wouldn't know an atom from an artichoke and they could care less. They don't understand scientific abstractions; what they do understand are crimes and criminals. You want stricter regulations for the vendors? You'll get them. But before you get them, the Congress will want a sacrificial goat – the Man Responsible. And it doesn't matter who.'

In the silence that followed, Parks could hear the low murmur of conversation out in the rotunda and the occasional cry from an injured man. Cushing waited a moment for his speech to sink in, then turned back to Brandt. 'Are you absolutely sure it *wasn't* sabotage, Hilary?'

Brandt wavered. He glanced at Parks for support and found none, then reluctantly turned back to Cushing. He sounded old and defeated. 'There's ... no way of saying that it definitely wasn't.'

'Thank you, Hilary,' Cushing said sardonically.

Parks stood up, pushing his chair back so it fell over behind him. 'It's so easy to finger one man. It's not the fault of the goddamned system, it's not because we built the plant hoping to wing it when it came to solving the problems; it's because of some unknown individual – and if we don't know who it is, all the better. You buy it and then everybody's off the hook. For what it's worth, I think it stinks.' He walked to the door, stopping briefly in front of Walton. 'Congratulations, Jerry, you just earned yourself a pension.'

The rotunda was crowded and from the far end, where Lerner had isolated the wounded, there came the faint sounds of moaning. Parks glanced around at the little knots of workers and technicians, some of them asleep on the tiled floor, others talking in low tones among themselves. He walked to the entrance again. Just as he was about to leave, a naked Kormanski came in leading Stewart, wrapped in a technician's smock.

Parks stared. Lerner hadn't told him that Stewart had been blinded.

He stepped outside, for the moment his mind on Kormanski again. Brave kid, he thought. And then, bitterly: He could afford to be. It was only his life that he had to account for. He didn't have to face a board of directors, or a Congressional committee or a legion of angry stockholders. They were what had gradually turned Brandt into a coward, not the threat of losing his life.

The cold air and the chill rain and the glow of the containment dome were a few hundred yards away ... He closed his eyes and tried to imagine that only the rain and the cool night air were real.

'Mr Parks?' It was Cassidy, the gate guard. 'Somebody's coming up the road.'

Parks felt a surge of relief. The detachment of CBR marines from Fort Nicholson. He ran down to the highway, then slowed. Dozens of cars were streaming from the town, their headlights boring small, bright holes in the darkness.

The townspeople, he thought. Coming out of curiosity because they had heard the explosions or had seen the burning plant from across the inlet. Coming to check on relatives who worked there.

And he was the one who was going to have to read them the list of the dead and the dying, the injured and the missing.

57

MIROS had never been meant for this kind of duty, Tebbets thought – quartering the ocean and searching for cargo ships and small craft and trying to warn them away from the shore near Cardenas Bay. It was slow, tedious work, complicated by the scheduling of the various MIROS satellites.

'What about aircraft, Captain?'

Kloster glanced up from his clipboard. 'COMSAC's been informed; all military planes will avoid the area.'

'What about civilian?'

'Civilian?' It was obvious they hadn't been uppermost in Kloster's mind. 'All the major airlines will be notified.'

'And light planes like Cubs and Cessnas?'

'For Christ's sakes, Tebbets, we can't watch out for everybody.'

The voice in Tebbets' headset suddenly came to life. 'Screen three, thirty miles northwest of Cardenas.'

Tebbets and Kloster stared at the screen in silence. Four small red dots crawled slowly across a mottled sea of glass.

'Visual on screen three, zoom seven.'

The small red dots abruptly became four small ships, barely visible in the fitful Pacific moonlight.

'Russian fishing trawlers,' Kloster said slowly. 'They come in close and fish just outside the territorial limits. American fishermen always complain.'

'So why do we let them do it?'

'Nothing illegal about it, according to International Law. Just annoying.'

'They'll be sorry they did this time,' Tebbets said. 'My guess is they've been sitting under the Cardenas fallout for quite a while. They'll have to be notified; I'll bet nobody knows the frequency.'

'*We* know but we can't let them know we know.' He suddenly cocked his head, getting a message for his ears only. 'They've contacted the Russian Embassy. You should start seeing those ships pile on the steam any minute.'

'Sorry we can't stay and watch,' Tebbets said, 'but there are probably others out there.' The screen shifted back to infrared scan. He settled back in his chair, concentrating on sloshing half an inch of cold coffee around the bottom of his cup. 'Think they'll ever make it home, Captain?'

Kloster looked up in surprise. 'Do I think who will ever make it home?'

'The Russian fishing fleet. The ships are probably old, lots of wood fittings, rusting metal. Difficult to decontaminate something like that, damned difficult. You can try washing them off but the particles have a habit of sticking. And there's the problem of their catch. They won't want to dump their fish.' He finished the coffee and squashed the cup down into a stack in front of him. 'If I were running their home port, I wouldn't let them in. As bad as letting Typhoid Mary into town.'

'That's the Russians' worry,' Kloster said. 'They'll think of something.' He jotted some more figures down on his note pad. 'Let me get hold of that forecaster again,' he muttered.

58

Senator Hoyt For the record, Captain Kohnke. You're attached to the Navy Department here in Washington, are you not?
Captain Kohnke That's right, sir. I'm with Naval Intelligence.
Senator Stone Captain, we would like to know the degree of cooperation we received from other countries during the period of the Cardenas disaster – and just how open we were with them.
Captain Kohnke We were very open, sir. There's no way you could hide a disaster of this nature and there was always the possibility that the fallout pattern would have affected other countries. I would say those nations we contacted cooperated completely – after all, many of them have atomic facilities, too. They all observed the media blackout and fed us what information they could on the Cardenas cloud.
Senator Stone I don't follow you there. What do you mean, they fed us information?
Captain Kohnke I think it safe to say they have their own equivalent of MIROS, Senator. I imagine they watch us as closely as we watch them. Considering the nature of the disaster, I think you could expect cooperation. We'd certainly cooperate with them.
Senator Marks As you must be aware, Captain, Washington is a city of rumours. One of the current ones is that a Russian fishing fleet was caught under the fallout from Cardenas and rather than allow the ships back into Russian ports – which they could possibly contaminate – Soviet submarines sank them, with the loss of all hands. To the best of your knowledge, is there any truth to this?
Captain Kohnke That's really not my area of expertise, Senator.

228

Senator Marks You don't even have an opinion?

Captain Kohnke If you're asking my opinion, Senator, I would have to say I think it's ridiculous.

Senator Stone You *have* to say it, Captain?

Senator Clarkson I've heard the same story around town and I think it's pure cock-and-bull. Ships have been sunk in storms before without leaving a trace and to slander the Soviets with this kind of rumour, I think, is reprehensible.

Captain Kohnke I quite agree, sir.

RepresWentative Holmburg I think we should have offered our condolences. After all, it wasn't one of their plants that blew its cork; it was one of ours.

Senator Stone You did know the Russian fleet was there; am I right, Captain?

Captain Kohnke Of course, sir.

Senator Stone And they did abruptly disappear from radar contact, am I right?

Captain Kohnke That's correct, sir.

Senator Stone And you have no idea why?

Captain Kohnke None whatsoever, Senator.

Senator Stone None of our Coast Guard vessels investigated to try and pick up survivors?

Captain Kohnke I believe the Coast Guard considered it too dangerous. They would have had to sail directly into the pattern of fallout.

Senator Stone If a ship had been caught in the fallout from Cardenas Bay, how difficult would it be to decontaminate it?

Captain Kohnke Very difficult, sir.

Senator Stone Then it might be very dangerous to allow that ship into port; correct, Captain?

Captain Kohnke That would have to be the decision of the Port Director, sir.

Senator Stone Really? If it was one of our ships, what do you think we would do if it was steaming towards its home port, say, of Oakland or San Diego?

Captain Kohnke I see what you're driving at, Senator, but I would have to remind you that Americans have always had a reverence for human life.

Senator Stone I don't need reminding, Captain – and you're not answering my question.

Captain Kohnke I'm not sure what we would do, sir.

59

There were fifty people or more standing in the rain, all of them frightened and angry. Cassidy had brought the electric lantern from the gatehouse and hung it from the overhead of the Information Building so they could see Parks. A few had tried to get into the building and had to be held back.

'What the hell happened, Parks?'

'Is Jim Roberts all right? Is my Jim all right?'

'Has anybody seen Tom Peterson?'

Parks held up a hand. 'I'm sorry—'

'Louder, we can't hear you!'

'Level with us, Parks!'

'How come you won't let us in?'

He lost his composure then, his words coming out harsh and choked. 'There's been an accident!' he shouted. There was sudden silence; he could hear the wind whipping past the edge of the building. It rustled the papers in his hands and he sensed everybody's eyes going to the white sheets.

'For God's sakes, Parks, we know there's been an accident!'

It was a little old lady in front who quietly asked the question that Parks had been dreading. 'Was anybody killed, Mr Parks?'

'We'll notify the next of kin—' he started.

'The next of kin are here!' somebody roared. 'What the hell's going on, Parks?'

He stepped forward from the shelter of the building into the rain. 'The reactors!' he shouted. 'They're gone, they're melting down! People have died; we've got injured here! A lot of the men are contaminated with radioactives – we can't let you in.' There was silence again and he lowered his voice. 'A detachmen of marines from Fort Nicholson is on its way. When they get here, they'll take over.'

He glanced out at the highway where the cars were lined up and then back to the people in front of him, some of them holding umbrellas, others in raincoats. His throat felt thick; he wasn't sure he could read the list . . .

A woman three feet away said in a firm voice that carried over the crowd, 'I want to know about my husband.'

Behind her, a man forced his way through the crowd and came up the steps. It was Cole Levant, a mountain of a man whom Parks had liked the few times he had met him. 'They have a right to know,' he said quietly.

Parks nodded. 'I'm not trying to keep the names from them,' he said, his voice cracking. He squinted at the list in the pale light from the lantern and began. For the next few minutes, there was only the sound of the wind and the rain and Parks' ragged voice, tolling off the names of the dead and the injured and the missing. Occasionally there would be a cry from the crowd. It was a scene he had seen a dozen times in newsreels; the mine disaster and the crowd of relatives and children gathered at the head of the tipple.

The total was a dozen known dead – verified by fellow workers who had seen them – and twenty-two missing. And God only knew how many would die in the weeks ahead.

Out on the highway, the clanging of a fire engine sounded suddenly. The crowd cleared a path for it and the town's one pumper ran up the lawn towards the containment dome. Parks had a mental image of a toy Chihuahua attacking a Great Dane. He dashed down the steps after it.

They were uncoiling the hoses when he ran up. 'What the hell do you think you're doing?'

The lead hoseman turned. 'What the hell's it look like, Jack?'

Parks waved him back. 'You might as well piss on it for all the good that's going to do. You'll dump more water on it and just create more steam. Go a dozen feet closer and you'll start catching the fallout. If you don't care how you die, go right ahead!'

The fireman hesitated. 'You're just going to let it burn?'

'What the hell do you think you can do with one engine? And it wouldn't help if you had a dozen. Spray water on it and you'll make it all the worse.'

'Chemical fire?'

'Radioactive.'

The fireman backed away and one of them started rolling up his hose. Abrams suddenly appeared at Parks' elbow. 'Lerner wants to see you back at the Information Building. Important.'

Parks turned and followed him back. Levant and the crowd were still there but it had broken up into small knots. Lerner was in the doorway; he motioned Parks quickly inside. He was holding the Geiger counter and looked oddly tense and nervous.

'Greg, let's check those cars on the highway.'

'Serious?'

'Yeah.'

They slipped around the side of the building and walked out to the highway. The first car they came to caused a roar of clicks from the counter. Lerner checked another car; if anything, the drone was louder. 'They're hot as a pistol. And I'll bet the people who drove them out here are, too. You might as well let them in to see their relatives, Greg; that crowd would probably send the counter right off the scale.' While he was talking, Lerner walked along the line of cars parked on the shoulder of the highway. There was a steady rush of clicks from the counter.

'The town's right across the inlet,' Parks reflected. 'It's directly beneath the fallout. Everybody in town probably has a dose – and if they drove out here, it's probably a serious dose. Really serious.'

They walked back to the Information Building and pushed through the crowd. Parks pulled Levant aside. 'Come in a minute, Cole.' They drew Levant over to a corner and Lerner silently held the counter out and walked around him; the counter clicks sounded like fast-popping corn.

Parks said, 'You're hot, Cole. Your truck was covered with fallout when you drove out here.'

Levant looked puzzled. 'I don't get it.'

'You know what fallout is, Cole? It's tiny radioctive particles from the reactor debris. It's fallout like in atomic-bomb fallout. Little radioactive specks of metal, metal oxide, and concrete that have settled out of the atmosphere over your car and you. If you don't wash them off, they can cause radiation poisoning, destroy your white blood cells, cause leukaemias and cancers later on in life. The particles may be too small for you to see or feel; this counter tells if they're present. And they're present on you, Cole.'

'Rob and I were inside the truck cab all the way,' Levant said defensively.

'You never opened the window? Your truck's completely sealed?'

Lerner added, 'Cardenas Bay is right under the fallout pattern. It'll have to be evacuated, everybody in it. They'll have to be checked out and, if necessary, decontaminated.'

Levant looked from one to the other and slowly shook his head. 'You're crazy. That's more than three thousand people. They're supposed to just leave everything behind, get in their cars and come out here? Because of something they can't feel

232

or hear or smell? Because something might kill them a year or ten years from now?'

'It might kill them one helluva lot sooner than that,' Parks said.

'You're out of your mind,' Levant said softly. 'Half of them wouldn't leave if the town were burning down.' He frowned. 'Wouldn't they be safer just staying indoors? If I got a dose, it was from driving out here, right?'

'Houses are sieves,' Lerner said. 'The wind blows through them all the time. There's nobody in town who doesn't have a dose by now. And it will just get worse; they couldn't stay indoors forever anyways.'

'You don't have the facilities here,' Levant said, still protesting. 'You couldn't get anywhere near that many people into this building. And coming out here could be dangerous in itself.'

'Take the side roads, away from the wind,' Parks said. 'In the meantime I'll try and commandeer a barn for decontamination – maybe a milking barn that has artesian water.'

'Parks, there's no way they're going to leave!'

'If they don't,' Parks said, 'they'll die. Some tomorrow, some next week, some next month and the rest maybe years from now. Everybody loses a little of their time. Some lose a lot of it. But everybody loses, Levant. No exceptions.'

Levant glanced around the rotunda at the huddled groups of technicians and at the back, where he could hear the cries of the injured. 'If I were a farmer and realized what had happened, I wouldn't let the townspeople within a mile of my place.'

'Neither would I,' Parks admitted. 'I'd get a gun and probably shoot to kill. I said we'd have to commandeer a place.'

'You got the guns so you can do the commandeering?'

Lerner was at the door, impatient. 'Things aren't getting any better out there.'

'OK,' Levant said. 'I'll round up some men. You show us how to decontaminate ourselves and we'll see what we can do.' On the porch, his words were almost swallowed by the wind. 'They won't leave, Parks – I know them. And if I do convince them, they're going to hate your guts.'

'You'll run the risk of recontaminating yourself!' Parks shouted. 'If you go, you're volunteering.'

'Sure, that's what they told me in the Army.'

Parks watched him slip away into the crowd. 'Thirty years ago,' he mused to Lerner, 'you mentioned "fallout" and you scared half the population shitless. Almost everybody had a shelter in his basement stocked with food and water and maybe a shotgun to keep his neighbours out. I never thought people would forget.'

'You so sure they have?' Lerner stared at the clouds spreading over the collapsing containment dome. 'I think Levant will tell them what happened and they'll panic.'

60

Karen said, 'Can you get through?' She held the electric lantern higher so she could see Glidden's face. The sweat had begun to bead on his upper lip and he brushed it impatiently away. 'If I could, I wouldn't be keeping it a secret, Miss Gruen.' He tried once more, then hooked the walkie-talkie back on his belt. 'We'll try again later.'

Bildor was bitter. 'Nobody gives a damn about us.'

'Parks knows we're down here,' Glidden said shortly.

'Then why doesn't somebody answer?'

It was funny how much you could tell just from voice inflection, Karen thought. Glidden was keeping his face carefully blank but she knew instinctively that he was lying; no one knew they were in the storage caverns. And even if they did, Parks undoubtedly had his hands full. Probably Barney did, too. Up above it must be— She cut the line of thought. She didn't want to think about the dangers that Greg and Barney must be facing. It was frightening enough to realize that somewhere just beyond the maze of darkened corridors were ten thousand tons of molten steel and reactor fuel. In the dark, with only the electric lantern, she had the horrible feeling that she was living in an air bubble at the bottom of an ocean.

Tremayne began to cough and Karen said, 'Put him down for a minute.'

They lowered the stretcher and Rossi massaged his biceps. 'He wouldn't be a problem if the batteries in the electricar hadn't crapped out. How much further, Mr Glidden?'

'Not far. Two corridors over and then to the right; the access door is at the far end.'

Bildor shivered in the darkness. 'We're kidding ourselves. We can make it to the access door, but if it's rough going after that, we won't be able to carry Tremayne very far.' Glidden made a noise in the back of his throat and Rossi turned away. 'I know what you're thinking,' Bildor said, his voice rising. 'But you know goddamned well we can't take him with us all the way. All we'll do is endanger our own lives. It's a dumb equation – any way you look at it!'

'For Christ's sake, shut up.' Karen put the lantern on the floor, then knelt down and felt Tremayne's pulse. Little things, comparatively speaking, could cause shock and it looked as if Tremayne were going into shock. 'Pick him up and let's go.'

They walked another fifty feet, Karen in front with the electric lantern. Rossi said, 'We're almost back to where we started.'

How long had it been? Karen wondered. An hour, maybe more? She was losing track of time. Up ahead she saw a glow in the main corridor. Bildor said, 'I guess all the lights didn't go – unless that's an emergency lantern.'

But the lights had already shifted over to emergency, Karen thought, puzzled, and then they, too, had gone. They were a dozen feet from the main corridor when she heard a slow, steady hiss. Glidden started to say, 'Wait a min—' but they were already rounding the corner.

The heavy emergency doors that led to the main reactor room were a shimmering white; they were starting to slump like melting wax. Bildor saw them first. He let go of his corner of the stretcher and gasped, *'Jesus Christ!'*

Karen screamed and turned to run back the way they had come. Glidden grabbed her and shouted, 'There's no way out back there. Run for the access door!'

They darted across the main corridor. Glidden twisted frantically at the dogged-down door. Then it was open and they lunged through. Karen hung back suddenly.

'Tremayne!'

Glidden clutched her wrist. 'You'll never get to him in time. You'll just get a heavy gamma-ray exposure.'

She clung to the doorway a moment longer. On the floor in the main corridor, Tremayne had regained consciousness and raised himself up on one elbow to stare at the doors she couldn't see. A tearing sound echoed through the corridor. Tremayne sat all the way up on the stretcher and started to scream. The glow in front of him blossomed, painting his face with a brilliant radiance.

Then Glidden had pulled her through the entrance and

started dogging down the door, cutting off Tremayne's screams.

'You couldn't have helped him.'

She leaned against the corridor bulkhead and tried to control the sobs pumping her chest. 'You just don't ... walk away.'

'Sure you do,' Glidden said harshly. 'The first thing a good doctor learns is when to give up.' His voice softened. 'Quit feeling guilty, Miss Gruen. We probably couldn't have carried him to the sea exit in any case.'

'It was quixotic even to try, wasn't it?'

'That's not my word for it. It just couldn't be done, that's all.'

'We could have rested along the way.'

'No, we couldn't have,' Glidden said, his voice grim. 'We don't have the time.'

She held up the lantern. Bildor had wet his pants, the stain spreading down the front of his technician's uniform. He was shaking. 'We've got to get out of here. That melt's going to keep right on flowing. It will flood the storage corridors.'

In the darkness, Rossi said, 'What happens then?'

Bildor looked as if he wanted to run again. 'It'll get bigger. The fissionables in the storage corridors will add to it. There may even be low-level explosions.' He turned. 'Let's go, *let's go!*'

Glidden shook his head. 'We'll need protective suits first. Maybe not right now, but we'll sure as hell need them later.'

'Where are we going to find them down here?' Rossi asked.

'There's a maintenance locker with suits a hundred yards down the path.'

Glidden took the lantern and started down the rocky pathway to the locker. Halfway there, Karen glanced curiously behind her, back the way they had come.

The access door was now a deep cherry red.

61

Ed had just started the car when Abby suddenly said, 'Just a minute – I forgot something.' She got out and ran back up the steps, through the hastily ransacked living room and into the bedroom. The photo album was in the bottom drawer of the dressing table. She pulled it out from under the neat stacks of cotton slips and flannel nightgowns, took a hasty look around for anything else she might have missed and paused in the centre of the room, caught up in momentary indecision. The sepia portrait of Aunt Helen that had been in the family for years, the set of Rosenthal china that had been her mother's wedding present, the quilt she had made when she was a high school girl ...

She hugged the photo album to her chest. All the memories she could take were in it; anything else would be too much to carry. They couldn't take everything, she thought, almost in tears. Besides, they'd be back. It was foolish running like this; she only half believed Cole Levant anyway.

No, that wasn't true; she had believed him completely. Down deep, she had always worried about the plant. She remembered the Korean War when they had built the fallout shelters. Of course, that had been in case of an atomic-bomb attack and this was hardly the case but still ...

They'd be back; she had to believe that. Somehow the authorities would get the plant under control and then she and Ed could come back ...

'Abby? What's taking you, woman?'

She glanced around the room once more, made a tentative move towards Aunt Helen's photograph, then turned and ran back to the car. Outside, the rain was heavier, and she swore she could smell the heavy, ashy odour of fire. Ed was holding the car door open for her. Quickly she got in, placing the photo album on top of the load in the back seat. That was her life, she thought. Faded snapshots of picnics and parties and babies and relatives whose names she could no longer even remember ...

'We never look through that any more, Abby. I'm surprised you went back for it.'

'I wish we'd had time for the china,' she said wistfully.

He started the car up with a jerk and they pulled out of the driveway into the street. Shadowy shapes of other cars filled the street now, all of them heading for the state highway; many of them had luggage lashed to the top or loaded into the trunk with the lid tied down.

'We never used the china except for company, Abby, and when's the last time we had company?'

She didn't answer. Instead she turned for a final look at their home, a gaunt building of brown shingles and sad-eyed windows huddling in the rainy darkness. She wasn't ever going to see it again, she thought. She was as sure of that as she was of anything.

'Ed, you still keep those mints in the glove compartment?'

'Stomach acting up?' He was suddenly solicitous, as he always was when anything was wrong with her. 'Can't blame you. First the lights all go out and then you get rousted out in the middle of the night on a wild-goose chase like this. You remember to lock the door?'

She nodded yes and fumbled around for the antacid mints. She was feeling a little nauseous and weak; probably a reaction from trying to pack so many things on the spur of the moment. And the pain of making up your mind what you really wanted to take with you.

There were more cars on the highway now and they slowed as they hit the edge of town. Ed rolled down the window so he could spit. 'Abby, we should have stayed right where we were until we heard something on the radio or the electricity came back on and we could get the late news on TV. I don't think that fisherman fella really knew what he was talking about; you know they've never liked the plant . . .'

He was talking like that, Abby decided, because he believed what Cole Levant had said even more than she did – but he didn't want to admit it.

It was open country now and gusts of rain were beating against the car. What was it Levant had talked about? Fallout? Stay away from it, he had said, but the way the wind was whipping around, there was fat chance of that.

She could see the plant from the highway, see it better than she could from the back porch, and the sight took her breath away. Half of it had melted down and bright clouds billowed from it into the night sky. She didn't doubt what Levant had said now.

The traffic slowed to a halt. There was an open area ahead – meadows where they used to go for occasional picnics. Trucks were parked at the edge of the area with groups of men standing nearby.

Overhead the sudden *whop-whop-whop* of helicopters sliced the night air. Three looming shadows, almost invisible behind bright landing lights, settled down in the meadows. For a moment the moon peeked from behind an ancient galleon cloud. She saw men climb quickly out of the 'copters to join those standing around the trucks. The men from the 'copters were dressed in white with helmet-like hoods and carrying rifles.

238

'What the hell ...! Sorry, Abby. Look like men from Mars, don't they?'

She nodded. 'Troops.'

'I can tell that; I ain't blind.'

Several of the white-clad soldiers started walking down the line of cars, speaking to each driver. Ed rolled down the window in time to hear one of them address the line of cars with a bullhorn. With his white uniform and faceless hood, he looked almost mechanical, Abby thought. Like a machine in human form.

'Keep on the freeway; all exit ramps have been blocked! Form up at the staging area down the road for decontamination!'

Ahead of them, the driver of an old Volkswagen was arguing with one of the soldiers. 'Look, fella, I'm driving right on through to San Diego, I've had enough of this town. I've got relatives in Diego and—'

The soldier brought his rifle up to the ready. 'The staging area's two miles down the pike, mister, and that's where you're going. We've got a roadblock down there and nobody goes beyond it.'

The voice was oddly reassuring, Abby thought. A young, perfectly human voice. She had half expected him to talk with a metallic screech.

A jeep bounced along the shoulder of the highway and stopped for a moment by the soldier at the stalled car. An officer – Abby guessed he had to be; there were some kind of patches on the shoulders of his white uniform – leaned out and said, 'Corporal? Cardenas Bay is under Quarantine. Nobody gets back in. Everybody goes to the staging area. Absolutely no exceptions. Use your weapon if you have to.'

He leaned back in the jeep; the vehicle roared off. The Volkswagen driver gunned his car. The young soldier shouted, 'O'Halloran? Up front!' He turned back to the car as another soldier came running up, automatic carbine at high port. 'That's as far as you go, mister!'

The Volkswagen pulled over on the shoulder. 'Outta my way, soldier boy!'

The corporal stepped aside and said calmly, 'Put some APs through the hood, O'Halloran.' The other soldier brought up his carbine and let loose a brief burst at the car's hood. The VW bucked to a halt; flame suddenly gushed from the punctured gas tank. The door abruptly popped open and the screaming driver tumbled out, beating at his flaming clothing and rolling in the dirt on the shoulder. Another soldier ran up and the corporal said, 'Sims, get a blanket. Wrap him up; then put him under arrest and take him to Colonel Burgess at the staging area.'

He took the bullhorn from his belt and turned to the angry crowd gathered at the edge of the highway. *'OK, folks, everybody back in their cars and head for the staging area right up the road.'* For a moment nobody moved. *'We're not fooling, folks – move it!'*

Abby had gotten out of the car. She ran over to the soldier helping the Volkswagen's driver beat out his burning clothes. 'I'm a nurse – he'll need some medical help.'

The corporal with the bullhorn trotted up, took her firmly by the arm and walked her back to the cars lined up on the highway. 'Back in your car, lady; no exceptions. He'll get medical attention; don't worry about it.'

'But I'm a—'

'Get moving, lady!'

Ed helped her back in the car. 'They've got no right to talk to you like that,' he said angrily. 'No right at all!'

She sat back in her seat and pulled her coat tighter around her. She felt old and tired and useless. 'He's just following orders, Ed. Don't blame the boy.'

'Then his orders don't make any sense, Abby. That man was probably pretty badly burned.'

Ahead of them the cars started again and a moment later they were inching up the highway. The wind had picked up. Abby could feel it cut right through her, even in the car. The cold and the dampness, that must be it, she thought.

She was starting to feel a whole lot sicker.

62

Colonel Avery Burgess turned the kitchen chair around and sat so he could lean his elbows on the back of it. He watched intently while the corpsman worked on the farmer's arm. How did the poem go again? *Under the spreading chestnut tree, the village smithy stands; the smith a mighty man is he, with large and sinewy hands* ... Larson's hands were large and sinewy, all right – the better to strangle Burgess with if he ever got the chance.

'That was a very foolish thing to do, you know. You could have been seriously hurt.'

Larson winced as the corpsman cleaned his upper arm where one round had laid open the flesh in a ragged wound. 'If your goddamned marines were half as good as you keep saying all the time, I'd be dead.'

Burgess smiled cheerfully. 'I know; they don't make them like they used to but then they don't make anything like they used to.' The smile faded. 'Gilroy's a sharpshooter. He hit you exactly where he wanted to hit you, or else you *would* be dead.' He glanced over at the farmer's son, standing by the stove, looking sullen. The boy was a duplicate of his father but thirty years younger. 'Your boy would make a great marine – the Corps could use him. Ever think of joining up, son?'

'Fat goddamned chance,' the boy mumbled.

'Make a man out of you,' Burgess said, cheerful again. 'If you already were, you would have taken a potshot at us like your old man did. It took guts to do that.' He briefly inspected Larson's wife, standing by her husband's side. She had obviously been a beauty in her day. 'Any coffee, Mrs Larson? It's cold as hell out there.'

'You took over our farm,' she said bitterly. 'Make your own coffee.'

Larson twisted slightly in his chair to look up at her. 'Martha, make the man some coffee. I could use a cup myself.'

She stalked over to the stove. 'When it's made, you can hand him his cup. Be damned if I will.'

'I guess I wouldn't win any popularity contest here,' Burgess sighed. He glanced curiously around the kitchen. 'How come you've got electricity? Your own power supply?'

'We've got a gasoline-powered motor-generator setup. Same thing for the stove and heating. They work off a propane tank.'

'You know,' Burgess said, 'it's really not my idea to do all of this. But the Cardenas Bay plant let go and—' He shrugged. 'Not much help for it. We need your barn. You've got artesian water, so we know it's uncontaminated, and you've got shower stalls out there. Couldn't ask for anything better, really.' He lit a cigarette and blew the smoke towards the ceiling. 'Why the hell did you try to hold us off?'

Larson winced again and glanced up at the corpsman. 'Take it easy, goddamnit – I'm more gentle when I handle one of my

241

cows.' He turned back to Burgess. 'A year ago the Government inspectors came through. Had to dump all my milk and they monitored my cows for two months. Strontium something. All the fault of your damned plant; something was wrong with it even then.'

'Not *our* plant, Larson. We don't go around building those things.'

'What are you going to do?'

'With the barn? Give a lot of showers – something over three thousand of them. That's why we need your cattle stalls and your well water. We can fly in drums of detergent but wash water would be a problem. Where do those drains empty out, by the way?'

Larson jerked his head towards the west. 'The creek, further down. It empties out into the ocean.'

Burgess noted it down on a card and stuck it back in his pocket. They'd have to quarantine all the farms along the creek until it had cleansed itself, if it ever did.

'You know,' Burgess mused, 'I was raised on a farm myself. Near Muncie, Indiana. Two hundred acres, most of it in corn. Now they're showing X-rated movies on it.' Larson grunted but didn't answer. They weren't going to be friendly, Burgess thought. Well, win some, lose some. 'You've got a nice layout here. Well kept up, modern equipment, your own tank truck—'

There was a sudden burst of gunfire outside. Larson and his son tensed. Burgess took in a lungful of smoke and blew it slowly out in a perfect ring.

'What the hell was that, Colonel?'

'Not sure, really.' Burgess was thoughtful for a moment. 'Some of your cows ever come back late?'

'There's always stragglers.'

'Then I suspect some of them probably straggled too far. They must have wandered into the fallout pattern.' He looked at Larson and slowly shook his head. 'I'm sorry, Mr Larson, there's just no way we're going to take the time to shave and wash down a cow.'

'You bastard!'

He ducked just in time to miss the thrown pot of coffee. He didn't move from his chair or even indicate he was aware of the pool of hot water and grounds running between his boots. 'The Government will compensate you, of course. I'll see that the form is mailed to you. It was probably only one or two cows.' There was another burst of gunfire. He sighed and stood up. 'My mistake. You ought to teach your cows to stick closer to home.' He nodded at the corpsman. 'You want me for anything, I'll be out in the barn.'

He walked out, idly wondering if Larson's wife was any better at throwing knives than pots of hot coffee. Couldn't blame her, really. And she only knew the half of it.

In the barn, white-clad marines were hanging heavy twill curtains around the shower area. There wasn't time for the niceties, Burgess thought: They could spend the entire night dividing up the whole area into individual showers. Besides, it was more efficient this way. People would get hit on all sides by the sprays.

A marine came running over. 'The barbers are set up and the choppers are bringing in fatigues. Should be here any minute. We're ready to go anytime, sir.'

'Fine. Where's the brass from Cardenas Bay?' The marine pointed to a group of men talking in a corner and Burgess strode over.

'Which one of you is Parks?' He started to hold out his hand, then suddenly pulled it back and smiled wryly. 'Not quite yet, I guess. Did you people pass inspection? I know you did the best you could back at your Information Centre but I'm afraid we can't rely on that.'

While he talked, Burgess weighed the group in front of him. He had thought at first that the older, heavier-set man was Parks but the man introduced himself as Brandt, the VIP from Western Gas. He looked as if he had been through hell and probably had been. Parks seemed more the engineering sort, the kind who wasn't afraid to get his hands dirty. Good, competent type.

'It's a low count but we're still contaminated,' Parks said.

Burgess nodded towards one end of the barn. 'The barbers are over there. Strip down and they'll cut your hair. We'll run you through the showers first.'

Parks looked uneasy. 'I thought we'd let the others go through first.'

Burgess shook his head. 'Noble of you but a little impractical. We need you as soon as we can have you, which was at least a good half hour ago.'

Cushing edged forward. 'My name's Eliot Cushing, I'm from—'

'The formalities can wait,' Burgess cut in. He knew who Cushing was. He had sized him up immediately; the man literally reeked of Washington. When he was old and grey and sitting behind a desk in DC, Burgess thought, this was the type he would have to work with. Maybe he'd get lucky and there'd be a war he could die in. 'Please strip down and go through with the rest of them; we'll need you, too.' Cushing froze and Burgess smiled pleasantly at him. 'I'll tell you how to spell my name for your report later. But right now – *if* you please!'

As they turned to leave, Burgess said, 'Just a moment. You there, you're Lerner? As soon as you get through, you'll be in charge here. My file on you says you've had more experience with decontamination than anybody else. They tell me the Israelis are very thorough in that sort of thing.' He looked at Lerner speculatively. 'You're listed in the emergency plan manning chart as the man who *should* be in charge in case of an accident. I'm glad you survived.' He looked around. 'There should be another man – Kormanski? He's supposed to have had some training, too.'

'He's back at the Information Building,' Lerner said.

'We'll send a jeep for him. He'll be your second in command. As soon as you go through the decon, I'll introduce you to the sergeant who's running things now. He'll take his orders from you. You've got six barbers, a gaggle of medics, and clothing's being flown in. Anything you need and don't have, see me.' He pointed at their soaked suits and technician's smocks. 'You'll have to go outside to strip – use the south pasture. Take everything off: hats, shoes, watches, wedding bands; it'll all have to be burned and buried. The same goes for the townspeople. Everything they've brought with them will have to be confiscated.'

'Everything?' Parks asked.

Burgess nodded. 'Of course – we don't have the equipment or the time to check out everybody's personal possessions to see if they're clean, Mr Parks. And we're not dealing with something that's going to go away in the next week or even in the next hundred years – or thousand years. *You* know that. Even the dust on a book could be deadly for somebody who might read it a dozen years from now.' He shook his head. 'I'm sorry; everything will have to be burned and then we'll bury the ashes.'

'The smoke—' Parks started to protest.

'—is blowing out to sea. We should be through before the wind shifts. God help us if we aren't.'

Parks didn't move. 'Then the grass grows over it and the roots pick up the radioactives and the cows eat the grass and we drink the milk and it will be just as bad.'

Burgess' smile faded. 'This won't be a farm after tonight, I'm afraid. It will be fenced off – quarantined and turned into a national preserve. I imagine that the job of watching over it will become one of the longer-lasting institutions of the human race. Eventually we'll probably have a priesthood that cares for taboo places like this.'

Burgess turned to walk away, then hesitated. 'When you're through, Parks, come and see me. We have to do something about that plant of yours – tonight.' He glanced through the windows at the clouds scudding across the sky. 'We've got monitors ready to go up but I suspect I already know what they're going to tell me. If the wind shifts . . .' He shrugged.

A corporal appeared at a run and saluted. 'Colonel, we're monitoring an unauthorized broadcast. We think it's a mobile unit from the highway just outside of town, probably a mobile news unit.'

'Tell Lieutenant Paxton to intercept it and take the men in custody.' He thought for a second. 'Do it the hard way if you have to.'

The corporal saluted and left on the run.

'What are you going to do?' Parks asked sarcastically. 'Shoot them?'

'Only if I have to,' Burgess said pleasantly. His smile faded back in again. 'You should have stripped and taken your shower minutes ago, Parks. You're not shy, are you?'

63

You could feel the tension building, Tebbets thought. Nothing you could put your finger on, just the extra snap in the reports that trickled through on his headset – and little things like no sugar in his coffee. He wasn't a boozer; what the hell did they think he ran on anyway? He sipped at his cup and stared thoughtfully at screen three. The infrared signature of Cardenas Bay was enormous, the bright haze drifting out to sea was only slightly less so.

Kloster's desk-chair was an island in a sea of crumpled

sheets from his note pad. He looked over at Tebbets. 'Have we got an update on the fallout pattern?'

'It's coming from the computer now.'

'How long will the wind direction hold?'

'Last I heard, five hours, maybe ten. Maybe less.'

'Which way will it shift?'

'South – towards Los Angeles.' Tebbets blew on his coffee. Goddamnit, the place was really falling apart; they knew he liked it lukewarm. 'Evacuating LA is going to be a bitch.'

'They're not going to try.'

Tebbets thought about that for one long, disbelieving moment, then put his coffee cup carefully down among the empties on the arm of his chair. 'They're just going to let the people sit there and take their lumps?'

Kloster looked both angry and frustrated. 'The city's blacked out. That means no street lamps, no television, no radio and no lighted green signs reading "This Way To The Fwy". Maybe something can be done in the morning but we sure as hell can't do anything now. All we'd do is cause panic in the middle of the night.'

Christ, Tebbets thought, they weren't going to do anything. Just sit tight and pray the damned wind didn't change. On the other hand, even if they could evacuate the city, where the hell would they move everybody? Then another thought struck him. 'Didn't you say your family lived in LA?'

'Glendale. And I don't need reminding.' Kloster stared at his note pad for a moment longer, then abruptly got up and walked towards the rear of the room.

'Hey, I didn't mean—!' Tebbets let the sentence die in his throat. Kloster had already left.

Out in the hallway, Kloster paused a moment and felt in his pockets for change. By the feel of it, he had more than enough. He looked up and down the deserted corridor, then walked quickly to the pay phone just outside the men's room. He emptied his pockets, piling the change on the little ledge below the phone, then dropped in a dime and dialled. Area code two-one-three ...

An operator's voice came on the line. 'This is a security intercept. I'm sorry but we cannot allow your call without authorization.'

Kloster stared at the phone blankly.

'Do you have security authorization?'

He started to clear his throat, then thought better of it.

'Please state your name and authorization.'

He reluctantly hung up the phone.

Back in the monitoring room, Tebbets glanced over sympathetically when he resumed his seat. 'Nobody home, huh?'

64

A huge bonfire of automobiles and blankets and furniture and clothing blazed in the centre of the pasture. Everything the townspeople had brought with them had been thrown into the flames. The marines had confiscated everything but their gold teeth, Lerner thought. And maybe they'd come back for those.

He watched for a moment longer: the stream of cars entering the farmyard, the confiscation of all goods and possessions and the enforced stripping, and then the shouts of outrage and complaint. Occasionally fights broke out; he saw one marine take a rifle butt to a teenager who didn't want to part with his hot-rodded Chevy. Moments later four marines shoved the car to the edge of the bonfire. A marine hunched under the burden of a flame thrower raised the muzzle of his weapon. An oily ball of flame rolled over the car. The flames leaped towards the darkened sky, the smoke twisting and coiling away towards the west.

Lerner shivered. Didn't they know you couldn't burn away contamination? The flames merely spread it – not that it made much difference now. The cold and the rain were getting to him. He ducked back into the barn. From the door, he had a panoramic view of the entire building. Inside, the townspeople were being searched once again by white-uniformed marines, checking for wallets and rings and watches and the small mementos that people carried with them. The next stop was the barber stalls; then the shorn and naked men, women and children were herded through the showers. At the far end of the barn they towelled off and dressed in olive-drab fatigues; then they were herded outside once more where they boarded buses that rattled off into the night.

His parents had been through the same thing when they were young, he thought, along with his grandparents. They had lived through the horror but his grandparents had died – stripped of their wedding rings and their gold teeth and even of their dignity as human beings. Their sole legacy had been a small stock of yellowing newspaper clippings that until that moment had carried no real meaning for Lerner.

The cold draught from the distant past of Dachau and Buchenwald made him shiver. Did the windows of the buses open? he wondered. Or were they sealed shut? Did the hiss of gas mingle with the mumble of conversation? Was the process of decontamination just a sham? Where did the buses go? To a graveyard where the bones of the passengers would lie guarded for millennia?

He felt paranoia and panic build deep within himself. How often had his parents felt the same? *'The Nazis were right; they should've burned them all.'*

Lerner suddenly found himself drawn to the cubicles in the barn as irresistibly as a piece of iron to a magnet.

In front of one of the barber stalls milled a group of teenagers, most of them cowed by the turn of events, a few of them belligerent. All the boys were staring at a long-haired, dishwater blonde slumped on an upended milk can; soft rolls of grey fat roped around her waist. Lerner wondered wryly if the showers would be a novelty to her. Too many burgers and fries and too many nights at the drive-in making joyless, sullen love, he thought. He looked at the boys again; their mouths slightly open, staring at the girl nervously. The perennial losers who lurked just beyond the light of the campfire, too frightened to approach the flames.

The girl was aware of her nakedness and angry at the sudden loss of mystery. 'Goddamnit, do you have to cut it all off?'

The barber ran his clippers expertly up the nape of her neck and a twist of hair fell limply into the lead-lined bucket at his feet. 'You should have worn a hat when you left the house. Radioactive particles are lodged in your hair and we don't have time for a thorough shampoo.' He shaved her head, then took a counter and held it briefly between her legs. He lowered the clippers. 'OK, spread 'em.' Two fast, long strokes. The girl was suddenly very near tears. 'You sure picked the wrong night to ball outdoors,' the barber said. One of the boys giggled self-consciously.

The showers were just as grim as Lerner thought they would be. Kormanski was herding the townspeople through; a marine with a counter was checking those who came out to make sure they were clean. Men, women and children were jammed in the stalls together, scrubbing at their bodies with stiff brushes white

248

with detergent foam. The scenes in the showers fused into one huge panorama before Lerner's eyes; people scrubbing each other's backs and then themsleves until they were pink, a small boy inspecting the men around him with obvious envy, a young girl clinging to her mother and crying as much from newly discovered shame as from fright.

An old lady, skirt slightly askew and stockings hanging limply over her thin, corded shanks, tugged at Kormanski's sleeve.

'Do I have to undress and shower with everybody else?' Her voice was frail, almost lost in the mumble of conversation from the stalls.

Kormanski looked surprised that she had gotten this far still partly clothed. 'Sorry, ma'am, we didn't have time to make other arrangements.' He tried to jolly her. 'After all these years, you're still bashful?'

'I had an operation,' she half whispered.

Kormanski's face smoothed. He was learning how to be hard, Lerner thought. 'I'm sorry, ma'am – orders.'

She started to undress; the people in the stall became suddenly quiet. A young woman stepped out to help her, compassion fleeting across her face as she unsnapped the old lady's cotton brassière. The others in the shower jostled silently aside to make room for her and then the casual banter started up again.

Lerner turned away. In the far part of the barn a mixed group of men and women were dressing in marine fatigues. Nothing fancy and nothing really warm, he thought.

But then, his grandparents hadn't enjoyed the luxury of underwear and overcoats, either.

A dumpy young woman with a white rag tied around her head babushka-style wandered around the benches where people were dressing, talking briefly to each of the men. She looked oddly intent and tragic. Another face from the past, Lerner thought; he knew her question before she ever asked it.

'Has anybody seen Paul Marical? He worked in the reprocessing plant.'

One of the men looked up from the bench where he was trying to stuff a size-eleven foot into a size-ten marine boot. 'If he was down in the storage corridors and you haven't seen him here, forget it, lady – those corridors were sealed off.' He suddenly shook his head and looked away. 'Ah, shit, lady, I'm sorry – you related?'

She hesitated. 'Just a friend.' She turned to another knot of men. 'You sure none of you saw him ...?' They shook their heads and her voice trailed off. She sat on one of the benches and hid her face in her hands.

Lerner felt as if he were flashing back and forth between the present and the past, a past that should have been locked safely away in the history books forever.

He walked to the entrance, where Kormanski stood with one of the marine medics. The elderly woman in front of them had already removed part of her clothing with a surprising lack of modesty. The medic put away his counter, shook his head and moved away as Lerner walked up.

'Sorry about the communal showers, Abby.'

'That's all right, Mr Lerner – I've helped give enough physicals in my life; I'm not about to complain because I have to take one.' Her voice sounded faintly forced and with a weariness to it that brought Lerner up short.

'What's the matter, Abby?'

'They wanted to check me over a little more closely.' She turned back to Kormanski, fear in her voice. 'You won't tell Ed?'

Oh, Jesus, not Abby ...

Kormanski looked as if he would break into tears. 'He should know, Mrs Dalton.'

'How much time do you think?'

'It's hard to say – we're not real experts here.'

She drew herself up, her voice a little stronger. 'I've been a nurse all my life, I've had to tell people bad news at times, too.'

A vein pulsed in Kormanski's throat. 'You were pretty badly exposed. The rain and the bird you picked up—'

'How much time?'

'Maybe a week, maybe a month.'

She nodded. He had only confirmed what she already suspected. 'They took away my photograph album.' Hesitation. 'Would it be possible to get it back?'

A last visit, Lerner thought. He and Kormanski looked at each other helplessly. Finally he said, 'I'm sorry, Abby. I can check but chances are they threw it on the fire right away for fear it was contaminated.'

She was silent a moment. 'Can I sit outside? I'd like to sit by the bonfire; I'd like to feel warm again. Maybe Ed could come out and talk to me.' Then she shook her head. 'No, he probably shouldn't. The rain and everything would be too much for him.' The tired old eyes caught Lerner's and held them for a moment. 'And I'm not very safe to be around, am I?'

Kormanski brushed past Lerner and swept Abby gently into his arms. She clung to him for a moment, crying, then pushed his arms away and stepped back. 'You mustn't,' she said.

'I'll make arrangements for the helicopter to evacuate you to a hospital,' Lerner said. He had to get back to the showers and check with the medics. *I am Lazarus, come from the dead to tell you all,'* Lerner thought sadly; *'I will tell you all.'*

Abby started to walk away, turned and asked, 'How is your young lady?'

He had avoided facing it all evening but now that it was out in the open, he was surprised at how unemotionally he accepted it. There had been too much death and disaster that night; you could only take so much grief and after that it was a way of life. His grandparents must have realized that.

'Karen's dead,' he said simply.

65

Representative Holmburg I still don't understand why some people died so quickly. We live with radiation all our lives, don't we?

Colonel Burgess As the ads used to put it, Representative, radioactivity has been in the family for generations. We're surrounded by it all the time. In the first thirty years of his life, the average person absorbs perhaps five roentgens—

Representative Holmburg Don't explain the units to me again; I didn't understand them the first time. What I was trying to get at was why, if we're absorbing radiation every day, a person can suddenly die from it.

Colonel Burgess It's like influenza compared to a simple cold, Representative. In cases where the whole-body dose might run as high as three thousand 'r' or more, you can die in a day and a half. They call it the 'central nervous system death' – the nervous tissue functions simply break down. At a thousand 'r' and up, a person might live as long as a week but would die the 'intestinal death.' The most common is the 'marrow death,' which occurs after a minimum lethal dose – say, six hundred 'r'.

Senator Hoyt I'm not sure just what illness goes with each name.

Colonel Burgess I didn't want to be graphic.

Senator Stone Colonel, we asked you to testify, we didn't ask you to spare our feelings.

Colonel Burgess Sorry, Senator. In the marrow death, the first symptoms are nausea and vomiting and sometimes a bloody diarrhoea. You suffer exhaustion and run a fever. If you linger to the third or fourth week, you'll notice haemorrhages in the skin and loss of hair. Your white blood cell count declines to a point where you're susceptible to almost any disease or infection – a trivial illness can kill you.

Senator Clarkson You're not only graphic, you're grisly, Colonel.

Colonel Burgess A case of radiation illness is hard to forget once you've seen it, Senator.

Representative Holmburg Barring direct exposure in massive amounts, I'm not sure just what dangers fallout poses.

Colonel Burgess Plants and animals concentrate radioactives so they enter the food chain, Congressman. By the time our children drink the milk or eat the meat, the concentration may have reached really dangerous levels.

Representative Holmburg The health-food nuts are no better off than the rest of us then?

Colonel Burgess We're all in the same food basket, Congressman.

Representative Holmburg Everybody at these hearings keeps talking about plutonium – is it really as bad as they say?

Colonel Burgess Weight for weight, it's thirty-five thousand times more lethal than cyanide. And it has a long half-life. It remains dangerous for a long time.

Senator Stone Was the possible presence of plutonium the reason for quarantining the Larson farm?

Colonel Burgess One of the reasons. There are other radioactives than plutonium. There was no way of decontaminating the Larson barn after we had processed the townspeople, no way we could be absolutely sure it was clean. And then there was the surrounding area and the pasture where we burned all of the townspeople's possessions.

Representative Holmburg Why didn't you just bury everything and be done with it?

Colonel Burgess We were afraid that people would come back and try and dig up mementos, things that held a high emotional attachment for them.

Senator Hoyt When will the farm revert back to the Larsons?
We've received inquiries from their lawyers.
Colonel Burgess That's out of the question, Senator. I
understand it's to be made a national preserve. The Government
will post it and place it under perpetual care.
Senator Hoyt You mean like a perpetual-care cemetery?
Colonel Burgess I think the analogy's a correct one.
Representative Holmburg Well, that's a matter of opinion.
Two or three hundred years from now, I rather doubt my
descendants will still be putting roses on my headstone. What
do you mean by 'perpetual?' A hundred years or so?
Colonel Burgess We're talking about a quarter of a million
years, Congressman. We might not have roses then. Or
congressmen, either.

66

The radiation suit was too big for her but the last thing she was
going to do was complain, Karen thought. They should have
been wearing them an hour ago.

They dressed quickly; then Glidden tried once more to
raise somebody in the main plant. There was still no response.

Rossi zipped up his hood. 'Isn't this a little like locking the
barn door after the horse has been stolen? What's been our
radiation exposure so far?' His voice was muffled by his air-
filtering mask.

'I don't know,' Glidden said. 'Do you have any idea, Miss
Gruen?'

They were all looking at her; she was the only one with any
real training. She shook her head. 'No real way of knowing.
It's probably quite high, considering we were still in the corridor when the melt broke through. We won't know how high
until after we get out of here and our film badges can be
checked.'

'We could be dead and not know it,' Bildor said.

'That's right, Bildor; you could be dead and not know it.'
The bitch in her was coming up like vomit, she thought. She
closed her eyes, then immediately opened them again. In the
dark behind her lids, she could see Tremayne and the molten
fuel flowing towards him.

253

'I've never been down to the sea exit,' Glidden said hesitantly. 'But there's only one and I'm certain the lights will lead us to it.'

'They're all out,' Bildor objected logically.

'We've got the electric lantern. We can follow the cord to the exit.' His voice held a false confidence. Karen decided that was one of the many differences between Glidden and Parks. Parks would admit his uncertainty. Glidden tried to hide his, with the result that it showed even more.

'It may not be the only way out,' Glidden suddenly added.

Behind his hood, Rossi looked surprised. 'There's another way?'

'Not really another way. We could try and go back through the corridors. There are other access ports and the reprocessing plant exit may be open now. Or we could try and bypass the emergency doors by climbing through one of the air shafts.'

Rossi said, 'You're not really serious? You're just suggesting that as a possibility.' Glidden nodded.

Karen said, 'If we make the wrong decision, we won't get another chance.'

'How do you mean?' Rossi asked.

'The access port we came through was glowing red five minutes later,' Karen explained. 'The melt will probably hit this part of the caverns ten, fifteen minutes from now.' She held up the electric lantern so they could see the light cord and the nearby path that disappeared into the darkness. 'It's all downhill. We can probably stay ahead of the melt but it will follow us all the way. If we do make it to the sea exit, any return will be blocked. And if we go back to the corridors and don't make it around the emergency doors, we'll be stuck there. There'll be no backtracking; the melt will be in front of us.'

'So why the hell go back?' Rossi sounded confused.

Glidden hesitated. 'We might not be able to get out by the sea exit,' he finally admitted. 'There's grillwork over the port itself; somebody on the outside would have to remove it.'

'I don't believe it,' Karen said slowly. 'You knew it all the time.'

'What the hell would you have done?' Glidden exploded. 'Stayed where we were? For all I know, the grillwork's rusted through. And I might raise some help on the walkie-talkie before we get there.'

There was silence for a moment; then Karen said, 'I'm sorry. I guess it's long odds no matter what we do.'

'It's dumb, it's really dumb,' Bildor chattered. 'Nobody

knows we're down here. Nobody knows we'll be heading that way. And even if the grill's rusted out, what do we do then? Swim around the point? For Christ's sake, I can't swim! And if the grillwork's still there, then we'll be pinned against it by the melt!'

'You can do whatever you want to,' Glidden said shortly. 'I'll take my chances.'

Karen remembered the glowing access port and the melt just behind it. She shivered. 'I don't want to go back to the corridors. I know what's there.'

'Rossi?'

'I'm for it.'

'Bildor?'

The little man slowly backed away from them, then turned and ran back towards the corridors. 'You'll never get out that way. It's dumb, it's just plain dumb!'

Glidden shouted, 'Bildor! Don't be a goddamned fool – you've got no lantern!'

The little man didn't stop. 'Go screw yourself!'

They watched him race back up the rocky path. Karen wondered if the feelings of the others were as mixed as her own. She had felt only contempt for Bildor but hadn't wanted to analyse it, afraid she was blaming him for her own guilt feelings about deserting Tremayne. It was one of the things she liked about Barney, she thought. He seldom had ambivalent feelings. Maybe it was because of the time he had spent in the Israeli Army, where he had to make immediate decisions with no regrets ...

Her last reservations gave way then. *Oh, God, how she wished she were with Barney* ... All the things she had always protested that she didn't want were suddenly the most desirable: the strong ties of a Jewish family, somebody whose domination she would have to fight but to whom she could also surrender half of her life, a man who might make mistakes but wouldn't spend hours vacillating, a man who used his roughness to hide his passion ...

Glidden had turned and started to walk downhill, following the string of dead light bulbs. 'Let's get out of here; that damned melt's right behind us. And God help us if Bildor was right about the storage corridors ...'

Karen held up the lantern and followed him, occasionally slipping on the stones that covered the path. Behind her hood she could feel tears leaking from the corners of her eyes but she couldn't reach up to wipe them away. Let them stay there, she thought. For the first time in her life, let them stay there. She wasn't that strong; she never really had been. The trait that Parks had always admired so much didn't really exist. She had just been playing a game. But now there was no time for games and nobody to admire her skill in playing them ...

A hundred feet behind them, Bildor was running the other way. He took a path away from the access port they had come through, then slowed when he reached the rough outer walls of the corridor complex. He started to search for another access port. Then the faint light from Karen's distant lantern faded and he was in complete darkness. The air under his hood was hot and stifling and he began to have second thoughts about leaving the others. There was a crushing sense of loneliness in the blackness of the caverns ...

But it was sure death to have stayed with them, he thought nervously. The melt would pin them against the grating. At least this way, he had a chance ...

He felt his way around a corner, then spotted a faint light up ahead. Part of the emergency lighting system was still working for some reason, he thought. Or maybe an access port was open and there were lights somewhere inside the corridor complex. He ran towards it, slowing when he realized it was acting oddly, that it was bobbing up and down.

As if somebody was carrying it, he thought, his heart jumping. 'Hey, you! Wait! Wait for me!'

The lantern stopped moving and he jogged towards it. What the hell ... a man in a radiation suit like his own, pulling a small wagon. He walked closer somewhat hesitantly. 'It's me, Martin Bildor – I'm one of the technicians in the reprocessing plant.'

The man stood there, inspecting him for a moment, the expression on his face hidden by his hood. Bildor began to feel uneasy.

Finally: 'Hello, Bildor.'

Bildor recognized the voice. He didn't particularly like the man but now he was dearly glad to see him. 'Marical! What the hell are you doing down here?'

'Same thing you are,' Marical said cautiously.

Bildor glanced at the wagon curiously, wondering what he had in it.

'You didn't know I was down here, did you?'

Bildor's uneasiness was growing by the moment. It looked like there were lead casks in the wagon. Which didn't make any sense unless ...

'Bildor?'

He glanced up, trying to hide his nervousness. 'Hell, no – none of us knew you were down here.'

'Us?'

'Glidden, Rossi and Miss Gruen. We didn't think anybody else was down here at all.'

'Thanks, Bildor.'

He hadn't seen the gun. He gaped in astonishment as Marical raised it and pulled the trigger twice.

The sound of the shots echoed and re-echoed through the caverns. Bildor, the look of surprise still arching his eyebrows, collapsed on the rocky floor.

67

Corporal Robert Allen dropped off the back of the truck before it had stopped rolling. Two privates followed him, their carbines at the ready. The dock area was black and deserted; nothing was moving except for one fishing trawler that had just slipped its lines and was gliding slowly out into the bay.

'Get a light on that boat, Murphy.' He waited until the powerful beam of the hand beacon picked out the name on the bow. *Taraval.* He pressed the button on his bullhorn.

'Ahoy, the *Taraval*! Get that tub back in here. The town's under quarantine! All inhabitants have to report to the staging area; you're contaminated!'

The sound of a motor starting belowdecks interrupted him. 'A couple of rounds over the bow, Davis,' Allen ordered. Two sharp cracks cut the air in succession.

'We're not kidding; turn that scow around!'

'Who you calling a scow?' someone yelled from the deckhouse.

'Chip wood, Davis, but don't aim at the deckhouse area.'

Davis fired two more shots; Allen heard the sound of splinters flying from the railing.

'OK, OK, we're coming about!'

'You've got thirty seconds or we'll put a round through your deckhouse!'

The *Taraval* made a slow circle in the bay and came in bumping against the rope fenders along the side of the pier. A man jumped onto the pier and made the lines fast, then sauntered over towards Allen. Another man vaulted over the side of the boat and followed him.

'Who the hell you shooting at, sonny? It's bad enough with all the lights out. You could've killed us!'

'No danger of hitting you in the dark; it's a sniperscope.' Allen held up a hand. 'That's close enough; you're probably hot as a pistol.' He noted they were both wearing slickers, which would help a lot. Contamination would be minimal.

'I want to know why you were shooting at us.'

'US Marines,' Allen said, bored. 'We're evacuating the town. Your power plant blew its lid and the area is covered with fallout.' He took a small pad and flashlight-pen from his radiation-suit pocket. 'Let's see who we're talking to, Murphy.'

The marine with the hand beacon turned it back on. Two sailors stood blinking in the sudden light. The oldest was about fifty and looked as if he were left over from the days of sailing ships. The other was thin and sinewy with nervous eyes, maybe in his early thirties. He could take him, Allen thought automatically; when it came to the old man, he might need a knife or a rifle butt.

'Names, please. Last one first.' They didn't say anything. He looked up at them. 'OK, fellas, we can stand here all night but I think I ought to tell you that you're breathing poison. Let's get it over with and see whether you rate a hospital or the last rites.' They answered reluctantly.

'Jefferson, Clint.'

'Halsam, Frank.'

'OK, Davis, call for the truck.'

He turned back to the sailors. 'You're both under arrest. Strictly a technicality. All it means is that if you try to go back to cruising on your boat, Murphy here can shoot you.'

The truck was already coming up the street. It slowed to a halt and they climbed in back. 'Next stop's the centre of town, driver.'

The youngest sailor said, 'How bad is it? Looked like everybody was leaving town there for a while.'

'Everybody did – except you guys. How come you didn't?'

'Waiting for the captain to come back. He never showed. We figured out what was happening and decided to split.'

They hadn't figured everything out or they would have left

a long time ago, Allen thought. The truck slowed and he tensed to jump out the back. Not much of a town ... Then he and Murphy had dropped off and the truck roared on. They had ten minutes in the business district and then another truck would pick them up. They were right under the fallout cloud and even with the radiation suits, their time was strictly limited.

'Take the right side of the street, Murphy; I'll take the left. Shoot looters if they don't stop and remember what the Colonel said about dogs and cats – or anything else that moves.'

He was halfway down the block when Murphy fired off a round. He started to lope over and Murphy waved him back. 'Somebody left a schnauzer behind.'

'Did you kill it?'

Murphy's voice, slightly muffled: 'Don't think so.'

'Do it.'

There was another shot and Allen continued down the street. His younger brother had a schnauzer. Cute dogs ...

He was almost to the corner when he heard the sound of breaking glass down a cross street. He froze. Looters, had to be. Always somebody willing to fleece their neighbours. He kept to the side of the building and edged up to the corner, then glanced around.

He couldn't see anything moving and then he caught it: halfway down the block, the glitter of broken glass in the moonlight where somebody had broken into a store. He waited a moment until the figure of a man appeared in the window and dropped to the street; then he stepped around the corner.

'Halt! United States Marines – this town is under quarantine!'

The figure scrambled to his feet.

'Halt – or I'll shoot!'

The shadowy figure started to run down the block, clutching what looked like a stack of books.

The asshole was going to run for it, Allen thought. The goddamned fool. He threw up his carbine. It would be tricky with the lighting, the moon was dodging in and out of the clouds, but he might be able to wing him in the legs.

'Halt!'

The man was almost at the end of the block. A moment more and he'd be around the corner. Allen's fingers tightened on the trigger. He squeezed off a single shot. The books exploded out of the figure's arms as the man stumbled and sprawled face down on the sidewalk.

Allen and Murphy ran up. Murphy switched on the hand beacon. Allen felt like throwing up. The lighting had been trickier than he had thought: he had caught the man square in the upper back.

Murphy toed him over and Allen caught his breath. A kid, just a kid. Maybe seventeen, maybe eighteen. Skinny, with glasses, he didn't look like a street type at all. And the books were really phonograph records, a few pop and several classical. Maybe he played in the school orchestra, Allen thought. Maybe he was a music student and couldn't afford records. Maybe it had been just plain old temptation ... Who knew; who the hell cared?

Murphy was on the radio: the meat wagon would be there any minute.

The beacon was still on and Allen took a last look at the figure on the sidewalk, the rainwater washing the blood into the gutter.

The kid probably would have died in a week anyway but somehow that didn't help a bit.

68

The echoes died away and Karen slowly let her breath out. 'Two shots,' she whispered.

Glidden held up his hand for silence. Karen strained her ears. Nothing could be heard but the slow drip of water nearby.

'Bildor,' Rossi said quietly. 'The shots came from the direction he was going.' His voice started to shake. 'Jesus, somebody else is down here and killed him.'

'We don't know that,' Glidden said. He started to turn back when there was a sudden, faint hissing from the direction of the access port, the same general direction Bildor had taken.

Despite the chill of the caverns, Karen felt the sweat begin to gather in her armpits. 'It's broken through.'

Rossi had started to follow Glidden and now he stopped, looking uncertain. 'What are we going to do about Bildor?'

Glidden cleared his throat but said nothing. Both he and Rossi were looking at her, waiting for her to make the decision. It was unfair, she thought. She didn't want the power of life and death, she didn't want to have to make that kind of decision. The difference between a doctor and a nurse, she thought; that was the reason why she had never tried for an MD. 'We can't go back,' she said finally. 'It's too risky.' The image of Tremayne loomed up in her mind and she shivered. 'There's not a damned thing we can do for him.'

It was exactly what Bildor himself would have said, she thought bitterly. Save yourself. It had a mean logic all its own.

They turned and followed the string of dead light bulbs down the water-discharge channel. They were running now, Glidden shuffling along as best he could, occasionally slipping down small slopes and stumbling over the rocks that cluttered the rough pathway. Behind them the ominous sound of rumbling built in volume.

'Smaller caverns collapsing under the weight of the melt,' Glidden explained. He sounded winded and out of breath. 'We're well ahead of it.'

They'd be OK, Karen thought. If the grillwork had rusted out. If somebody was there to meet them. If they could raise somebody on the walkie-talkie. If . . .

Rossi, who was leading the way with the electric lantern, suddenly stopped and held up his hand. 'Trouble.'

Karen and Glidden came up behind him. At Rossi's feet, a crevasse opened up across the path. Boards had been placed over it for a rough bridge but these had fallen to the bottom. Rossi held the lantern up higher. The trench was perhaps forty feet deep; one end butted up against a rock wall; the other widened and disappeared into the distance.

'Where's the light cable?' Glidden asked, glancing around. Rossi swung the lantern; the heavy Romex cable was stapled along the near wall. 'Lower the lantern a moment – there.' Six feet below the cable was a thin ledge a few inches wide that hugged the wall.

Glidden tugged on the cable, then put his weight on it. It held; the heavy-duty staples had been driven deep into the limestone.

'You first, Miss Gruen. Hang on to the wire and edge across.'

She could just reach the ledge with her feet and still hang on to the taut cable overhead; it was wet and slippery and it was difficult to keep a grip on it. She started to inch slowly across. At one point she felt herself begin to slide, hesitated, then continued forward. On the other side, she let go of the line too soon, slipped on a pebble, then sprawled forward on the rocky floor. Her whole body felt stretched and her shoulder flared with pain.

Rossi was next; he edged quickly across, his feet barely finding purchase on the thin ledge. He had tied the electric lantern to his waist and the swaying light cast shadows that fingered deep into the ravine at his feet. Then he was standing beside Karen, holding the lantern up so Glidden could see his way across.

When Glidden was three feet out, Karen saw he was in trouble. He was older than he looked and he had been winded by the run through the cavern. Now he was having difficulty getting his thick fingers between the wire and the rock. He was taking longer and longer between handholds and was resolutely not looking down. Karen caught her breath. Glidden was obviously afraid of heights, probably even of relatively short drops.

He was almost to their side when several staples suddenly pulled out of the rock leaving Glidden hanging on the wire, a few feet out from the edge. He closed his eyes. Karen saw him catch his breath, then try a convulsive hand-over-hand along the sagging cord. Rossi knelt at the edge of the drop and held out his hand; he touched Glidden's wrist, then grabbed it and heaved him onto the other side.

Glidden was sick for a moment. Karen quickly felt his pulse. Jumping but slowing down; he'd be OK. After a moment he sighed and sat up. 'We should try the radio again,' he said thickly. He unclipped it from his belt and handed it to Rossi. 'Here, you do it. You know how?'

Rossi nodded, studied it for a moment, then put the lantern on a rock and knelt down with the radio, his back to the ravine.

Karen could never quite recall what happened next. Later she thought it was because the rock Rossi was kneeling on was slick from the constant overhead dripping and had a gentle slope to it. Suddenly Rossi started to slide. His arms shot out as he scrabbled for a hold; then he disappeared silently over the edge of the trench.

Glidden grabbed the lantern and ran to the edge immediately. They could see Rossi lying at the bottom, forty feet down. He wasn't moving.

Karen glanced along the rocky sides. There were no visible hand- or footholds. She looked back at Glidden, his face pasty in the lantern light. He couldn't do it, she thought. He was too old and with his fear of heights, one look down would finish him. 'I'll have to go down,' she said.

Glidden slowly shook his head, his voice firm. 'We're only a few minutes ahead of the melt.'

Karen ignored him. 'We'll have to cut some of the cable free; you can let me down to the bottom with it.'

'There's no time,' Glidden said harshly. 'You coming?'

Karen didn't move. 'We'll need help to get out,' she said. 'And the radio's down there. Help me cut the cord loose.'

She deliberately kept her voice level and professional and fought him with her eyes. He finally lowered his and said, 'OK, I'll go down and get the radio.'

She shook her head. 'If he's alive, you'll need to pull him up – I don't have the strength for that.'

He hesitated again, then nodded and pulled the rest of the cable free of its staples. It parted at a splice on the opposite side when Glidden threw his weight on it. They tied one end to an outcropping of rock and dropped the rest into the ravine. Karen tugged on it to make sure it was secure, then let herself quickly down to the bottom. Glidden's voice floated above her: 'Hurry up; I can hear the melt.'

She felt Rossi's pulse, then did a fast body check. It had been quick. He had severed his spine on a sharp rock at the bottom; she hadn't seen the pool of blood from above. She gently loosened his fingers from the radio and closed his eyes, then prepared to climb back up.

There was no helping anybody, she thought dully. There had been no helping Bildor. There had been no helping Tremayne, either. For the first time she knew what a doctor must often feel with terminal patients; for some diseases, there are no cures.

She tucked the radio in her waistband and pulled on the rope. 'Coming up!' It could have been her imagination but she could hear more rumbles in the distance and over them the faint, almost subliminal sound of hissing. She gripped the cord and quickly climbed back up to the path. Silently she thanked God for the back-pack trips to the mountains with Parks, where he had taught her the rudiments of climbing, along with the pleasures of outdoor love.

They had stumbled another hundred yards down the path when she suddenly stopped, tugging at Glidden with one hand. 'Wait. Wait a minute!' She pulled at the walkie-talkie in her waistband. The speaker crackled, followed by a small, tinny voice asking for their location.

Glidden grabbed the radio and answered briefly. There was

more crackling and Glidden slumped against the cavern wall while Karen collapsed on a nearby rock. There was no sense crying, she was cried out. With all the interference and the bad reception, she had recognized the voice at the other end. Barney had found her.

She might have guessed he would.

69

You could tell just by looking, Kamrath thought: one shot through the heart, another just behind the left ear. Nevertheless, he went through the formalities of feeling for a pulse. The lantern Kamrath had found in an emergency locker flickered, then brightened.

One through the heart, one through the head, he thought. Doc Seyboldt had been murdered like that.

He stripped off the dead man's hood and white uniform, pausing a moment to look at the label inside the collar. 'Radiation suit.' He'd probably been working with hot stuff when the siren sounded. Kamrath quickly went through the pockets in the man's street clothes. The usual collection of odds and ends, keys and coins. And a film badge pinned to his shirt front. *Austin Bildor*. Kamrath recalled that he worked in the reprocessing plant; so he must have known Marical.

What had they talked about before Marical pulled the trigger? he wondered. Why had Marical bothered to do it? Because, of course, Marical had been carrying something with him and Bildor had seen it, or Marical was afraid that Bildor *would* see it. That *had* to be it. Marical had as much right to be down there as anybody else; there would have been no questions raised on that score. And Marical had no reason to believe he was suspected of anything or being sought for questioning.

He had something with him and Bildor had seen it. So Marical had shot him.

Fissionables, of course. But they'd be shielded and they'd be heavy. Marical wouldn't be lugging them out in shopping bags.

Kamrath stood up and lowered the lantern until there was a two-foot spotlight on the floor then walked slowly around the body in increasingly wider circles. He stopped. There were two parallel trails in the dust of the cavern floor. He knelt down again, setting the lantern on the floor. One of the trails ran over what had been a small rock; it lay in smashed fragments on either side of the track.

Marical had been pulling something with wheels, probably a cart. Otherwise the rock would just have been pushed out of the way. As it was, something had crushed it. Something damned heavy.

Marical had loaded a cart or a wagon with his stolen fissionables and was taking advantage of the confusion above to get them out. He wondered for a moment if Marical had had anything to do with the disaster. Well, when he found Marical, he thought grimly, he'd ask him.

He lifted the lantern again and carefully inspected the floor. There were faint scuff marks for a few feet where Marical had obviously walked towards Bildor to administer the *coup de grâce*, then back to the cart.

But were the tracks coming or going?

He went down on his knees again, searching for the faint telltale marks. The heel marks made by a man pulling a heavy load, the faint half-moons in the dust left by a man trying for a greater purchase on the ground.

The marks weren't hard to find. He stood up, holding the lantern high. Marical had gone that way. He sniffed the air. Maybe it was only his imagination but he had lived near the ocean too long not to be able to tell the smell of salt water. Marical was heading for an exit by the sea.

Kamrath clutched the riot gun and trotted silently along the almost indistinct parallel tracks. Behind him he could hear faint rumbling sounds.

70

Parks watched the bonfire without actually seeing it; he was only vaguely aware of its warmth. He stared blindly at the flames and ran equations through his head once more. There were no insoluble problems, he thought, not even this one, but time was working against them and no bright ideas had yet flashed into his mind.

He debated going back inside, then decided against it. Inside, it was Lerner's show and there was little he could do to help. And he didn't want to argue with Cushing and Brandt and Walton about whom or what they could blame it all on.

He saw a figure standing closer by the bonfire and he started to walk over; then he recognized Abby and stayed in the shadow of the barn. There wasn't anything he could tell her. How did one cheer up the dying? Too much tragedy, he thought, and you blanked on it.

But it still hurt to think about Karen.

It hadn't been the perfect relationship, there had always been something missing. Maybe the fault had been a mutual one: they had both tried to make a close friendship into something else. Perhaps they had worked too hard at it. Barney had always been more natural, more spontaneous with her. Karen could confide in him but it was Barney whom she really needed ... He grimaced. He and Karen had functioned well in bed together but that said more for the body than the heart.

He stared into the flames again, suddenly ashamed of himself. People were selfish, he mused. You thought of somebody who had died and you thought of what you had lost. You didn't think of what they had lost, of the life they might have led—

Something caught his eye in the woods, just beyond the firelight. A glimmer of brown and white in the moonlit darkness of the nearby woods. Simultaneously he heard a shot. The patch of colour leaped, then dropped down in the underbrush, where there was the brief sound of thrashing.

'Did you get it, Gilroy?'

Burgess was outlined in the open door of the barn, shading his eyes and staring out towards the woods.

'I think I did, sir.'

'Let's check.' Burgess strode towards the woods and Parks followed him. At the edge of the clearing a marine spread the bushes and shone his flashlight into them. A young fawn, less than a year old, lay on its side, its eyes just beginning to glaze in the light.

'Check it with the counter, Gilroy,' Burgess ordered.

The young marine unclipped a Geiger counter from his belt and held it out towards the animal. The steady background clicking increased to a jumbled roar.

'I don't like to kill animals or see them killed, Parks. But

266

there are a lot of animals under that cloud and they travel. They usually have a thick fur or hair, which holds radioactive particles. It's impossible to catch them all and decontaminate them; it's the same problem we had with the cows. We'll be lucky if we find all the people in the area and manage to take care of them. I'm afraid that most of the animals will have to be killed.'

'Most of them?'

'All of them, of course.' Burgess stood up and stared into the woods. 'Do you have any idea what kind of game is in the area?'

'A few deer, rabbits, wood rats. Some mice, maybe a few snakes.'

'And birds,' Burgess added thoughtfully. 'Insects of all types. And you can throw in pets like cats and dogs that have been allowed to run free. Then add the farm animals on those farms beneath the clouds.' He sighed and turned to Gilroy. 'Call base for a four-point-two-mortar company and G-gas rounds.'

'What are you going to do?' Parks asked.

'Only thing we can do. Once we move the people out, we'll sterilize the valley.'

They were walking back to the barn when a marine ran up to Burgess. 'Colonel, the commo sergeant reports they've picked up a radio transmission from the plant.'

Parks felt stunned, then blurted, 'That's impossible! There's nobody back there; there's nobody who *could* be back there!'

'Let him talk, Parks,' Burgess ordered curtly.

The marine looked confused. 'I don't know the details – the transmission mentioned something about caverns.'

Parks gripped him by the shoulder. 'How did they pick it up?'

'I don't know – somebody remembered the plant superintendent had a hand transmitter.'

Parks started running then. He should have thought of it. Glidden had a walkie-talkie and, of course, he would try and report in. Glidden had been reporting in all of his life; he'd still be reporting in after he retired.

Radio communications had been set up on the porch of the farmhouse. Parks took the steps two at a time, followed by Burgess and the marines. Lerner was already there, as well as Brandt and Cushing. He knew what the news was by the look on Lerner's face.

'Who besides Karen?'

'Glidden. They made it through an access port into the caverns. There may be others. We couldn't get all of the transmission.'

There had been another man, Parks remembered. Tremayne. Karen had gone down to help him. That made three names he could take off the casualty list, three weights he could subtract from his load of guilt.

Then he had a frightening thought and turned quickly to Burgess. 'You'll have to hold up your G-gas, Colonel. The area's riddled with small holes that feed into the caverns. Once you fire your canisters, the gas will seep into the cave area and you'll kill everybody down there.'

Burgess looked blank. 'You can get them out, can't you?'

Parks hesitated. 'I don't know. I don't know the area down there.'

'There's the sea exit,' Brandt volunteered. 'You can probably get them out that way.'

'We'll have to get a boat,' Parks said slowly. 'And it will take time for Karen and the others to get to the exit. Colonel, can you have your radioman contact the party and tell them to get to the sea exit?'

'How long will it take your people to get there?'

'I'm not sure – why?'

'If we're going to use the gas, we'll have to use it before the wind shifts.'

Parks felt the skin tighten on the back of his neck. 'How much time does that give us?'

Burgess shrugged. 'Maybe until morning; we can't pinpoint it.'

'And if our people aren't at the exit by then?'

Burgess' face was blank. 'I'm sorry, Parks; my orders are that anything in the area that walks or crawls or flies can't leave here unless it's radiologically clean. Anything or anybody that's left after we decontaminate the townspeople and leave will die. Sorry – you've got a couple of hours and that's it.'

'And if we can't raise them?'

Burgess shook his head. 'Until just before the wind shifts, that's the best I can do. I'm also assuming that we can do something about the plant before then as well, though that will probably take an act of God. But if we can't, the fat will be in the fire for a far larger area than just Cardenas Bay.'

Parks closed his eyes for a moment. If the wind were right, maybe an area ten miles wide and a hundred miles long. Maybe more … Little bit by little bit, he thought. Not too much at any one time or he'd overload his circuits and wind up slashing his wrists. 'What about the fish in the ocean? You going to sterilize it, too?'

'That's funny, Parks. The Pacific's big enough to dilute the fallout but there won't be any fishing in the area for a dozen years or more.' He hesitated. 'Look, I feel sorry for your friends. We probably missed some people in town – the sick, shut-ins, people who never got the word – and I feel sorry for them, too. It's like war: I'm sorry for everybody connected with it but feeling sorry's not the business I'm in.'

Parks glanced over at Lerner. Even in the moonlight, the man's face was paler than usual. 'They'll use defoliants, too, Greg. You can't allow the flowers to grow and have the birds and the bees and the insects come back into the area. By the time they get through, the land will look like it had been scrubbed with steel wool.'

'Karen?'

'We'll have to get her out, that's all.'

The trouble with problems, Parks thought, was that you tried to solve them all at once. It seldom worked that way; you had to take them a step at a time. There were few instant miracles; all there really was, was hard work and slow progress.

'Colonel, do you know if the farm has a donkey engine?'

'I think I saw one out in back – why?'

'The model back at the Information Centre. If we have power, we can at least see where the melt is.'

Burgess studied him. 'You'll be risking recontamination.'

'We can cut it down with radiation suits.'

Burgess hesitated, then nodded. 'All right.' A brief smile flickered across his face. 'How many do you want?'

Parks turned to Brandt, Cushing and Walton clustered behind him. 'You gentlemen coming? I have no monopoly on bright ideas.' Brandt nodded. Cushing was icy. 'I doubt that I can contribute much.'

'A man of your expertise would be invaluable,' Parks said sarcastically. 'What do you think, Colonel?'

Burgess was poker-faced. 'I think Washington would expect Mr Cushing to be there.'

Cushing's expression didn't change. 'You want me there, I'll be there.'

Walton looked sick. 'Not you, Jerry,' Parks said. 'You stay behind and work on the casualty lists.'

They put on radiation suits and Parks started walking towards one of the trucks parked near the highway. Lerner caught up with him. Parks said quietly, 'She's a fine woman, Barney – you're lucky.'

Lerner looked at him oddly. 'She's pure bitch, Greg – and both she and I know it.' There was friendly contempt in his voice. 'You two would never have gotten along. We'll fight each other the rest of our lives. We'll make each other miserable long before we'll make each other happy.'

Parks wondered for a moment about himself. Was he just being a good loser, or had he known it all the time? Psychologically speaking, he and Karen had always made sure the bed was made and the furniture was dusted before the other walked into the room. He had never seen Karen in an old bathrobe and curlers. But he was willing to bet money that Lerner had seldom seen her any other way.

And then once again he blanked Karen from his mind. The farm was on a slight rise and from the road he could see the plant and what was left of the containment dome. The dome itself was glowing red and white and streaming from it was a radiant opalescent haze that fingered the night sky, then flowed out towards the ocean.

He stared at it for a long moment, acutely aware of the freezing chill in the night air. Then he got in the front seat of the waiting jeep after the others climbed in back. Burgess squeezed in beside him in the driver's seat.

A moment later they were bouncing down the road back to the Information Building. In the rear-view mirror Parks could see marines back at the farmhouse, tugging the donkey engine out to the road. There was a familiar figure working with them – Cole Levant. He watched them hoist the engine aboard another truck; Levant climbed in after it. Good idea, Parks thought. Levant not only knew the countryside, he also had a boat.

With good luck, they should be hooked up in half an hour or so. And then he'd be face to face with the problems of the melt and the fact that all of the formulas and equations he had ever been taught weren't worth a tinker's damn.

Beside him, in the darkness, Burgess asked, 'Parks, what the hell really went wrong? Off the record, I don't mean the technical details.' He fumbled with a cigarette, trying to put into words what he was thinking. 'I guess I'm trying to fit it into some kind of philosophical framework. Your friends think it was sabotage but I have the feeling that the whole concept of the power programme was wrong.' He was silent for a moment, his face briefly lit by the flaring of a match. 'I'm not sure I'm making myself clear. I guess what I'm trying to say is that I think the accident – *an* accident – would have happened no matter what.'

Parks stared at the glow in the sky ahead of them and finally said, 'We pushed the technology too hard and too fast, Colonel. We thought we knew more than we did and when the questions came up, we just didn't have the right answers. It's as simple as that.'

71

The model slowly came to life as the donkey engine outside the Information Building provided the power for it. The sensors themselves were self-powered and would continue to transmit as long as they were undamaged. Parks watched intently as the shadowy details began to build up. The areas where the sensors had been destroyed were black; the rest of the model showed the familiar outlines of rooms and corridors and even suggested the rugged passageways of the caverns. Knowing the layout of the plant, he could assume that the black area indicated roughly the size of the melt. He could also determine if the melt was travelling – and where.

Brandt covered the black area with his hand. 'How large do you think it is?'

Parks ran various estimates through his mind. 'No way of really knowing. I'd say the front is about a hundred, maybe a hundred and fifty feet wide. And growing.'

Brandt paled. 'That's larger than any computer-study forecast.'

Nothing had fit the computer studies, Parks thought. Nothing would. He drew a line with his finger across the leading edge of the black area. 'The main body of the melt is about fifty feet down. It's probably as big as it is because the radioactives from the storage cells have added to it. It must have wiped those out half an hour ago.'

As they watched, the area in black suddenly jumped by half an inch, then another half. 'It's broken through into the

271

caverns,' Parks said quietly. For the next minute there was dead silence in the room as they stared intently at the model.

'You sure there's no way of cooling it?' Cushing asked. For some reason it struck Parks that the question was rhetorical, almost a challenge.

'I don't know of any. Maybe when the experts arrive from Washington, they'll have some ideas.' He glanced up at the group around him. It was almost like being back on the balcony – how many short hours ago? Only Brandt and Cushing were now dressed in marine fatigues and radiation suits, and Lerner – still back at the commo station in the farmhouse – had been replaced by Levant. And there was Colonel Burgess, fascinated by the model and bored by the interplay between the rest of them, substituting for the Greek chorus of newsmen.

'How large did you say the melt was, Parks?'

'Probably more than ten thousand tons. Say three thousand for each reactor, plus whatever the storage caverns might have contributed. And God help us if they contributed as much as I think they did.'

There was a slight tremor and the building shook a little, causing the jury-rigged overhead light to swing gently back and forth. Without looking up from the model, Burgess asked, 'What's causing those? That's the second one.'

'Probably the heat and weight of the melt are fracturing some of the limestone formations in the caverns.'

'And possibility of criticality?' Brandt asked, white-faced.

Parks nodded. 'There could be – low-level.'

Burgess glanced from one to the other. 'What happens then?'

Parks sucked in his breath. 'If there were low-level atomic reactions, it could peel away the entire front of the cliff.'

'And?'

'The amount of radioactive debris you'd be adding to the fallout would be staggering.'

'Parks.' Burgess hesitated, trying to read his face. 'What if we dynamited the cooling pond above the plant – let the water drain into the pit. There are sixty million gallons in the pond, that should cool the melt.'

Parks stared, appalled. 'It would also drain into the caverns. There are people there, remember?'

Burgess looked uncomfortable. 'We'll get them out in time.'

Parks had a sudden flash of intuition. 'You've already sent a demolition team, haven't you?'

'They can be called back.'

'You never asked my opinion,' Parks said, unbelieving.

Cushing said stiffly, 'There'll be casualties in any event. The choice is between a few or a few hundred thousand.'

Parks whirled on him. 'You gave the orders, Cushing? By whose authority?'

Cushing bridled. 'The Secretary of the Commission—'

'—is not a scientist nor a nuclear engineer! He's a lawyer, he's a professional ass-kisser!'

'Parks, can we afford to wait until the Washington team gets here?' Burgess asked.

'No, goddamnit!'

'Mr Cushing, will it work?'

Cushing licked suddenly dry lips. He looked uncertain. 'It should have the same effect as the emergency cooling system—'

Parks cut in. 'The hell it will. What we've got now is decay heat. Pour the pond water on it and you run the risk that the water will act as a moderator so the melt becomes self-sustaining. You'd also have steam explosions and God knows what else.'

'And if it did work?' Burgess persisted.

'If it did?' Parks asked bitterly. 'Then we'd really have problems. Sixty million gallons of contaminated water washing thousands of tons of radioactives into the ocean just offshore. We could pollute the continental shelf for centuries. You wouldn't be able to fish; you wouldn't be able to swim. You wouldn't even be able to walk on the beach. Compared to it, the biggest oil spill imaginable would be trivial.'

'You've got a better idea?' Burgess asked mildly.

Parks made a noise. 'That isn't even an idea.'

'No matter what happens,' Levant asked quietly, 'fishing off the coast is through?'

'For generations.' Parks brooded about it for a moment. 'Blow the cooling pond and I'm not sure that's all that would be through. I don't think the plankton in the ocean would survive. Kill them off and you kill off the plants that make two-thirds of the oxygen in the world. We'd all slowly suffocate.'

Cushing suddenly leaned across the model towards him, his voice savage. 'Your reports about the plant, Parks. You should have started sending them in long before you did. There's no way you can stop a multi-billion-dollar project in the middle, no possible way.' He included Brandt in his glare. 'And goddamnit, both of you knew it.'

Parks stared coldly back at him. 'If you're looking for a villain, Cushing, forget it – I won't play.'

Brandt began to tremble. He was no longer the Man in Charge, he was only a pudgy executive in his fifties whose granite face had suddenly developed wattles and a double chin, who was dressed incongruously in a white radiation suit that was two sizes too small for him, making him look oddly like the little dough man in the television commercials. 'What were we supposed to have done, Eliot? We didn't manufacture anything ourselves; we relied on outside suppliers. You know what they're like. How many feet of defective pipe did we have? How many valves didn't meet specs? We policed it as best we could; we inspected every part that came in. We did the best job possible.'

His voice held a note of pleading that turned Parks' stomach.

'It obviously wasn't good enough, Hilary.' Cushing's voice was acid.

It was all a show, Parks thought, carefully staged for Burgess' benefit to be used in case Cushing failed to make his sabotage story stick. *And what were Mr Cushing's reactions, Colonel? Tell the members of the Committee in your own words . . .*

Burgess pulled over a high-topped stool and sat down. He looked disgusted. 'I rather think all you people will have a chance to tell your side of things. Unfortunately, the longer we sit here, the closer we come to committing suicide. The air must be contaminated and I don't know what the hell is falling on the roof. The worst thing is that I'll die just as soon as you and right now you're using up *my* time.' He lit a cigarette and turned to Parks. 'You're sure about the cooling pond?'

'You run the risk of starting up the reaction all over again. Besides, you'd be pouring water down a rathole.'

Burgess sighed. 'Jesus, Parks, I thought better of you than that.'

'Then why the hell didn't you ask me in the first place?' Parks closed his eyes and kneaded the bridge of his nose. 'OK, I know; we're all tired.'

'What I would like to say is: "Let's all go home and get a good night's sleep so we'll be fresh in the morning." But I can't say that, can I?' Burgess looked frustrated.

'What about evacuating Los Angeles?' Levant asked. 'Some of the marines were talking about it back at the farm.'

'Evacuate Los Angeles,' Burgess repeated dryly. 'In the

middle of the night and with no place to send anybody? No way. It wouldn't solve the problems here in any event.' He looked down at the model. 'How long will the pit stay active, Parks?'

Parks felt helpless. 'A few years. Perhaps even longer.'

Cushing wandered over to the window and stared out at the burning reactor building. His thin, worried face looked almost skeletal in the ruddy light. 'The Congressional committee will tear us apart,' he said to no one in particular.

The problems were too big, Parks thought. They had been too big for years now. Your mind couldn't deal with the possibility of millions of people exposed to fatal doses of radiation. It was a study in hypotheses, a problem in statistics. When it came down to the immediate and the personal, you had to think about something small, something you could grasp, something you were familiar with. Maybe the only sane re-actions were for Brandt to complain about incompetent vendors, for Cushing to worry about a future Congressional investigation, for himself to be obsessed with Karen and the others below. None of them could really look at the larger picture and assume the guilt for it. Who could? The now-forgotten Congressmen and business leaders who had made all the decisions years ago?

He was suddenly aware that Burgess was staring at him.

'Time's up,' Burgess said. 'We're between a rock and a hard place, gentlemen. What are we going to do, just sit on our ass?'

72

Tebbets listened carefully over his headset, his coffee cup for-gotten. The reports were streaming in now from all over the world; it was like somebody had kicked over an anthill, he thought. He glanced over at Kloster, busily lighting a cigar-ette.

'Why not smoke the one you lit a minute ago?'

Kloster glanced down at the cigarette still glowing in his ash-tray. 'Thanks.' He snuffed out the spare and stuffed it back in the pack.

'What's the wind look like?'

'A high-pressure area is moving in. The wind should start

shifting in another two hours or so.' The screens before them now held a constant weather picture; they were patching in photographs from a dozen different reconnaissance satellites. Even the Russians were broadcasting their satellite overviews – they were slightly fuzzy, which Tebbets guessed was deliberate: the Soviets didn't want to reveal their true capabilities.

'How's it look?' Kloster asked.

'We're making top-secret news all over the world. Everybody's scared shitless that the cork will come all the way out of the bottle. If the rain stops, the fallout could carry around the globe.'

'We must really be making friends.'

Tebbets was suddenly alert to a voice in his headset. He listened a moment, then said, 'It's more like we're influencing people. The Mexicans just dropped the other shoe. They're threatening to break off diplomatic relations if it blows far enough south.'

'And if it blows north, the Canadians will do the same thing.'

The rain had been a godsend, Tebbets thought. So far the moist air had kept the radioactive fallout relatively close to the ground. With a dry wind, the pollutants could rise and circle the globe like the dust cloud after the explosions at Krakatoa.

'What about the spotter plane?'

'It's up there.' Kloster was working with a sheet of figures again. 'We should be getting reports any minute. Composition of the cloud, elements present, level of radioactivity – that sort of thing. Don't expect to be cheered up.'

There was the sound of many footsteps in the corridor outside and Tebbets turned, craning his neck towards the rear of the room. 'What the hell—'

The door at the back opened and half a dozen MPs filed down the aisle and took up parade-rest positions by the screening boards. The mumble of conversation stopped and all of the technicians stared towards the rear. Tebbets couldn't make out whether the officer who followed them in was a captain or a bird colonel. The officer walked to the front and motioned one of the technicians away from the commo mike. Jesus, he looks grim, Tebbets thought. A moment later his headset was buzzing. The voice sounded tired and bored but there was no doubting the authority in it.

'Gentlemen, several hours ago we had a security intercept from this building.'

Tebbets glanced suspiciously at a suddenly pale Kloster.

'—remind all of you of the appropriate sections of the National Espionage Act. This installation is top secret. Anything you may see or hear in the next twelve hours will not be discussed further, even among yourselves. None of you will be permitted to leave for that period of time nor will you attempt to contact friends or relations. We have provided living quarters for you here at the centre. We have also notified the wives of you who are married that you will be working overtime. I am not prepared to discuss the reason for these orders. You may consider that this installation is now operating under a SAC yellow alert ...'

The old order changeth, Tebbets thought cynically, giving way to the new. The next thing they'd do, they'd start serving him decaffeinated coffee.

73

McCloskey grabbed at his seat as the light Cessna dropped a sickening second, then shuddered in the buffeting wind. Rain drummed against the cabin roof above him. He concentrated harder on the gear in front of him, valiantly trying to control his stomach. God help him if he had been in the Navy, the mere thought of the ocean made him seasick.

Boruck, the pilot, turned his head slightly. 'How's the count?'

'It's high but I can't tell how high. You'll have to get closer, I need a better sample. I don't dare let the probe down further; in this wind we'd lose it.'

'Closer, shit, we're as close as we're going to get. It's all I can do to control this thing now. Why the hell they sent us up, I'll never know.'

'Because we were on duty call and the plane already had the gear in it. Quit bitching.' McCloskey wiped his eyes and tried to focus on the meters. The count mounted as he watched. The probe samples would be analysed later in a mass spectrograph. Strontium and caesium were present, probably – and in large quantities. Certainly iodine 131, also in large amounts. His heart began to beat faster. If he could believe the instruments, astronomically large amounts. Iodine 131 had a half-life of eight days, thank God, but a lot of people below would still come down with thyroid cancer in the years ahead. There'd be a lot of U-235 and – he winced – plutonium. But they'd have to get closer to the cloud to get an accurate sample.

He adjusted the instruments again, then started to mumble to himself. There'd probably be a lot of krypton 85, too. A half-life of ten years and a tendency to dissolve in the fatty tissues, so the overall body dose would go up. And there'd be a lot of it, a whole helluva lot of it . . .

'We'll have to get closer,' he repeated absently.

Boruck shook his head. 'I told you, it's too risky. We could hit a downdraught and that'd be all she wrote, buddy.'

'We're paid to take risks, Boruck.'

'No tickee, no washee? Not worth it.'

But McCloskey could feel the little plane buck as it started a slow turn that would take it closer to the cloud. 'Try and get above it.'

'Sure.' Then they were over it and McCloskey craned his head towards the window. It was like flying over an opalescent river. In the distance, he could make out the ruddy glow of the plant. It must have been hell when that let go, he thought.

'McCloskey, what were you doing when you got the call?'

'Eating a late dinner.' For a moment his mind strayed from the instruments in front of him and his stomach lurched. 'Lamb chops, and I'd just as soon not think about them. Why?'

'I hope those goddamned chops have wool on them when you get back.'

McCloskey laughed. 'Don't sweat it; we'll be OK. Head up-wind, towards the plant '

He could sense it coming then. A slight rise, like going over the top of a hill in a roller coaster, and then a sudden drop that must have been several hundred feet – the downdraught that Boruck had been worried about. He grabbed at some papers whirling towards the roof of the craft and said quietly, 'That did it. We flew right through the middle of it; every meter back here is pinned. Even the ionization chamber is overloaded.'

He started to jot down figures while Boruck reported in. For a minute he didn't pay any attention to what was being said; then gradually he became aware that Boruck was arguing with the General. The last thing he caught was: 'It's a rough sea, General.' Then Boruck angrily hit the off switch on the radio.

McCloskey looked up in alarm. 'What was that all about?'

'They want us to go for a swim.'

'Ditch? In this weather? That's suicide!'

'That's what I told the man.' The plane started to dip towards the ocean below. 'Secure your gear and put your papers in an oilskin.'

McCloskey fumbled for a moment with the instruments, then said, 'I signed up to do a job, not to kill myself. I'm a lousy swimmer.'

Boruck shrugged, preoccupied with the plane. 'Sorry, old buddy. We're now a hot number as the saying goes and we've got orders to take a bath. The Coast Guard is going to pick us up.'

'Why don't we wait until they get here?'

'There's a ship in the area, should be here any minute. They don't want to stay under the cloud any longer than necessary.'

'They won't let us land back at base?'

'We're too hot.'

McCloskey scrambled around stuffing his papers in an oilskin bag, then curled up by the door, close to the raft and the survival gear. He glanced out the window, trying to see through the sleeting rain. The heavy, oily waves were fifty feet below them now. It would be like setting down in a school of angry whales, he thought.

'Brace yourself!'

He ducked his head. They struck, bounced once, then settled sluggishly onto the rolling ocean. Something hit him in the back of the head, momentarily stunning him; then he was shoving hard against the cabin door. It flew open; the cold air and wet wind slapped him in the face. He shoved the raft out and watched it quickly inflate. The plane was settling fast now; waves were sloshing in the door. Behind him he could hear Boruck swearing. He turned. The front of the plane had been smashed in; Boruck was pinned in his seat. McCloskey struggled towards him, water washing around his ankles. He pushed aside a piece of metal cowling and Boruck eased out from underneath it. 'OK, let's go.' Boruck's voice sounded weak with an odd whistle to it.

McCloskey fought his way back to the door. The line securing the lift raft to the plane had parted and the raft was bobbing in the heavy seas, a good hundred feet away. No helping that now, he thought. A hundred feet was nothing to swim, except he was no longer a kid and he had never taken a dip in open seas.

He started to dive, caught his foot on the side of the door

and ended in a painful belly flop, strangling in the foam swirling about the plane's undercarriage. A hundred feet but the raft was bobbing further and further away. He doubled up, face down in the water, and worked his shoes and pants off, then struck out for the raft. The water was icy; he felt his chest and arms start to grow numb. He had lost sight of the raft in the grey void of the ocean when his head thumped against it. He reached up and caught a line on the side of the raft and pulled himself into it.

He lay for a moment on the plastic surface, sobbing, then glanced around for the plane. It was several hundred feet away now, tilted so that one wing was high in the air, the cabin door a good ten feet above the waves. Boruck, bracing himself in the opening, was screaming at him but the words lost themselves in the wind.

McCloskey searched frantically around the sides of the raft for a paddle, hoping to edge closer to the plane. He was at the far end, weighing down one side, when a large swell hit the other end. The raft rose straight in the air, then flipped over. He struggled in the water beneath, coughing. Another wave lifted him up; the raft slid over him.

He was high in the air now, on the crest of the wave; he could see the dark ocean around him. The plane and Boruck had disappeared from view. The raft was sliding down the steep slope of the wave, away from him.

He treaded water for a minute, searching the ocean around him for the oilskin with the papers. Then he realized that it didn't matter. The raft was a hundred yards away and he no longer had the strength to swim for it.

74

Senator Hoyt General, I understand you were responsible for sending up a spotter plane to determine the radioactivity of the Cardenas Bay cloud?

General Whitmore That's right, sir.

Senator Hoyt Then you were also responsible for ordering the plane to ditch in the open seas?

General Whitmore It's actually a chain-of-command thing,

sir. You could say that I was at the bottom of the chain, so to speak.

Representative Holmburg I may be a country boy, General, but I recognize buck passing when I hear it. It's a simple question: Did you or didn't you give the orders for the plane to be ditched?

General Whitmore I was trying to explain that the chain of command provides—

Senator Stone Somebody higher up ordered you to have the plane ditched?

General Whitmore Well, no—

Senator Stone Then the orders originated with you, isn't that correct, General?

General Whitmore Put like that, sir, I wouldn't deny it.

Senator Hoyt A Coast Guard vessel was reported en route to pick up the pilot and the observer but it never appeared on the scene.

General Whitmore I'm not sure that's completely correct.

Senator Stone I have to agree with you there, General – it isn't completely correct. A ham operator in Sacramento picked up the radio transmissions between the plane and its base. As a matter of fact, he reported that the plane was down to the police and the local papers. Our office queried the Coast Guard and on that night there was no vessel in the immediate vicinity of the plane. Nor did they have orders to send one. Did you know this, General?

General Whitmore Well, yes. Actually there was no Coast Guard vessel in the area that night.

Representative Holmburg I'll be damned – General, how could you justify telling those men that a ship was standing by? Did you know how rough that sea was?

General Whitmore I was well aware of it, sir.

Senator Hoyt I can't believe what you're telling us.

General Whitmore It seemed advisable to let the men believe a ship was close by and would pick them up. I doubt that they would have ditched the plane otherwise.

Senator Stone I think you owe the members of this Committee more of an explanation than that, General.

General Whitmore Senator, the men in that plane were already dead in one sense. The dose of radiation they took when they flew through the cloud would have been fatal within a week or two. There was no way that plane could have been safely decontaminated; it would have endangered the personnel at whatever base it landed at. We traded the lives of two men who were already dead for those of any number of men at the airport. It was a painful decision.

Representative Holmburg I'm glad I'm not you, General. I don't think I would sleep very well at night.

General Whitmore If it's any satisfaction, sir, I sleep very badly.

75

'What are they saying?' Karen asked.

Glidden motioned her to silence as he listened intently to the walkie-talkie, then shoved the radio back in his web belt. 'They're sending demolition men to the sea-exit grill and blowing it out. We're supposed to meet them down there.' He helped her up from the rock. 'You OK?'

She nodded. 'You?'

'Tired. Damned tired.' The strain showed in his face. Karen wondered how his heart was holding up.

They worked their way across another gully. Glidden said, 'The man who killed Bildor—'

'I thought you said we didn't know that for a fact,' Karen cut in. She had a feeling she knew what was on Glidden's mind but didn't want to think about it.

'He didn't commit suicide,' Glidden grunted. 'And those were shots – I know guns, I used to collect them. Hard to tell in here but I would say a small calibre pistol.'

The lantern was growing dim and she kept one hand on the wire as she walked; if the light went out and she lost her hold, they'd never find the exit.

'Whoever shot him has to get out, too,' Glidden continued. 'And there's only one way out.'

'That we know of,' Karen amended.

Glidden shook his head. 'There's only one way out,' he repeated grimly. 'The sea exit. All of us will meet down there – and we're unarmed.'

'If there's nothing we can do about it, then why worry?'

Glidden sounded contrite. 'I didn't bring it up to worry you.

I was going to suggest that when we see the exit, we turn off the lantern. Keep in the shadows as much as we can and see what happens.' He hesitated. 'There should be marines.'

Marines. She thought about that for a moment. 'It's pretty bad up above, isn't it?'

He nodded. 'About as bad as it can get.'

For some reason she felt closer to him then. The we're-all-in-the-same-boat syndrome, she thought. He was a curious man, too strong in appearance and actions to be labelled a fuss-budget, too lacking in real authority to be the company whip. Always good for a cheerful 'good morning' and a friendly smile. The man everybody went to if they needed something but for whom they still felt contempt. He wore the invisible stamp of the loser, the good grey man who had been there for-ever and whom everyone took for granted.

'Oh,' he said, 'if it helps any, that was Barney on the radio the last time.' He was feeling his way carefully down the slope, swinging the electric lantern beam ahead to pick out the foot-ings.

'You don't like him, do you?' Karen asked.

'Lerner? Not particularly.' She could sense him frowning in the dark. 'He rubs me the wrong way. I don't like noisy radi-cals, especially the know-it-all kind.'

'Barney's not as bad as all that,' she said.

'Probably not,' Glidden admitted. 'Twenty years from now, after he's taken his lumps, I'll probably like him. Maybe it's just that I'm thirty years older. That's what Parks told me once.'

'Greg?' she said thoughtfully. 'I wonder how he's making out.'

'God help him,' Glidden said. 'Quite apart from the wolves he's facing now, I feel sorry for him.'

It wasn't what she had expected. Glidden held out his hand to help her across a rough stretch of rock. She scrambled over it, then said, 'How do you mean, "sorry for him"?'

Glidden stopped for a moment and put down the lantern while he caught his breath. 'I feel sorry for him in two re-spects. When he was going to school, everybody thought highly of engineers – particularly of nuclear engineers. You were a grind, you never had time to get involved in politics or issues or campus fads. But it was all worth it. Oppenheimer was your hero and you were going to make the brave new world of the future come true; you were going to Make A Contribution.

By the early seventies, that had all changed. You were a villain raping the environment and endangering the world itself. I imagine a lot of young engineers were confused by it all, probably bitter.'

He was quiet for a moment, lost in thought, and Karen said, 'You said you felt sorry for him in two respects. What's the other one?'

'Maybe I'm talking about myself now,' he said slowly. 'If you don't make it by the time you're forty, they start bringing in younger men to work underneath you. Before you know it, they're working over you and you end up shuffling papers until it's time to retire.' He held up a hand. 'I know what they say about me; it's amazing how much you can hear when your back's turned. Greg's at the turning point. He's the right age and they've got Abrams in the office now. Abrams is a real New York knife; he could slit your throat and you wouldn't know it until you went to turn your head. Whether or not Greg brought Prometheus on stream was to be the big deciding factor.' He shrugged. 'It wasn't going well; it didn't go well right from the start. Not his fault but he'll take the blame. He'll shuffle papers from now on.'

She had never looked at it from that angle, Karen thought. She had always complained that Parks didn't pay enough attention to her, that he was married to his job. Yet if Glidden was right – and she knew instinctively that he was – it was the time of life when he had to be totally committed to the job. It had been make-or-break time for him but she had never taken that into consideration. Barney was younger but someday it would be the same for him, too. There would come a time when he would have to put his job first and she would have to take it without complaint.

'How much further?' She didn't want to talk any more about Barney or Parks or think about herself. Nor did she wish to think about Bildor or Tremayne or Rossi or what must be happening on the outside; if she did, she would either have hysterics or freeze with fear. There was only one thing she wanted now and that was to get out.

'It can't be too much further – I can smell sea air.'

They had hit a fairly easy stretch. The hissing and the rumbling from the caverns behind them was fading further and further in the distance, though it wouldn't take more than a five- or ten-minute delay to lose their lead. Without thinking now she was helping the winded Glidden over the rough spots and the small gullies that broke up the path. He didn't protest.

Then once again there was a faint, tinny crackling from the radio, dimmer this time. Glidden stopped and pulled the radio out of his belt, listening at the small speaker for a moment. He suddenly jammed the radio back in his belt and turned to her, urgent.

'We'll have to run for it,' he said, almost apologetically. 'They're going to use G-gas in an hour and if any of it seeps down here, we're finished.'

Karen wondered if it really made any difference after all. If the caverns had filled with radioactive gases from the melt, then it was all over with already, though she might not know it for another week or two.

76

'Sealing the site might work,' Burgess said slowly. 'Our demolition men can close the pit.'

'It'll probably only add to the debris in the fallout cloud,' Parks said.

Burgess drummed his fingers on the top of the model. 'There aren't many options open to us. We've got about an hour before the wind shifts, maybe less. We've got to do something about your melt before then, no ifs, ands or buts.'

He turned to Cushing. 'When the hell do your experts get here?'

Cushing looked uncomfortable. 'The morning, that's the latest I've heard.'

'No real hurry, hmm? That's four hours away.' He thought for a moment, then glanced up at the faces around him. 'OK, gentlemen, that's it then. We'll close the exit port and seal the pit. If that doesn't work—' He shrugged. 'Well, I guess it'll have to work; otherwise it's goodbye Los Angeles.'

'If the wind shifts before your hour is up?' Parks asked.

Burgess shook his head. 'Demolition men are already in position. The first indication of a wind shift, we'll blow everything in sight.'

'The people in the caverns?'

'Last we heard, they were on their way. If they don't get there in time ... I've done my best.'

He didn't meet Parks' eyes and Parks said, 'Do you have a location on them?'

Burgess studied the model in front of him. 'I'm afraid not, Parks. Haven't been able to raise them for a while. My guess is that their batteries are down. If you've got any other ideas, I'd like to hear them.'

'If you can't seal it, what about the cities downwind?' Cushing asked.

'We've been over that,' Burgess said crisply. 'There are no plans to evacuate; it'd be impossible.'

There were no rabbits he could pull out of the hat, Parks thought. No trick, no sudden solutions ... Or were there?

In the silence, Parks ran his forefinger down the streak of black on the model. 'The melt's moving fairly fast now; it's on a straight line right to the ocean.'

Karen and the others were ahead of it, he hoped, but now he realized that Burgess was right. If they weren't at the sea exit before the wind shifted, the demo men would have to seal the opening to prevent the melt from reaching the sea.

'I don't understand,' Levant said suddenly.

Parks looked up at him, almost resenting the statement. Levant was the outsider in the group, the one who knew the least about what was happening. 'You don't understand what?'

'You said it was flowing in a straight line through the caverns. That doesn't make sense.'

Everybody was staring at Levant now.

'Why not?'

'I used to play in those caverns when I was a kid. Those cliffs are honeycombed, branching caverns all over the place.' He held up his hand and spread the fingers. 'Your melt should be running in a dozen different streams.'

'We had most of the side caverns sealed off,' Brandt cut in. 'In case of a waste pipe leak, we wanted to make sure everything was funnelled down to the sea exit and didn't accumulate in pools.'

Parks stared down at the model, an idea swimming in his mind like a fish in a pond. Then he had it hooked. 'We've all been a bunch of dumb bastards,' he said slowly. 'If we could split the melt into a large number of streams and small pockets—'

286

Burgess interrupted. 'Like separating hot coals – they'll cool faster then; is that what you mean?'

Parks nodded, feeling sudden enthusiasm well up within him. 'If we could do that, it'd make more sense to try and seal off the pit and the sea exit then. Break the melt up into enough small pools and you also reduce the chance of criticality, of there being a self-sustaining reaction.'

'There's only one sea exit?' Burgess asked.

'I've been down there,' Levant insisted. 'There's only one.'

Brandt leaned over the model, inspecting the area of the melt. 'It's a problem in volume versus area,' he mused. 'You increase the surface area as much as possible – the larger the surface area, the greater the cooling effect.'

Parks said, 'We'll need a boat and explosives.'

Burgess nodded. 'We've already commandeered one. A couple of sailors were trying to leave the bay in it.'

Levant suddenly said, 'Their names wouldn't be Halsam and Jefferson?'

'Your boat?'

'We'll be taking it right in under the fallout cloud, won't we?'

Burgess shrugged. 'It's been sitting under the fallout anyway. Probably have to be broken up and buried afterwards.'

Levant looked at him shrewdly. 'I'll get a new boat out of it?'

'Of course.' Burgess was weighing Levant now. 'We'll need some people who know the caverns. My men can lay the charges but they won't know where.' He paused. 'You said you knew the caverns well, that you used to play in them when you were a child?'

Levant nodded, resigned. 'OK, sure, I'll go.'

Parks said, 'I'd like to go along.'

'The more the merrier.'

'And bring Barney Lerner.'

Burgess looked surprised. 'He's running the decon station.'

'Kormanski's qualified.'

'Any special reason?'

Parks hesitated. 'Personal.'

'That's a lousy reason. All right, it's OK by me if it's OK with him.' Burgess glanced at his watch. 'We've got less than an hour – maybe. The explosives are already at the dock with demo men waiting.'

Parks stared. 'Anticipating us?'

Burgess shook his head. 'We would have blown the sea exit

in any event. They would have been on their way in another five minutes.' He turned to Levant. 'Your men are on the boat, everything's set.'

He fixed all of them with a curious look. 'If it works, it will have been such a simple solution. I can't understand why it took you so long.'

It was Brandt who said, 'It's not always easy to see the obvious – in anything.' He was staring at Cushing when he said it and on his face was a look of sudden understanding.

77

They couldn't be far; she could smell it herself – that peculiar combination of salt water, cold air and rotting fish that laymen called 'fresh sea air'. It was hot inside the caverns now. Both she and Glidden had put on their hoods with the air filters. The melt was behind them; she could hear it growling along with the sharp crack of an occasional bit of exploding concrete or limestone. Pray to God that somebody was there, she thought. And another fast prayer that they got there before anybody else.

'Will the radio work any more?'

Glidden paused a moment, as much to get his breath as to try and operate the radio. He pressed the various buttons, spoke into it and listened intently for a reply. No crackle, no sign that it was working at all. 'The batteries are dead,' he said.

There was another smell now. Karen quickly identified it. The smell of hot metal. She prayed that the filters in her hood were working; if she could smell something, it sure as hell meant that *something* was getting through.

She almost cracked then. She had seen too many people die, and it all seemed so hopeless. And she was tired and there wasn't any point—

Glidden stumbled and fell. She was by his side in a second, helping him up.

She not only had to get herself out; she had to get him out, too, she thought. Left foot, then right ... Ignore the smell of burning metal and the rumbling and the hissing behind her, ignore what was probably happening on the inside of her. Left foot—

And then she could see the sea exit blocked by the steel grill-work at the end of the rocky passageway. Glidden saw it, too; they dropped the lantern and ran towards it. There might be somebody else there, Karen thought suddenly, somebody else with a gun.

But it didn't matter. The sea exit was just ahead and she could see the sparkle as a torch cut into one of the heavy bars of the grillwork.

Fourth Day

78

It was the hour before dawn. False dawn, Parks thought, when there was no light but only a glow in the sky, a glow on the horizon that didn't come from the plant. The only activity on the wharf was that around Levant's boat, the *Taraval*, where half a dozen marines in white suits loaded satchels of explosives.

Lerner was waiting for him.

'The Colonel told me that if I wanted to come along, I could.'

'Karen's there. I thought you might want to be present when she gets out.'

'Sure. Thanks a lot.' His eyes were haunted by something that Parks couldn't quite figure out.

'You don't want to go, you don't have to.'

Lerner shook his head. 'I'm OK; it's the decon station.' He hesitated, fighting with himself. 'A lot of those people are going to die.' He had to have it out then. 'The plant should never have gone on stream, Parks. You knew that.'

'I tried to stop it,' Parks said, tired.

'You didn't try hard enough!' Lerner's voice was close to cracking.

'Talk to Brandt, not to me. Or better, talk to Cushing.'

Lerner laughed quietly. 'If I started, I think I would end up trying to kill them.' He turned towards the wharf. 'I know what happened; all of you were gutless wonders.' Parks didn't bother answering and Lerner reluctantly abandoned the conversation. 'You coming along?'

'It's my show. I want to be there when Karen and Glidden and the others come out. And I want to see the end of it.'

'You sure this will be the end of it?'

'Of this part of it.'

Lerner nodded thoughtfully, once again sizing him up. 'Levant and I will be setting charges along with the marine demo men.'

The Renaissance man, Parks thought. 'You know how to do that, too?'

'You'd be surprised what you can learn in the service, Parks.'

'I was never in – lucky, I guess.' Then: 'Karen will be glad to see you.'

Lerner nodded. 'She'll be glad to see anybody, I don't think it's been pleasant down there.' His calm façade crumbled a little then. 'How bad would the melt be down there? As far as exposure goes?'

Parks didn't want to think about it and wished Lerner hadn't brought it up. 'Depends. If they managed to get hold of some radiation suits, maybe not too bad. If they didn't – What the hell can I say, Barney?'

Lerner searched his face. 'Were you really interested in Karen, Parks? I mean seriously interested?'

'I liked her a lot,' Parks said evenly. 'If I had been divorced or if I could have gotten one easily, I probably would have married her.'

'Would she have married you?' Lerner asked.

Lerner wasn't quite so confident of Karen after all, Parks thought. He let his own contempt show then. 'Jealousy's a lousy emotion, Barney. I don't know whether she would have or not. I never asked her. But I'll give you one bit of advice: if you want to lose her, just keep on doubting her loyalty.'

Somebody called from the boat; he walked over, ignoring Lerner. Cushing, who managed to look natty even in a radiation suit, was waiting for him. The deep lines were gone from his eyes and he had the faintly distracted air of a bureaucrat, worried about what was going to happen the day after tomorrow.

'In another hour, it will all be over with, won't it?'

'If everything goes right.'

'I'm sure it will.' The cool eyes were steady on his face, trying to read whatever he could from any passing flicker of emotion. 'You'll be leaving in a few minutes. When you get back, I imagine the team from Washington will be here – investigators as well as the think-tank people. I wouldn't ... tell them a great deal. Talk too soon and they may hang you for it later.' He was all charm and confidence now. 'You don't have to agree with me on anything; it's still good advice to follow.'

'I'll remember that,' Parks said, amazed at the note of gratitude that crept into his voice.

'If there's anything I can do for you – later, I mean – please don't hesitate to ask.' Cushing suddenly reached out and squeezed his shoulder, then turned and walked back to one of the trucks. The pressures on him must have been great, too, Parks thought. You kept looking for supermen and you found ordinary people but that was hardly something to hold against them.

Then he realized that without even half trying, Cushing had made points with him. Like any good politician, his charm was his stock in trade. Press the flesh and show you *care*. See me when you get back from the war, boy; the company will always have a spot for you ...

Then he was on board and they were heading out into the bay. Lerner sat next to him, under the overhang of the deck-house. They were moving in towards the cliff, under the cloud now, and Parks imagined that the deck was getting gritty. Impossible, he thought, too many waves were breaking over it ... Then he remembered, with sudden acuteness, how susceptible he was to seasickness.

Lerner said suddenly, 'I think a lot of Karen, Parks. I'm jealous of her, I know that. I think about her all the time; I keep forgetting what's going on, what's really going on ... What happens if this doesn't work? I don't believe any of us think about that. Maybe we can't.'

Parks sighed. 'We think about small things, Barney. We think about a few people; we worry about ourselves. What are we supposed to do? Hold history in our heads, be fully aware all the time of everything that's happening? Maybe a De Gaulle or a Churchill could do it; I can't. I'd go crazy. Who said, "A single death is a tragedy; a million deaths is a statistic"? Von Clausewitz?'

'Wrong war, wrong tyrant,' Lerner said dryly. 'It was Joseph Stalin.' He shivered in memory. 'The decon station looked like photographs of Buchenwald; I kept seeing my own grandfather and grandmother there.' He glanced at the small flag at the bow, whipping in the wind. 'If we fail and the wind shifts, I swear to God I'll imagine that I see the ovens.'

Parks looked at him sharply. 'What's wrong, Barney?'

'What's wrong?' Lerner asked, almost to himself. 'My grandparents died at Buchenwald. It's like a birthmark; you carry the knowledge with you the rest of your life. I've always wondered what they talked about at the end. Up to the very last, they must have thought something would save them. I keep thinking that's a lot like us.'

Parks didn't bother to answer. He wondered if Karen really understood Lerner, then dropped the thought.

'Hey, Parks.' Levant was looking out from the deckhouse. 'You sure the Government will buy me a new boat?'

'That's what the Colonel said.'

'What'll it take? Two years and a lawsuit?'

Even Levant, Parks thought. The world could end tomorrow and people would still be worried about next month's paycheck. 'I've got a hunch all you'll have to do is squawk and they'll pay off in twenty-four hours.'

Levant thought about it for a moment, then turned back to the wheel, relieving Halsam. 'OK, Parks, I won't hold it against you when it doesn't work out that way.'

They were laying off the cliff front now and the boat was dead in the water, bobbing up and down on the waves. A marine with a torch climbed up on the ledge opposite the grill, lit the torch and started cutting the metal grillwork.

Parks watched him for a long moment, seeing the cliff front rise and fall with every passing swell.

He felt the motion churn the contents of his stomach. The next instant he was hanging on to the railing and vomiting into the green seas below. His mind emptied itself along with his stomach; for the first time in a dozen hours, he didn't think about the plant and what might happen in the morning.

79

Tebbets said quietly, 'Vandenberg's meteorological team is reporting a shifting wind pattern.'

Kloster nodded. 'The high-pressure centre is accelerating about five miles an hour.'

'Do you have an estimate on the wind shift?'

'Half an hour, maybe less.'

When that happened, the cloud would be hitting Los Angeles and heading towards the Mexican border, Tebbets thought. A lot of the fallout was probably being washed out by the rain within ten or fifteen miles of the plant, but once the rain stopped, the radioactive particles would carry that extra distance.

Kloster was half shrouded in a haze of cigarette smoke. Tebbets wondered what he was thinking about, then decided he already knew. His wife and family undoubtedly, just as he was thinking about Susan, very much remarried and with two kids now, living in Pacoima. Probably everybody in the room had relatives or friends or knew somebody living in southern California.

He glanced about. Not with a bang but a whimper, he thought. None of the usual offhand comments, none of the banter that sometimes filled the room when official duties were light. The MPs were still there but they had faded into the background. There was only the steady succession of coastal views on the screens and the monotonous flow of weather information. There was nothing they could do, he thought. They were as helpless to change anything as the people who lived in the path of the cloud.

He hadn't seen Susan in – how long – four years now? He probably never would have seen her again, given her own choices as well as his. But now he probably never *could*, and the thought made him want to see her very badly. He had missed her for a long time and now he was going to miss her even more – and for a much longer time.

'The wind's starting to change,' Kloster said quietly.

Tebbets picked up his coffee again, sipped at it, then changed his mind and poured it into a nearby wastebasket. It suddenly tasted like crap.

80

Senator Hoyt Mr Reiss, you're a member of the National Security Council, are you not?

Martin Reiss The terminology's incorrect, Senator. As you know, the members of the Council are the President, the Vice-President and the Secretaries of Defense and State. I'm associated with the Council as the recording secretary.

Senator Hoyt Thank you, Mr Reiss – I was, of course, referring to your official position. But to continue. On the eve of the Cardenas Bay disaster, is it correct to assume that the White House knew of the extent of the disaster shortly after it occurred?

Mr Reiss Not exactly, Senator. The original blowdown of Prometheus One occurred in the early hours of the evening, with the other reactors at the complex failing shortly thereafter.

No really complete report was made to the White House until close to midnight.

Senator Stone Standard bureaucratic lag.

Mr Reiss The original reports were made to department heads and the military chain of command. And then we had to contact scientific advisers for an interpretation of both the event and the available data.

Senator Stone The President couldn't have evaluated the information on his own?

Mr Reiss He could have but his interpretation may not have been correct. He's no more a physicist than Representative Holmburg is.

Representative Holmburg I don't know whether that's intended as flattery or not. What was the President's reaction?

Mr Reiss As you might imagine, he was deeply disturbed. One of his first acts was to convene the National Security Council, as well as to call in members of the Environmental Protection Agency.

Senator Stone I would assume that recommendations were made to the President and that one of them was the evacuation of Los Angeles and southern California.

Mr Reiss Evacuating LA was one of the first alternatives explored, Senator. It was rejected as not being feasible.

Senator Stone I don't understand, Mr Reiss.

Mr Reiss It would have been totally impractical, Senator. Los Angeles was blacked out at the time because of the failure of the coastal portion of the national grid. There was no way we could have passed the order to evacuate, no way we could have notified the populace. Radio and television sets – as well as stations – simply weren't working. The only viable route east, US Highway 66, would have been totally inadequate for even a small fraction of the traffic. And there was no place to send the people. I'm sorry, Senator, the evacuation of Los Angeles was not one of the contingency plans seriously considered. Aside from the other drawbacks, there was also the likelihood of panic and the projected number of casualties because of it was deemed unacceptable.

Senator Stone In the light of what he has just said, I would like to ask the witness a crucial question. Does a workable plan exist for the evacuation of any major American city on a few hours' notice?

Mr Reiss Under the circumstances you describe, Senator, it doesn't; it probably never will.

81

Karen held her breath as the cutting torch ate its way through the rusted metal rods of the grating. She and Glidden were in the shadows, waiting for the torch man to finish his work. She wondered if anybody else was waiting, too, ready to run for the exit once it was open. Foolish, she thought. The marines were there; she was safe. But her nerves were gone; she realized it would take very little for her to panic.

Then the white-suited figures were lifting out a large section of the grill. She ran then, and a moment later she was standing on the ledge outside, feeling the rain and the cold wind beat against her face.

'Karen?'

Parks was standing a few feet away. She stared at him for a moment, wanting to throw herself into his arms but still not sure what he would do. Before she could say anything, Barney appeared beside him and stood there, just looking at her. She didn't hesitate then; the expression on his face was enough. Barney held her close for a long moment, then abruptly moved away.

'Better get in the boat. We're going to dynamite the caverns and there's not much time.' He was crisp and almost impersonal; he had given her no time to cry, no time to become over-emotional. He wouldn't have in any event; he didn't approve. Only the slight touch of his hand on her arm told her what he felt.

She looked at Parks mutely. There was so much to be said that now never would be said. Then she let herself be handed down to the boat. The last she saw, Parks was talking to Glidden ...

'How bad is it, Greg?' Glidden asked.

'There's nothing left,' Parks croaked. 'They all went, starting with Prometheus One.'

Glidden blinked in the muted daylight, not really understanding. 'Many dead?'

'A dozen, another dozen unaccounted for.' Parks licked his lips, glad to be back on dry land if only for a few moments. 'There's lots of fallout. It's blowing out to sea but the wind is shifting. We're going to blow the cavern floor and try and divide the melt.'

'You were right,' Glidden said in a tired voice. He couldn't meet Parks' eyes. 'We never should have tried to take the plant on stream.'

He didn't want to be told that he had been right, Parks thought. Not now. 'Where are the others?'

'We had to abandon Tremayne,' Glidden said slowly. 'Rossi's dead and so is Bildor.' He paused. 'Somebody shot Bildor. There's somebody in there with a gun.'

Parks didn't pursue the matter. He knew what Glidden was saying but there was no time to worry about that now, however. Several of the marines started to help Glidden down to the boat. He turned just before he stepped off the ledge, timing his step to coincide with the rise of the boat on the swells.

'It was too big to stop, Greg. Prometheus was like a boulder rolling downhill. Every day that went by, they were counting on it more and more.' And then he turned and disappeared into the deckhouse. He was favouring his left leg and his shoulders slumped. He had never realized it before, Parks thought. Glidden was an old man.

Then Levant and the demolition men were on the ledge. 'You going back on board, Parks?'

It wasn't over yet, Parks thought. He wanted to see the end of it; my God, how he wanted to see the end of it.

'I'd like to go with you,' Parks said. Levant shrugged. Lerner and several of the demo men had already disappeared into the mouth of the cavern; Levant and Parks followed.

Inside the cavern, one of the marines said quietly, 'We've got ten minutes to set charges and get back to the boat. The wind's starting to shift.'

82

'Set several charges here,' Levant said, standing by a wall of concrete, his face twisted with memory. 'There's a whole series of small caves behind this.' Lerner set the charges looped with primacord and played out the cord to a central strand. Then he loped after Levant as he moved further back into the cavern. Parks and the other demolition men were several hundred feet behind them, busily setting charges where Levant had indicated, reeling out primacord for each charge and taping it to the central strand.

The further back they went, Lerner noticed, the warmer it seemed to get. And somewhere ahead of them, he heard a hissing sound accompanied by a deep rumble. The melt, he thought. And Karen had been racing that for hours ...

'How much time?' Levant grunted.

'Five minutes, maybe a little less.'

'Christ, it's hot.'

Lerner cocked his head and listened carefully, then pointed to a turn in the passageway about three hundred yards ahead. 'It looks like the cavern is collapsed up there; my guess is the melt's right behind it.'

Levant glanced around carefully at the walls, then nodded. 'Let's get closer. The walls between this and the next caverns are pretty thin. We should be able to drop the floor there, too.' They raced forward and Levant set the charges, then looked suddenly around. 'What the hell did I do with my knife?'

'You leave it back at the bend?'

Levant quickly checked his pockets. 'Must've.'

'I'll get it.' Lerner turned and jogged back down the passageway. Levant had left a satchel charge at the end and the knife was beneath it. Lerner put his torch on the floor and bent down to pick it up. Somebody was coming up from a side passage. One of the marines, he thought; maybe time was shorter than he had estimated.

He straightened up and stared at the man in front of him in silence for a moment. Then he said, 'Hello, Paul.'

'Hello, Barney.'

Marical held one hand behind him and Lerner knew instinctively what he was hiding. His eyes strayed beyond Marical for just a fraction of a second. In the side passage was a toy wagon, lead casks piled in it.

Marical watched his eyes flick to the wagon, smiled slyly and brought the pistol from behind his back. He quickly raised it before Lerner could jump him.

'What happened up there, Barney?'

'Prometheus One had a LOCA. The others followed – China syndrome.'

'No shit. Bad?'

'If the wind shifts, the fallout could wipe out half the state.'

Marical laughed quietly and shook his head. 'How'd it happen?'

'Probably sabotage,' Lerner said coldly. 'By you.'

'Me?' Marical seemed genuinely surprised. 'It never occurred

298

to me, Barney.' For a moment he looked contemptuous. 'It would have been easy to do. How many dead?'

'A dozen – and there'll be more. Peterson, the guys in Control Central, Stewart ... And a lot of radioactivity scattered around the landscape. They had to evacuate the town, decontaminate the people.'

He kept a careful watch for an opening; Marical was just as carefully watching him. The smiling Nazi, Lerner thought.

'Everybody wearing radiation suits?' Marical asked.

If only his eyes weren't so alert, Lerner thought. One small shift, somebody coming up the passageway, anything to distract Marical for a split second. 'Mostly the marines.'

Something struck him about Marical then. He was leaning comfortably against the rocky wall but occasionally he'd lift his free hand to wipe away the sweat. It was hot but it wasn't that hot. And there was a curious lack of fear or even concern in his voice. 'You feel OK?'

Marical shook his head. 'I feel like shit. Sweats, headaches, fever. It's radiation poisoning.'

Lerner had a sudden hunch. 'Is that why you killed Doc?'

'Doc? Yeah. I was always sick and he finally took a blood test. About a day later, I figured out what I had myself. I knew when he saw the results he'd report it and there would be an investigation.' He laughed wryly. 'I should have been more careful in the first place. I feel like the bartender who couldn't hold his liquor.'

'That was a rough way for Doc to go.'

Marical frowned, as if Lerner didn't understand something. 'Any way is a rough way to go. I did it clean and neat and instantaneous.'

Lerner stared at Marical, unbelieving, then pointed at the wagon. 'You were trying to get that stuff out through the sea exit?'

'I had contacts meeting me there.' Marical looked at him quizzically. 'No way it's going to work out, is there?'

'No way. The wind's been blowing directly from the plant site to the sea. Anybody on a boat coming this way would get a dose. And then there's the marines.'

'That figures. It was a screwed-up deal from the start.' He suddenly changed the subject. 'What were you doing with the charges?'

'Getting ready to blow the caverns. Parks thinks it's the only way to stop the melt.'

'He's probably right.' Marical was silent for a moment. 'I guess I've got nothing more to say.' He aimed the pistol carefully at Lerner's head. 'Sorry, Barney.'

'You can't get out, Paul,' Lerner protested quickly. He pointed to the wagon. 'Not with that.'

'No need for it now.' Marical shrugged.

Somebody come along, Lerner prayed. 'The exit's crawling with marines, Paul.'

Marical gestured at his own white suit and hood. 'It's not that bad a gamble. If I wear my hood, nobody will recognize me.'

'Karen will. She's on the boat.'

Marical hesitated. 'It'll still work. Everybody will be too busy to notice. Besides, I don't have many choices.'

'You're sick,' Lerner said, fast. 'You've got a bad dose; you can't make it more than a few days.'

'A few days is a few days,' Marical said dryly.

'What were you going to do, Paul – build a bomb?'

'Not me – I guess my contacts were.'

'Terrorists?'

Marical looked nervous. 'You're talking a lot, Barney.' He wiped his forehead with his free hand. 'Nobody overseas, nothing that exotic. Strictly homegrown. We've got our own terrorists now.'

Anybody, Lerner breathed . . . 'What'd you do it for, money?'

Marical changed then. Suddenly he was no longer casually friendly. Lerner could now imagine him standing over Doc on the beach, placing the gun behind his ear and pulling the trigger. The little man's muscles were tense, his gun hand a study in sweaty marble. His eyes were large and luminous.

'Money, Barney? No, only partly. More than that, it was a chance to hit back at something that robbed me of the most important thing in my life.' Lerner could sense a sick rage just below the surface. 'My wife and I met at Mohawk Bluffs; we both worked in the lab there. She kept her job after we were married, even after the kids were born. But they were sloppy at the plant – they usually are. Management never bothered to tighten up.' His face was now carefully blank of any emotion. 'She took one damn long time to die and every minute was painful. There were a lot of doctor bills, then the expense of taking care of the kids . . .' He paused for a moment, remembering. 'Mohawk disclaimed all responsibility. They couldn't afford to admit they were wrong. I never saw a dime.'

Marical cocked his head and smiled bitterly. 'See, Barney?

Nothing fancy after all – just plain old-fashioned revenge. It's easy to steal fissionables from a nuclear power plant. I figured once a bomb or two went off, they'd stop building the plants.' He shrugged. 'And I needed the cash to pay all those bills. It seemed only fair.'

'You'll kill a helluva lot of people just to make a point.'

Marical half smiled. 'A lot of people are going to die out there anyway, aren't they?'

Lerner knew instinctively that the conversation was over. He dodged to one side and launched himself at Marical, trying to tackle him around the knees. Marical easily sidestepped him, reversed the pistol and clubbed him on the head with the butt. Lerner went to his knees, stunned, still trying to feel in front of him for Marical. He couldn't see; blood was streaming into his eyes. Dumb thing to do, he thought. He should've tried his luck the moment he had seen Marical; talking had been a bad mistake. He had forgotten everything he had learned in the Israeli Army. You don't talk first; you never talk first.

He could sense Marical circling him. Then he felt something cold pressed against his head just behind his left ear.

Running feet sounded in the passage far away. *'Barney? Where the hell are you? We've got to get out of here!'* Parks' voice.

Cold metal against his head. The goddamned Nazi was going to—

83

Levant said, 'Is he dead?'

Parks tried to stanch the flow of blood, then gave up. 'I don't think so. Let's get him out of here; Karen will know what to do.'

He picked Lerner up in his arms and Levant said, 'On the double – the timer is set.'

They jogged back to the exit. Suddenly Parks felt Lerner stir in his arms. His eyes flickered open for a second and Parks said, 'Who was it?'

'Goddamn Nazi,' Lerner whispered. 'Marical.' Then his body went limp and his head lolled to one side. At the exit, the marines took Lerner and lowered him gently into the boat. A moment later there was an audible gasp and a half-muffled scream. Parks *guessed* that Karen had discovered who it was.

He jumped into the boat. Levant followed, ducking into the deckhouse and taking the helm from Halsam. The *Taraval* leaped away from the cliffside and fled towards the open sea. Half a mile out a heavy rumble from the cliff front beat the air. The limestone bluff dissolved slowly in a waterfall of rubble. On the deck one of the Marines let out a halfhearted cheer. No one joined him.

Parks turned away then and went to the deckhouse where Karen and Lerner were. Karen had bandaged Lerner's head and was holding him in her arms. Lerner was mumbling incoherently in a low, heavy voice.

She looked up at Parks, her eyes trapped and frantic. 'He's saying everything he always wanted to, everything he was always afraid to. Everything seems so simple to him now.'

Parks shifted uncomfortably. 'How is he?' he asked. He had seen her nude before but he had never seen her quite so naked.

'He's dying,' she whispered.

84

Marical didn't know where he was. He had heard Parks and the others come up the passageway, fired the one shot into Lerner's head, then fled back up the corridor. He must have taken a wrong turn, he thought, and gotten turned around somehow. He was heading again for the sea exit; the floor was sloping down. The boat would have left by now and he could either swim for it or try to make it up to the top of the cliff. That was probably the best bet; it would be too long and hairy a swim.

Something was wrong. The floor had tilted down for a while but now he was climbing a slope again. And it was warm, warmer than he had remembered it earlier. He had been right the first time but hadn't trusted his judgement; he had walked right back to the melt.

The explosion caught him by surprise. There was a *crrrump* and the rocky floor rose up to meet him. He lay there, half stunned, for a long moment, listening to the roar of the limestone caverns collapsing around him. The dust began to clear. He realized he was now lying on a ledge with a sheer drop in front of him. Thirty feet away, on the other side of the chasm, he saw a slow movement. Something very bright was edging closer and closer to the lip of the abyss.

He stood up, shielding his eyes. The melt. It flowed sluggishly towards the edge, started to drip over, and then became a slowly growing torrent. It was blinding – and warm. More than warm, hot – hotter than he could ever remember the sun down in Florida or Mexico.

He let his arms drop down to his sides. He could feel the heat blister his face. Vaguely he wondered how many sunshine units he was absorbing – that's what they had called them at Mohawk Bluffs, he thought bitterly.

The melt was now a waterfall cascading over the edge of the chasm and splintering into a dozen little rivulets as it fell into the various smaller caverns and openings below. It was blinding him. Dark splotches spread before his eyes and he knew his optic nerves were burning out. Then the scene faded into black.

Funny, he thought he heard somebody calling his name.

Doc and Lerner and Wanda. He had deep regrets about all of them now, especially about Wanda. Homely girl but she had always done everything he had ever asked. And she had loved him. Just as Marie had loved him through those agonizing months as she had died slowly before his eyes.

It was hotter than he could stand but he was no longer able to scream. He knew that his hair was burning, but he felt no pain. The waterfall of searing metal had now become a torrent of sound.

Sunshine, he thought for the last time. He could feel it in his bones.

Kamrath stood frozen halfway down the passageway, his face bloody from where the explosions had thrown him against a rocky wall, and watched in horror. Marical was standing on a ledge facing a blinding white waterfall of metal. At first he had shielded his face but now his arms hung limply at his sides. He hadn't moved, though his hair was burning. As Kamrath watched, Marical's white uniform burst into flames.

'Marical! It's me, Kamrath!'

The figure didn't move. Marical couldn't hear him over the cascade of hot metal. Kamrath stood a moment longer in agonized indecision, then ran forward. He had come too far to be cheated, he thought. The heat had begun to blister his own face when he felt the pathway shiver beneath his feet. He stumbled to a halt, clutching at the rocky wall for support. Just in front of him, the trail crumbled, to be swept away by a river of metal.

Marical was now isolated on the rocky ledge; there was no way to get to him. Kamrath shouted again, then dropped to one knee and brought up the shotgun. He aimed just above Marical's head and squeezed the trigger. Marical had to know he was there!

The sound was swallowed up by the roar of the molten cascade. Marical still didn't move. He couldn't hear him, Kamrath thought again. Marical would never know that he had been tracked down, that he was going to have to pay for Doc's death.

His eyelids were beginning to puff. Kamrath threw up an arm to protect his face against the heat. Marical was paying, but it wasn't the right way. God was meting out justice instead of him.

It was blasphemy but he couldn't help it. He had come this far and now he was being cheated.

Marical would never know, he thought in anguish.

And then the figure on the ledge crumpled to its knees, swayed for a second and dropped soundlessly into the pit before it.

Kamrath blinked, once again aware of the intense heat … and something else. He let the riot gun slip from his hands and slowly walked back along the path. The blisters on his face had begun to ooze and his coat was hot to the touch. He'd have to find a way out, if there still was one.

The heat and the roar slowly faded behind him and gradually even the image of Marical paled in his mind.

Odd, he felt so goddamned weak and sick to his stomach.

85

Senator Stone You were Chief of Personnel at Cardenas Bay?
Robert Hoffman For all of Western Gas and Electric, Senator, not just the complex at Cardenas Bay.
Senator Stone But you did the hiring at Cardenas Bay?
Mr Hoffman No, sir, not exactly, I wouldn't want to mislead the Committee on that score. Depending on the position,

management at Cardenas Bay might do their own interviewing and hiring. We would process the paper work.

Senator Hoyt Did you process Paul Marical's application?

Mr Hoffman I've had that matter looked into and, yes, his papers did cross our desk.

Representative Holmburg Did you check him out?

Mr Hoffman I'm not sure what you mean when you say 'check him out'.

Representative Holmburg My God, man, you must do some checking to make sure you're not hiring card-carrying Communists or psychopaths, don't you?

Mr Hoffman We go pretty much by previous recommendations, sir. If a man has worked for another power company or a related industry, I think it would be a waste of time to conduct another security check.

Senator Stone So you take their previous employer's word for it.

Mr Hoffman Personnel departments are not particularly large, Senator, and Western's perhaps isn't as large as it should be. We don't have the manpower to check everybody out. And there's no point in running security checks on file clerks.

Senator Stone Paul Marical didn't apply for a job as a file clerk. He was working in a sensitive area, handling dangerous materials.

Senator Hoyt Did you check his background?

Mr Hoffman I don't recall ever seeing his records, Senator. I believe he had arranged to carry his personnel records with him from his previous job and was going to turn them over to the people at the Cardenas Bay plant. We saw no reason to double-check.

Senator Hoyt Then you didn't know that his wife had been seriously exposed in an accident at Mohawk Bluffs, that she died of pancreatic cancer a year later?

Mr Hoffman Not having seen his records personally, there was no way of my knowing that, Senator.

Senator Hoyt It wouldn't have done you any good if you had seen them, Mr Hoffman. The reason he carried them with him was so he could falsify them.

Senator Stone Did you talk to anybody at all at Mohawk Bluffs before hiring Marical, Mr Hoffman?

Mr Hoffman I didn't think it was necessary, sir. That's a formality that I'm sure was taken care of directly by the people who hired him at Cardenas Bay.

Senator Stone It may interest you to know, Mr Hoffman, that management at Cardenas Bay believes you check back on all recommendations and previous places of employment as a matter of course.

Mr Hoffman They have no reason to believe that, sir.

Representative Holmburg The Committee will pardon my levity, but you can say that again.

Senator Stone You have no idea then whether or not Paul Marical carried a deep hatred for nuclear plants because of his wife's death as a result of the accident at Mohawk Bluffs.

Mr Hoffman I know nothing about that, Senator.

Senator Hoyt Then you would also have no idea whether or not Paul Marical might have sabotaged the Cardenas Bay plant.

Mr Hoffmann No idea whatsoever, Senator. I'm hardly qualified to judge but from what you've told me – and this is the first time I've heard any of this – I suppose it's possible. Maybe even probable.

Hiatus – Sixth Day

86

'How are you?' the voice said.

It was difficult abandoning the dream and waking up. His mind was still fogged with the transition period between waking and sleeping, when dreams are still more real than reality. Parks blinked a couple of times and struggled up on the cot. The rest of the hospital tent was empty. He blinked a couple of times, then groaned and started to burrow beneath the blankets. Just a few minutes more . . .

A little more urgently: 'Are you awake?'

He snapped alert then and sat up. Cushing was sitting in a chair by the side of the cot. He was wearing a civilian suit and, except for his shaved head, looked remarkably as he had the first time they had met. 'How do you feel?'

Parks yawned. 'Raw. Like I've been flayed alive. How long have I been asleep?'

'You've been out two days. You were sick for a while. You'd sleep, eat, then go back to sleep again.' Cushing looked properly sympathetic.

Things were floating back in his memory now, a lot of things he wished he could forget. 'Lerner,' he asked suddenly. 'Did he make it?'

Cushing shook his head. 'He died shortly after they got him to the hospital. There was nothing they could have done.'

Parks studied the pattern of sunlight on the blankets. 'Anybody else?'

Cushing hesitated, then said, 'Not everybody got out of town in time. And so far as we've been able to check, Sheriff Kamrath was either trapped in the plant or possibly in the caverns. He apparently had gone there looking for Paul Marical.'

Parks looked surprised. 'Marical?'

'I'm not sure why. I think he thought Marical was responsible for Dr Seyboldt's death. I'm sorry he's not here to ask.' Cushing looked a little bored and Parks guessed he actually wanted to talk about something else.

'What about the plant?'

Again, a slight hesitation. 'There's no need to worry; everything's sealed off now. The gas apparently killed all animal life and we'll keep the site sprayed with defoliants.'

There was something wrong with the answer but Parks was still groggy and couldn't put his finger on it. He didn't want to think about it any more. Lerner was dead. Others had died; others *would* die ... Cushing wanted to talk about something else.

'You've got something on your mind.'

'A team of investigators flew in, as I thought they would.'

'No reporters?'

'There won't be any.'

Parks started searching for his boots. 'The lid's on?'

'For the moment.' Hesitation again. 'At least until we get everything sorted out.'

'People will talk,' Parks said.

'It doesn't matter what they say,' Cushing said slowly. 'It depends more on who they are.'

Parks stared. 'You better sort me out now.'

Cushing teetered back in his chair and locked his fingers behind his head. His eyes were wary and searching as always. 'I'll spell it out very frankly, Parks. It's very important – more so than you might realize right now – what people in authority say. As for the men who worked in the plant, we'll see to it that they get other jobs – at other plants. And the fishermen will be compensated. In stages.'

'In hopes that everybody will dummy up. At least for a while.'

Cushing nodded. 'That's exactly it.'

'It's all small potatoes in the overall picture?'

'That's right.'

'And you've got something planned for me.'

Cushing's chair came down with a crash. 'Come off it, Parks – I'm not from the KGB or even the CIA. You can walk out of here and say anything you want to. All I'm trying to do is help you figure out what you really want to say.'

'That it was sabotage and not an accident?'

'Parks, first things first. Regardless of anything that's happened – *anything* – we're not going to scrap a hundred billion dollars' worth of nuclear plants and go back to living in caves because of one accident.'

'There have been hundreds of accidents.'

Cushing nodded, tired. Parks guessed that he wanted to get out of there and catch a plane back to Washington. 'If you want to count every stripped screw, that's your privilege.' The eyes were colder now, the voice faintly threatening. 'You've got a right to your say. We've certainly got a right to ours.'

'Like what?' Parks asked bitterly. 'That you closed your eyes to a hundred different violations? That you deliberately put a plant on stream when you knew it wasn't ready?'

'Parks,' Cushing said quietly, 'I don't know if the Government will want a scapegoat or not. But if they do, we've already found one. You. Go ahead and blame the vendors, Government harassment and pressure or incompetent workmen – the unions will love that one. You think you'll find that many people to back you up? I told you once before that your letters to the Commission have probably disappeared by now. Your own records are ashes that have been scattered over half the ocean. Complain all you want. The more bitter you get, the more people will think you're trying to shift the blame.'

Parks was on his feet, balling Cushing's coat in his fist and lifting him half off the chair. Cushing didn't change his expression. 'One punch, Parks, and you'll have ruined your case and saved me a lot of trouble.'

Parks relaxed his grip and sat down on the cot, suddenly dizzy. 'I'm sorry, Cushing.'

Cushing shrugged. He said softly, 'It was your plant, you ran the show and whether you like it or not, the buck stops with you. So you didn't think it should go on stream. You knew what was at stake. Did you honestly think a few letters to Washington would stop it? You did everything that was in the rule books but that's all you did. God *damn* it, there are a lot of men like you in industry! Bright, calm, efficient, a little bewildered when it comes to finding your way around government or politics. You have everything going for you except passion. If you want to change the world, Parks, you have to want to change it passionately.'

He leaned forward in his chair. 'You like machinery, Parks; you're proud of machines that operate as they should. Well, yours didn't and nobody's going to believe you if you try and blame it on somebody else. It was *your* machine that screwed up, Parks.'

Parks lit a cigarette and stared at the floor for a moment. Finally he said, 'You think I'm dangerous?'

'You could be – in the sense that you could make some things more difficult. The country has to bite the bullet. We have no alternative, and you could make it a lot harder to bite. People are going to have to live with nuclear power. It would be nice if they weren't frightened to death every minute they were doing so.'

'They won't be frightened if they think the plant failed because it was sabotaged?'

'We can offer more guarantees against sabotage than we can against poor design or machines that, basically, just won't work because we don't know enough or the number of variables is too great.'

Parks looked up at him, startled. 'Then you agree with me?'

Cushing shook his head. 'Not at all. It's just that the human race has entered a period of history where it can no longer play it safe, where it will just have to gamble on the odds and hope for the best.'

'I don't like the odds or the gamble,' Parks said. 'Why should I keep quiet?'

Cushing glanced at his watch. Parks could see him mentally calculate the time to the airport. 'Western's building a new breeder reactor in Oregon. They'll need a manager up there in about six months.'

Parks thought about it for a moment. 'I see, the carrot and the stick. How come Brandt isn't here offering the carrot?'

'He will be.' Cushing stood up and reached for his hat. 'The country can't live without energy, Parks. We've got to have it and we need men like you to help us get it.'

When Cushing was at the door, Parks said, 'You know I won't go along. If something goes wrong with a breeder, it doesn't just melt down. It blows up. But I wouldn't go along in any event.'

Cushing looked surprised, then half smiled. 'For a while, there, I wondered.' The smile vanished. 'I levelled, Parks. I meant everything I said.'

Parks shook his head. 'Too many people died, Cushing. I have to say why I think they did.'

Cushing nodded, suddenly sombre. 'You might be able to convince people. But if you do, life is going to be goddamned hard; nobody's going to thank you, Parks.' He fingered his hat, trying to think of a last argument, then realized there wasn't any. He stood in the doorway a moment longer, brooding. 'When we accepted the convenience of the automobile, we also accepted fifty thousand highway deaths a year. They're unfortunate but nobody thinks anything about them. We have to live with nuclear power and that means running the risk of an occasional disaster. We won't want to but we'll learn to accept that, too.'

He put on his hat and picked up his briefcase. 'I'm sure you don't care, Parks, but I respect you even if I don't like you.' He hesitated, then said softly, 'From here on in, it's going to be down and dirty.'

87

Senator Hoyt Then you think that the disaster at Cardenas Bay was due to sabotage?

Eliot Cushing I don't think there's much question of it, Senator. In the months since the incident, investigators have turned up a good deal of information about Paul Marical. We know he lost his wife through an accident at Mohawk Bluffs. We know he carried a grudge against nuclear plants afterwards. We have reason to believe now that he sabotaged the plant to cover his own tracks and to create a diversion while he smuggled out the stolen fissionables.

Senator Stone If the witness will permit the observation, that was some diversion.

Mr Cushing I think it unlikely that he meant it to turn out quite as it did; it obviously got out of hand.

Representative Holmburg Mr Cushing, we've had quite a parade of witnesses before this Committee, some of whom have been very impressive. A few of them – Mr Parks, in particular – have presented a lot of testimony to the effect that the plant was basically unsafe, that there was too much of a rush, that vendors were supplying defective parts, that sort of thing. Do you have any comments on that?

Mr Cushing I'm sure that Mr Parks was sincere and testified to the best of his ability. But I would like to remind the Committee that for a number of years, I passed on all reactor safety problems. Almost all of the complaints passed over my desk – after the first year, I doubt that I saw a new and original one. When complaints and warnings were justified, we investigated and shut plants down and fined the vendors and frequently the plant itself. The Commission never tolerated sloppy work or unsafe procedures. And that's why I have to disagree with the conclusion that Mr Parks drew from his own testimony. Though the records have unfortunately disappeared, I was quite familiar with the troubles at Cardenas Bay. None of them were unique; we had seen them all before and they had never led to anything like this. There are numerous built-in safeguards; granted that one might fail but it's difficult to conceive of all of them going.

Representative Holmburg You were actually on the scene throughout the disaster and before, right?

Mr Cushing That's correct, sir.

Representative Holmburg Then you worked with Mr Parks during that time?

Mr Cushing We were on the scene together, yes, sir.

Representative Holmburg You must have formed some sort of opinion of Mr Parks' abilities during that time.

Mr Cushing I came to appreciate Mr Parks' capabilities, which are considerable. In my opinion, he's a very competent man. Beyond that, I don't think I should comment.

Senator Hoyt The situation is a little too serious for you to be coy, Mr Cushing. You've paid your compliments to Mr Parks. Now I think if you have any reservations about Mr Parks' past actions or decisions, we should also know about them.

Mr Cushing I don't believe I could fault any of his decisions. If I had any adverse comment, it would be that I considered him too excitable at times – though under the circumstances, that's hardly a black mark against him. I also considered him a devoted engineer. Perhaps too much so.

Representative Holmburg Too much devotion to your job is a bad thing? You'll have to explain that one. My constituents would find that hard to follow.

Mr Cushing Demanding perfection from a machine can sometimes be like demanding it from a human being. You can look for it but I think it's a mistake to expect to find it.

Senator Clarkson You're implying that Mr Parks was a perfectionist?

Mr Cushing I think he expected too much from the Cardenas Bay facility, that the small things that went wrong – things you could expect to go wrong in the normal course of operation of any plant – were magnified out of all proportion in his mind.

Senator Stone I think you're damning with faint praise, Mr Cushing. And things obviously did go wrong. Major things.

Mr Cushing I didn't volunteer my remarks about Mr Parks, Senator; I was asked for them. But let me rephrase some of my testimony here: I don't believe that the Cardenas Bay plant failed because of the nature of the plant or because of the shortcomings of the vendors or because of inexperienced workmen; we've dealt with all of those before, in other plants, both singly and in combination. From testimony given, I think it reasonable to assume that a far more likely cause for the failure at Cardenas Bay was relatively prosaic – sabotage. Though conclusive evidence is lacking, we do have both a suspect and a motive.

Senator Marks It's unfortunate that the suspect is no longer alive to testify.

Senator Stone Mr Cushing, if I can ask you to repeat information already given, your position at the time of the disaster was Vice-Chairman for the Reactor Safety Subcommittee under the Committee on Reactor Design, am I right?

Mr Cushing That's correct, Senator.

Senator Stone And what is it now?

Mr Cushing As the Committee already knows, I am now Vice-President for Nuclear Development for Western Gas and Electric.

Senator Stone And Hilary Brandt?

Mr Cushing I'm glad to say that Mr Brandt is still with us in an advisory capacity. I'm sorry that his health precluded his testifying here today, though I don't know what he could add to the testimony he's already given.

Senator Stone You don't think that your testimony before this Committee reflects a possible conflict of interest?

Mr Cushing The events at Cardenas Bay occurred almost a year ago, Senator. I wasn't connected with Western then. They approached me a short time ago when Mr Brandt's failing health made it imperative that Western find a new vice-president. I would like to stress at this time that I'm proud of my present position and also that my service in the Government was instrumental in qualifying me for it. The history of American industry is full of examples where individuals who have served their country either in government or in the military have gone on to render further service in industry itself.

Senator Stone I believe President Eisenhower referred to it as the 'military-industrial complex'.

Senator Hoyt My esteemed colleague from Pennsylvania is badgering the witness.

Senator Stone My apologies to the witness if he construes my natural curiosity as badgering. Mr Cushing, in previous testimony Mr Parks has recommended that the nuclear programme be abandoned. What would you recommend?

Mr Cushing Senator Stone, I can't think of a more tragic act than the abandonment of the programme. American military power, as well as economic independence, relies heavily on nuclear energy. Despite the circumstances, I consider the present outcry against nuclear power as both irresponsible and shortsighted. What would we replace it with? We cannot mine enough coal; there is not enough natural gas and our existing geothermal and hydroelectric power simply couldn't replace the energy currently supplied by nuclear plants. Solar power and fusion, to be blunt, are pie-in-the-sky. Abandon our present nuclear programme, as Mr Parks suggests, and once again we would be dependent on sources overseas for our fuel needs. It would bankrupt us financially and lay us open once more to oil blackmail. The most logical course – in fact, the only course – is to continue with the present programme and to increase security safeguards at all our plants to make sure another Paul Marical can't cause a repeat of the Cardenas Bay incident. As I've stated a number of times before this Committee, I personally respect Mr Parks' view but to discontinue the nuclear power programme would simply be throwing out the baby with the bathwater.

Senator Stone That's quite a speech, Mr Cushing. However, I would like to protest your continuing faint praise of Gregory Parks while you slit his throat. I also think you've dismissed out of hand several possible long-term solutions to the energy crisis and tried to frighten us into continuing a programme which has resulted in one of the most tragic disasters in American history. In short, I consider your testimony before this Committee as completely self-serving.

Representative Holmburg I hate to say it but the Senator from Pennsylvania and I have just parted company. I can't see throwing half my constituents out of work for fear of something that's not only preventable but probably wouldn't happen again in a thousand years. I've got to agree with Mr Cushing. To shut down the programme would be to deliver our beloved country into the hands of a bunch of desert despots.

Senator Hoyt The role of this Committee is to recommend

to the Congress as a whole, not to make policy. But Senator Stone's opinion notwithstanding, I think I speak for the majority of Committee members when I say that Mr Cushing's views are not only cogent but overwhelming in their thoughtfulness and considered logic.

88

Parks finished lacing his shoes, then stood up and put on the khaki shirt lying on the chair. Before he left, he noticed a small business card on the blankets. It read simply: *Eliot Cushing.* And in small engraved script beneath, a phone number. He studied it for a moment, then tore it in two and let the pieces flutter to the floor.

Outside, the winter sun was blinding. He stood in the shadow of the tent to let his eyes adjust while he got his bearings. The tent was on a shallow bluff overlooking the bay. He thought he recognized the spot; he and Karen used to have an occasional office lunch there. Cole Levant appeared in front of a neighbouring tent. Parks waved and turned to look at the town in the distance.

The town wasn't there any more. Rather, part of it was; the other half of it had been smashed flat. Parks watched quietly as tiny bulldozers levelled the toy buildings. He wasn't sure but it looked like the drivers were wearing white suits. Other bulldozers were working in the ruins and he guessed what they were doing: scraping the wood and cement and plaster into piles where the debris could be loaded into fifty-five-gallon drums.

Levant walked over. 'They're canning what's left of our town, Parks.'

On the other side of the tent, a small line of people were waiting to get on the bus.

'What's happening, Cole?'

A few feet away, a flatbed truck, the driver in white, rumbled by on the highway. Rows of drums were stacked two high on the back.

Levant looked pale and somewhat weak. 'They're stripping the whole area down to a depth of two feet. They're going to bury the drums in a national preserve.' He looked bitter. 'Sort

315

of a radioactive Arlington. They tell me it happened in Spain once.'

Parks watched the bulldozers weave methodically back and forth on the horizon. 'What about your boat?'

Levant fumbled in his pocket for a pair of steel-frame glasses, then pulled out a set of soiled forms. 'I was told to fill these out in triplicate. In six months, I should have a new boat – maybe. I'm not holding my breath. Don't know where I'd fish anyway; the coastal waters are off-limits now.'

Parks watched the destruction of the town a moment longer, then asked, 'Where's Karen?'

Levant jerked his thumb down the line. 'Over there. Waiting.'

She was standing in the line, dressed in a shapeless marine jump suit. She wore no make-up; her shorn head was protected from the sun with a large blue handkerchief folded into a babushka. She saw him but didn't wave. He walked over; it was only when he got closer that he noticed the black arm-band against the green twill.

'I was afraid I'd miss you.'

'I'm glad you didn't.'

'I'm sorry about Barney,' he said.

She shrugged, her face a mask. There was an awkward silence.

'I had a long talk with Cushing.'

'All of us saw him go in your tent,' she said. There was a trace of bitterness in her voice. 'I imagine he took you to the top of the mountain and showed you all the kingdoms of the world.'

'That sounds Biblical.'

'It is. Luke, four-five. Barney once quoted it to me.'

Lerner was with them like a shadow, Parks thought without rancour. 'They need a manager for a breeder plant in Oregon.'

'And they offered it to you.'

'That's right.'

'We were talking in line,' she said slowly. 'When we saw him go in, I bet they couldn't buy you. I guess I lost.'

Parks studied her face. She shouldn't use make-up again, he thought; she was far prettier without it. Or maybe wholesome was the over-used word. 'You think people should live in tents and go back to wood stoves?'

'If that's the only alternative.' She shivered with sudden memory. 'Anybody who worked in the plant would agree with me.'

'So do I,' he said.

316

'You mean that?' He nodded and she said thoughtfully, 'You're finding yourself.'

'I've had a lot of help recently.'

Levant came up then and said, 'Has anybody seen Rob? Damn kid, we're supposed to leave in a few minutes.'

They found Rob and a friend playing on the beach a short distance away. They were squatting in the sand, Rob holding a magnifying glass and focusing the sun's rays on a piece of paper. The paper started to smoke just as they walked up.

'Let's go, boys,' Levant said gruffly. 'I thought I told you the beaches were posted; you want to go through the showers again?'

Parks stared at the smouldering sheet of paper. '"If wars were fought with sunbeams",' he mused, ' "we would have had solar power years ago."'

Karen looked at him. 'Who said that?'

Parks shrugged. 'Can't remember. A pretty bright man, whoever he was.' He touched her lightly on the arm. 'Will I see you again?'

She nodded and pressed a piece of paper into his hand. 'If you want to. As a friend – at least at first. I'll be going home to Seattle. My sister works in a hospital there and they might have an opening. You?'

He thought about it then for the first time. 'I'm not sure. I'll be blackballed from the power industry but I don't think I'd go back anyway.' He paused, thinking. 'Someplace along the line, I guess I'll pick up a divorce. Then maybe I'll just visit Seattle. But first, I want to spend a few weeks with my brother's family in Long Beach. Sort of dry out – no excitement and lots of sun.'

Karen's face had suddenly gone blank. 'Nobody told you?' she asked. 'Cushing never said anything?'

Parks stared. 'About what?'

89

Senator Hoyt Mr Tebbets, you were on duty at the MIROS tracking centre in Denver at the time of the Cardenas Bay disaster. Can you tell the Committee what happened at the time of the wind change?

Mr Tebbets We were watching the screens, looking at an overview of the entire coast. The fallout cloud had been growing all night; by morning it was approximately a hundred and sixty miles long and maybe thirty miles at its widest. Just before the wind changed, we were notified that they had set off charges to seal the pit where the reactors had been.

Senator Stone What happened then?

Mr Tebbets Nothing, Senator.

Senator Stone What do you mean, 'nothing'?

Mr Tebbets We expected the cloud would be cut off and that the winds would dissipate it. Instead, the cloud continued to spread to the south. We were told later that they had underestimated the amount of dynamite needed to close the pit. They had based their original estimate on some computer study. I don't believe the pit was fully sealed off until noon.

Senator Hoyt Could you describe the situation as it appeared on your screens?

Mr Tebbets The cloud shifted over fairly fast, sir – we barely had time to warn shipping and aircraft in the vicinity. Within an hour or so, it reached as far south as Oceanside and as far east as San Bernardino.

Senator Stone It covered the entire Los Angeles basin, then.

Mr Tebbets Yes, sir, eventually it did.

Robert Katz and George Pan Cosmatos
The Cassandra Crossing 60p

As the Transcontinental Express gathers speed, a brilliant surgeon and a beautiful photographer race against time as they search for the suspected carrier of a killer disease which could spread throughout Europe.

At the top-secret international health centre, Stephen MacKenzie must decide whether or not to use the Cassandra Crossing: a rickety bridge, unused for decades, suspended over a deep chasm . . .

Spencer Dunmore
Collision 75p

Two giant jets crammed with passengers – a Boeing 707 and a Douglas DC-8 – converge over Toronto in a violent thunderstorm. Suddenly a lightweight Aeronca flown by an amateur dives out of the clouds, and a seasoned pilot blunders . . . In a shuddering, end-of-the-world eruption of sound the two jets collide – to become one terrifying, unstable monster.

'Breathtaking story of danger in the air . . . it will make your blood run cold but you'll find it difficult to stop reading' DAILY MIRROR

Berton Roueché
The Cats 60p

Too many city folk have been turning their cuddly kittens loose when they leave their holiday homes on Long Island. Out in the woods, the cat colony has been growing and changing . . . They used to prey on rats and birds. Suddenly packs of blood-crazed mutant wildcats, with razor-claws and inch-long teeth are attacking homes and humans . . .

'Very nasty indeed . . . invites comparison with *The Birds* and it is more terrifying because more believable'
TIMES LITERARY SUPPLEMENT

Selected bestsellers

☐ **The Eagle Has Landed** Jack Higgins 80p
☐ **The Moneychangers** Arthur Hailey 95p
☐ **Marathon Man** William Goldman 70p
☐ **Nightwork** Irwin Shaw 75p
☐ **Tropic of Ruislip** Leslie Thomas 75p
☐ **One Flew Over The Cuckoo's Nest** Ken Kesey 75p
☐ **Collision** Spencer Dunmore 70p
☐ **Perdita's Prince** Jean Plaidy 70p
☐ **The Eye of the Tiger** Wilbur Smith 80p
☐ **The Shootist** Glendon Swarthout 60p
☐ **Of Human Bondage** Somerset Maugham 95p
☐ **Rebecca** Daphne du Maurier 80p
☐ **Slay Ride** Dick Francis 60p
☐ **Jaws** Peter Benchley 70p
☐ **Let Sleeping Vets Lie** James Herriot 60p
☐ **If Only They Could Talk** James Herriot 60p
☐ **It Shouldn't Happen to a Vet** James Herriot 60p
☐ **Vet In Harness** James Herriot 60p
☐ **Tinker Tailor Soldier Spy** John le Carré 75p
☐ **Gone with the Wind** Margaret Mitchell £1.75
☐ **Cashelmara** Susan Howatch £1.25
☐ **The Nonesuch** Georgette Heyer 60p
☐ **The Grapes of Wrath** John Steinbeck 95p
☐ **Drum** Kyle Onstott 60p

All these books are available at your bookshop or newsagent:
or can be obtained direct from the publisher
Pan Books, Sales Office, Cavaye Place, London SW10 9PG
Just tick the titles you want and fill in the form below
Prices quoted are applicable in UK
Send purchase price plus 20p for the first book and 10p for each
additional book, to allow for postage and packing

Name _____
(block letters please)
Address _____

_____

While every effort is made to keep prices low, it is sometimes
necessary to increase prices at short notice. Pan Books reserve the
right to show on covers new retail prices which may differ from
those advertised in the text or elsewhere